THE DARK WE SEEK

KYLA STONE

The Dark We Seek

Printed in the United States of America

Cover design by Christian Bentulan

Book formatting by Vellum

First Printed in 2022

ISBN: 978-1-945410-92-5

Created with Vellum

To David Kepford, the fictional identity of a real American hero. He probably would not consider himself a hero, but I do. Thank you to all who have served and sacrificed so much for the citizens of this country.

"Light can devour the darkness but darkness cannot consume the light."

— **Ken Poirot**

FOREWORD

This book takes place in the rugged, beautiful Upper Peninsula of Michigan. The towns and cities mentioned are real, though the author has taken a few liberties for the sake of the story. Thank you in advance for understanding a writer's creative prerogative. If you get a chance to visit the UP, make sure you try a pasty!

1

LENA EASTON

DAY TWENTY

Lena Easton stood at the bow of the emergency rescue boat, searching for Cody Easton's body.

Tendrils of long chestnut waves whipped against her face as she scanned the limestone bluffs with her binoculars. A thousand coves, inlets, and watery caves lined a hundred miles of Lake Superior coastline.

The Alger County Undersheriff and her longtime friend, Jackson Cross, stood beside her, searching the water. The wind tousled his sandy hair as he anxiously rubbed the stubble along his square jaw.

Tall and handsome, Jackson had always drawn the eyes of the ladies, but he barely noticed. He was too dedicated to the job and still in love with the ghost of Lena's dead sister.

Beneath the water, huge boulders and toppled timber were scattered like jackstraws on the lake bottom. On clear days, spears of sunlight penetrated the crystal-clear waters; you could see fifty feet straight to the bottom.

Beneath her spectacular beauty, Lake Superior held tight to her secrets. A corpse might be taken by the surf and deposited in a tangle of driftwood on a beach miles away or more likely, drawn down to the bottom of the lake hundreds of feet below the surface, never to be found.

"We've searched this area already," said one of the two park rangers, a skinny redhead named Eddy Forester who was assisting them at the behest of the sheriff. "We didn't find anything."

"You didn't search with Bear," Lena said with confidence. "Bear can find him."

The massive 150-pound Newfoundland perched at the bow, his big front paws on the gunwale as he leaned over the port side, the SAR vest he wore bright orange against his cinnamon fur.

He sniffed the water eagerly, searching for Cody's scent from the T-shirt Lena kept in a brown paper bag in her pack. Bear resembled an oversized teddy bear—with teeth. He was also smart, loyal, goofy, and utterly dedicated to his duties as a certified search-and-rescue dog.

"How does it work?" Jackson asked. "He's not even in the water."

"Bear can detect the scent of human remains beneath ninety feet of water. He can also detect traces as small as a shard of bone or a drop of blood."

The park ranger whistled. "How will we know he doesn't smell a dead fish? Or say, a dead raccoon washed out by the tide?"

"The decomposition scent is unique to humans. When he alerts, it'll be for a human corpse, not a raccoon."

The ranger folded his arms across his chest as if unconvinced. He looked like he wanted to be anywhere but here, searching the great lake for another dead body.

Two days ago, they'd recovered the corpse of the victim that Walter Boone had thrown overboard, the crime Cody had witnessed that had led to Amos Easton's murder and Cody's death.

The boat scythed through the emerald water. Seagulls wheeled against the bright blue sky. They headed east, hugging the miles of rugged coastline between Amos' home and South Bay in the small town of Munising, Michigan.

To their left, Grand Island rose like a great sleeping giant.

Growing up, she'd spent weekends camping, hiking, and kayaking on the island.

Everything was painfully familiar and simultaneously different, both home and not.

Jackson stepped closer to Lena. He spoke quietly but loud enough to be heard over the wind and the rumble of the engine. "How are you doing?"

It was an almost impossible question to answer. Three weeks ago, half of the world had been plunged into darkness, thrusting the entire planet into chaos.

Brilliant auroras had lit up the heavens for almost two weeks as a series of powerful super-flares erupted from the surface of the sun, known as coronal mass ejections, or CMEs. A scientist on TV had called it a triple CME, each classified as X50, stronger by many magnitudes than Earth had experienced in modern times.

Clouds of scorching hot plasma had struck Earth, causing devastating geomagnetic storms. As the massive bursts of radiation struck the Earth's magnetosphere, power grids were destroyed as transformers were overloaded and power lines burst into flames. Satellites in orbit were damaged when induced currents burned out their circuit boards, affecting GPS, telephone, internet, television, and high-frequency communication systems such as ground-to-air and shortwave radio.

Unlike an EMP, or electromagnetic pulse, the solar storms had significantly impacted long conductors such as power lines, internet cables, and magnetic gas lines, while small-scale electronics hadn't been affected, like computers, cell phones, or microchips in vehicles.

Phones worked if you could charge them, but cell towers were down. Vehicles drove as usual, but gas stations were left without power to pump the fuel. Laptops switched on, but the internet had gone dark.

The world was in turmoil. Every supply system had been disrupted on a global scale. Grocery stores were gathering dust. Gas stations were low on fuel and rationing heavily if not outright empty. Hospitals were running out of critical care meds and supplies. Banks had closed. The stock market had been erased in a blink; worldwide financial systems were in utter disarray.

Then there was Shiloh's kidnapping, Lena's exhausting 1600-mile cross-country journey to the Upper Peninsula, and the capture and death of Walter Boone, a serial predator. The graveyard of bodies they'd discovered behind his derelict cabin held the key to her sister's murder.

And then, of course, there was the unexpected return of Eli Pope.

"I'm taking each day as it comes," Lena said.

"And Shiloh?"

"I don't know," she said honestly. "That girl is a hard nut to crack."

"Is she still sleeping in the tent?"

"She refuses to come into the house."

A week ago, Lena had moved back into her father's house. Though Amos Easton had been murdered in the junk yard rather than the farmhouse, Shiloh wouldn't step foot inside the doorway.

Instead, she'd set up a tent in the woods, a hundred yards from the house. Lena had tried to bribe her with treats, a Snickers bar and Pop-tarts, Shiloh's favorites, but Shiloh had staunchly refused.

In the end, Lena hadn't forced it. If the girl felt more at home among the trees, then who was Lena to stop her? Lena endured her share of nightmares, waking in a cold sweat, her pulse pounding, as her dead sister called out to her and she could not answer.

They shared the same grief, faced the same fears, knew the same devastating loss. And yet, they were essentially strangers. But she'd be damned if she would let her niece down again. The world might be coming apart at the seams, but Lena was bound and determined to be the mother Shiloh had never had.

Lena sighed. "I don't blame her, not one bit."

"She's a survivor. She'll figure it out."

Lena nodded, then tugged up her windbreaker and checked her insulin pump, a habitual act she performed dozens of times a day. Her blood sugar numbers were running lower than normal. The constant stress made it difficult to assess her blood sugar and keep her Type I diabetes in check.

Jackson withdrew a small object from the bag at his feet and handed it to her. "This is the last one in my stash."

Gratefully, she took the juice box, unwrapped the straw, and sipped the sweet apple juice. Jackson knew it was her favorite snack to raise her numbers. As kids, he'd always kept several juice boxes on hand in case she forgot—or more accurately, her perpetually drunken father forgot—to keep them stocked.

Now, she'd have to figure out how to make homemade apple juice or switch to something else, like the tubs of frosting she kept in her solar-powered mini-fridge along with her precious supply of insulin. Twenty-three months left.

And then what? It was a constant worry in the back of her mind, a disconcerting feeling that time was running out, sand dribbling through the hourglass with no way to stop it.

Lena shoved the dark thoughts from her mind and focused on Jackson, studying her friend's careworn face. He'd aged half a decade since he'd realized that he had sent an innocent man to prison. "You haven't been sleeping."

"Like you should be talking."

"Jackson."

"I can't sleep. There's no time. There's too much to do."

"And the nightmares?"

He shrugged as if to say, of course.

Unlike Jackson and the rest of the town, she'd always believed that Eli was innocent of her sister's death. All these years, the killer had continued to kill. He'd never stopped. He was out there, somewhere.

She lowered her voice. "You can't save a ghost."

He looked away. "I know that."

"Be careful, Jackson." Of what exactly, she couldn't quite say. But she knew how driven he was, how merciless he could be, especially against himself. He was haunted by Lily's death, consumed by what he'd done to Eli. Guilt drove him. Guilt could be a dangerous, reckless thing.

"I will," he said, but she didn't quite believe him.

At the bow of the boat, Bear's body went rigid. He ducked, dropping his head low over the gunwale, his bushy tail standing straight out as he frantically sniffed the water. He barked, deep and loud.

Lena patted Bear's back. "You found something. Good boy."

Her bones felt heavy, her limbs like cement. She simultaneously longed to find Cody and dreaded it. Walter Boone had confessed that he'd chased the boy over the bluff, that he'd watched Cody fall, his body broken on the rocks.

And yet, until he was found, Lena grasped a slender thread of hope.

As she'd held out hope for every missing person she'd searched for, as days passed and faith dwindled, as despair settled into her mind and body.

In the end, it was hope that destroyed you.

"Bear just alerted," Lena said. "We need to search here."

Jackson waved at the captain. "Stop the boat!"

The boat slowed. One of the park rangers threw the anchor. Bear barked again, mournful now, his tail drooping. He'd done his job, but like Lena, he dreaded it.

With her heart in her throat, she knelt on the seat next to Bear and rubbed his favorite spot behind his floppy ears. "Good job, boy. You did good. So good."

Jackson's face was pale, drained of color, but he was determined to see this through, as she was. He touched her shoulder. "If he's down there, we'll find him."

She nodded, emotion thick in her throat, unable to speak.

Jackson was cold-water scuba certified, as were the park rangers. Lena remained on the boat with the captain while the divers suited up in dry suits, wriggled into their buoyancy control device vests, checked their tanks and gear, and put on their regulators and masks.

They sat on the gunwale, toppled backward off the stern of the boat, and disappeared beneath the surface of the water.

At the end of May, temperatures in the Upper Peninsula hit the sixties in the afternoons. The water temperature was in the low forties, ice-cold and frigid. It was the freezing waters that kept bodies infamously preserved in Lake Superior.

Due to the unusually low temperatures of the water, the bacteria that typically caused a body to bloat, then float, were inhibited. The myth that Lake Superior never gave up her dead was both folklore and fact.

Lena moved to the stern of the boat and waited. Sensing her anxiety, Bear bounded off the seat and stayed close to her side.

She lifted her face, the sun on her cheeks, the breeze tugging at her hair. On either side of them, the great cliffs reared from the water, boulders the size of cars dotting the shoreline. The ball of the sun descended toward the horizon, the limestone bluffs tinged golden in the late afternoon light.

They'd reached Pictured Rocks National Lakeshore. Emerald waters reflected the dramatic cliffs tinted vibrant shades of browns and reds from iron, black from manganese, and greens and blues from copper, as if some great unseen hand had painted them.

The day was too lovely for the darkness that had invaded the world. Mother Nature didn't care. She'd wreaked her devastation; now sated, she basked in beauty.

Lena shielded her eyes and watched the gulls soaring above the shoreline. A lighthouse perched on the hill just north of Munising. The white tower topped by a lantern room and red cupola roof stood at least eight stories tall. Built into the base of the tower was a single-story brick cottage, the light keeper's home.

A splash came from the water as one of the divers surfaced. Jackson bobbed to the surface first. He appeared strangely alien in his dry suit with the regulator in his mouth, the mask obscuring his eyes. She couldn't see his face or read his expression.

He handed her his fins and she helped him onto the stern of the boat. Bending forward with the weight of the tank, he sat on the bench, removed his regulator, and pushed the mask up onto his forehead. Water dripped down his face.

Bear whined and pressed his bulk against her thigh. She dug her fingers into his fur for support. "What did you find?"

Jackson met her gaze without flinching. "They're bringing up the body now. It's him, Lena. It's Cody."

2

ELI POPE

DAY TWENTY-ONE

Eli Pope stood at the back of the crowd against the wall close to the nearest exit and wished he were anywhere but here. Anxiety hummed through the room, palpable tension in the air.

Three hundred people had crammed into the Munising Community Center, where the Alger County Sheriff had called an emergency town meeting along with the Munising Police Chief, Sarah McCallister, and the Munising superintendent, Johnny Jessop. The assistant district attorney, Larry Keys, was also present, as was Eli's old friend, Undersheriff Jackson Cross.

No reporters were present, since there were no television stations to broadcast, no social media profiles to update, and no newspapers to print. The massive geomagnetic storms caused by the super-flares had been so powerful that they'd damaged HF radio frequencies, including most ham radios. Satellite phones didn't work, either. All forms of mass communication had been obliterated.

Eli wiped the sweat from his brow. The community center didn't have a generator. Without air conditioning, the air was stifling and stank of sweat, B.O., and fear. Instinctively, he scanned the room, checking for exits and watching the restless crowd for potential agitators, for armed individuals who might pose a threat.

Who was he kidding? Everyone posed a threat to him.

Eli shifted uncomfortably, aware of dozens of pairs of eyes watching his every move. He recognized many of the townspeople: Scott Smith, Elmer Dunn, Dana Lutz, Fred Combs, and Mrs. Grady, the long-time librarian. All former classmates and acquaintances, men and women he'd known his entire life.

People flashed him suspicious glances. When he returned their gazes with a steely one of his own, they looked down and away, anywhere but at him, their faces red, their eyes darting with shame and guilt, curiosity and resentment.

Not much remained secret in a small town. They'd heard the rumors spreading like wildfire, that perhaps he was innocent. It didn't matter. They couldn't let go of their hatred so easily.

Especially not someone like Gideon Crawford. Eli recognized the man standing a row ahead of him, a few spots to the left. He was half-turned, glaring over his shoulder at Eli, pure revulsion in his gaze. Instinctively, Eli scanned him for the telltale bulge of weapons but found nothing.

Gideon was a big man, boasting a barrel chest and ham-sized fists. There was something unkempt in his wrinkled clothes, greasy coal-black hair, and scruffy goatee. His broad face and slanting cheekbones hinted at his Native heritage.

Once upon a time, Eli and Gideon had been friends. Gideon had been Lily's boyfriend when she was murdered. He should have been the primary suspect; instead, it was Eli who'd found himself in the crosshairs.

Eli wondered, not for the first time, if Gideon had it in him to kill. Jealousy and betrayal were potent motivators. Gideon had been at the Northwoods Bar that night, along with Sawyer and Cyrus Lee.

Gideon could've easily followed him to Lily's afterward, could have seen them together, waited for Eli to leave, and then killed her in a jealous rage. It was possible.

Eli didn't care whether Gideon hated him or not, whether any of them did. He didn't care how they felt, one way or the other, as long as they left him the hell alone. Or so he told himself.

Eli returned his attention to the front of the room as Sheriff Bradley Underwood stepped up to the lectern, a megaphone in his right hand. He was a stern, formidable black man in his early fifties with ramrod straight posture and a clean-shaven jaw.

While most people in town were disheveled after three weeks without electricity, Underwood's crisp uniform appeared freshly pressed. He hadn't been sheriff when Eli had been arrested eight years ago; back then it was Horatio Cross who'd ruled Alger County with an iron fist.

Sheriff Underwood leaned forward and spoke loudly into the megaphone, his booming voice commanding attention. "Thank you, everyone, for coming. Give me your attention for a few minutes."

The crowd quieted down, their faces upturned toward the stage.

Underwood cleared his throat. He looked like he'd rather peel off his fingernails than say the words he spoke next: "We have reason to believe that Eli Pope did not murder Lily Easton, the crime for which he was convicted."

Audible gasps echoed. It was one thing to hear rumors, quite another to hear them validated. "What the hell is going on?" someone shouted.

"How do you know it wasn't Pope?"

"How'd you get things so wrong, Sheriff?"

Underwood ran a hand over his bald head and pursed his lips. "Eli Pope has the sincerest of apologies from Alger County, from the Sheriff's Office, the DA, and the Munising Police Department. A terrible mistake occurred, a miscarriage of justice. This was a grave error which we are investigating to the fullest."

Eli stiffened. What did he expect? Eight years of suffering and misery reduced to "a mistake." He bristled with dark fury. His hands balled into fists at his sides. It'd give him immense satisfaction to punch that pompous jerk in the face.

The DA, Larry Keys, leaned toward the megaphone. "Mr. Pope will receive restitution for his time served while incarcerated. He has the right to live in peace and we should give him that peace."

Eli felt dozens of eyes on him: curious, scrutinizing, pitying, prying. He despised them all. His face grew hot. Nausea churned in his stomach. His gaze flicked to Jackson, who met his eyes for a brief moment then looked away.

"If it wasn't Pope, who the hell did it?" a woman in the back yelled.

"It was that freak Walter Boone!" someone shouted back.

"The investigation is not complete—"

"What about the graves you found?" someone shouted. "Who are the other victims?"

"Did Boone kill all those girls, too?"

Underwood cleared his throat. "As some of you have heard, we have uncovered the graves of seven deceased individuals. Alger County is currently working to identify the deceased and notify the next of kin, at which time we will release the names to the community—"

"Did Boone kill Lily Easton, then?" Dana Lutz shouted. "Or do we have a serial killer in Alger County?"

The crowd stirred in alarm, restless and edgy. Whispers and gasps of dismay rippled from one end of the room to the other.

"There is no serial killer in Alger County." Sheriff Underwood clasped the megaphone with both hands. Sweat beaded his brow. "Our deputies apprehended our primary suspect, a man named Walter Boone. He was killed during the rescue of Shiloh Easton and Ruby Carpenter. Both girls were saved. That's what we should focus on here. The Sheriff's Office and the Munising Police Department are working to keep the citizens of Alger County safe."

"So, you're saying Boone *was* a serial killer?" Dana Lutz asked. "That he's the one who killed all those girls?"

"The investigation is ongoing," Underwood insisted. His Adam's apple moved up and down as he swallowed. He was nervous. He had every reason to be. Eli did not envy the sheriff his job. He didn't envy any of them. "Let me be absolutely clear. Our investigation points to a single suspect, and that suspect is dead. You may rest easy in your beds tonight."

"Rest easy?" asked an incredulous woman bouncing a crying, snot-nosed toddler on her hip. "Are you kidding me? After everything that just happened?"

"What about the grocery stores?" a man in a hunting jacket shouted.

"I can't get gas!"

"We haven't had water in five days!"

"Where the hell is FEMA?"

"My kids haven't eaten since yesterday. What are you doing about it?"

"I can't get my refill of beta-blockers!" Elmer Dunn yelled. "Without it, I'm a dead man! I won't last two months!"

Eli had had enough. The walls were closing in, stifling and claustrophobic. The jostling, agitated crowd pressed too close. He couldn't breathe.

He inched toward the exit. He checked his six again and noted that Gideon Crawford still stared at him with naked hatred in his eyes.

Eli ignored him and pushed his way through the double doors, out into the fresh air. Blinking in the afternoon sunlight, he took a deep breath and steadied his nerves.

A middle-aged woman leaned against the brick wall to the right of the front doors, smoking a cigarette, a duffle bag at her feet. She glanced over at him and offered a grim smile.

"There you are," she said as if she'd been expecting him.

Michelle Carpenter owned the IGA country store in Christmas, the next town over, where he'd shopped for years. Once upon a time, she'd traveled across the International Bridge to procure his favorite beer. Now, her red hair was threaded with silver, worry lines bracketing her mouth.

"It's funny. I haven't smoked since college. When the power

went down, I saved all the cigarette cartons I had at the store, figuring they'd be a valuable commodity to trade if it came to that." She exhaled a puff of smoke and stared across the street at the shuttered bank on the corner. "When Ruby went missing, I started up again to deal with the stress, and now I can't seem to stop."

Eli didn't know what to say. He had no clue what she wanted from him. The last time they'd met, she'd accused him of murder and kicked him out of her store.

Michelle gestured toward the community center behind them. "I couldn't go in there. I know they're talking about him...about what he did to Ruby. I just couldn't do it."

"You don't have to explain anything to me."

"I do. I was awful to you. I'm sorry, Eli. You're probably sick of hearing it, but I am."

"You don't owe me anything."

"You saved my daughter."

"Shiloh saved your daughter."

"You shot Walter Boone. You made sure he couldn't come after Ruby, that he wouldn't hurt any other girls after her. She doesn't have to go through the trauma of a trial. A trial would've broken her. He's dead and frankly, I'm glad of it. If I was there, I would have shot him myself."

She said it with such conviction that he glanced at her. Her eyes were hard and tired, her features drawn.

"Ruby is alive, thanks to you." Michelle took a final drag of her cigarette, dropped it, and stamped it out with her sneaker. "I have something for you. Truth be told, I came hoping you would show up." She reached down, rummaged in the duffle bag at her feet, and pulled out a six-pack of bottled beer. Instantly, he recognized the amber bottle, the white label emblazoned with the red maple leaf.

"You found Molson Canadian?"

"I've had it for a while. My husband used to drink it, so I've kept it around, but I don't keep it in stock in the store anymore, after...after what happened." She shifted from foot to foot, clearly nervous. "Maybe this was a bad idea. Maybe you never want to see one of these things for the rest of your life."

He shook his head, his throat abruptly thick with emotion at the unexpected act of kindness. He didn't trust himself to speak.

She held out the six-pack and offered a wan smile that held more despair than joy. "Please don't judge us too harshly, Eli Pope. I hope someday you can find it in your heart to forgive us."

"Forgiveness has nothing to do with it." He turned on his heel and strode from the weed-infested parking lot, leaving the community center and Michelle Carpenter behind. He took the Molson Canadian with him.

3

JACKSON CROSS

DAY TWENTY-ONE

"I was wrong," Jackson said.

Jackson's father stared at him with hard unflinching eyes. "What is done is done. Do you understand? The past is dead and buried. What you need to do now is take care of business."

They stood on the back deck of Horatio and Dolores Cross' palatial home, which was designed to resemble a grand Tahoe lodge. The stone and cedar house perched on a bluff with 500 feet of shoreline and boasted spectacular views of Lake Superior.

Jackson wasn't in the mood to appreciate the view. He had barely been home in days. He was burning the candle at both ends, often sleeping in his truck or at the Sheriff's Office.

Yesterday, they'd dragged Cody Easton's small body from the lake. Jackson was rattled, shaken to his core, eaten alive with guilt. "I planted evidence against my best friend. I put him in prison for eight years. God only knows what horrific things happened to him there. Even worse, my actions allowed a killer to go free, to keep killing—"

His father shook his head and gave him an incredulous look. Tall, square-shouldered, and fit in his mid-sixties, he wore khaki slacks and a button-up shirt, his distinguished white hair brushed back from his high forehead. "Stop wallowing, son. What's done is done. You did the best that you could at the time. What good is your remorse now?"

Jackson blanched. His father, the illustrious former Alger County sheriff, had ruled the county for eighteen years. Jackson never imagined he'd hear such words from his mouth. "I've been wrestling with this decision for weeks. I think I should turn myself in. I should resign—"

Horatio seized his shoulders. "You will do no such thing. Do you hear me? Get it together, son! That's not what you should be thinking about. The town depends on you. This family depends on you."

"You don't understand—"

"This is not the time for moral waffling. Resign? You're not thinking clearly. The department needs you more than ever. You can't quit. And above all, you can't show weakness. You can't show a shred of doubt. They need someone strong to follow until things get straightened out again."

Jackson nodded numbly. How wrong he'd been. The consequences had been astronomical. All those dead girls, while Eli rotted in prison, an innocent man.

Eli wanted to kill him for what he'd done. He knew that. He felt it. His old friend longed for vengeance, and he wasn't wrong. Whether or not Eli would seek that vengeance, or when—remained to be seen.

Guilt and shame wormed inside of him. "But I...what I did..."

"We all make mistakes, son. Guilt will only cripple you. And for what? You can't go back and save those girls. You can't undo what happened. Eli Pope was an unfortunate situation, a mistake. It's done. It's over."

"An unfortunate situation? An innocent man rotting in prison is far more than unfortunate."

"Why should you throw away an entire career, all the good you've done, all the good you will do? That's not right. That's not justice. All we can do now is look forward."

"I am looking forward."

Horatio's blue eyes were sharp and cunning in his weathered face. He leaned in close, merciless. "Protect this town. Protect the county. But your first and last priority is only this: take care of your family. Take care of us. Do what you have to do to protect us from whatever's coming. You think you can handle that?"

Jackson suppressed a flinch. He thought he'd become inured to the frequent barbs from his father. For some reason, this one hurt more than usual. "I got it."

"You have an opportunity, here. Don't squander it."

"An opportunity? What are you talking about?"

Horatio's grip tightened on his shoulders, fingers digging like claws into his trapezius muscle. "Sheriff Underwood doesn't have what it takes. He thinks he does, but he's weak. He doesn't have the guts to do what will be required to survive in this world. The other deputies already look to you. When the time is right, you'll take the mantle of sheriff and lead this county out of the darkness. You must be strong for your mother, for your sister. They need you."

His father was a political animal through and through; even now, he was playing politics, turning disaster to his advantage. "I understand."

"Do you?"

Jackson shifted his gaze across the deck through the open French doors to the kitchen, where his sister ate a leisurely late-morning breakfast at the dining room table.

Astrid sat tall and imposing in her wheelchair. At 5'11", broad-shouldered and sturdy, she exuded a striking beauty with her silky blonde hair and strong Nordic features. The accident had done nothing to diminish her looks.

Though she could walk, due to the chronic pain in her legs from the car accident fifteen years ago, she used a wheelchair as if to soak up the constant pity from those around her with an insatiable greed.

Through the screen door, her icy eyes locked onto his. She tipped an empty glass in his direction as if mocking him. For what, he'd never understood.

Her long-term boyfriend, Cyrus Lee, sat at the table beside her. Though reserved, he was always hovering around her, subservient but sharp-eyed, like a crow hunting for something shiny to filch.

Where Astrid was blonde and broad, Cyrus was thin, wiry, and bristled with restless energy. His great-grandfather had been the owner of a prosperous copper mine in Keweenaw County, but the family had squandered their fortune in poor investments in the late 90s and never recovered.

Cyrus nodded at him with a sly smile. Jackson had the sneaking suspicion that Cyrus knew full well that Jackson despised him and relished making him uncomfortable in his own home. "How's the case going, Undersheriff? You closed the Boone murders yet?"

"Everything's spectacular," Jackson muttered. He didn't want to discuss the case with anyone here, let alone Cyrus Lee.

He turned his attention to his mother, who scurried about the gleaming kitchen, opening cupboards and pulling out spices. Flour was scattered across the counter, a platter of eggs and pancakes set on the table.

Surprisingly, the generator still had fuel. Once again, the lights were on, the power wasted.

Frustration curdled Jackson's stomach. They were supposed to be conserving their rations. He'd gone over this with them, repeatedly. A heavy defeated feeling spread over him.

"Mom, you need a break," he called.

His mother opened the screen door and shuffled onto the deck, enveloping Jackson in an airy hug and kissing his cheeks. "Jackson! It's so lovely to see you, dear. You're the one who has been so busy, burning the candle at both ends."

In her late fifties, Dolores wore a sundress dotted with yellow daisies and high heels. Her favorite strand of pearls encircled her pale white throat. Her silver-streaked hair was swept in an elegant French twist.

"I'm fine." Jackson hugged her back. She was so thin, so small; she reminded him of a tiny-boned bird. She looked ready for an afternoon lunching with the ladies at a posh beachfront restaurant.

He pulled back and glanced out at the manicured yard, at the flowers blooming from mulched beds, then toward the gazebo overlooking the lake. He frowned. "Mother, where is the garden we talked about? You love to plant things. I gave you seeds—tomatoes, lettuce, cucumbers, zucchini."

"Pruning the roses is practically a full-time job, and we've lost Jed, the gardener, you know. I planted the petunias and the daffodils around the gazebo. Don't you see them? They look lovely."

"We need to be planting food, remember?"

Dolores stared at him blankly. Her eyes were glassy and slightly unfocused. She wrapped her thin arms protectively across her chest.

"Mom? Are you listening to me?"

"Jackson, stop." Horatio's voice was commanding. "Let your poor mother be."

"Mother, I need more orange juice," Astrid demanded from the kitchen.

"In a moment, dear."

"I'm thirsty!" Astrid called, loud and petulant.

"Her boyfriend is right there." The old feelings stirred: resentment, impatience, pettiness. "He can get it for her. Or better yet, she can get it herself. Why does he have to be here all the time, eating our food?"

His mother frowned, wrinkles radiating from the corners of her eyes. "That poor Jefferson boy. It's the least I can do for him."

Before he could ask what she meant, she tugged at his arm. "Come lunch with us. We'll take the boat out on the lake. It's going to be a beautiful day."

"Not today, Mom. I have a lot of work to do. And the boat wastes fuel. We need to conserve everything we have, remember?"

"A pity, dear." Dolores ignored his words as if she hadn't even heard him. Instead, she kissed Jackson's cheek again and hurried back into the house to do her daughter's bidding.

Jackson watched her leave, struggling to rein in his anger, irritation, and a growing sense of powerlessness. They still didn't get it. They'd been coddled their entire lives and they expected nothing to change now, three weeks into a worldwide disaster.

The entire Northern Hemisphere had lost power. There would be tremendous suffering before life would return to any semblance of normality. The aftershocks would last for years, for decades.

But what could he do? They were his family. If they refused to take care of themselves, it was up to him. Wasn't it?

"Don't rile your mother," Horatio said. "Why do you insist on making this harder on her?"

"Make this harder?" Jackson hissed. "I'm not making it harder. Reality will do that just fine. What is she going to do when the generator runs out and she expects the lights to turn on with the flip of a switch? Or when she opens the pantry one morning and there is nothing left to eat?"

"That won't happen," Horatio said evenly, "because you will not allow it to happen."

Jackson shook his head. "She's planting daffodils instead of a life-sustaining garden. She has to understand—"

"No! You have to understand. She is fragile. She can't handle certain...realities. You know that."

Years ago, Jackson's brother had disappeared. Then Astrid's car accident left her paralyzed. It had been a difficult time for everyone. To survive, his mother had cultivated her reality, refusing to accept certain ugly truths.

He lowered his voice. "Are you medicating her?"

"Some Zoloft keeps her calm."

"She doesn't need—"

"It's exactly what she needs."

"Where are you getting the meds? The pharmacy got cleaned out a week ago."

Horatio shrugged and gave him an enigmatic smile.

"What about Astrid?"

His sister took multiple prescriptions for pain relief; it was how she'd gotten hooked on uppers years ago. His parents had enabled the addiction. Over time, she'd added prescriptions for a variety of ailments.

"I'm keeping an eye on it. She's good for a while."

"Who's your source?" Jackson repeated. He wouldn't be put off this time.

Horatio sighed. "Cyrus Lee gets what we need."

"What? Where's he getting it?"

"He was a pharmaceutical rep for years before he started day trading. Obviously, day trading is off the table these days, but he still has connections."

"Cyrus Lee is getting drugs without prescriptions?"

"Don't be so judgmental, Jackson. That's why I didn't tell you. Don't worry about it. I've taken care of it."

"What happens when they run out?"

"They won't. You'll make sure of that, won't you?"

Jackson gritted his teeth. He had bigger problems to deal with than his mother's and sister's pharmaceutical addictions. He felt the weight of obligation upon his shoulders, the seemingly impossible burdens looming over him. He needed to protect the town, keep Shiloh and Lena safe, and take care of his family. He also had to prevent Eli from exacting revenge and find the killer lurking among them.

His father leaned in close. Jackson smelled the bourbon on his breath. "I need to make sure we're on the same page. That you'll do what needs doing."

Jackson straightened. "I will."

His father peered into his face, his thin lips tight with disapproval. Jackson resisted that familiar urge to cringe, to make himself as small as possible. He couldn't recall a time when Horatio had looked at him differently.

He shouldn't have confessed to his father. He should have

known he would find no absolution here. Horatio was correct in one aspect, however: Jackson's resignation would help nothing.

Everything had changed and Jackson needed to change with it; he just wasn't sure how yet.

His father wanted him to look forward, to seize the next opportunity to take control, to seize power. He wanted Jackson to forget the dead girls who called out to him for justice. To forget Eli Pope.

"Thank you, father, for clarifying things for me." He felt his throat closing. He had to get out of this stifling house, to get away from these insufferable people. Jackson turned on his heel and strode across the cedar deck toward the driveway.

"Where do you think you're going?" Horatio said to his back.

Jackson said, "To right a wrong."

4

JACKSON CROSS

DAY TWENTY-TWO

The acorn struck Jackson on the back of his head.

Jackson sighed. He should be grateful it wasn't a bullet. He turned around, scanning the tree line, one hand on the butt of his service weapon. He wore his uniform though he wasn't here on official business as the undersheriff.

"You win, Eli. Come out."

Nothing. No sounds. No movement. He'd managed not to snag Eli's tripwire, but Eli still knew he was there. Jackson did not doubt that.

A blue jay lectured him from the branch of a white oak above his head. Thirty feet to his right, the river burbled over moss-covered stones and fallen logs. Tall trees cast cool shadows across the clearing while mosquitos and black flies swarmed in the sunlight.

Jackson studied the empty campsite: the tent in the center of the clearing, the second almost invisible shelter hidden behind a boulder, the Dakota fire pit, a log for seating, and the shirts hung to dry on a clothesline strung between two trees.

He understood why Eli preferred it out here. He longed to go fly fishing, to lose himself in the tranquil peace of the river, to forget the chaos in town, the fear reflected in the eyes of everyone he saw.

He couldn't do that. Jackson had a duty to the people, the county, and his town.

Jackson bent, picked up the acorn, and rubbed it between his fingers, thinking of the old game they'd played as boys, to see which one could sneak up on the other. Eli always won.

The hairs on the back of his neck rose. He sensed Eli watching him. Try as he might, he could see nothing in the woods. Jackson was good at his job, but Eli was something special, the kind of man who survived in the wilderness, who could kill a hundred different ways.

Jackson wasn't naïve. He and Eli had worked together to rescue Shiloh and bring down Walter Boone, but the bad blood between them hadn't cleared, not by a long shot.

Devon Harris, a deputy in the Sheriff's Office, knew his location. Not that it would matter if Eli decided to take his vengeance. Eight years in prison changed a man. Eight years for hatred to fester and poison a soul.

Eli Pope was more dangerous than ever.

Still, Jackson believed they could talk this out as men. He had no choice but to believe that. Whether he walked out of there alive or not was the question.

"We need to talk, Eli. I know you're here."

Sunlight reflected off of the limestone outcroppings. The verdant trees rose on either side of the river, lush ferns hugging the riverbank. Ten yards to Jackson's left, a shadow flitted among two birch trees. Eli stepped soundlessly from the woods.

Ropy muscles rippled beneath his army green T-shirt, his dog tags hanging from his neck. His movements were smooth and oiled as a panther—confident, efficient, and powerful. His sharp cheekbones, tanned skin, and fierce jet-black eyes revealed his Ojibwe heritage.

He wore boots and tactical cargo pants, a holstered VP9 at one hip, a sheathed combat knife on the opposite side, and a utility belt hung with spare magazine pouches slung across his waist. The muzzle of his AK-47 was aimed at Jackson's chest.

Jackson revealed both hands and kept them in plain view, the acorn displayed in his open palm. He'd feel more comfortable with his Glock in hand, but beggars couldn't be choosers.

He didn't come for a pissing contest. If he were honest, he would lose.

"Put down your weapon, Eli."

"I don't think so."

Jackson waited him out, sweating profusely, but Eli didn't budge. "I'm here to talk, Eli."

Eli's unflinching gaze studied Jackson, taking everything in without blinking. "So talk."

The two men faced each other, fifteen feet apart. Old friends. Now enemies. Huge oak trees rose all around them, their branches scraping the cobalt sky. Grasshoppers and cicadas buzzed in the grass.

Jackson breathed in the scents of pine sap and damp earth, steadying himself. "I owe you an explanation."

Eli stared at him. He was still, contained, every movement efficient and purposeful. A watcher, a hunter. He studied Jackson like he was imagining sawing off his head with a dull knife.

"I was wrong, Eli."

Eli's lip curled in scorn. "You were *wrong*? I went to prison. For eight years, I suffered, every minute of every day. I was locked in a cage with killers. Do you have any idea what that's like?"

"There is nothing I can say to make it up to you. I know that. I'm not here to try, but I owe you the truth."

Eli offered a thin, humorless smile. "Jackson Cross, the principled cop, always with the moral high ground. Lena used to say you were the best of us. But you compromised your precious ethics. Tell me, what made you betray your best friend?"

Jackson winced. He deserved that. "I was devastated. We all were. The whole town was in shock. Amos Easton believed it was you from day one. I was so consumed with grief, so desperate to solve the case, that I...I thought I was doing the right thing. I believed it then, but I was wrong. I felt I had no choice."

"You always had a choice."

"I know that. I know."

Eli kept his rifle aimed at Jackson, his finger on the trigger guard. He spat out a single word. "Why?"

Jackson closed his hand over the acorn and tightened his grip until the nut dug into his flesh. Guilt knifed him. The past surged back with the intensity of Technicolor. Here it was, the moment of confession. He hated himself with every word he spoke, but he pushed onward.

"There was a darkness inside you I didn't understand. We were best friends, and then suddenly, we'd become strangers. Lena had moved away, so she couldn't help. And Lily...it was like Lily brought it out in you, that darkness. You brought it out in each other. She told me how you would drink together, too much too fast, that you both liked things wild, intense...dark."

He hesitated.

Eli's eyes narrowed. "There has to be more."

"Your DNA was all over the house. On the condom left in the trash."

"I never lied about being there that night."

"I know," Jackson said in a strangled voice. "I know. We had no reason to believe there was a serial killer involved. There was no indication—"

"Because you stopped looking."

Eli's words hit him like a blow to the solar plexus. "Yes," he said. "Yes."

"What else?"

"There was Shiloh," Jackson said.

Eli hunched his shoulders as if deflecting a blow. "What about her?"

The crime scene flashed through his mind. The red-stained sheets, Lily's beaten face, her dark hair spread across the satin pillow. The little girl rocking back and forth, her skinny arms wrapped around her knees, dried blood on her face, her eyes dull with shock.

"I found her."

Eli stiffened, his features going rigid. Jackson had noticed how he looked at Shiloh like he'd kill anyone who dared hurt her, would tear them apart with his bare hands.

"Shiloh didn't speak for days, except for a few words when I found her."

"What did she say?"

"Your name. I asked her to say it again, to make sure, but she shut down. And then she wouldn't talk at all. The child psychologist couldn't get anything out of her."

"I was there that night. I had dinner with them. I used to color her My Little Pony coloring books with her, for Pete's sake. Maybe she was asking for me. She was terrified and alone and desperate for someone she knew. Did you consider that?"

"She whispered your name. In the same breath, she said the word, 'windigo.' "

"That could mean anything."

"The windigo is a Native American monster who kills and eats people."

Eli's face darkened. "I'm fully aware of my ethnicity and what it means. Is that it? Is that all you had?"

"I know how it sounds. But coupled with what else we knew, or thought we knew, it was the strongest lead. Still, it wasn't enough for a search warrant. The DA said that a traumatized five-year-old child was unreliable, they couldn't use it, it wouldn't hold up in court."

"Big surprise."

"I tried to talk to you first. I was desperate, grieving, floundering with little evidence and no leads. There was tremendous pressure to make an arrest. I went to your father's house, but no one was home. Your leave was almost up. I knew you'd be back to a Ranger Battalion out of my reach, so I used the key your dad kept beneath the broken shed board behind the house. I went inside, telling myself I was checking on your welfare, that I had a legitimate reason to enter that house as I'd done a million times before. I found a desktop computer in the bedroom you were staying in. I went through the search history and found nothing recent within the previous thirty days, but I did find dozens of websites visited earlier in the year. Dark, disturbing things. Violence against women. Then I found the handcuffs, duct tape, and a blindfold in your room."

Jackson's palms had gone clammy. Nauseous, he let the acorn drop and balled his hands into fists to keep them from trembling, to keep Eli from seeing. "I went to your favorite campsite to talk to you, but if you recall, you pointed a gun at my face and screamed at me to leave. I wanted to believe you. I wanted to ask about what I had found, to get your side of things, but you turned me away."

Eli gave a bitter snort. "I know how the law works. I know how justice gets railroaded for a quick conviction, especially for people like me. History is littered with scapegoats. We're always the criminals, the degenerates, targeted by lazy or corrupt cops." A muscle bulged in his jaw as he stared Jackson down. "I never thought it would be you."

Jackson licked his lips. "The evidence—"

"What evidence? That computer was my father's. You know he used to rent my old room to a trucker who'd use it every month or so when he had a couple of days layover. If you'd bothered to check, you would have found that I was on deployment when those sites were visited. That wasn't me. It was never me."

"And the cuffs, blindfold, and duct tape?"

"On leave, I always kept a sling pack with me for my essentials. Back then, I carried a 1911 45 Remington Rand, four magazines, a set of handcuffs, a sleep mask for long flights, and duct tape that I used for torn straps, covering holes or rips in my gear, whatever. I had a lighter with some duct tape wrapped around it.

"On my last deployment, my company was supporting an ODA, a Special Forces A team, along with foreign soldiers and contractors looking to execute arrest warrants on the Serbian-

Kosovo border. We were searching for war criminals. I kept the cuffs in my chest rig and the sling pack, even when I was off."

Jackson swallowed. "Lily told me once that you hurt her."

"I never harmed her. Not like that. I would never hurt her or any woman."

"She said that you put your hands around her throat."

"It was a nightmare. I was sleeping, dreaming of—" He shook his head as if he could shake the memories right out of his skull. "I've never regretted a single man I've killed. Not once. They were bad men who deserved to die. Doesn't mean that doesn't stay with you, that it doesn't stain you. It'll ruin you if you let it. I let it ruin me. It was like the nightmare overpowered me and I couldn't wake myself up. I didn't know what I was doing."

Jackson searched his old friend's face for signs of deception but found none. What he saw was pain. Sheer, unadulterated pain.

"I was scared of myself," Eli said. "That's why I left that night instead of sleeping over. I didn't trust myself when I slept. We fought. She wanted me to...to do it again."

"Do what again?"

"Choke her. To do it for real. I refused, and she would not accept that. I tried to leave, and she slapped me. It was a game to her. Or maybe it was her self-imposed punishment, I don't know. Lily wanted it rougher and rougher. She wanted pain, to be in pain. I wouldn't give that to her."

Eli looked at Jackson with a haunted expression, like every word he spoke came at a cost, naked torment on his face he couldn't hide. "I wanted her to move on. I wanted to move on, but I couldn't seem to do it. We made each other miserable, we made each other forget. She was a lost soul. You only saw the good in her, Jackson. You didn't want to see the brokenness. Those jagged edges would cut you. They cut Lena. They cut me. But they cut Lily herself the deepest."

Jackson clenched his jaw. Eli wasn't wrong. He'd seen the darkness in Eli and discounted it in Lily, allowing unrequited love to blind him from things he hadn't wanted to acknowledge.

He recalled that sun-kissed day at the lake years ago, when Eli had pushed Lily beneath the water, how she'd come up cursing at him in one breath and cajoling him the next, taunting and teasing. Her emotions had been volatile and shifting like mercury, one minute hot and the next ice cold, like Jekyll and Hyde, manipulating others for her own capricious needs.

He saw them in his mind's eye: two sisters raised alone in the woods by a bitter alcoholic who took out his drunken rages on his daughters. To survive, Lena had developed a savior complex, trying to save everyone but herself, while Lily had spiraled into self-destruction, dragging the people she loved down with her.

Jackson understood how children raised in violence adapted in any way they could. He understood how a person could be blinded to their own wounds, but also to the sharp edges of the ones closest to them.

Emotions shifted like shadows across Eli's features—remorse, regret, anger. "The last time we were together, she said if I wouldn't do what she wanted, she knew someone who would. Before we found Boone and his graveyard, I always wondered if it was Gideon Crawford she meant. He had more of a motive than I did. Or someone else I didn't know about. That was your job, but you didn't bother to look. Did you even check if Gideon had an alibi?"

The words crumbled like ash on his tongue. "I believed you had done it. God forgive me, but I did, Eli. I did. I still had the bottle of Molson Canadian you'd left at my house the night of the murder. I had access to a sample of Lily's blood. I thought I was doing the right thing. I thought I was sacrificing everything for justice, but I was wrong, so wrong."

Eli stared at him without speaking, indignation a black fire in his gaze. The muzzle of the rifle hadn't moved a fraction, his finger resting on the trigger guard. His powerful biceps flexed as if he was imagining what squeezing the trigger might feel like.

Jackson tensed. Fear stabbed his gut like an icepick. Would Eli try to kill him? Not try, Eli *would* kill him. Eli had hunted men for a living, after all. He could chew him up, spit him out, and wouldn't taste a damn thing.

"There it is," he forced out. "That's everything." The shadows grew longer, stretching like ghastly fingers across the clearing as mosquitos bit at Jackson's exposed skin. He ignored them. "You told me you would kill whoever framed you. Now you know the truth."

Eli gave a harsh, hollow laugh. "I've dreamed of this moment. Every night for eight years, trapped in that concrete prison, with the stench of sweat and violence and fear permeating the air. The things I would do to the person who'd stolen my life. I've dreamed of tying you up, putting a rope around your neck, tying the other end to the Bonneville, then pouring gasoline over your head and going for a drive. Your skin would peel off before the sparks set you ablaze."

Jackson tried not to flinch. He knew better than to seek forgiveness. He would never ask. He would never receive it. Neither did he deserve it. He offered the only thing he could. "I need to know if you're going to let me do my job."

Eli's expression was flat, unreadable. "You're going to find Lily's killer."

"If it's the last thing I do."

For a long minute, Eli didn't move. Finally, he gave a brisk nod, as if deciding something, settling an internal debate within himself. Seemingly with tremendous effort, he lowered the rifle. "Then go do it."

Jackson didn't ask what would happen afterward. He already knew. In Eli's dark eyes, vengeance still burned.

5

LENA EASTON

DAY TWENTY-TWO

Lena ran. Her legs pumped like pistons, sneakers thudding along the gravel road. Sweat dripped into her eyes, her lungs on fire.

Jack pines, white oaks, and maples stretched far above her. Mosquitos swirled in the panels of light sifting through the canopy of trees, the ragged sky above her the deepest blue. Crows cawed angrily as she trespassed beneath them.

She ran like she could outrun her demons. Five miles a day since she'd arrived in Munising, just as she'd done in Tampa. Rage, grief, and helplessness drove her on, mile after mile.

Summer, winter, rain or shine—it didn't matter. She needed to run, had to run. The empty space inside her chest expanded, the fire burning her clean again.

Only it didn't burn her clean. Not this time.

Cody was dead. She'd believed it, but now she knew it in her heart, within her soul, down to her bones. Knowing and believing were two entirely different things.

Lena had to tell Shiloh. The girl had been gone all day, wandering the woods, checking snares, and hauling firewood, Bear frolicking beside her. As she'd requested, Shiloh had left

Lena a note—scrawled in crayon on a fragment of paper, nailed to one of the porch posts with a crossbow bolt.

Let it never be said that Shiloh didn't possess a wicked sense of humor.

Lena turned toward the Easton property and jogged up the driveway, breathing hard. The rambling farmhouse of her childhood had crumbled into disrepair. Leaves clogged the gutters. Vines crept up the right side of the house and strangled the wide front porch. The front door sagged, paint peeling.

For a moment, she imagined Mother Nature reclaiming houses and buildings, swamping roads and telephone poles, swallowing entire towns, then cities, gradually erasing humanity's very existence.

She slowed to a walk and drank deeply from the hydration pack strapped to her back, which held Smarties, dried fruit, and granola bars along with glucose tabs. The pack contained her M&P 9 EZ Shield pistol, which added weight, but she didn't go anywhere without it.

After checking her blood sugar numbers on her pump, she ate a granola bar, bolused herself with insulin for the carbs, and made a mental note to figure out how to make homemade snacks that she could take with her.

Like everything else, pre-packaged food was running out fast with no resupply in sight.

Wildflowers had sprung up overnight, clusters of wild columbine, goldenrod, and black-eyed Susans bursting into color. The camo-green nylon tent peeked between the jack pines and wild raspberry bushes that lined the property to the west. Leaves, twigs, and pine boughs layered the tent roof.

Lena suppressed a grim smile. Shiloh adored Eli and imitated practically everything he did or said. They were good for each other. They needed one another in ways they didn't yet comprehend.

At the thought of Eli, something flickered deep down inside

her. She pushed it away. Now was not the time. Steeling herself, she headed for Shiloh's hideout.

"Shiloh, I'm here!" She announced her presence since sneaking up on a firecracker like Shiloh was a bad idea. That crossbow was no child's weapon.

Lena unzipped the fabric door and Bear thrust his big head through the opening, his fluffy rump wriggling in greeting, his tail beating against the nylon walls.

Lena rubbed his ears as she bent and peered into the tent behind him. "Can I come in?"

She received a morose grunt in response. At least it was a response.

Lena crawled inside. Slanting afternoon sunlight bathed the cramped interior of the tent with an orangish glow. Shiloh sat cross-legged atop her sleeping bag. Her crossbow leaned against the tent wall next to a quiver of bolts. Sitting in front of her was a travel book opened to a full-page photo of the Eiffel Tower.

Thin and small, thirteen-year-old Shiloh made up for her size with a fierce attitude. She wore ratty jeans with holes in the knees, black combat boots, and one of Cody's shirts: an oversized charcoal T-shirt emblazoned with the Death Star, the words "Out of Service" printed beneath it.

Shiloh shut the book and tucked it under her sleeping bag. "What do you want?"

Lena didn't waste time. "We have to talk."

"Spit it out, then."

Her lungs constricted. "We found Cody. We found his body in the lake. I'm so sorry."

Shiloh went rigid. Her raven-black hair was tugged back in a braid, tendrils sticking to her cheeks. Her dark eyes glistened with a lifetime of heartache, but she didn't cry. She didn't moan or scream. She didn't make a sound.

Still as a statue, her shoulders clenched as a dozen emotions flickered across her features—sorrow, anger, grief, resignation.

Lena was trained to deal with loss, but this was different, like a part of her soul had been ripped from its moorings. She longed to crawl across the tent and wrap her niece in her arms and never let go, but Shiloh hadn't allowed Lena to touch her since that terrible night at the cabin.

Everything inside the traumatized girl was sharp and jagged as broken glass. It would take time. Time and patience, and trust.

"I'm sorry, honey. I'm so sorry."

Bear gave a mournful whine. He went to Shiloh, nosed her face, and licked her cheeks. The Newfie was gifted with an uncanny ability to read and respond to human emotions. Since he was a puppy, he'd known when Lena was sad or stressed.

The big dog turned in a circle in the three-person tent, then flopped 150 pounds of Newfoundland across the girl's legs. Shiloh gave an involuntary *oomph,* scowling for an instant, but only an instant.

Bear's softness, gentleness, and sweetness won her over, and Shiloh sagged into him. She wrapped her arms around his broad shoulders and buried her head in his furry neck.

"We'll have a funeral—" Lena started.

"No funeral."

"What?"

Her words were brittle, hollow, easily cracked. "No funeral. No dumb flowers. No dumb music. No dumb sermon by a dumb pastor who doesn't even know Cody."

"Okay."

"Cody will hate that." Her small, elfin features contorted.

Cody wasn't here any longer; he no longer had opinions, likes or dislikes. He was gone. Lena didn't correct Shiloh, didn't judge her in her grief. Lena swallowed back her own sadness.

Shiloh shook her head wildly, her fingers like claws in Bear's fur. He didn't seem to mind. His tongue lolled, tail wagging. "That's not Cody. It's not him."

"I said okay."

Shiloh narrowed her eyes with suspicion. "Okay, what?"

"We'll figure it out. If you don't want a funeral, we won't do a funeral. It's your choice, Shiloh."

Shiloh said nothing. They listened to Bear's panting. His tail thumped the sleeping bag.

Lena inhaled the scent of dog breath and damp fur, along with pine sap and that earthy smell she loved. She watched her niece, thinking of her sister, how similar they were, how they shared that same dark fierceness. A wave of regret washed over her, the familiar shame over the things she'd missed.

"We should do something, though," Lena said. "It's important to say goodbye, to mark his passing."

Death was about to become the new normal. As the corpses of the sick and starved piled up, would funerals become a relic of the past? She hoped not. Rituals were important; they reminded us of the things we shouldn't forget.

"Fine," Shiloh said.

"You knew Cody better than anyone. What would he have wanted?"

Shiloh gave a sullen shrug. "He loved the water, and his boat. He liked the old Norse stories, where the slain heroes were set alight and sailed out to sea."

Lena frowned. "Well, that's...unconventional. Let's think about it."

Shiloh grunted, noncommittal.

Bear lifted his head and his ears pricked. He let out a low growl.

Lena tensed. "What is it, Bear?"

Then she heard it, the rumble of an engine approaching.

6

LENA EASTON

DAY TWENTY-TWO

Lena put a finger to her lips, adrenaline spiking her veins. Perhaps Jackson had come for a visit, but he would have called ahead on the handheld radio. Maybe it was a false alarm; maybe it wasn't.

Shiloh nodded and scrambled to her knees, one hand on Bear's ruff, the other reaching for her crossbow.

Lena gave a sharp shake of her head and gestured for Shiloh to stay put. She was safest here in the tent, hidden by the trees. The girl was brave, but she was reckless, and she was still a child.

Shiloh scowled at her, but Lena was already out of the tent, her M&P in hand. Bear rose to his feet to follow her. A low growl started deep in his chest. Lena signaled for him to stay with Shiloh.

Bear chuffed in vehement disagreement, but he obeyed. Unlike humans, he always obeyed.

Outside the tent, Lena crept from a maple to a big jack pine, using the trees for cover, her footfalls loud in her ears.

Holding the pistol in both hands, she snuck behind an oak and peered around the trunk. The farmhouse was located north of her position at the top of the hill. Below the house, a section of the driveway led to the gravel parking lot for the salvage yard down the hill.

The rickety, ugly as sin Honda Pilot that she had affectionately nicknamed the Tan Turd stood in the driveway. It was dented and battered; its bumper held together with duct tape. The mini-fridge that held her supply of insulin sat on the overgrown grass in the front yard in a patch of shade, an extension cord attached to a pair of portable solar panels lying in the sun.

Far down the driveway, a rusty pick-up appeared. It gunned closer, approaching rapidly.

The hairs on the back of Lena's neck prickled. She didn't recognize the truck. Keeping low, she darted from the tree line to the Tan Turd's front bumper and hunkered down. She wanted space between herself and Shiloh. If their visitors had ill intent, let them come after her.

The truck roared up the driveway and came to a halt in the middle of the gravel parking lot, about forty yards to the south of the Tan Turd. The engine ticked in the sudden silence.

The occupants sat in the vehicle. They didn't open the doors or get out.

Lena's unease grew. With one hand, she tugged the radio Jackson had given her from her leggings pocket and tried his channel. Static filled her ear. Damn it! He was out of range.

They were on their own. No communication. No 911 to call. No police to respond within minutes, coming to the rescue with sirens blaring and lights flashing.

A minute passed, then another. Two people sat in the cab, a large figure on the driver's side, and a smaller person in the passenger seat, probably a woman. They waited and watched the house as if scoping it out.

She sucked in her breath, forced herself to calm down, to be smart, to steady her hands. She peered around the bumper, careful to stay hidden. Who were these people? And what the hell did they want?

The driver's door swung open. A big, burly guy hopped out. He wore a dirty T-shirt, his greasy hair pulled back in a man-bun, a gold ring punched through both nostrils of his nose like a bull. He carried a shotgun.

The passenger door opened and a woman exited. Her stringy, dishwater-blonde hair curtained her long, narrow face. Oozing sores peppered her lips. A ratty fuchsia-pink dress hung from her bony frame. She looked sickly, likely on meth. She gripped a tire iron, not a gun.

They spread about five feet apart and started toward the Tan Turd. Their movements were jerky and shaky, like tweakers strung out on drugs. That made them dangerous.

"I know you're there," said the guy with the bull ring. "Give us what we want."

Lena stiffened. Her heart bucked in her chest. "I don't know what you're talking about."

"The stash of insulin you've got. We heard you have years' worth. Give it up."

She waited for the clichéd *and no one gets hurt,* line but it didn't come.

Her heart thundered in her ears. How the hell did these tweakers know she had insulin? She'd never seen them before. "Not gonna happen. You're trespassing on private property. Leave now."

Footsteps crunched on gravel. One moved left around the Tan Turd; the other to the right, attempting to catch her in a pincer move, two on one.

"Don't move or we'll kill you," the woman in the pink dress said.

Lena ducked down to remain out of sight. "I don't have any insulin. Whatever you heard, it's wrong."

As they spoke, she got a bead on their location in her mind. They were about thirty feet back from the rear of the SUV and creeping closer.

A cold sweat broke out on her forehead. She'd let them steal whatever they wanted to preserve life first and foremost, but not that; anything but that.

If they took the insulin, she'd be dead in a week or two, maybe less. Without it, she'd soon develop severe abdominal pain, start vomiting, and suffer terrible headaches and blurred vision as her brain swelled, then delirium, followed by coma and death.

That insulin was her lifeline.

Lena would have to fight them, some way, somehow. She had no choice.

"I will shoot!" she called out. "This is your last chance! I have cover. You're both in the open. This is about to end badly for you. If you take another step forward, you're the ones about to die."

Bull Ring screamed more insults at her. Fear replaced the anger in his voice from only moments before to chemically-infused anxiety and paranoia. He yelled at the woman in pink. "We're about to be attacked!"

"I don't see anyone else. She's alone."

"It's a trap! I know it is!"

"It's just one lady. That's what she told me," Pinky insisted. "Don't trip out on me! Take her out! She's just a dumb housewife. Come on!"

"Okay, okay!" Bull Ring whined.

"Let's grab the prize and get out of here!"

They sounded half-crazy, hyped up on meth, paranoid and delusional, which made them unpredictable—and dangerous. Lena's pulse thudded in her ears, her palms damp and clammy, her body ice-cold.

Fear threatened to derail her thoughts. She fought to remain focused and present, to think through her options. Getting low, she peered beneath the Tan Turd to keep track of their movements and make sure they didn't sneak up on her. If she needed to abandon the car, she'd flee eastward toward the house to lure them away from Shiloh and Bear, and the insulin.

"Give it up or we kill you, right here and now," Pinky yelled. Her voice was closer now—maybe twenty feet. As she drew nearer,

Lena realized she was younger than she'd first thought, nineteen or twenty, tops.

Pinky's voice went up an octave in excitement. "Look what's sitting right there in the yard! I bet the pot of gold is right there in that fridge, ain't it?"

Sweat broke out on her forehead. Lena tightened her grip on her pistol. Any closer and she'd be forced to fire. One more step. She held her breath.

"I can't get a good bead on her," Bull Ring growled. His footsteps pounded closer, circling her to the right. "She's hiding behind that damn van—"

"Shoot her already!" Pinky shouted.

A cinnamon-brown streak burst from the woods in a blur of fur, muscle, and teeth. Bear gave a savage bark, his hackles raised.

He ran into the driveway and stood bristling between the Tan Turd and the guy with the bull ring, between Lena and imminent danger. He had never appeared so ferocious.

Startled, the intruders spun toward him.

Bull Ring raised his shotgun at the dog.

Fear lanced through Lena. Without thinking, she stood and aimed, finger on the trigger. "Don't you dare hurt my dog!"

Before she could fire, a twang and a whoosh came from the direction of the woods.

Bull Ring screamed. He collapsed to the gravel, writhing in agony. The shotgun went skittering. A bolt stuck out of his upper left thigh where a widening circle of blood darkened his pants.

A second whoosh sounded from the direction of the woods.

Pinky shrieked, dropped the tire iron, and clutched at her arm, staring at her hand in horror. A second bolt quivered from the center of her right hand, several inches of the shaft protruding from either side of her palm.

"What the hell!" The woman cursed. She stared at her pierced hand in shock, like she couldn't believe what had just happened, how swiftly her reality had shifted for the worse.

Shiloh stepped between two trees parallel to the driveway. She held the crossbow's buttstock nestled tight against her shoulder, feet spread in a fighting stance. Her cheek was pressed to the stock, her dominant eye in line with the sight, her trigger hand on the grip, index finger balanced on the trigger.

A fiberglass bolt was cocked and aimed at the woman's chest.

Shiloh looked determined and fearless, ready to squeeze that trigger without hesitation. "You losers don't learn, do you? Never shoot the dog."

7

LENA EASTON

DAY TWENTY-TWO

"You stupid slut! Look what you did!" Pinky screeched, her blood-shot eyeballs nearly bugging out of her head.

"Next one goes through your face," Shiloh said, calm and nonchalant. "I wouldn't move if I were you. Trust me, I could use the practice on real targets."

Pinky panicked. She turned and fled, didn't even glance back at her downed partner as she dashed back toward the truck, her gait jerky and uneven, hunched over, blood dripping from her injured hand and staining the pink dress crimson.

"I've got her!" Lena called. "Watch the guy."

Shiloh swiveled and aimed the crossbow at Bull Ring on the ground ten feet behind the Tan Turd. "Someone told me once that I could catch more flies with honey, but I think I can catch a hell of a lot more with your hollowed-out carcass."

Bull Ring cursed at her.

Shiloh simply smiled. "Care to find out who's right?"

With the first meth head down, Lena moved to the right, both arms up and holding the pistol in a two-handed grip, keeping Pinky between her sights. Her arms shook and she felt cold all over. Her blood sugar was dropping fast.

The tweaker stumbled to the truck, ripped open the driver's

door one-handed, and toppled inside. After a minute of struggling, she managed to start it and wield the steering wheel one-handed.

"We should shoot her," Shiloh said.

"Only if we have to."

"I have to!"

"No, you don't. She's running. Let her run."

The pick-up's tires squealed and spit gravel as it swung into reverse, bouncing off the driveway into the overgrown weeds, nearly hitting several trees before the woman got it turned around. She peeled down the drive at eighty miles an hour.

Bear dashed down the driveway after the retreating truck, barking up a storm.

"Bear, that's enough." Lena strode back to Bull Ring, who groaned and writhed on the ground. She looked down at him. "How the hell did you know to come here?"

He glared up at her. "Help me! I'm dying!"

"I will help you," Lena said, "if you tell me what I need to know. Otherwise, I will stand here and let you bleed out right in front of me. Your femoral artery has been nicked, possibly severed. What blood can't escape through the wound is pooling inside your bodily cavities. Your heart rate is increasing rapidly to compensate for the blood loss as your heart attempts to supply your vital organs. Do you feel cold? Right now, you're going into hypovolemic shock."

"Don't let me die!"

"Shiloh, watch and make sure that woman doesn't come back. I don't think she will, but just in case. And get my first-in bag, my med kit. It's in the back of the van."

Shiloh was already moving. "Got it!"

Lena lowered her pistol but kept it on Bull Ring as she went for the radio. This time she got through to Jackson. "We were attacked. One fled; the other is here at the house. Shiloh shot him with her crossbow."

A moment of static. "This is Jackson. We'll be right there, Lena.

Hang tight. Over."

She tucked the radio back in her pocket, dropped to her knees beside the injured man, and patted him down for a hidden knife or second gun—there was nothing. He wasn't in any position to hurt anyone, but it was worth checking.

"You're a nurse! You have to help me! You have to!"

"I'm a paramedic. And I do not have to help you. You came to my house. You threatened me and my family." She aimed the pistol at the man's head. It felt incredibly heavy in her hands. "I have every right to shoot you dead right now."

"Please," he whimpered. "I'm begging you."

She knew what Eli would do. Eli would shoot him without a second thought. Or he'd watch the tweaker bleed out to save the ammo. Either way, he'd walk away without guilt.

She cursed under her breath. She wasn't Eli. This creep didn't deserve to live, but that didn't mean she was prepared to take his life. Not now, not like this.

This was about her, not this drugged-up waste of oxygen. She had vowed to first, do no harm. The creed was bred into every cell of her body. Even in this broken world, she would do what she thought was right.

"You have about ten seconds to decide." With her free hand, she reached out and snapped the bolt about two inches above the spot where it pierced his flesh.

Bull Ring shrieked in pain. "My girlfriend, okay! My girlfriend told me you had the stash. She said...insulin now is like...liquid gold...diabetics will do anything...will pay any price for it..."

"How did she know to come here?"

"I don't know, okay! I don't know. She said she heard it at the shelter. Someone told her."

"What shelter?"

The man grimaced. He panted, sucking in rapid, shallow breaths. His skin was losing color. The puddle of blood grew rapidly beneath him, staining the ground.

"What shelter?"

"The Harbor! Okay! The Harbor in Christmas. She stays there sometimes when her parents kick her out of her place and she don't got somewhere to go."

"What's her name?"

"J-Jasmine. Jasmine Wilkins! She said it would be an easy payday. It was supposed to be easy, just a snatch and grab. That's all I know. Help me, please!"

Shiloh brought Lena's bag and dropped it on the driveway next to her.

"Keep your crossbow on him, Shiloh. If he makes a move for a weapon or to hurt me, shoot him. And keep an eye out for the second intruder in case she comes back."

Shiloh scanned the driveway, alert and wary. "Already on it."

Lena set the pistol down next to her knees, tugged on a pair of latex gloves, then pulled a tourniquet from her trauma kit and wound it around the man's upper thigh, tightening until the spurting blood eased. The crossbow bolt couldn't be removed without medical care above what she could provide here.

The rumble of a vehicle approached. Shiloh swung around and faced the road, crossbow up and ready. Bear stood beside her, warning the entire forest with his booming bark. Lena felt the thundering vibration in the soles of her boots, in her chest.

The sheriff's department-issued truck appeared through the trees, driving too fast but with expert precision. Devon was behind the wheel, not Jackson.

Devon parked and Jackson leaped from the truck and raced toward them, his county-issued AR-15 in his hands, the stock pressed against his shoulder. He scanned the surroundings as he approached. "Any threats?"

"The woman took the truck and ran." Lena stood unsteadily and stripped her bloody gloves. Dizziness washed through her, nausea churning in her stomach. "Sorry, I need—I just need something—"

"Get a glucose tab from Lena's pack," Jackson ordered Shiloh. "In the front zippered pocket. Right there. That's it."

The girl obeyed. Lena couldn't seem to lift her arms, her body felt heavy, weighed down. Shiloh shouldered the crossbow and popped the glucose tab into Lena's mouth. "You need water?"

"She likes apple juice," Jackson said.

Shakily, Lena rolled her eyes. "He thinks he knows everything."

"She's still got her sense of humor, that's a good sign."

Devon crouched and held two fingers to Bull Ring's neck. "He's alive. Let's get him in the back of the truck and to the hospital."

"He doesn't deserve a hospital," Shiloh said.

"That's not for us to decide," Lena said.

"What about the tweaker that got away?" Shiloh demanded.

"She'll likely head to the hospital. We'll find her," Devon said.

Frowning, Jackson studied Bull Ring. "I know this perp. He's got a rap sheet longer than my right arm. Petty thievery. A drug addict and an occasional small-time dealer. He tried to start a meth lab a few years ago in the Hiawatha National Forest outside of Manistique and nearly blew himself up. His brother lost an arm and is currently incarcerated. He's bad news."

"What happens now?" Lena asked. "Do we have to make a report or something?"

"Clearly this is self-defense," Devon said. "You aren't going to get in trouble on our end.

I'll write up a report, but I doubt the DA wants to hear it. He's a bit overwhelmed at the moment."

"What the hell did they want?" Jackson asked. "There's nothing here worth anything."

Lena patted the dented hood of the Tan Turd. Duct tape wrapped the front and rear bumper. It looked like it was a thousand years old. "We take offense at that."

"They were after Lena's insulin," Shiloh said. "He said the pharmacies were all empty, and that diabetics were willing to pay anything for a vial."

"That's true about the pharmacies. But why come here?"

Lena repeated what Bull Ring had said about the shelter.

Jackson's expression darkened. He cursed under his breath; a muscle in his jaw twitched.

"What is it, boss?" Devon asked.

Without a word, Jackson turned and stormed toward the truck. "Get this tweaker loaded up so we can get out of here. I've got something to take care of."

Five minutes later, they were gone. The late afternoon sun slanted through the trees, a pleasant breeze sighing through the branches. The sudden quiet was disconcerting.

Lena went unsteadily to the mini-fridge on the overgrown lawn and checked it, as she had compulsively checked it every single night, breathing a sigh of relief as the cold air hit her face. The vials were safe and protected.

She sank to her butt in the grass, checked her numbers, and ate two packages of Smarties. Then she sat and breathed in the fresh air, waiting for her blood sugar to stabilize, to feel normal again.

"You saved his life," Shiloh said in an accusing tone. "Why?"

"It's my job. It's what I do. I heal people. I don't hurt them unless I have to, and at that moment, I didn't have to keep hurting him. It was safe for me to help."

Shiloh made a dubious face.

"I'm not comfortable allowing someone to die when they no longer pose a direct threat."

"How can you know? What if someone comes back and poses a bigger threat later?"

Lena looked at her. "That's a good question."

"Eli would've killed them both."

"You're not wrong. My moral and ethical choices might be different from someone else's. You'll have to decide that for yourself. In the end, I have to make choices that I can live with. Does that make sense?"

"Whatever." Shiloh kicked at a rock. "She's lucky I didn't shoot her in the face."

Lena sighed. The girl was just like Eli, through and through. It wasn't necessarily a bad thing. "You okay? You did shoot two people with your crossbow this afternoon."

She scrunched up her nose. "That reminds me, I need those bolts back. We've gotta conserve in the apocalypse. Isn't that what you're always telling me?"

"Shiloh. Be serious. This is a lot—"

Shiloh shot Lena a peevish look. "This isn't the bad stuff. This is nothing."

"Okay." Lena studied her for a moment and then nodded. "Okay. Then, let's go."

"What do you mean?"

"This house holds bad memories for both of us. Sometimes, what we need to heal is time. And sometimes, all the time in the world won't make a difference. What do you think about a fresh start somewhere else? It's still in town, but a new place to call our own."

"There's nowhere else to go."

"Yes, there is."

Shiloh took that in. The girl had never lived anywhere but here. This place was her life, her universe. It was time for a new beginning for Shiloh, and her too. Lena could see it, could envision them making a go of it, thriving, even.

"I know it's a big change—"

"I'm in."

An ember sparked to life in her chest. "I haven't even told you where it is yet."

"Doesn't matter. I wanna go." She hesitated. "With you."

Lena smiled. "Okay."

"Okay."

"How long do you need to pack?"

"You mean, like right now?"

"Yes. Right now."

Shiloh looked back at the farmhouse she'd grown up in. "I need ten minutes."

Lena hauled herself to her feet, a smile on her lips. "We're leaving in five."

8

JACKSON CROSS

DAY TWENTY-TWO

Jackson burst into his parents' home and stormed into the living room, incandescent with rage. "What the hell did you do?"

Astrid stared up at him with a sweetly innocent smile. "Whatever do you mean, brother?"

"Stand up," he said. "I know you can. Stand up and face me and admit what you did!"

His mother gasped. "Jackson!"

He stood in the center of the expansive family room, reclaimed rafter beams stretching across the twenty-foot ceiling. A massive stone fireplace encased in a marble mantle rose to his right. Hunting trophies hung on the wall to his left—deer, moose, and bear.

His mother sat on the velvet sofa beside Astrid, who leaned against plumped pillows, her legs stretched across Dolores' lap as she massaged her daughter's shins, calves, and ankles. Faded purple scars zigzagged across Astrid's withered legs.

Astrid experienced severe pain from the accident; their mother would give her hour-long massages each day. Cyrus Lee would do it on occasion, but only if Dolores couldn't. Jackson looked away. "Mom, this is between me and Astrid."

"I planned to make your favorite chocolate chip cookies this afternoon, but we're out of chocolate chips. And butter. Your father promised me he'd head to the store."

From his armchair where he was reading a leather-bound classic edition of *Moby Dick*, Horatio shot Jackson a look of warning. "I will, Dolores. I've been busy."

Jackson ignored him. He was too angry to play their little mind games, to coddle them any longer. "The stores are closed. The shelves are empty, just like I said they would be."

Dolores blinked at him, confusion in her eyes. "I'll bake something delicious for you tomorrow, dear. Don't you worry."

"That's not what I'm worried about, mother."

Dolores finished rubbing Astrid's feet and helped her into her wheelchair. Astrid groaned as if she were in immense pain. Her cane leaned against the sofa within easy reach, but Astrid relished being doted on. Dolores was half Astrid's size, and her thin arms strained to lift her daughter, who could lift herself just fine.

"Where's your boyfriend? Can't he help you?"

Astrid glared at him. "He's busy taking care of us. What are you doing?"

"Keeping the whole county safe, what do you think I've been doing?" He hated his sister's ability to get under his skin, to find his weakness, stick a knife in, and twist it.

Once in her wheelchair, Astrid kissed Dolores on her papery cheek without taking her eyes off Jackson. "May I have a blanket? I'm cold."

"Of course, darling."

"Whatever would I do without you, Mom? You're a lifesaver."

Dolores brought her an Afghan blanket and wrapped it gently around her shoulders before patting her head with a shaky hand. His mother looked suddenly old, her shoulder blades hunched inward like wings, her silvery hair frazzled, and her eyes dim and bleary.

Horatio had her on a high dose of antidepressants, but Jackson was too upset with Astrid to focus on his mother now. "Lena was attacked by two tweakers high on meth. They knew she had extra insulin and seemed to think they could sell it for more drugs."

Astrid stared at him with wide unblinking eyes. Her cheeks were pink and flushed. She wore no makeup; she had never needed it. Her beauty masked her pettiness, her tendency toward casual cruelty, like a child with a magnifying glass, frying ants on the sidewalk.

She was both fragile and sharp as a blade.

With a practiced hand, Astrid brushed her silky blonde hair behind her shoulders. "That's truly awful, Jackson. Is she alright?"

"No thanks to you."

She stuck out her lower lip in a pout. "Why would I have anything to do with that?"

"Lena stayed here her first night. You knew she had her insulin with her. And you volunteered at the Harbor two nights ago. I checked."

"The homeless need food and water too, Jackson."

"One of them confirmed they got the information from the shelter."

"Did they say my name?" Her voice had gone distinctly chilly. "Are you accusing me of something you can't prove? Isn't that a big no-no for a sheriff? I mean, an undersheriff."

"No one needs to name you, Astrid. You are the only one who knew."

Astrid crossed her arms over her chest and stared him down.

"They came with weapons. Lena could have been hurt or killed. Shiloh was there, a thirteen-year-old girl. How could you?"

"These are baseless accusations and frankly, I'm hurt. To think my own brother would accuse me of such a horrible, absurd thing. Why would I do that?"

"Is this necessary, Jackson?" Horatio asked.

Jackson ignored his father. "Why indeed? Why do you need a reason for any of the callous and hateful things you've done over the years?"

"Hateful? You go too far, brother."

"You never liked Lena, or Lily for that matter. You were always jealous of them—"

Astrid's ice-blue eyes went hard, and her mouth flattened. "Don't you dare speak of Lily Easton in this house."

He had never understood why she'd hated Lily so much. He knew better than to ask. Astrid said much but revealed little; she kept her cards close to her chest, her true self hidden by her charming smile. She acted weak for the pity she craved, but if anyone messed with her, she'd destroy them. Not physically, of course, but with cruel insults, vicious rumors, and scandal.

Jackson's hands balled into fists at his sides. Anger roiled through him, sharp and bitter. He struggled to control himself. "I know it was you."

"Everyone knows she's back in town. It's not like that ugly-as-sin beater van of hers is hard to miss. Everyone knows she's diabetic. And everyone knows the Easton place. Do you think it's some big conspiracy to believe that a couple of meth heads would decide to hit her up for her insulin stash? You're delusional."

"Don't be cruel, Jackson." Dolores stood behind Astrid's wheelchair and rubbed her shoulders, her expression reproachful. "How can you say such awful things to your sister?"

"They could have been killed! You have no idea what you might've done." He paused, meeting Astrid's gaze, her eyes pretty as a doll's and just as empty. "Or maybe you do know what you did. Maybe it's what you wanted."

"That's enough!" Horatio thundered.

Astrid did not break his gaze, as if she wanted him to know that she knew the truth. More games. More twisted manipulations. Bitterness had consumed Astrid after the accident that had stolen her legs, her dreams, and her future.

She was always this way, a voice whispered in his mind. He'd pitied her and allowed it to excuse her behavior, but no longer.

Deep inside him, something snapped. Without a word, Jackson spun and headed through the vast living room for the kitchen and the door to the basement.

"Where do you think you're going?" Horatio asked.

"Don't leave us!" Dolores called after him, her voice plaintive. Then, to Astrid, she said, "He wouldn't leave us, would he? Not when we need him."

"Jackson only cares about himself." Astrid's cutting words were the last thing he heard.

His sense of duty almost forced him to turn back. Almost. Even after Astrid had carelessly donated his hard-earned supplies, he'd gone out again and retrieved more. He'd done it for them, always for them.

His feelings for his family were bound up in a tangled knot of guilt and resentment, obligation and love. It was slowly unraveling.

Horatio followed him into the immaculate kitchen, not a speck of dust or crumb left anywhere. "Stop."

Jackson turned to face his father.

"If you leave, you leave with nothing. You aren't taking a single can of beans. Nothing. You understand me, son?"

"The generator should be out of propane. It should have run out a week ago, the way everyone has been draining electricity in this house. But it hasn't. I checked the tank. You had it filled. Sawyer ambushed a propane truck in Chatham last week. You got it from him."

Horatio stared at him without blinking. "I will not apologize for taking care of this family."

"Publicly, you condemn Sawyer, while privately you contract with him to keep yourself cushy and comfortable, is that it?"

"Get off your high horse before you fall off and bring the people you care about down with you. You must be willing to do what it takes, especially now." Horatio looked him up and down as if assessing his worth then shook his head in derision. "No wonder Underwood thinks you're incompetent."

Jackson couldn't help it. The comment stung someplace deep down, in that wounded, vulnerable spot he'd always hated in himself. Wounds inflicted by the people who were supposed to love you most were difficult arrows to dodge, no matter how much you expected them, or convinced yourself to endure them. They hurt, every time.

"I'll take a duffle bag of clothes and a backpack of supplies. The rest, I'll leave to you," he said stiffly. As angry as he was, he didn't wish to see his family members starve. "I'm leaving, and I am not coming back."

Horatio made a disbelieving grunt in the back of his throat. "You'll come back groveling."

Jackson had never groveled. Reinventing history was a honed skill in his family. He'd simply submitted in the past, but no longer. The world was changing and demanded that he change with it. "I will not."

Horatio did a half-turn, showing Jackson his back in dismissal.

Jackson refused to be made small. He stood his ground and said nothing, refusing to beg, to capitulate, to make pathetic excuses that would only further diminish him in his own eyes.

At his silence, Horatio turned back. Jackson held his gaze and did not blink. It was his father who dropped his gaze first.

His family was slowly tearing itself apart. Horatio saw all things only in relation to how they affected him. His mother was fragile and needy, his sister selfish and cruel.

There were cracks all over the place. The center would not hold.

Jackson had to get out before they took him down with them.

9

JACKSON CROSS

DAY TWENTY-THREE

"Hurry it up, I don't have all day." The county medical examiner wore PPE from head to foot as she gestured for them to enter the makeshift morgue.

Jackson and Devon had arrived at the Munising Hospital where the bodies of the seven victims found behind Boone's cabin were held in cold storage. The corpses would normally be delivered to the University of Michigan's forensic lab, but they weren't conducting autopsies and would not say when they might do so again.

It felt like walking into a massive refrigerator. The frigid air raised goosebumps on Jackson's arms. Corpses in black body bags were stacked nearly to the ceiling and covered every available inch of space.

The hospital itself was bedlam. Parked vehicles overflowed the parking lot, spilled onto the road, and jammed the ER entrance. Gurneys of patients crammed the hallways. They were operating well over capacity, the nurses and doctors hurrying to and fro, frazzled and exhausted.

The generator rumbled. Overhead, the fluorescent tube lights flickered.

"Damn lights," the ME grumbled. Venla Virtanen was a stout,

no-nonsense Finnish woman in her fifties with short, white-blonde hair. "They do that every day now. I'm waiting for the moment they don't come back on."

Jackson inhaled the familiar smells of bleach and antiseptic. "How are things here?"

"Terrible," Dr. Virtanen said. "Intake is up over fifty percent. We've already seen a marked increase in heart attacks, strokes, accidents, and drug overdoses. People are starting to run out of the medications that keep them alive. We have the generators, but how long will we have fuel? Then what?"

The ME shook her head in resignation. "Hospital staff is already down thirty percent. We're losing doctors and nurses by the hour. And who can blame them? Everyone is quitting, everywhere. How can you go to work when you don't have gas to drive your car? Your kids are at home without food. You're not getting a paycheck. Everything's changed in the blink of an eye and no one knows what to do."

"You're still here," Devon said.

Dr. Virtanen made a noncommittal sound in the back of her throat. "My daughter lives over in Paradise with my two grandkids and her useless husband. He can't even change a light bulb properly." She frowned. "I worry about them constantly, but I'm committed to my job. I love what I do. But this...I don't know. I just don't know."

"I know what you mean," Devon said. "There are still crimes being committed. We're still here, as long as it takes."

"Talk to me in a month and we'll see."

Devon and Jackson exchanged a disconcerting glance. If they lost their medical examiner, their ability to solve cases would be severely hampered.

They'd already lost access to the National Crime Information Center, NCIC, which they had used to check criminal backgrounds, search outstanding arrest warrants, and track terrorists. They'd also lost access to the CODIS DNA Crime Database, which collected DNA information and location tracking extracted from facial recognition software, security cameras, and phone tracking.

Normally, the state police or the FBI would've been up their asses if not outright asserting jurisdiction. The Alger County Sheriff's Office had requested aid from the federal field office and the State Police Department in Detroit, but the state police had been deployed to handle food riots throughout Detroit and Grand Rapids. There were also riots in Kalamazoo, Lansing, and even as far north as Traverse City.

Everyone else had their hands full, so this case was theirs. For now.

This was their chance to do something right, to make one small difference in the sea of chaos, with a world fast sliding into something ugly and unrecognizable.

The ME straightened her shoulders and got back to business. "You're not here to listen to me grouse. You're here about the seven deceased females. I have twenty other corpses on the docket to process. I don't have all day, so let's get to it."

"What about Cody Easton?" Jackson asked.

"I've not gotten to him yet. Get in line." Dr. Virtanen led them past an array of body bags on gurneys and a rolling medical tray covered in shiny steel instruments, including a Stryker saw to cut through bone.

Devon pulled out her notebook. "What can you tell us about the victims?"

Dr. Virtanen moved to a stretcher along the far wall and pulled the papery sheet back from the corpse. The remains had been reduced to a skeleton. Patchy wisps of long brunette hair clung to the ochre-colored cranium.

"The deceased were females. Judging from bone development and pelvic shape, they varied in age from mid-teens through the early twenties. Five were probably teenagers, while the other two are likely to be twenty to twenty-three. None had given birth."

Jackson frowned. Lily Easton had been twenty-seven when

she'd died, at least five years older than the other victims. She also had two children. It was an anomaly.

"Do you know when they died?" Devon asked.

"Approximately." The ME tilted her chin toward a file folder on the counter. "I've included the data in my report. I have ordered the Jane Does according to the estimated time of death. Jane Doe One perished about fourteen years ago. Jane Doe Two, about eleven years ago, while Three and Four died approximately seven and six years ago. Jane Doe Five died around four years ago. Jane Doe Six was killed within the last two years. And Jane Doe Seven approximately one to two months ago."

Devon's skin went ashen. "Our unsub has been killing for that long? Undetected? Holy hell."

Jackson kept his focus on the details, his mind whirring. He frowned. "Most of the victims died after Lily Easton, except for two."

"That is correct."

"You're sure that Jane Doe One was killed first?"

"Generally, it takes ten to fifteen years to decompose to a skeletal state. According to advanced decay and skeletonization typical of a human body buried underground without a coffin, yes."

Jackson made a mental note. A serial killer's first kill was often someone they knew, before graduating to strangers and potentially before they developed sophisticated measures to avoid detection.

"As you know, a tox report is impossible now. I can't provide information on whether they died while intoxicated or drugged, or whether they were poisoned. I can tell you that the likely cause of death for the seven victims is strangulation. The hyoid bone is typically broken in only a third of strangulation cases. Here, we have five Jane Does with fractured hyoid bones. Two of the victims retained enough tissue to determine blunt force injuries to the neck.

"Strangulation often produces evidence of asphyxiation, as determined by pinpoint hemorrhages, or petechiae, in the skin, eyes, and deep internal organs. Three of your Jane Does showed evidence of petechiae, but to be clear, petechiae is a non-specific finding, which means it could occur due to hanging, drowning, profound drug intoxication, et cetera. The details are in the report."

Dr. Virtanen moved to the next victim. "All of the Jane Does suffered several facial fractures, the maxilla and mandible bones to the nasal and palatine bones. See here and here. The force required to do this is considerable."

"He beat them in the face before strangling them," Devon said. "To stun them. To take the fight out of them. Or it's part of the control and domination aspect of the act."

Jackson gazed down at the crushed facial bones of what was once Jane Doe One's face, her identity. This unsub, or unknown subject, had hated everything that she was, that she represented.

He said, "I don't think it's for control or any practical purpose. A man who does this to a woman's face is driven by hatred. He detests his victims. He hates women. They've spurned him, ignored him, taunted him. During the act, he's enraged. It's revenge, getting vengeance on each victim, getting even. He feels vindicated after each kill. It's not for the sake of controlling them but eradicating their identity, utterly destroying them. The violence is for the sake of violence. That is the purpose."

"He's a sadist," Devon said.

Jackson nodded. "Whereas Boone was a power and control rapist. That's why he kept them in the pit for weeks, why he played mind games with them, treated them like his toys, like dolls. This unsub's M.O. is distinct from his partner's."

"The bodies were too decomposed to determine whether the injuries were sustained antemortem or postmortem," Dr. Virtanen said.

"I would think antemortem," Jackson said. "You can't hurt a corpse. And he wants to hurt them."

"Were there other injuries?" Devon asked.

"None that I could detect," the ME said. "Jane Doe Three had a healed fracture of the ulna, and Jane Doe One broke her left ankle as a child. The growth plate was stunted."

"What about the necklaces?" Jackson asked.

"Each locket contained a lock of hair, which we DNA-matched to each of the deceased. They're in the evidence envelope."

"His calling card," Devon said.

The ME covered the corpse of Jane Doe One and moved to the next corpse. "During the excavation of Jane Doe seven another object was discovered. We found a ring."

Devon raised her eyebrows. "The victim's?"

"Judging by the size, it's a man's ring. It's similar to a class or sports ring. I could not determine its origin." The ME gave Jackson an appraising glance. "That's your department."

Devon retrieved the ring from the evidence envelope with gloved fingers. She held it out in her palm.

Jackson examined it. The thick band was constructed of black steel with Celtic markings. Twin titanium snakes circled the circumference of the band, their bodies intertwined. The wide face of the ring featured an intricately carved wolf's head, the snakes' heads caught between its jaws.

"The ring was recovered two inches distal to her right hand, beneath the corpse, approximately four feet deep, which implies the girl and ring were buried at the same time, during the same event."

"It might have slipped off while he buried her."

"It's possible." Jackson squinted, his brow furrowed. A tingling sensation started at the back of his neck and spread across his scalp.

"It might have belonged to Boone," Devon said.

"Maybe."

Devon studied him. "What is it, boss? You recognize it?"

"Perhaps." A memory pricked the back of his mind. Exhaustion pulled at him, but he forced himself to focus, to think. The wolf eating the snakes...it was familiar, too familiar. "I've seen a tattoo of this image. Maybe the ring, too. I can't place it."

"Walter Boone didn't have any tattoos." The ME briskly covered the remaining bodies of the Jane Does, already moving on to her next case, the next victim. At least a dozen waited for her. How many would there be next week? Two dozen? Even more?

"Whose ring is it, then?" Devon asked as she signed the Chain of Custody log, tucked the evidence envelope under her arm, and headed for the morgue exit.

Jackson fell into step beside her. "That's one of many questions we need to answer."

10

SHILOH EASTON

DAY TWENTY-FOUR

Lena hovered nervously in the doorway behind Shiloh. "What do you think?"

Shiloh took it in with wide eyes. "You sure it's empty?"

"I asked around. This lighthouse was privately run by the volunteer historical society. They've got other things to worry about now. I'm sure they'd appreciate someone taking care of it. Do you like it?" Lena asked, anxiousness in her voice.

Shiloh stepped through the doorway. She hadn't even seen the whole thing and she already loved it; no way was she admitting that, though. "Jury's still out."

The light keeper's house was a small brick cottage attached to an eight-story whitewashed stone tower. A gallery catwalk ringed the lantern room. The cupola was painted bright red to match the red brick of the cottage. At the top, a lightning rod pierced the sky.

"The cottage is on well and septic," Lena said, "with a spring that feeds a creek as a secondary water source. There's an old caretaker's cabin, too. And someone built a greenhouse in the backyard. It's gone to seed, but we can get it up and operational again. We can grow tomatoes, cucumbers, lettuce, carrots, and potatoes year-round. The spring that feeds the creek is cold enough that we can build a springhouse for refrigeration."

Shiloh went inside. Bear followed close at her heels, his paws clicking across the wood floor. He sneezed as their footsteps kicked up dust. "How old is this place?"

"It was built in the 1880s."

It looked ancient. There were no lights, no outlets, no electricity wired into this place at all. Luckily, it boasted indoor plumbing. With the septic system, they could lug buckets of water from the creek or lake to fill and flush the toilet.

Wood paneling lined the walls, and the floors were constructed of rustic pine planks. In one corner stood an ancient contraption, a Singer treadle sewing machine.

There was a tiny kitchen, an even tinier bathroom, and two bedrooms with hand-hewn wooden beds and homemade quilts. The kitchen boasted an authentic woodstove for cooking, which made Lena even more excited. A second woodstove in the living room provided heat in the winter. Lanterns hung from hooks on the walls for lighting.

A wooden door in the kitchen separated the cottage from the lighthouse tower.

"You wanna go up?" Lena asked, grinning like a little kid.

Her enthusiasm was catching. Shiloh grinned back. "Hell, yes."

"Language, missy."

Shiloh rolled her eyes and scampered past Lena as she forced open the rickety wooden door. The stone tower was tall and narrowed at the summit, the iron staircase spiraling at least eighty feet straight up.

A landing was located every fifteen feet or so. Two tiny rectangular windows were cut into the stone two-thirds of the way up, which were used to cool the interior of the lighthouse and provide natural light.

At the base of the stairs, Bear balked.

"Come on," Shiloh said. "You can come, too."

The hackles rose on Bear's spine. He growled at the staircase like it might transform into a snake and bite him.

"He doesn't like the stairs," Lena said. "He's special like that."

They climbed the rickety stairs without him. The Newfie gazed forlornly up at them as if upset that they dared to go somewhere without him. At each landing, Shiloh tried to coax him up, but Bear circled the base of the tower, whimpering his displeasure from below.

"We'll come back down, I promise."

Dust tickled her nose. Shiloh sneezed. The air smelled faintly of mildew. At the second to last landing, she used her lockpick set to unlock a rusty steel door.

An old plaque labeled the tiny four by six foot room as the service room, where keepers stored cleaning equipment, spare parts, tools, and a log book. A bunch of old kerosene lanterns lined one shelf, with extra wicks and a few dozen candles.

Her gaze was drawn to an object encased in glass sitting on a bookcase shelf next to a collection of ancient journals. A sign said "Do not touch" but Shiloh, of course, ignored it. The sole benefit to the world crashing in on itself was the opportunity to abolish dumb rules.

She glanced behind her. Lena stood a level below, reading a plaque about the construction of the tower. Shiloh picked up the glass case, opened the back, and removed the authentic arrowhead.

Constructed of hammered flint, the arrowhead was attached to a three-inch length rod, bound to the arrowhead with dried sinew. Smiling, she pressed the tip to her finger. It was still sharp.

Tugging the elastic band from her braid, Shiloh wound it around the arrow. With one hand, she pulled her thick black hair into a messy bun and stuck the arrow through it.

Now, that was badass. Besides, it wasn't as if the Lighthouse Historical Society needed it. There would be no more school tours for a very long time.

Lena came up behind her. "Cool, right?"

"It's not terrible," she admitted as she ran a finger along a dusty telescope in the corner. The lantern room would be a fantastic spot to watch the stars. "I bet Ruby would like to see this."

"We'll bring her over for a visit. Ready to go up? The best is yet to come."

Shiloh pilfered one of the logbooks and slipped it into the front pocket of her hoodie—Cody's old hoodie. She'd taken to wearing his clothes, especially when she slept. They still had his scent, that woodsy, artsy smell that was distinctly her brother. "After you."

Together, they scaled an upright ladder to reach the lantern room through a hatch in the floor. The walls of the lantern room were constructed entirely of glass. Shiloh whistled, taking in the spectacular 360-degree view.

"That's the beacon." Lena pointed to a strange object constructed of steel and glass in the center of the lantern room. "The Fresnel lens uses prisms to magnify a small amount of light so it casts a beam over long distances, twenty miles or more."

Shiloh crossed the room to a small door, opened it, and stepped out onto the gallery deck, a catwalk that circled the tower at the level of the lantern room.

Lena followed her out. "Be careful."

"I'm not scared of heights."

The cool breeze tickled her cheeks. The sun warmed her face. Almost ninety feet up, she felt as high as the seagulls that circled the bluffs, riding the currents of the wind. From here, she could see the beach, the woods, the greenhouse and caretaker assistant's cabin, the winding creek emptying into Superior.

Long fingers of land protruded into the lake. Lime and sandstone bluffs jutted a hundred feet above the waterline, layers of rock molded by centuries of glaciers. The waves broke against the shore, foaming into lacy patterns in the pebble-strewn sand.

The great lake stretched out as far as the eye could see, the skyline broken only by Grand Island in the distance. Lighthouse keepers from a hundred years ago would have scanned the same horizon for ships in distress.

Cody would've loved to draw this scene. Her chest ached at the thought; she swiped at her eyes to keep Lena from seeing, and then cleared her throat. "Boats still need lighthouses to guide them into shore during storms and fog, to avoid wrecking against the shoals and rocks."

"That's correct."

"Is that what we're going to do? Run the lighthouse?"

"It's an idea."

Shiloh tried to remain non-committal. "Not the worst one I've ever heard."

"I think we can make a go of this," Lena said. "It's going to take a lot of work, but this has potential. It's got the woodstove, the generator for the lighthouse beacon, and the greenhouse we can fix up. There are cisterns for rainwater collection. And the spring can keep some of my insulin refrigerated as a backup in case something happens to the mini-fridge. If we can keep the beacon lit, we could help people, too."

Shiloh couldn't help it. Her whole body thrummed with excitement. For half a second, she forgot the bad stuff: the nightmares, the feeling of Boone's hands on her throat, the bone-crushing grief for the dead brother she hadn't saved.

"There's one big problem. How the hell do we figure out how to work this thing?"

"Did you notice the room downstairs with the bookcase of books about lighthouses? I saw some manuals. Plus, I know the woman who used to run this place as a volunteer when I was in school, Mrs. Grady. She's the librarian now. You might know her?"

Shiloh nodded. Mrs. Grady was an old friend.

"I think she'd be willing to help." Lena looked around. "As far as fuel for the generator, there's some in the tank now, but I can't tell how much. With GPS navigation gone, this lighthouse is critical for every tugboat, fishing boat, yacht, ferry, and shipping barge out there. Maybe we talk to the Sheriff's Office, FEMA, or the superintendent. I'm sure we can work out a way to get fuel in exchange for manning the lighthouse. It's a public service. No one wants to run aground in the middle of a storm."

"It's worth a shot."

"Okay. We're off to a good start, but we need some ground rules." Lena ticked them off with her fingers. "I need to know where you are. We eat dinner together each night. You use a fork and spoon, not your fingers. Personal hygiene is a thing. You sleep in the house. And there's a curfew."

Shiloh made a face. "More dumb rules? Seriously?"

"Oh, yes, young lady. You're used to frolicking through the wilderness at all hours, but some things need to change around here. Things like a curfew are non-negotiable."

Her grandfather had never cared where she was or when she came home. When he'd been on a bender, she and Cody had been safer in the woods.

Shiloh crossed her arms over her chest. "Midnight."

"Nine p.m."

"Ten."

"Nine thirty. Privileges must be earned."

"I want to sleep in the tower, in the lantern room."

She expected Lena to balk, but she didn't even blink. "Deal."

Lena stuck out her hand. Shiloh rolled her eyes but shook it.

"This is a big responsibility."

"I'm not scared."

Lena smiled. "Good."

11

ELI POPE

DAY TWENTY-FIVE

"Howdy, stranger." Lena stood on the porch, hands on her hips. She wore jeans and a fitted white T-shirt, her long, chestnut waves pulled back into a ponytail. Sweat beaded her forehead, dirt smudged her cheek.

Eli's face warmed; he averted his gaze and cleared his throat. "I heard what happened. I came to make sure you were okay, you and Shiloh."

"You want to come in?"

Yes. Yes, he did. "Sure."

Eli followed her into the cottage. It felt like stepping back in time. Most of the furnishings were original to the 1800s.

She led him to the small, sunlit kitchen where she glanced out the back window to check on Shiloh, then turned to face him. "How are you at construction?"

"Depends on what it is."

"We found a creek leading to a freshwater spring. We're trying to figure out how to build a springhouse for refrigeration. I've got the solar panels for the mini-fridge, but I want a backup. I don't want to store everything in one place, either, in case something happens. Besides, with a springhouse, we can refrigerate milk, meat, cheese, or whatever we need to."

"Good idea."

She beamed. "I know."

"I'll help."

"Are you sure? All I can promise you is some of that aforementioned milk and cheese."

"I want to help." He looked her over, scanning for injuries but saw none. "You're both okay? Did they hurt you?"

"They were unsuccessful, thanks to Shiloh. Things could have gone badly." She looked shaken but not scared. "I don't want to be taken by surprise again. I want to be smart and strong. We have to prepare. I know you have...skills." She gestured at the lighthouse. "I want to make this place a fortress. I want to protect her."

"So do I." He held out an object folded in a hand towel to hide it from prying eyes. He'd retrieved it from one of the caches he'd buried years ago. "Start with this. It's cleaned and oiled, loaded, and ready to go."

She unwrapped the Taurus 357 Magnum revolver. "I already have my M&P 9 Shield."

"Keep it in the house somewhere close. You might need it someday. You won't have your holster on you at all times. It's a good backup option."

Soberly, she nodded. "Thank you."

"I used to keep mine in the junk drawer in the kitchen, next to the stove. I had a pistol taped under the coffee table, and one in the bedside table."

"Back when you had a house." She offered him a small smile. "Now you're a wild man who lives in the woods."

"Houses are overrated."

Even under the circumstances, her smile lit up her eyes, her entire face. He couldn't help himself; he smiled in return.

He didn't want to make her uncomfortable, to make her bolt like a startled doe, but he couldn't help himself; he longed to be near her, to catch that smile. She had such warmth to her, like a glow that lit her up from the inside that you could feel like heat, simply being near her.

He said, "I hope you never have to use it."

"I will if I have to."

"I know."

Lena was tough, brave, and practical. She was not built to kill, but to heal, to help others. He knew that the very thought of taking a life was anathema to her very being. As a little girl, she used to rescue every kitten and bedraggled baby bird she came across.

Everything in him wanted to protect her from that choice, that darkness. Let her bind wounds and tend the injured, to use her strength for good where he could not.

Lena was nothing like him. Where she was light, he was darkness. He was the monster that stood between the innocent and the worse monsters. He had accepted that role. He felt no remorse, no shame, and no guilt over the bad men he had put in the ground.

Occasionally, he wondered what kind of person that made him. In the end, he did not care that he didn't care.

"How is Shiloh?" he asked.

"She's traumatized. But she's a tough kid. She's strong. I'm trying to give her a safe place where she can heal. But I'm worried, Eli. I'm worried we can't promise anywhere is safe anymore."

"We never could."

"I know. But I'll be damned if I don't try."

He joined Lena at the rear window. A grassy backyard dropped off to a pebble-strewn stretch of beach fifty yards to the north. He scanned the property, taking in the cottage, the lighthouse tower, and the little assistant's cabin. Fifty-plus yards of clearance surrounding the lighthouse offered a clear line of sight. That was good.

To the east of the lighthouse, a creek meandered across the property before spilling into Lake Superior. Shiloh was hard at work unloading a wheelbarrow stacked with cinder blocks they'd found at an abandoned landscaping shop.

Bear lay stretched out on his side on the grassy bank next to the growing pile of blocks, panting as if exhausted from a long day of labor. His big head swiveled to follow Shiloh's movements, his ears pricked, tongue lolling.

Lena's eyes went hard. "I never want to feel that helpless again. I have to protect her. I know you understand that."

"I do." He wanted to be here to protect them both, though he had no right to either of them. He wanted to touch her, to offer comfort, but knew he couldn't. She smelled like vanilla and cinnamon, the smell achingly familiar. It was abruptly difficult to breathe. "I'll help you. I'll come by tomorrow and work on some security protocols. Whatever you need, just ask."

Lena pulled two cans of peaches and two bowls from the cupboard and set them on the table. "You hungry? I need to eat something."

"I'm good." In truth, he hadn't eaten much the last few days, but Lena needed every calorie she could get.

"Suit yourself."

She checked her pump, then perused the back of the can, brow furrowed as she calculated the carbohydrates in her head and matched it to the insulin dose she bolused herself with at every meal.

He'd watched her do this a thousand times. It was as normal to her as breathing. But there was nothing normal about living with Type 1 diabetes now.

Behind her, her diabetic supplies were neatly organized on the counter beside a bucket of sudsy dishwater and a Coleman lantern: infusion sets, sensors, rechargeable batteries for her pump, a sharps container, the glucometer, and her emergency glucagon kit.

He looked at the paraphernalia for a long time, thinking about her illness, about what would happen a year from now. Or two years from now. How was she going to get the medication that kept her alive?

Dread formed a stone in the pit of his stomach. He couldn't imagine a world without her in it, he truly couldn't.

She caught him looking and made a face. "I'm fine," she said quickly, too quickly. "Don't worry about me."

Easier said than done. "Who said I'm worried?"

She rolled her eyes and took a big bite of peach. Syrup dripped down her chin, and she wiped it with a laugh. "I'm trying to take things a day at a time, okay?"

"Okay," he said, but things weren't okay, and they both knew it.

She changed the subject, and they chatted about nothing for a while. After she finished eating, she cleared the table and sat down again. Her lips pursed as she studied him with that familiar tilt to her head he knew so well.

"What is it?" he asked. "Something's bothering you."

"I need to tell you something."

"What?"

"You might want to sit down for this."

Eli remained standing. "Tell me."

She cleared her throat, smoothed her ponytail, and looked anywhere but at him.

"Lena," he said.

"Okay, fine." She huffed a breath, faced him, and met his gaze. "Shiloh...she's yours."

He stared at her blankly. "What do you mean?"

She gave him a look. "Men."

"Lena—"

"She's your daughter, Eli."

Eli sat down hard.

Luckily, there was a chair to catch him. Shock rushed through him. He stared at her in astonishment. "What?"

"You're a father. Congratulations."

He blinked. "Lily told me it was a security guard at Kewadin Casino in Sault Ste. Marie. I don't remember his name."

"She lied. Big surprise."

At the time, he'd suspected that Gideon Crawford was Shiloh's biological father. He was half Ojibwe; his mother had the black hair, the cheekbones, the tawny skin. He'd thought that Lily hadn't wanted Eli to know that she was playing them both, but he'd known anyway.

He shook his head. "We were off and on, more off than on. The timing doesn't work."

Lena cocked her brows. "Oh? Did you bother to count the months?"

She had him there. "I was deployed when Shiloh was born. I didn't come back home on leave until she was a toddler."

Lena's expression softened. "I didn't even know until Shiloh was four. Lily didn't want me to tell you, she made me swear it. After she died and you were arrested, I was afraid it would hurt you more. I didn't know if the DA could use it against you."

"We used protection," he said dully.

"Protection doesn't always work. And Lily was terrible with birth control pills. Exhibits A and B, Cody and Shiloh." She winced at Cody's name, then rubbed her face. "I apologize for dropping this bomb on you, but you need to know. You deserve to know. I should have told you earlier, but there was so much going on. This isn't something you just blurt out in passing."

He heard Lena's words, but his mind still struggled to process the meaning. "Why didn't Lily tell me?"

Lena sank into the kitchen chair beside him. "Lily had her reasons for things. They didn't have to make sense to other people. Truth be told, sometimes she used information to hurt people. You know that. Besides, she knew you were deployed much of the time. You hardly visited—"

"I would have. Every chance I got if I'd known. I'd have sent her money. I'd have sent birthday gifts, cards, and video messages. I would have wanted to be in her life. In...my daughter's life."

He rolled the words on his tongue, still astonished at their meaning. He was flabbergasted, amazed. He had a daughter. He was a father.

It didn't make sense and it made all the sense in the world.

"I'm sorry I didn't tell you sooner."

"You don't have to apologize to me, Lena. You never have to apologize."

He looked at her across the table. Afternoon sunlight slanted through the window over the sink. The light haloed Lena's wavy chestnut hair. Even tired, her skin glowed, her eyes cobalt blue.

She watched him carefully. "You aren't upset?"

"I'm...surprised. But upset? No. Never."

The corners of her mouth twitched. "Eli Pope, you never cease to amaze me."

"I'm a father," he said, awed.

"Shiloh needs you in her life."

"Does she know?"

"Not yet. You should be the one to tell her when you're ready. Don't wait too long."

"I know."

Suddenly, he couldn't wait to see her. He shoved back his chair and stood. Emotions too big to name swelled in his chest. He'd never felt anything like this; he had no idea how to quantify it. It was beyond anything in his experience.

He strode across the kitchen, opened the back door, and headed into the backyard. The wind whipped at his clothes. The emerald water rippled in frothing wavelets like lace, lapping the pebbly shoreline.

Bear roused himself and trotted over to Eli with a welcome woof. Eli absently scratched the top of his head, but he had eyes for only one person.

On the eastern edge of the yard, the creek burbled over mossy rocks. Shiloh hefted a concrete block from the wheelbarrow and dropped it onto the ground next to a pile of two-by-fours. Sweat soaked her T-shirt and plastered her hair to her forehead. She fisted her hands on her hips and glared at him. "Took you long enough."

A bewildering sensation passed through him like a cool breeze, a shadow rippling over deep water. He recognized himself in her sharp features, her coal-black eyes, that glossy raven hair. "Shiloh."

"What?"

He couldn't take his eyes off of her.

She glared at him. "WHAT?"

He shook his head.

She huffed. "You're weirding me out."

"Sorry." He took several steps toward her and halted. He couldn't stop staring. "Lena told me you drove away those tweakers."

Her dark eyes glittered. "I nailed one in the thigh, got the other one in her hand, right through her palm. You should've seen it. Neither of 'em will be robbing anybody for a while. I should have killed them. To make sure they never came back."

She wasn't wrong.

"People have the right to defend their home and their property, their lives, and their loved ones. You did good."

She nodded, tough and unflinching. Thirteen years old but damn if she didn't have the heart of a warrior. That reckless courage needed to be trained and tempered with wisdom, or she'd dash straight into the lion's den wielding nothing but that crossbow, a lone child facing down a pride of lions with bared teeth and sharpened claws.

He would not allow anything to happen to her. He'd missed thirteen years; he didn't want to miss a second more.

He opened his mouth, closed it, his tongue thick, his mouth like wet paper towels.

The English language had deserted him. He didn't know what to say, or how to say it.

He didn't have the words yet to tell her the truth, but he would, and soon. He just needed to figure out how.

12

JACKSON CROSS

DAY TWENTY-FIVE

Jackson stopped abruptly. Shocked, he stared at the door. A cold chill crept over him.

He'd left his parents' house the night before in a rage, too upset to pack his things. He'd slept in his truck and was up early the next morning to interview the ME with Devon.

He'd spent the rest of the day responding to multiple reports of break-ins, carjackings, and robberies across the county. People were running out of supplies. With the store shelves gathering dust, they'd resorted to stealing and plundering from their neighbors.

Golden shadows lengthened across the lawn as bats swooped and darted through the indigo sky. The setting sun cast the horizon in scarves of brilliant color—tangerine and orange, scarlet and crimson.

Yesterday, he'd entered the house through the main front door upstairs. He had not seen the basement entry door he typically used until now. He'd returned to gather a few personal belongings and depart his parents' home for good.

The hairs rose on the back of Jackson's neck as he took in the large red letters scrawling a message across the door: *Stop or She Dies.*

He touched the scarlet letters. They were dry, slightly tacky. For half a second, his brain registered the liquid as blood, but no, he could smell the paint fumes. This act of vandalism occurred within the last twenty-four hours.

He stared at the words, rigid and unmoving. Anger and apprehension melded into a white-hot fire and ignited in his brain.

What a juvenile act to leave a warning on someone's door in dripping blood-red paint. And yet, it had the desired effect: a gut punch of dread, of outright fear. The message was a warning meant to intimidate him, to scare him into backing down.

He knew exactly which case the trespasser referred to. There was only one that mattered. Who could have done this? And the more pressing question—how the hell did they know that Jackson was still pursuing his mysterious unsub?

The threat itself could be targeted at multiple people. Who was *she*? His sister? His mother? His best friend, Lena? His partner, Devon?

Or was it Shiloh, the child at the beating heart of both cases, past and present?

It didn't matter to him whether he received a paycheck, whether Underwood authorized the investigation, or whether he was threatened. Jackson would follow the trail to its horrible, bloody conclusion. He'd hunt monsters even as the world crashed down around him.

Nothing would stop him. Not threats, not anything.

He was on the right track. And the killer knew it.

13

SHILOH EASTON

DAY TWENTY-SIX

Shiloh hesitated in the doorway of Ruby Carpenter's bedroom, uncertain. It wasn't a feeling she was used to.

She couldn't take her eyes off the small shape curled like a comma beneath a mound of blankets. The navy-painted bedroom walls closed in: dark, stuffy, and claustrophobic.

Shiloh moved to the bed, Bear at her side. "Hey."

The shape didn't move.

"It's me."

The quilt stirred, then nothing. A musty scent wafted from the bedding—the smell of unwashed sheets and greasy hair. When was the last time Ruby had taken a shower? Shiloh and Lena didn't have electricity in the cottage, but they took sponge baths with rainwater from the cisterns, which they could warm on the woodstove. It took forever, but it worked.

"Ruby?"

No answer.

Not even Bear could get a rise out of her. He whimpered, nosing the girl's shoulder. She didn't respond, didn't even open her eyes.

Worry gnawed at Shiloh's belly. She'd seen it in Mrs. Carpenter's eyes, too—that haunted, half-panicked look, that terrible unspoken fear that she'd gotten her daughter back only to lose her again.

The truth was that it didn't matter how tightly you held on; you could still lose the thing most important to you. Trauma was like an obliteration of your very self. It was an untethering, a fraying at the center of your being.

Shiloh knew that better than anybody.

"Ruby," Shiloh repeated. "Look at me."

Finally, the girl in the bed turned toward her. Stringy copper-colored hair clung to her gaunt cheeks. Her lips were cracked, her eyes glassy and unfocused. She looked like she hadn't eaten in days.

Ruby Carpenter had transformed into a ghost of herself.

"You're letting him win," Shiloh said. "Don't let him win. He's dead. He can't hurt us anymore."

"He's inside my head." Ruby spoke so low that Shiloh had to crouch beside her to hear. Her voice was raspy, like dead leaves scraping across concrete. "I can't get him out of my head."

Shiloh hated Walter Boone with the fury of a thousand burning suns. Boone had killed Cody. And he'd locked Ruby underground and tortured her. He had broken more than her body, he'd broken her mind.

Shiloh wanted to punch something, claw at it, kick and hit, use her crossbow and shoot bolts at this invisible horror until it was full of holes. It wasn't something physical, something you could touch or defeat or eradicate. It was a poison that got inside you and destroyed every good thing from the inside out.

Shiloh was helpless against it, and she despised that helplessness with every fiber of her being. A part of her didn't know why she bothered, why she cared so damn much for this girl who was mostly a stranger.

They'd survived this thing together, this terrible thing. Shiloh had tried to save Cody and had failed, but she hadn't failed with Ruby. She couldn't bear the thought of losing her, too.

Shiloh swallowed her fear, leaned close, and spoke into Ruby's ear to make certain she heard every word. "The girl I found was a girl who wanted to live." She tapped Ruby's chest beneath the piled blankets. Ruby flinched and pulled away. "Find that girl."

Shiloh stood there for long minutes staring at the girl curled into a fetal position, no more than a husk of her former self. And then she walked out of the dark, dank bedroom. Bear followed her, his head down, tail limp.

In the shadowed kitchen, Lena sat across from Mrs. Carpenter at the kitchen table, her hands folded over the woman's hand. Bear padded across the linoleum floor, placed his head in Lena's lap, and gave a sorrowful whine. He felt the heaviness like they did.

Sorrow was a physical presence crouching in the corners of the house. It hugged the shadows and sank into your pores. Shiloh's skin prickled. It made her jumpy, like spiders crawling under her skin.

"She's barely spoken," Mrs. Carpenter said. "I can't get her to eat. She has nightmares. I don't know what to do."

"Keep trying," Lena said. "Don't give up on her."

"I don't know how to fix her."

"This isn't a broken bone or a laceration we can suture. It's deeper. We have to give her time, time and love. I'll ask the hospital about local psychologists in the area. Mental health is overlooked in a crisis, but we're going about it all wrong. It's as crucial as food, water, and shelter."

Mrs. Carpenter's face crumpled. "I don't know how to do this. I don't know how to face it. It's too much. It's overwhelming. All of it."

Lena squeezed her hand. "One day at a time. One hour at a time. One minute at a time if we have to. Step by step, okay?"

"I don't know if I can do it. There's a part of me that feels like giving up and giving in, like Ruby. I don't know if it's depression, but it scares me."

"We can't give up. Not on Ruby, not on ourselves. We'll get through this. We will."

A part of Shiloh wanted to believe Lena, too. She felt the darkness, pressing in from the outside, stretching her bones from the inside.

After a moment, Mrs. Carpenter nodded wearily. She rolled an unlit cigarette across the table, back and forth, with trembling fingers. "I'll try."

"That's a start." Lena rose from the table. "Shiloh and I will do the dishes for you. I brought over a couple of cans of chili and some zucchini from the garden. We'll make dinner."

Mrs. Carpenter stared at the wall, her shoulders hunched like she was shrinking in on herself. "Water...food...All the things we never thought twice about. Phones. Internet. Is it truly all gone?"

"For now. For a while."

"I saved some of the goods from my store. Ruby and I will be okay for a month or so, but then we'll have to figure something out. I saved several cartons of cigarettes and other items to trade."

"Don't tell people what you have," Shiloh warned. "They'll just want to take it from you."

Mrs. Carpenter's eyes widened. "I suppose you're right. We don't want to think that it could happen here, but I guess it'll happen everywhere before long."

"It already is," Shiloh said.

Mrs. Carpenter nodded. "May I ask what you guys are doing for water? We were on city water, so we've got nothing now."

"You can get water from the lake for washing dishes and flushing toilets," Lena said. "And rainwater for drinking and showering, but you've got to make sure it's sterilized. Consider all water contaminated and take precautions. Boil it for ten minutes and wait thirty minutes for it to cool."

Shiloh wrinkled her nose. "Boiled water tastes flat. It's disgusting."

"You can add a pinch of salt to a quart of water. That will help. Boiling uses a lot of fuel that you can better utilize for cooking. Another option is bleach, pool shock, or iodine. I used chlorine to disinfect our rain cisterns. Do you have any of that on hand?"

"I've got a couple of gallons of bleach in the laundry room."

"Good. Eight drops per gallon of water. Stir and let it sit for thirty minutes. And don't forget to sterilize the lid and neck of any bottle you use as well. E. Coli isn't something anyone can afford."

"Thank you. Truly."

"We're fixing up the greenhouse. Maybe Ruby would like to help with the garden. Fresh air will be good for her, and we'd be glad to share some produce."

Shiloh wanted to shoot bad guys, not grow lettuce or weed all day. Gardens were last on the list of her concerns. For once, she held her tongue.

As Lena said, you had to start somewhere.

14

JACKSON CROSS

DAY TWENTY-SIX

"Alger County is a dumpster fire." Sheriff Underwood stood behind a lectern in the Sheriff's Office debriefing room and glared at the deputies and cops sitting around the conference table. "I hope you're all prepared for what's about to rain down upon our heads."

The Munising Police Department and the Alger County Sheriff's Office were located in downtown Munising near Munising Bay, where tourists flocked by the thousands in the summer for boating cruises to tour the famed Pictured Rocks. Well, they used to.

At the police chief's suggestion, the two law enforcement agencies had pooled their resources for the foreseeable future. Sheriff Underwood had taken control, no surprise there.

Underwood's suit stank of smoke and his fingers were stained with nicotine. He'd been trying to quit smoking for the last ten years. He'd failed.

He scowled. "In the last forty-eight hours, we've had reports of three burglaries, two carjackings, and six armed robberies at gunpoint."

"People are getting hungry," Jackson said. "And they're scared."

Everyone had a dull, shell-shocked expression. Every day that passed, the glaze etched itself deeper into their countenances.

"It's going to be fine," the police chief, Sarah McCallister, said. "People existed for thousands of years without electricity and did just fine. So will we."

Devon raised her brows. "With what tools? With what skills and expertise? It's not that simple. Everything is automated, computerized, and run by mega corporations, including food production."

It wasn't the end. But the hell between here and the other side appeared insurmountable. It was insurmountable to millions of people who did not have the seeds or knowledge to grow food, to those who could not build fires or find wood to provide life-giving heat, or had no access to fresh water. It was insurmountable to those who needed modern medicines to survive heart disease, diabetes, Addison's, and a host of ailments that were death sentences a hundred years ago and would become so again, or those who might have learned to survive but that chance would be cruelly stolen from them, victims of greed and desperation, murdered and left to rot in the empty streets.

"What about FEMA?" Alexis asked.

"I met with Superintendent Jessop last night," Underwood said. "Michigan National Guard will make the next FEMA delivery tomorrow morning. They'll distribute emergency rations, water, medical equipment, and toiletries. They've requested local law enforcement assistance to bolster security in case folks get out of hand. Hart and Nash, take point on that."

"On it," Nash said.

"The governor promised FEMA will keep up with the deliveries, but Jessop calculated supplies will be depleted within two weeks. FEMA never intended to resupply the entire country in a disaster of this scale. They prepared for regional emergencies."

"Figures," Moreno muttered.

"Oh, the news gets even better. The governor insists the prison gets the first drop."

A flurry of disgruntled murmurs circulated through the briefing room.

"What the hell?" Moreno said. "Felons over little kids—is that what we're doing now?"

"Convicts are under state jurisdiction; it's not my call."

"You'd let them starve?" Devon asked.

"Hell yes," Moreno said, "in a hot second. They're the leeches civilization needs to rid themselves of first. Upstanding citizens need that food, not the dregs of society."

"They can't release violent offenders into the populace. They'd wreak havoc."

Moreno shrugged. "Let them die in their cages. Who cares? Who's going to cry over them? Let those bleeding-heart activists feed them food from their own kids' mouths if that's what they care so much about."

"The federal government is not going to starve prisoners to death as a matter of policy." Underwood tapped the lectern with impatient fingers. "Not yet, anyway."

"Good riddance," Moreno muttered.

"FEMA says everyone will get fed," Underwood repeated like even he didn't believe it.

"For two weeks. Then what?" Alexis Chilton asked.

No one had an answer for that. Several of the officers shook their heads. Fear and anxiety pervaded the room. How could it not? It was like facing a war with an enemy you couldn't see. Like hemorrhaging from the inside; you were bleeding out but couldn't staunch the wound.

Underwood glanced down at his list. "Good news is we've established repeaters throughout Munising to expand our radio communication radius. We will continue to expand throughout the county as equipment and manpower allow. The local gas stations have closed to civilians; the remaining fuel has been reserved for first responders and government use only. Conserve your gas. No wasted trips. Soon we'll be following the Mounties' lead. Anybody know how to ride a horse?"

Several hands went up. Underwood snorted. "Settle down, cowboys. That question was facetious."

"What about our ongoing cases?" Jackson asked.

Underwood turned his sharp gaze on Jackson. "Alger County just cracked a serial murder case. A predator is off the streets. Frankly, the timing couldn't be better. This is exactly what we want to keep in the forefront of the minds of the citizenry. We get the job done. We'll keep them safe and sound so they can sleep at night."

"We have evidence that Boone did not act alone. We think—"

Underwood raised a hand, palm up as if warding Jackson off. "I don't give a damn what you think. That fear-mongering right there is what needs to stop, Cross. People have enough to fear. We cannot afford to inject panic into a volatile situation."

Jackson frowned. "Surely, the people should be afraid. If it's true, then—"

"Put this whole ugly thing behind you. Pat yourselves on the back. You did it. You caught a psychotic monster and put him down. Now we have monsters of another sort to deal with."

"Sir—"

Underwood shot him a scathing look. "What part of shut the hell up did you not understand?"

Devon side-eyed Jackson and shook her head, as if to say, *Not now*.

"Understood, sir." Jackson pressed his lips together, leaned back in his seat, and crossed his arms over his chest. He said nothing more. Underwood saw his concerns as a direct challenge to his authority and control. And control was what Underwood desperately desired now more than ever.

There were other ways to circumvent the problem of the sheriff. Jackson didn't plan to stop. He had already followed up on the threat painted on his door. He'd checked with the neighbors. No one saw anything—no DNA, no hairs, no fibers. The perpetrator had worn gloves.

Jackson had checked with the local store owners to see who

might have sold crimson paint in the last few weeks. Again, he came up empty.

Moreno cleared his throat. "Speaking of monsters, Sawyer is becoming a problem."

"He's a thorn in our collective asses," Underwood said. "He's been making moves while we've been caught with our pants down. Three days ago, his men took over the gasoline storage facility west of Munising."

"We gonna take it back?" Jim Hart asked.

"Add it to the list. Sixty mercenaries with submachine guns are guarding it. He's got an army of cockroaches. Do you want to go in there with ten deputies with shotguns? We need back-up from the state police department or the National Guard, but they're too busy right now trying to maintain control of the cities and the natural gas storage fields downstate, all fifty-eight of them, the most of any state. We'll deal with him, trust me."

He glanced down at the list in his hand, the line between his brows deepening. "Next item on the agenda. The Sheriff's Office will assist the Munising police in setting up checkpoints along the major roads into and out of Munising. We will also continue to patrol the county."

Underwood gave a hollow laugh. "Thank God this didn't happen during high season. Can you imagine dealing with thousands of whining, hungry families with no way to get home? People think they have a summer cabin they visit a few times a year and they get to take refuge here. No and no. Year-round residents only. No one other than government entities goes in or out."

Devon's hand shot up. "Ah, isn't that against the law? Refusing access to lawful landowners? They won't like that."

Underwood's expression darkened for a moment, then cleared, his jaw muscles bulging as he worked through the options. Above all, he was a political creature, always thinking of upcoming elections, voters, and promotions. "If they can prove ownership, they can come in. Otherwise, send them packing."

"What about the dozens of stranded tourists we've already got?" Alexis asked.

"Kick 'em out." Moreno spun in his chair. "We've got no responsibility to take care of them."

"Where are they going to go?" Alexis asked.

"Not our problem."

"We don't have the manpower for roadblocks and checkpoints," Devon said.

"We could set up volunteer teams," Jackson said. "Citizen patrols, that sort of thing. This is their home, too."

Underwood scowled as if he'd rather undergo a colonoscopy than deal with John Q. Public. "Fine. Alexis, that's your department."

Alexis made a face. "I'm tech support. Since when—"

"Since your position is no longer relevant now that computers are no longer a thing, make yourself useful."

Beneath the table, Alexis gave him the finger. Oblivious, Underwood turned his attention to the next item on his list. "We need a few folks to beef up security at the hospital. Dr. Larson told me they've had to turn patients away. They've run out of beds. Worse, they're running out of meds. People are dying. Loved ones are going crazy with grief. Richard Park's mother died without her stroke meds last night. He was so distraught that he tried to choke one of the nurses."

"Oh hell," Devon whispered.

Hasting raised a hand. "I'd love to, but I haven't gotten a paycheck since the sun blew a gasket. We're expected to keep doing our jobs, but where the hell is our pay?"

Discontent rumbled through the room.

"And what about our pensions?" Hart asked.

Moreno shot him an incredulous look. "Down the toilet, man. You can kiss that nest egg goodbye. It's gone."

Hart looked stricken.

A police officer named Nick Fuller groaned and hunched

forward, elbows on his knees, head down. He was an old-timer, less than a year from retirement.

Underwood stood at the front of the room, broad shoulders rigid, his hands like claws on either side of the lectern, his eyes bulging. "McCallister, you wanna take this?"

The police chief had listened quietly until now. She leaned forward, her elbows on the table. "Listen, we can't tell you exactly when you'll get paid, but you will. This is a temporary crisis. We will get through it and come out the other side."

"How?" Hasting asked. "That's what we keep hearing, but come on. It's just lies piled on more lies to keep us in line, keep us coming to work for free. The governor has no way to pay us. The banking system collapsed overnight. They can't get those 0s and 1s into our accounts and we can't access them even if they could. The stock market collapsed. The dollar collapsed. Cryptocurrencies are useless. We should wipe our butts with those worthless C-notes, that's all they're good for now."

"How we gonna do our jobs with no pay?" Hart asked.

"Same way we did them before, numbnuts," Underwood snapped. "I've had enough whining. Don't get your panties in a wad and do your damn jobs."

Jackson shook his head at the irony. He'd thought Underwood would be the first to check out, but he was still here, as crabby as ever, stubbornly showing up each day, pension or not. Sheer vindictive stubbornness must be driving the man, an obsessive desire to win at all costs.

Alexis did not back down. "Why should we keep coming to work? Give me one reason."

"It's the right thing to do," Jackson said.

"You can shove the right thing up your ass, Cross," Hasting said. "When everyone else was emptying the store shelves, we were doing 'the right thing.' Now we've got no food and no money."

"No retirement," Hart said mournfully. "No pension. That was the only thing that got me out of bed in the morning."

"That and pasties," Devon deadpanned, referring to the infamous Upper Peninsula delicacy.

No one laughed. Most officers wanted to believe the police chief. They needed to believe it was temporary, that the government would find a solution to avert a catastrophic loss of life. Deep down, it was unfathomable to believe the doom and gloom perpetually exploited by the media could ever happen. Not here.

It happened in Venezuela and Syria and Ukraine. It did not happen here. But it had. Now, they'd been confronted with their mortality whether or not they were prepared.

Charles Payne, one of the Munising police officers, rose to his feet. "I have a family. Our neighbors were robbed last night. The thieves poisoned their German Shepherd and made off with everything they had in the pantry, every last can of beans. Mark's got nothing to feed his kids today. I wasn't there to stop it. I was on the night shift. What happens when it's my house next?"

His eyes were wide and glassy, like he was watching a horror movie playing out in front of him, the stuff of nightmares. "You people need to wake the hell up."

"What do you propose we do?" Alexis asked.

"Take care of yourself first. No one else is gonna do it for you. The governor certainly isn't. Protect yourself and your family before someone takes it away from you. And they will."

Moreno and Hasting exchanged uneasy glances. Jackson couldn't read their expressions.

People had to make that decision for themselves and their families. When faced with the choice between working for nothing to save ungrateful strangers or saving your family, there wasn't much of a choice. Right and wrong were fading into shades of gray.

Everyone watched in silence as Fuller strode around the conference table and walked out the door, which closed quietly behind him. Cops and deputies squirmed in discomfort. Who would be next?

"Coward," Moreno muttered under his breath.

Devon whirled on him. "Shut up."

"Anyone else?" Underwood asked.

Utter silence descended. No one else moved, not even Hasting.

Underwood banged the lectern with his fist. "Then what are y'all sitting on your butts for? Get the hell to work."

15

JACKSON CROSS

DAY TWENTY-SEVEN

The dense, stifling air coated Jackson in sweat. The Sheriff's Office was silent. There was no heat or air conditioning, no electricity. The generator had run out last night.

A single LED lantern sat on his desk, casting wavering shadows into the far corners of the empty office.

Jackson leaned over his desk at his cubicle and rifled through the case files, the photocopied images of the seven victims splayed out before him. These were Walter Boone's murder victims, according to Sheriff Underwood.

He didn't believe it. Boone didn't fit the profile. He was disorganized, while the killer who had used Boone for his own purposes was organized, intelligent, cunning, and meticulous. Another type of predator entirely.

But Underwood couldn't hear it. He couldn't face the possibility, so he refused. He was overwhelmed, the system fracturing beneath the weight of unprecedented catastrophe. Let sleeping dogs lie. Don't panic the populace. Don't overturn rocks to see what lay beneath them in the middle of a hurricane.

He tried to conjure empathy for the sheriff but could not. The truth was the truth. Justice was still justice. The victims called out from their graves for answers. Jackson could still hear them, Lily's voice the loudest of all.

They haunted him. He could not forget or let them go.

Jackson rubbed his bloodshot eyes, his eyelids like sandpaper. He desperately needed a good night's sleep, but sleep eluded him.

Devon had left two hours ago. Moreno and Nash were long gone. It had been a stressful, tense, endless week. Things would only get worse.

Jackson had put in twelve hours a day every day for the past month. Everyone was anxious, frightened, and bewildered. They demanded answers he couldn't give them.

He had not anticipated the mental and psychological ruin that had laid waste to so many people before the food had even run out—depression, anxiety, suicidal urges, fear, dread, and helplessness.

And yet, he saw good people fighting it, refusing to give in, struggling to survive. For others, the mental strain was debilitating. And for those millions who needed anti-depressants, anti-anxiety meds, and anti-psychotics—God help them all.

Though it was past 10 p.m. and he was exhausted, Jackson couldn't leave. He sat with the case, picking at threads, working through it in his mind. He let the chaos of the day fade into the background as he considered the angles, the holes, the pieces he was missing.

The custom ring featuring the carved wolf eating the two snakes was sealed inside a clear evidence bag. He combed through the crime scene photos for clues to the victims' identities, then read and reread the crime reports, examined the missing persons' reports they'd managed to scrounge up, and studied the autopsies.

It was like forming the picture of a puzzle from pieces that were missing, the empty spaces, the thing that wasn't there.

There were seven victims, eight when you included Lily Easton. All had been strangled. All had been beaten around the face hard enough to fracture bone. All had been left with a gold half-heart locket with a lock of their hair tucked inside.

All eight were dark-haired girls, no blondes. Ruby Carpenter was a redhead, but Boone had admitted he took her for his own.

These lost girls had slipped through the cracks. It would be nearly impossible to track them down. They couldn't put out a description on the wires, couldn't issue an APB or post on the FBI Kidnappings and Missing Persons list. He couldn't access federal databases or request the aid of the FBI's Behavioral Analysis Unit.

He felt cut off from the world, isolated from resources and connections and all the things he and everyone else had taken for granted. Now all of it was gone.

It felt overwhelming, impossible, a needle in a haystack of needles.

Yesterday on his own time, Jackson had gone to Summer Tabasaw's house to notify her next of kin. He still carried the 5x7 photo of the Ojibwe girl with the glossy black hair, dark eyes, and high cheekbones, her arms crossed defiantly over her chest.

He remembered the promise he'd made to the old woman who ran the *Nindaanis* House Shelter outside of Marquette. *Who will stop the monsters? I will. I will stop them.*

The address was sixty-five miles north of Marquette outside of the Keweenaw Bay Indian Reservation, a long drive that used precious gas, but it was important. Her parents deserved to know what had happened to her.

The woman who'd answered the front door was a broken shell of a human being—bony, rail-thin, with sallow-tinged skin. There was a ravenous look about her. Track marks scarred her arms, a cold emptiness in her eyes that chilled Jackson to his core.

She'd refused to let him inside the dilapidated trailer until he'd offered a package of Twizzlers he kept in his truck for Shiloh, which she'd devoured like she was starving.

The trailer stank like accumulating garbage. Flies buzzed over a sink overflowing with food-encrusted dishes. Overstuffed trash bags bulged in the corners, the frayed carpet stained and scattered with crumbs.

In the end, the woman had given him nothing he didn't

already know. She'd barely known her daughter. He recalled the cigarette burns on Summer's arms. He'd left feeling bereft for a child he'd never met and never would.

Jackson shook the memory out of his head and flipped through the photos yet again. His mind kept circling back to two things.

First: the as-yet-unidentified first victim. It was a good bet that the killer had known her. They needed to find her, comb through her case, re-interview witnesses, searching for the overlooked clue that would break the investigation wide open.

Second: the custom ring. He'd seen it before. He'd been wracking his brain since the autopsy with the ME.

Abruptly, he stood. Case files were kept in the basement of the Sheriff's Office. Jackson grabbed his flashlight and made his way through the darkened rooms, down the long hallway, weaving between office cubicles and the reception desk to the stairwell.

Downstairs, dusty, stale air struck him. Within minutes, he'd pulled several evidence boxes, signed them out, and carried them upstairs to his cubicle.

Two hours later, he found what he'd been searching for: a file on James Sawyer's suspected criminal enterprises. Dozens of Sawyer's known associates were listed with photos and rap sheets.

One of Sawyer's top enforcers, Wes Vaughn, had been dishonorably discharged from the military a decade before. He'd grown up in Copper Harbor and had served a few stints in the Kinross Correctional Facility for battery and assault.

The hairs rose on the back of Jackson's neck. He leaned forward and held the photo closer to the light. On the right side of the man's neck, a tattoo peeked above his jacket collar—the wolf's head, jaws slavering as his fangs closed over two writhing snakes.

The tattoo was a near replica of the ring.

There was a connection. He felt it. He *knew* it.

Jackson needed to get to Sawyer.

"Knock, knock."

Jackson nearly jumped out of his skin. He'd been so focused

on the case that he hadn't heard the front door open or the approaching footsteps.

"Damn it, Devon! You trying to give me a heart attack?"

"I'm happy to see you, too. Lucky for you, I come bearing gifts." Devon thrust out a pasty wrapped in aluminum foil. Invented as portable meals for Cornish miners in the mid-nineteenth century, the famous pasty was pronounced with a soft "a" as in "pass."

Jackson hadn't realized he was starving until his stomach rumbled at the delicious scent of onions, diced beef, and rutabaga wrapped in a scrumptious pastry shell. "Where did you get these at this time of night?"

"I picked them up after work from the Falling Rock Café. They're practically the only restaurant still open. Annalise said she'll keep making pasties as long as they can source the ingredients. I think I love her."

Annelise Anders, the Finnish owner of Falling Rock Café in Munising, had continued to make her savory pasties. Annelise always saved one just for Devon. Instead of taking cash, Annelise had started trading for whatever she needed—Band-Aids, batteries, seeds, eggs.

The UP had a strong Finnish heritage. The Finns had crossed the ocean in the 1800s to mine copper and iron, along with a few Swedes and Norwegians. The UP alone was home to about 50,000 Finnish Americans.

"True confession," Devon mumbled around a mouthful of pastry, "I planned to eat them both myself, but when I saw the light wavering in the window, I knew you were still working like a deranged madman. So, here we are. Take it before I change my mind, boss."

Jackson did. "Thank you."

Devon perched on the edge of his desk as she inhaled her pasty. "I'd ask what you're working on, but I'm afraid I already know. Underwood will pitch a fit if he finds out you're still investigating the case."

"What I do on my time is my business. Underwood can take a long walk off a short pier."

Devon groaned. "You sound like Moreno."

Jackson finished his pasty, went to toss the aluminum foil in the trash, then thought better of it. Who knew when they'd be able to run to the store and grab whatever they needed? The conveniences of modern life were in the rearview mirror. Instead, he folded the foil into a rectangle, placed it on the edge of his desk to clean later, then returned his attention to the files.

The images of the victims' faces blurred. He blinked and rubbed his eyes. Fatigue pulled at him. He felt the exhaustion like lead in his bones.

"You okay, boss?"

"I'm fine. You should go home and get some sleep."

She didn't say anything for a minute. He could hear her steady breathing. She picked up Jane Doe Four's file and leafed through it. "I want to help."

He looked up at her. "You're not getting paid and you're offering to put in even more hours?"

"You're doing the same thing."

"I'm hounded by ghosts. I'm obsessive, like a dog with a bone, according to Lena. I have no choice. But you don't have to do this. You don't have to get dragged down with me."

She didn't take her eyes off the file in her hands. Her braids hung like curtains over her face, so he couldn't read her expression. "Why did you go into law enforcement?

"My father served as the county sheriff for eighteen years. My grandfather was a judge. My great-grandfather worked in the iron mines. This place is in my blood. So is the badge."

"It's more than that."

"My family is...complicated. I suppose I took comfort in the black-and-white nature of the law. Good and evil, right and wrong. I wanted to be a good guy, to make a difference, to help people."

The old ways were dying. The structures that held men to higher standards had collapsed long ago, held together with string and silly putty. Did justice matter if there was no law, no way to enforce the rules? No lawyers or judges or chain of command?

He said, "I guess I'm naïve, but I still believe the truth matters, even now."

"You're not naïve." Devon pushed back her braids with one hand and met his gaze. The lantern cast deep shadows beneath her eyes. "When I was ten, my dad died in a car accident. After that, my mom drifted from boyfriend to boyfriend. She was terrified of being alone. Bad men could smell the fear on her. It attracted them like flies to honey."

Her eyes hardened. There was toughness there, an iron will beneath her easy-going exterior. "When I was in my bedroom with the door locked, listening to the newest boyfriend shouting, my mom crying, I would fantasize about stopping him, being strong enough to pick him up and throw him out the front door. Once, he hit her and I called 911. When the police arrived, my mom lied for him. She refused to press charges. And the cops just left. I swore to myself that if I was law enforcement, I'd look harder, dig deeper. I wouldn't leave a twelve-year-old girl defenseless." She blinked rapidly and looked away. "It's silly."

"It's not silly. It's brave. You're a good deputy."

"Thanks, boss." She waved a nail-bitten hand in a vague direction. "Anyway, I don't have any strong ties back in Detroit. No family. Things weren't great in that department, either."

There was another story there, but not one she was willing to tell yet. He didn't pry.

"Tell me what you've found," she said.

So, he did. He filled her in on the tattoo matching the custom ring, his suspicion that this case led to Sawyer, some way, somehow.

Her eyes glittered with something like anticipation. "I believe you about Boone. I want in."

"You'll get in trouble if we're caught. We're off the books here."

"What's Underwood gonna do? Fire me? He can't fire you, either. There's no one to replace us."

"Even if he did, I can't let a killer get away with murder, apocalypse or not."

"We," she said with a lopsided grin. "We aren't letting a killer get away."

He smiled at her. For the first time in a long time he didn't feel quite so alone. "We."

16

JACKSON CROSS

DAY TWENTY-EIGHT

Jackson approached the docks at the Bayshore Marina.

Several security contractors hung around, looking formidable. Before he'd stepped foot on the first dock, two burly men exited the shuttered Sportfishing Charters shop to intercept him. Weapons bulged beneath their loose polo shirts.

He felt eyes on the back of his neck, too. Sawyer had eyes everywhere.

Several boats were moored along the dock, from sleek speedboats to weathered fishing crafts to a couple of sailboats. Out past the harbor, waves rippled like wrinkled tinfoil, glinting beneath the cloudless blue sky.

The first man halted five feet from Jackson, his right hand resting on the grip of a wicked-looking pistol. "Business is closed."

"I need to talk to Sawyer."

"Not gonna happen."

"Tell him it's Jackson Cross."

"Doesn't matter."

. . .

Jackson studied the docks. Sawyer's big yacht was gone. Several shirtless men busied themselves loading crates and boxes onto the ferry at the end of the dock.

He squinted and shielded his eyes. "I heard Sawyer moved his main operation to Grand Island."

Neither man answered. They stared at him, expressionless. The short, barrel-chested man glared at him with piggish eyes. His pockmarked nose was crooked, broken in bar fights or prison. He wore a thick gold chain around his fleshy neck.

The second one was tall, at least 6'3", rake-thin, and boasted a lazy eye. Tattoos of dragons and skulls sleeved his wiry arms. Jackson recognized him; Taylor Randall, a high school drop-out who'd had several run-ins with the law for armed robbery and assault and battery.

Neither wore rings or had visible wolf or snake tattoos.

"I need to see him."

Crooked Nose revealed his equally crooked teeth in a sneer. "The old rules don't apply. We're in charge, now."

"I have useful information for him."

"Sawyer has no interest in making deals with law enforcement. Not even you, Cross."

"Sawyer will want to talk to me, trust me. When he finds out you two bozos kept me from informing your boss of valuable intel, he'll have your heads on a spike."

"Nice try, but no cigar." Randall leaned in close. His breath smelled rancid, like he hadn't brushed his teeth in a few weeks. Cystic acne dotted his greasy chin. "Sawyer thought you might come sniffing around. He told us to send you packing. His specific directions were to 'send him away with his tail between his legs.'"

Jackson stiffened. He stared into Randall's cold soulless eyes and did not back down. "Take a step back, buddy."

Randall sneered. "Or what?"

"You don't want to find out."

For a tense moment, neither man moved a muscle. These were bad men capable of doing bad things. The threat of arrest and prison had stayed their hands in the past, but what would happen now? How soon would things devolve into the Wild West?

He didn't fear Sawyer's hired goons, not even the big silent Russian ones. Rumor had it that Sawyer had beefed up his protection team to include professional mercenaries, likely former military. These goons were tough but run-of-the-mill criminals.

Jackson had known this wouldn't be easy. He'd have to get to Sawyer another way. He wasn't sure how yet, but he'd think of something. He always did.

That island held the answer to Lily's death. He felt it down deep in his bones.

Jackson held Randall's stare. He knew better than to back down first, to show an ounce of weakness. His arms hung loose at his sides, his right hand close to his sidearm, his muscles tensed, prepared for anything.

Randall blinked first. He dropped his gaze and stepped back with a hard smile. "Guess it's your lucky day."

"I'd say it's yours," Jackson said.

"We'll be sure to pass on your message," Crooked Nose said, dripping sarcasm. "Have a good day, Undersheriff."

Jackson dipped his chin, his gaze hard. "I'll be seeing you, gentlemen. You can count on it."

17

LENA EASTON

DAY TWENTY-EIGHT

Lena planted her hands on her hips. "We're not moving."

Eli attempted to stare her down. "The lighthouse is well-known. It's easily seen from the water and land. It's not exactly hiding in plain sight."

"This is not a negotiation."

"From a tactical standpoint, you want to blend in, not stand out like a sore thumb."

They stood in the gravel driveway, facing off, the lighthouse behind them. Seagulls wheeled above the tower, squawking and squealing. Shiloh was off with Bear gathering firewood for the woodstove so they could cook chili for lunch.

Eli wore a pistol and a knife on his belt, with magazines attached to utility pouches. His AK-47 lay within easy reach against a tree two yards away. Even dressed in cargo pants and a T-shirt, he looked ready to go to war at any minute.

Lena sighed. "I know it's not your defend-the-castle wet dream, but there's nowhere that's one hundred percent safe. I'm not hiding. This is important to me and Shiloh. You've seen her. This place is good for her."

Eli frowned but said nothing, because he knew she was right.

On their first night, she and Shiloh had walked the beach for hours with Bear at their side. Shiloh had collected Petoskey stones; red, black, and yellow agate; Pudding stones composed of quartz, red jasper, and black chert; and smooth, colorful bits of sea glass.

She'd lined the windowsills in the lantern room with her collection.

Lena felt it, too, the pull of this place, the rugged beauty of the forest and beach, the calm of endless water. The dazzling view from the top of the lighthouse stretched for miles.

They both needed this.

"It's not just about the lighthouse. We're repairing the greenhouse. There's a diesel generator if we can get fuel, plus the woodstoves for heat and cooking indoors, and the springhouse we're building next to the creek. There's even a root cellar down in the basement. This is a good spot."

A shadow crossed Eli's features. It passed so swiftly that it might have been from the trees or a cloud, but she caught it. "There are always people who want to take what you have. And it's not always things they want."

"I know that." She spread her arms. "That's why I asked you to help, to do your magic."

"You won't change your mind, will you?"

She stared back at him, unperturbed. "Nope."

"I don't like you out here alone." He said it as if it pained him.

Lena glared at him, irritated. "I've got a shaggy pony with teeth. He happens to be an excellent alarm system. His bark will deter most intruders. For the rest, I'm armed with a gun I know how to use."

"Will you use it? If it comes to that?"

Lena hesitated. She liked to think that she would, but she still felt nauseous at the thought of taking the life of another human being.

"You got lucky with the tweakers. They were the type looking for easy prey. Now that they know you'll put up a fight, they'll leave you alone. Not everyone will be like that."

"I know," she said.

"Next time you face an assailant, you finish him off. Don't give him the chance to come back and kill you, because he will. Make sure he's eliminated before you do anything else. First, aim for an easier center mass shot to bring him down, and then a head shot to ensure it's done."

Lena swallowed. Before she could say anything else, Shiloh trotted up from the direction of the woods, a bundle of deadwood sticking out of the oversized beach bag slung over her shoulder, her crossbow across her opposite shoulder. In her free hand, she carried a dead hare by its ears.

She wore ragged jean shorts and a dirty tank top, her hair yanked back in a braid with an arrow woven into the strands. She looked half-wild, feral and fierce.

When she caught sight of Eli, her whole face brightened. For his part, Eli looked pleased to see her, though he couldn't be bothered to crack a smile. He hadn't told Shiloh yet. Lena didn't know what he was waiting for but understood his hesitance. Families, especially toxic ones, were complicated.

Bear tore across the yard after her in a streak of cinnamon fur, black jowls flapping, tongue lolling. Shiloh patted his head with a satisfied smirk. "It took me damn near forever to get one. Bear kept scaring 'em away, but I brought home dinner."

Lena forced herself to frown in disapproval. Someone had to be the adult around here. "You spent hours frolicking in the woods instead of working on the greenhouse as I asked you to this morning, I see."

"Frolicking? No way. Today I hunted"—she held up the rabbit, beaming—"and I gathered"—she jostled the firewood in her beach bag. "Who needs a garden?"

"You do, because you need fruits and vegetables."

"Fruits and vegetables are overrated."

"Not if you don't want to die of scurvy."

"Whatever." She rolled her eyes and grinned at Eli. "Wanna do target practice? I'll bet that AK-47 of yours that I can beat you with my crossbow at fifty paces."

"I'm not giving you my long gun."

Shiloh waggled her eyebrows. "You scared to get wasted by a girl?"

Eli snorted. "You talk a big game for someone whose feet don't touch the ground when you sit in a chair."

"I won't be sitting in a chair when I cut off your jingle bells and tie them in a bow around your throat." Shiloh shot him a devilish grin. "Now will I?"

Eli laughed. It was a rare, foreign thing, rumbling from his chest, low and deep and happy. Lena had not heard that sound in years.

Startled, she opened her mouth as if to say something, then thought better of it and simply shook her head. "You should laugh more often, Eli Pope. It makes you slightly less terrifying."

"I like him terrifying," Shiloh said.

"You think I'm terrifying?" Eli asked.

"No, of course not," Lena stammered. Her cheeks went hot. She'd never feared him, not like that. He would never lift a hand to hurt her or Shiloh. It was the flutter in her stomach she feared, the tightness in her chest whenever he was near.

Memories bubbled up, some good, some painful. She shoved them down deep and focused on the reason he was here—to fortify their home.

It was far safer to keep the past in the past.

Flustered, she clapped her hands to get everyone down to business. "We all have work to do. Let's get to it before lunchtime." Without looking at Eli, she said, "We're staying. That's final."

"I figured as much. At least you're a quarter-mile from the road. Guess that's better than nothing."

He stalked over to the battered Dodge Ram he'd gotten from who knew where, lowered the liftgate, and unloaded supplies: concrete mix, pails for water, bags of gravel, and two heavy-duty posts. A pair of large metal gates hung off the tailgate.

Lena frowned. "What's that?"

"First thing, we're putting in a gate. It won't stop anyone intent on getting to you, but it'll make things difficult for the riffraff. The common thief doesn't like difficult, especially when there are hundreds of houses offering easier pickings."

Eli gestured at the tangle of thorny raspberry bushes pressing in on either side of the rutted gravel driveway. "Don't trim these. Keep it looking wild. These big oaks and jack pines mean no one's bypassing the gate in a vehicle. That's good."

"Where did you get the gate?"

"The neighbors. They weren't using it. It's old and rusty and looks like it's been around for a hundred years. That's perfect."

"You...stole their gate?"

"Among other things." He shot her a sheepish glance. "The place was abandoned. Don't worry, I checked."

Lena shook her head, for once at a loss for words.

"I'm staying in the lantern room," Shiloh said almost shyly. "You wanna see it? I can provide overwatch from up there."

Eli turned, shielded his eyes, and gazed up at the catwalk that ringed the lantern room. "I don't like you up in that tower if something goes wrong. You'll be trapped."

Shiloh's face fell. "But I can do overwatch from up there."

Eli didn't say anything for a minute, thinking. "What do you think about rappelling?"

Shiloh's eyes widened. "You mean down the lighthouse? Are you serious?"

"Dead serious. I've got some rope and equipment in my truck."

The girl pumped her fist in the air and whooped.

"Hold up," Lena said, her parental instincts kicking in. "Is this safe?"

Eli met her gaze and did not look away. "Shiloh will be safe as long as she's with me."

Lena trusted him. God help her, but she did.

Shiloh looked from Lena to Eli and back to Lena. "Come on. Please? Pretty please?"

It was lovely to see Shiloh excited about something; that spark in her eyes had gone dark for so long. How could Lena deny her that? And she did trust Eli when it came to their safety, with their lives.

Lena sighed. "Fine. But only if you swear to weed the garden after."

"You're sucking out my soul, woman." Shiloh grinned from ear to ear. "When can we start?"

The corners of Eli's mouth twitched. "How about now?"

18

ELI POPE

DAY TWENTY-EIGHT

Eli lay prone in his observation post, hidden within the tree line, and watched the cottage, alert for any threat, for anything that did not belong.

He peered through the binoculars and zeroed in on the modest cottage attached to the lighthouse, seventy-five yards from his current position located on a small hill to the southwest of the lighthouse and parallel to the beach, where he had a good sight-line of the clearing and the building itself.

He'd constructed the observation post of chicken wire, covered it with thick underbrush and dense thorny bushes, and hollowed out a space wide enough for his body. Then he attached Mylar foil to the inner walls to protect against the elements and evade infrared scopes from potential enemies. Behind him, a narrow tunnel provided egress for coming and going.

Dried mud smeared his face; he wore dark green clothing to blend into his surroundings and obscure his human form from prying eyes. It wasn't glamorous, but like any long-term surveillance mission, he'd brought Ziplock bags to take care of necessary biological functions.

With him were his bivy sack for sleeping, his rucksack with

food and water, his pistol, and his AK-47 with plenty of ammo. If there was trouble, he'd be ready.

He wished he had better night vision, an SR 25 semi-automatic sniper rifle, and a Mark 19, a full-auto grenade launcher. In an open field, he could take out a squad even in armored vehicles.

He had none of those things, not even night vision.

He was only one man, a single operator in a hostile environment and limited by his humanity. He had to sleep, hunt and eat, gather supplies, and care for his physical needs.

From his experience on past operations, he knew he couldn't get close to providing serious protection for Lena and Shiloh.

Like all Tier One operators, he had received training in protecting high-value targets. More than once overseas, his unit had deployed to assist state department DSS agents protecting diplomats in high-risk areas. Then, he'd had a CAT, or counter-assault team, heavily-armed shock troops on stand-by, and counter-intelligence teams. And of course, there were sniper teams, intelligence groups consisting of the CIA, DEA, State Department personnel, air support, and CPOs, or close protection officers.

Eli only had Eli. Plus Bear as an unwitting member of his Security detail. He could not offer surveillance twenty-four seven to the standard he was accustomed to, but he would do what he could.

Though he far preferred a position inside the cottage, in a bedroom or on the couch or hell, even the floor, which best situated him to defend them, Lena would never go for it. He'd considered begging or bartering, but Lena was nothing if not incredibly stubborn.

Lena did not know he was here, and he damn well planned to keep it that way. Her pride and her broken heart would keep her from accepting him into her home, or her life. He knew her as he knew himself.

After the pain he had caused her, he no longer had the right. He could not blame her.

Gray clouds scudded across the sickle of the half-moon that hung in the star-studded sky. The beacon from the lighthouse swept across the land and the water in slow, measured arcs. The night was quiet but for the breeze rustling the leaves and bushes, the surge of the waves lapping the sand.

Again, he scanned from left to right, bumped the binoculars five degrees, and scanned back from right to left. Breathe in, breathe out. Steady and still, at one with his surroundings.

In addition to installing the locked gate at the bottom of the driveway, he'd reinforced the front door and instructed them to always keep weapons close at hand. Sandbags were piled beneath several windows to serve as shooting positions.

Every time they entered the house, he'd instructed them to check each room, pistol in hand, making sure no one had entered during their absence. He'd also suggested applying a piece of clear tape on the inside of the door jamb before exiting the cottage; if the tape was torn, they'd know someone had broken in.

He'd wanted to dig booby-trapped pits and bury punji sticks like the Vietnamese, but Lena rightly worried Bear might fall in and skewer himself. Eli questioned the Newfie's killing instinct, but his bark would serve as a good warning system. Perhaps he could lick intruders to death.

In truth, Bear was both a Godsend and a curse. On the plus side, Eli could eventually get some sleep, knowing that Bear would wake him up barking if the dog sensed anything amiss.

On the other hand, Bear was a trained tracker and Eli had to ensure the dog didn't beeline straight for his hiding spot. To keep Bear from detecting him, he'd smeared on deer and raccoon scent to scent-mask himself.

Even after all they'd done, he feared it wasn't enough. He could hide them in a reinforced fortress or underground bunker and it wouldn't be enough. In this world, there were too many ways to die.

He hated deceiving Lena, but his guilt would not dissuade him.

He had not sworn to tell her the complete truth. She didn't need to know everything.

He couldn't see Shiloh up in the lantern room, but he sensed her, awake and watchful. Whenever he thought of her, which was often, his chest expanded and he felt lighter somehow. He would tell her soon, he told himself, when the time was right.

Jackson would try to keep her childhood innocence. The rest of Shiloh's childhood had already been stolen. Eli could take that pain and transform it into strength, the way he had done with his own.

Across the clearing, the back door opened. A sliver of light spilled across the overgrown yard. Lena stepped onto the porch as Bear bounded past her. She wore jeans, sandals, and a faded pink flannel shirt tied at the waist. Her hair was tugged into a messy bun, a few tendrils escaping to frame her face.

She held an LED lantern in one hand and her pistol in the other, watching her surroundings, alert and attentive, while Bear nosed the sea grass, searching for the perfect spot to do his business.

Her voice carried in the crisp night air: "Come on, hurry up. It's freezing out here."

She'd paid attention to his lessons. His chest tightened at the sight of her, his hands went clammy. It was difficult to breathe.

Eli had been all in the second he'd laid eyes on her. Back in prison, when he'd told the sadistic killer Darius Sykes that he'd loved no one, he had lied. Lena had always held the top place in his heart. Well, until Shiloh, but that was a different kind of love.

Lena was kind and compassionate, smart and driven. She'd inspired him to become a better version of himself. She had offered him a chance at a different life, a life he desperately wanted but feared he did not deserve. There were things broken in him that he had not known how to fix.

And so, he had done the one thing that Lena could not forgive.

He hadn't intended it. Hadn't wanted it, not like that. He didn't know whether Lily had fallen into it as he had—a drunken lapse, a moment of terrible judgment—or if she had orchestrated it.

It didn't matter.

He had done it.

And then Lily had told Lena.

And in doing so, he had lost the best thing that had ever happened to him. And he'd known it, before, during, and after.

In the years since, each time he had returned home, he had gone back to Lily, again and again, a glutton for punishment.

He'd allowed himself to remain tangled with the sister of the girl he'd loved and lost, because Lily was the closest thing to Lena. Or maybe he and Lily had both taken comfort in the too-familiar taste of pain, shame, and regret.

He was not that man anymore. His battles as an elite soldier, spent in dangerous theaters around the world, and those tortured years surviving prison—those things changed a man.

He was not yet sure what he was. There was one thing he knew without a doubt: he would move mountains and swim oceans for her. He would tear down castles with his bare hands if she asked it of him.

The choice, as it had always been, was up to Lena.

He was not naïve enough to believe he would ever have a chance with her. He would watch, and wait, and do everything in his power to protect the woman he loved and the prickly thirteen-year-old who'd pushed her way into his heart long before he'd known to call her daughter.

Eli adjusted his position, stretching his shoulders and settling in. Mosquitos buzzed around his face. Insects whirred incessantly. It was going to be a long night.

19

LENA EASTON

DAY TWENTY-NINE

Lena stood with Jackson on the catwalk ringing the lantern room at the top of the lighthouse, eight dizzying stories high. Great gusts of wind tore at their hair and clothes and threatened to topple them over the edge.

Far below, the water surged against the sand and rocks, the waves forming lacy plumes. The chilly wind sliced at her exposed skin. Above them, a falcon soared with wings outstretched.

"I brought something for you." Jackson held out two small rectangular objects. "They're called Frio wallets. They're for diabetics."

Lena opened the thick fabric wallet. They were cooling packs. There was room to store four vials and four syringes in each one. "I've heard of these. I looked for some before I left Tampa but couldn't find them."

"I got them when I went supply shopping in Marquette and kept meaning to give them to you. I figured since refrigeration is a huge issue, you could use these. No ice packs required. They use crystals activated by water that cool via evaporation. They're reusable, just dip them in water for a few minutes every forty-five hours, and they're good for up to one hundred degrees."

"Thank you." She held the cooling packs to her chest like they were priceless treasures, which they were.

A month ago, she could've bought a dozen on Amazon and had them shipped to her door. Now? Now you made do with what you had or could scavenge.

"I'm going to split my stash between the fridge, the springhouse, and these. That way, if something happens to one supply, I'll still have some left."

"Good idea."

Lena tucked the cooling packs into the pocket of her cargo pants, then shoved her hands into the pockets of her windbreaker. "You didn't come out here just to give me these."

"How do you know?"

"I know you better than you know yourself. You've always got an agenda, Jackson."

He flashed her a sheepish grin. "You caught me. I need your advice."

Since they were kids, Jackson had come to her with his problems, his concerns, his fears. Neither of them had the kind of parents one could turn to for advice or a comforting hug. They'd depended on each other.

Jackson was the sensitive one, the one who cared too much. He couldn't let things go. That obsessive tendency made him an excellent cop, though he suffered, and suffered deeply. He tried to hide it, but she could always tell with him.

She said, "It's the case, isn't it?"

"We've had no breaks. We've been hamstrung at every turn by the lack of resources, communication, and the world falling apart. I have one clue, but I am unable to pursue it myself. I need...I need to ask Eli a favor."

She glanced at him in surprise, waiting for him to tell her more, but he shook his head in apology. "I'm sorry, I can't give more details. It's confidential. But it's important. It could be critical to solving the case, Lily's and the other victims."

At the mention of Lily, vertigo washed through her as if she were teetering on a precipice. It was a sense of loss like falling, falling forever with no way to stop yourself, dizzying in its intensity.

"The last time I saw Eli, he told me to leave and never come back. He's never going to forgive me. Not that I expect it or deserve it. There's no way in hell that he'll help me."

"Did he shoot at you?"

"If he shot at me, I'd be shot. Eli doesn't miss a target."

She snorted. He wasn't wrong. "If he didn't shoot you, then there's your answer."

Slowly, Jackson nodded.

"If Eli thinks he can help, he will. Give him some credit."

"I don't have the right to ask him to do more than he already has."

"All you can do is ask. Eli's answer is up to him. Let him decide whether your cause is worthy."

"He could betray me. It could go very, very badly."

"He went with you to Boone's cabin, didn't he?"

"He did."

"You had to trust him then."

"I had no choice. I'm pretty sure he came within a hair's breadth of shooting me in the back of the head."

She remembered that night, the fear and dread, that terrible sensation of everything unraveling at once as the auroras painted the sky blood-red. How close they'd come to losing Shiloh. "He won't betray you. That's not who he is."

Jackson stared down at the beach without speaking. She braced herself against the railing and followed his gaze. To the west, the rocky beach curved into a cove where seagulls nestled among the ragged black rocks. Further out, a fishing boat rolled the crests and swells, rising and then dropping away, the waves tinged scarlet as the sun sank lower in the sky.

"You're so certain." The wind took his words and hurled them over the edge into the ether.

"I know what he did, the mistakes he made. But I know him, Jackson. I know him."

"It's been eight years. Eight years he had to survive among monsters, had to become like them. That changes a person. And he has every reason in the world to despise me. How are you so sure that you know him?"

She paused. "Faith, I guess."

"Blind faith can be a mistake. I've learned that the hard way."

"There's a difference between blind faith and faith with your eyes wide open."

He frowned. "They look the same to me."

"Sometimes the faith we need is in ourselves. Trust your instincts."

"You always know the right thing to say."

"We're all stumbling around in the dark, trying to do our best. That's all we can do."

"I'm not giving up on Lily. I won't."

"I know."

The sun sank toward the horizon, setting the sky on fire. Jackson looked at her steadily, the wind ruffling his sandy-blond hair into his eyes, the sunset turning his skin golden, resolve in his gaze. "I know what I need to do."

20

JACKSON CROSS

DAY THIRTY

Jackson parked his patrol truck next to a glossy, cherry red M760i BMW in the Northwoods Inn parking lot.

He'd been sleeping in the truck for three days now. Sleeping was an overstatement. He was exhausted and in desperate need of a shower and a soft mattress, desperate enough to beg.

Built during the logging glory days of the nineteenth century, the mansion had been lovingly restored into a bed and breakfast and local bar. It was set on twenty pristine acres along the coast located a few miles northeast of Munising. Dozens of goats and chickens wandered the manicured yard beneath stately oaks, hemlocks, and maples, which were tapped for maple syrup in March.

A big white goat dozed on the roof of the red BMW. As Jackson exited the truck and slammed the door, the goat scrambled up, her hooves scraping the roof, and glared down at him. She bleated angrily at Jackson like he was an intruder, and she was anything but happy about it.

Jackson gave the goat a wave. "Sorry, Faith. The owners of that pretty car aren't gonna be happy you decided to take a nap on their expensive property, you know."

Faith bleated an impertinent response. As one of Lori's favorites, Faith was well-known at the Northwoods Inn. She was big, ill-mannered, and ornery. And for some reason, she loved cars.

"Don't get lippy with me, young lady. I could arrest you, you know."

Jackson turned his back on the cheeky goat, crossed the parking lot, and pushed through the oversized double doors. Designed to resemble a rustic lodge, dark wood paneling lined the walls of the grand foyer, with great cedar beams arching across the cathedral ceiling.

A floor-to-ceiling masonry fireplace stood in the center of the foyer, around which sat clusters of leather armchairs where guests could gather and converse or simply stare into the flames with a Jack Daniels and contemplate the existential problems of the universe.

Jackson strode past the stuffed black bear in the corner next to the cedar doors. It reared on its hind legs, paws outstretched in greeting; tourists loved to take pictures with it. Light flooded in kaleidoscopes of color through the two-story stained-glass windows and spilled across the slate floors.

He headed for the Northwoods Bar on the right-hand side of the foyer where locals communed with neighbors and friends, watched the Lions or the Redwings on the flat screens, or drank away their woes.

A pretty, rotund woman in her sixties met him before he'd made it to the reception desk, which was empty. Laugh lines and crow's feet spanned the corners of her cornflower blue eyes. She wore practical converse sneakers, worn jeans, and a plaid shirt rolled up at the elbows.

Lori Brooks greeted him warmly. "To what do we owe this pleasure?"

Jackson stuck out his hand but Lori opened her arms and pulled him into a bear hug. He let himself sink into her embrace. Lori Brooks knew how to hug the sadness out of a person.

Jackson squeezed her forearms and pulled away. "Thank you."

"You looked like you needed a hug, sweetheart."

Embarrassment colored his cheeks. Lori Brooks exuded grandmotherly charm from every pore. Jackson's grandparents had been cold and distant, much like his father. His mother's affection was smothering rather than comforting.

He cleared his throat. "I'm looking for a place to crash for a while. You got a room?"

Lori's smile widened. He half expected her to ruffle his hair, but she didn't. "For you, always."

Lori didn't ask why he'd left his parents' house, and for that, he was grateful. "Cash and credit cards are off the table, but I'll find a way to pay you for room and board. I'm a terrible cook and everything I try to grow dies on the vine, but I can moonlight security and I'm adept at construction."

"Of course. Gretchen will get you a room. Or, we still have one of the cabins available."

Tim and Lori ran the Northwoods Inn and Bar like a well-oiled, self-sustainable machine. Years ago, they'd constructed wind turbines along the bluff together with solar panels on the roof, so the inn had power. A gravity-fed well system provided running water, and the food they served was farm-to-table, picked from their ten-acre garden and small working farm.

They also had a soft spot for creative types and had built an additional six cabins on the property, where they invited writers, painters, and musicians to spend a week creating art, inspired by the stunning beauty of Lake Superior's coastline.

"A room will be fine," Jackson said.

"God bless you, Jackson." At his questioning look, she said, "I know you haven't been paid in weeks, and no payment is coming. And yet, here you are. You're doing God's work whether you know it or not."

"And what is God's work?"

Lori didn't hesitate. "Protecting the innocent and keeping the wolves at bay."

Jackson ducked his chin, embarrassed though he wasn't sure why. He was no hero. He wondered daily whether his presence made any difference at all. The world was sliding into chaos, and he couldn't hold it back.

Tim set down the glass he'd been polishing with a towel, came around the bar, and shook Jackson's hand. He'd been sober for twenty years though he still bartended when needed. "Whatever Lori says, I'm in full agreement. Anything we can do for you, you just let us know."

Jackson knew they meant it. These were good people, genuine, kind, salt-of-the-earth folks. They were real Yoopers, people who would give their coats off their backs if someone needed it. And now that folks did need help, Tim and Lori were the first to extend a hand.

"I don't expect food. I'll figure that out myself. But a roof over my head, running water, and indoor plumbing sound like real luxuries right now."

Tim chuckled. "A month ago, we took running water for granted. Can you imagine?"

"Unfortunately, I can, all too well."

Lori clucked her tongue. "Of course, we'll feed you. Don't think anything of it. Make yourself right at home."

Gratitude expanded inside his chest like a balloon. "Thank you, truly."

"Before you go, I need to apologize to you," Tim said in a gruff voice. He shifted, clearly uncomfortable, but the set of his jaw revealed his determination to see this conversation through. "And to Eli, too."

Jackson raised his brows. "I'm listening."

"That night we went to his father's house, up in arms and ready to do great bodily harm to protect our town. Our hearts were in the right place, but we were wrong, so wrong. We shouldn't have come after him like that. I should've known better."

He glanced at his wife with a guilty expression. Lori rubbed his arm in encouragement. "I do know better, and I've felt bad ever since. And he was innocent. We could have killed an innocent man." Tim pressed his lips together, regret on his face as he shook his head. "God forgive us."

"As far as I'm concerned, there's nothing to forgive. Eli Pope is another matter, though. We all owe him far more than an apology."

"Agreed. Do you know where he is? We haven't seen him since the sheriff's announcement last week. He slipped away before I could talk to him."

After his conversation with Lena, Jackson had made up his mind. Lena's friendship had that effect on him. Her insights could cut through his doubt and anxiety straight to the truth of a matter.

Tonight, he would ask Eli for a favor he had no right to ask but would ask anyway. Some things were bigger than either of them, more important than hatred, bitterness, or vengeance. He could only hope that Eli would see it the same way.

"He's a bit gun-shy, as you might expect. I'll relay a message to him if you'd like."

"We'd like to have him here for a meal," Lori said. "Home-baked bread spread with freshly churned butter, and my famous Pannukakku pancakes."

Jackson's mouth watered. The Finnish concoctions were an oven-baked cross between a big pancake and custard and could be topped with anything from sprinkled sugar and a squeeze of lemon to stewed venison and seared mushrooms.

Lori sighed. "Of course, that won't make up for a thing, but I think it's important that he knows the town isn't against him. We want to make amends in our small way."

"I'm sure he'd appreciate that." Jackson glanced around the foyer. It was busier than he'd expected. Most folks were headed in one direction or another, but several slumped in armchairs or hunched at the bar. "Seems like you've got a lot going on here."

"We've been taking people in," Tim said.

"That's kind of you."

Lori drew herself to her full height of 5'1" and gave him an affronted look. "How could we do otherwise and live with ourselves? Jeanine Harding is a single mom with four kids. We offered her a cabin in exchange for cleaning duties since we lost our cleaners once we couldn't pay them. Jed Miller is seventy years old and has stage four prostate cancer. He's got no one to take care of him. We have some stranded hikers and birders who've stayed on with us, too. Sandra and Maggie are doing great in the kitchen, while Johannes is a vet tech and helps us with the animals. We can't do much, but we can do this."

"You know, call me a hippie, but I always imagined that people would go back to a commune sort of lifestyle," Tim said. "More hands mean less work. More people to work together to create a safe and sustainable environment for everyone. The type of living we've gotten used to, houses are too far apart from each other. We need to be close to each other for true community, the way we used to live."

Jackson nodded. "You've got a good thing going. Pretty soon, more people will start noticing. You need to protect it."

"God told us to watch out for each other in the Bible, didn't he? We've tried to do that our whole lives, but now it's more important than ever. If we can help, we will."

"I'm serious. You need to protect what you're creating here. Some people want to destroy what others have built, to take what they won't bother making for themselves. That will only get worse."

Lori's eyes crinkled. "I'm not that much of a hippie. We understand that part, too. It's unfortunate, but it's reality. We've hired our head of security." She tilted her head at the bar. David Kepford sat half-turned on his stool, coffee cup in hand, spine straight and his back to the wall, with the rest of the room in his view.

"The Munising High School principal?" Jackson shouldn't have been surprised. He'd always wondered whether Kepford had served, though he'd never asked.

Lori fisted her hands on her ample hips. "Young man, I wasn't born yesterday. Kindness doesn't mean being naive or dumb as a box of rocks. If we allow this place to be taken, we will be in no position to help anyone, and we will in turn become a burden to others. I don't believe for a second that's what the good Lord intended. Be wise as serpents, He said."

"And harmless as doves," her husband reminded her.

She set her mouth stubbornly. "We are harmless, unless someone intends harm, and then we will stop them with the business end of a shotgun."

Jackson found himself smiling. "I like where your head's at."

Lori's gaze drifted toward the fireplace. Her eyes narrowed and she frowned.

"What is it?" Jackson asked, sensing trouble.

"I feel bad complaining..."

Tim put his arm around Lori's shoulder and gave her an affectionate squeeze. Even after forty years together, they were in love, and it showed. Tim lowered his voice and leaned in. "Lori doesn't like to speak ill of anyone, but sometimes a thing needs to be said."

"He's right," Jackson said. "I can't help if I don't know there's a problem."

"Most people are doing their best. We're all scared to death. We're shocked and worried and anxious. Most folks, here at the inn and in town, I see them working hard and helping each other. Doing what they can to prepare and make do, but not everyone. A few people are just sitting around, acting like the world only ended for them, no one else. They can't be bothered to lift a finger to help themselves or anyone else."

"Tell me who."

Tim nodded his chin at a couple slumped in leather armchairs before the hearth. They looked like they'd just stepped out of an Eddie Bauer catalog. A boy of eight or nine lay prone on the rug with his Gameboy clutched in both hands, glued to the screen. The mother stared down at her phone and tapped buttons like her Facebook and Instagram might reappear as though nothing had happened, as if this new reality was just a horrible dream.

"They won't do a thing, though they've been asked. Lori

doesn't have the heart to tell them to leave, but to be honest they're wearing out their welcome. And those three men over there at the bar are rude and disrespectful. They change the atmosphere, you know? Makes the other guests antsy. And frankly, me too."

"They get loud and belligerent," Lori said, sounding guilty for speaking the accusation aloud. "I try to give everyone the benefit of the doubt, but these guys."

"Lori likes everyone. If she doesn't like someone, you know they're bad news," Tim said.

Jackson gave them a reassuring smile. "No worries. I'll take care of it."

Lori squeezed his arm. "I know you will, honey."

Jackson approached the family first. To their credit, the parents rose to greet him. The mother glanced nervously back at her son as the husband shook Jackson's hand. They introduced themselves as Traci and Curt Tilton.

"Where are you folks from?" Jackson asked.

"Bloomfield Hills, a suburb of Detroit," Curt said. "I'm a corporate lawyer at Sandler and Associates. We come up here every year to fish, kayak, and get off the hamster wheel, you know. We ran out of gas and the gas station won't let us fill up. We don't have cash. We used it on food the first couple weeks after the credit card machines went down."

"The remaining fuel is reserved for first responder and government use. I'm sorry about that."

Curt's mouth tightened. "We're stranded here."

"I'm truly sorry for that, but you'll have to find accommodations elsewhere."

"You're kicking us out? We have a child!" Curt's voice rose in anger. Behind the anger lay radioactive fear. "What are we supposed to do? You want us to starve?"

"Tim and Lori don't want you to starve. They offered to let you do some chores in exchange for meals for your family. And they've been kind enough to allow you to stay at their inn for a month without pay. I'd say they've gone above and beyond."

"We're not servants," Curt said. "We're hungry and tired. My wife has fibromyalgia. We came here for peace and quiet, to relax and rejuvenate as a family. We did not sign up for this."

Traci stood beside her husband, her shoulders rigid, wringing her hands in front of her stomach, her face ashen. She did not say a word.

"I understand," Jackson said, feeling a pang of sympathy. "Truly, I do. But no one signed up for this. Other people can't be expected to carry your responsibilities for you. You're becoming a burden to those who are struggling to make ends meet, same as you. No one is forcing you to do a thing, but you do have a choice. You can pitch in and earn your keep, or you can leave."

The defiance fled from the husband's face. Panic crept in, a wild, barely controlled terror. "We just want to go home."

Jackson knew what Sheriff Underwood and his father would say. Good riddance. These people weren't citizens of Alger County, they weren't friends or family; they weren't his responsibility. He should wash his hands of them.

He glanced past the parents and caught sight of the little boy, who still clutched the Gameboy in his hands, staring at it in fierce concentration, as if he couldn't look away, as if he dared not look away. The screen was blank, the gaming console long dead.

Pity rushed through Jackson. He wanted to give them the benefit of the doubt; he understood they were paralyzed by fear, terrified for their child. At the same time, he couldn't allow them to continue to drain his county's resources.

"Look, I'll take you as far as Sault Ste. Marie. The National Guard has a presence there. Maybe they're busing people downstate."

"We just want to go home," Curt said.

"No." Traci had listened in silence with a stricken expression on her face. She placed a hand on her husband's arm and cleared her throat, then shot another glance back at her son. "That's not a good idea."

Startled, Curt shot her a confused look. "What are you talking about?"

Traci's anxious gaze flicked between her son playing on the floor and Jackson. "We've been listening to the emergency radio. It's the only station that isn't pure static. Things are getting bad, worse than I could have imagined. They're saying the stores are empty, the public water shut off two weeks ago, the hospitals are overflowing. Regular people are stealing food, robbing each other at gunpoint. There are shootings every single night, even during the day. Trash is piled in the streets."

Traci looked at her husband with a beseeching expression. "I know we want to go home, but I don't think we should. Not now. It's safer here. It's safer for Keagan."

The father's face drained of color. "We don't have a house here. We don't have clothes, toiletries, or our other car. We don't have—"

"Those are just things," Traci interrupted. "None of that matters. Who cares about your Tesla? What matters right now is keeping Keagan safe, and protecting our family."

"But work...I have a job and responsibilities. I can't just..." his voice trailed off.

"I doubt many company mergers are happening right now," Jackson said.

Traci raised her chin. "I'm not saying it's perfect here, but it's better than the city. It's not like we have family in the country we can stay with. We're on our own." When she met Jackson's gaze, her eyes were steady. "Please give us another chance. We understand how precious this opportunity is. We'll help, we'll pitch in. I promise."

Curt squeezed his wife's hand and gave a heavy nod. "I suppose she's right."

"There is plenty of work to do with the farm, the animals, the garden, general upkeep, food preparation, even security if you know your way around a gun."

"We can stay?" Traci asked, hope a fragile thing in her voice.

"On a trial basis. You will have to earn your keep."

"We will." Curt Tilton shook Jackson's hand, relief mixed with gratitude washing across his features. "Thank you."

"Don't thank me, thank the Brooks, and not just with words."

It remained to be seen whether they'd be true to their word, but if Tim and Lori were willing to give second chances, so was Jackson. If they rose to the occasion, great; if they didn't, then he'd kick them out himself.

He didn't have such high hopes for the next group.

The first man rose from his bar stool as Jackson approached. His two friends rose behind him. The other two were taller, both barrel-chested with physiques that hinted at past athletics—football players, or hockey—but the muscle had sagged and swelled to fat.

Their expressions were sullen. They looked tense, irritated, and miserable, the type itching for someone to blame and raring for a fight.

Lori's instincts were correct. These three were trouble.

21

JACKSON CROSS

DAY THIRTY

Jackson tensed, his heart rate accelerating, his hand hovering above his service pistol.

"How can I help you, Deputy...Cross?" the first man asked, reading his uniform tag and saying his name like an insult. Hostility exuded from his pores. He lifted his chin, nostrils flared, legs spread.

Jackson knew his type. He was short, 5'6" tops, the kind of guy who resented the hell out of the world for it, always had a swagger, attempting to compensate for his insecurities with puffy gym muscles, designer clothes, and a fancy car.

It was probably his cherry-red BMW in the parking lot.

Jackson remembered the goat plopped on the roof and suppressed a smile at the thought.

The guy halted less than two feet from Jackson, invading his personal space. "Something funny, officer?"

Jackson didn't react. "It's undersheriff. What are your names?"

The short, aggressive one was Greer. The largest man, Hershel, was heavily bearded with squinty eyes. The third guy sported a beer gut and called himself Buck. The men were in their late thirties, dressed in fancy hiking boots, camo pants, and Dri Fit T-shirts. They were bankers or accountants or CFOs practicing hunting and camping up here in the boonies, playing at the rugged life.

Now that things were getting real, rugged wasn't so enticing.

"The owners of this establishment told me they've asked you nicely to leave, but you're still here. It's time to move along."

"We can pay," Buck said. "We've got plenty of money. The banks are closed, that's not our fault. That hick gas station turned us away, too. We've got no cash left. Soon as the damn ATMs start working again, we're good for it."

"You really think things are going back to normal anytime soon?"

Greer blinked. "Damn straight. This is just a hiccup and everyone's going crazy, wettin' their panties in fear, believing everything they hear, damn pansies."

Jackson refrained from rolling his eyes. Some people refused to comprehend the predicament they were in because denial was far more comfortable. The truth was staring them in the face, but they refused to see it.

He kept his voice calm, even as he lowered his gaze and checked their clothing, particularly the waistband, searching for a bulge that signified a pistol or knife. "Gentlemen, you may leave on your own or you will be escorted off the premises and outside the town limits."

Greer lifted his chin. "These other people are staying. Why do we have to leave?"

"Things have changed. Those guests who remain have been invited to stay by the owners. You have not."

"They've got no right to do that!" Hershel said. "We're paying customers. We reserved this crappy lodge for three weeks. Our money is as good as everyone else's here."

Greer stepped forward and jabbed an aggressive finger at Jackson. "We got rights. You can't kick us out! We deserve shelter and a good hot meal and a warm shower as much as anyone else. We're paying customers. We pay damn taxes!"

Irritation flared through him. He had a hundred better things to do than waste time with these monkeys. "Remove your finger or I'll arrest you for assaulting an officer."

Greer didn't back down. "You country bumpkins think you're better than us, huh? You're all survivalists up here who think you know better, think you're smarter? Cause you can hunt and fish and start fires?" Greer's bloodshot eyes bulged with fury. He was on something, possibly opioids, but Vodka for sure. The stink of alcohol leaked from his pores. "We've got guns, too."

Jackson had had enough. His hand settled on the butt of his pistol, a warning he hoped would not go unheeded. "Get your things and be gone in thirty minutes or go to jail with me. Those are your choices. Choose wisely."

Greer sneered. "Big talk considering it's three of us against one cop. And you've got no radio or phone, do you? You're as SOL as the rest of us. No, I think we will stay right here."

He gave a slow smile as his gaze flicked around the foyer. "Such a nice place. It'd be a shame if someone had an accident smoking in bed and burned it down. How tragic that would be, don't you think?"

Greer glanced at his cronies for approval, growing more hostile with each passing second. The bar and foyer had gone silent. Three dozen pairs of eyes watched their every move.

He gave a self-satisfied smirk. "You're just a yokel backwoods cop. You're all alone, us against you."

"He's not alone," a deep voice rumbled.

Jackson didn't take his gaze from Greer and his cronies. Out of the corner of his eye, he glimpsed a figure sliding off a bar stool and striding toward them.

David Kepford tugged up his Green Bay Packers T-shirt to reveal a Sig 226 pistol in a concealed holster at his hip. He scanned the men, taking everything in, assessing for threats.

"You think you can take us both?" Jackson said evenly. "You lost. Now get out."

Buck took Kepford in with one awed glance, backed up, and

raised his hands in surrender. "Hey, man. I don't want any trouble. I'll go."

"What the hell!" Greer said. "You turning into a pussy on me?"

"We should just go, man. It's not worth it." Buck shook his head, eyes wide. "I'm out. I'll be gone in thirty."

Jackson turned to Greer. "This is your last chance—"

Growling in fury, Greer lunged. He threw a powerful round-house punch straight up at Jackson's skull.

Jackson dodged it, then seized the man's Dri Fit T-shirt, stepped inside the swing of the punch, and shoved Greer back against the bar. The stool fell to the floor with a noisy clatter.

Adrenaline surging, Jackson seized Greer's hand and bent his wrist backward until he cried out. He wrestled him around, so his chest and stomach were shoved against the bar. Jackson fumbled for the cuffs at his belt.

A furious blur shot at him from the left. Hershel rushed Jackson, one fist up and swinging, the other hand reaching for something at his waist. Jackson had no time to react. If Hershel had a weapon, he was done for—

Kepford moved from behind Hershel. His hand shot between the man's body and right shoulder. He seized Hershel's upper arm, twisting it hard, bringing his arm even with his shoulder in a painful compliance hold.

Hershel screamed, standing on tiptoes to avoid the agony shooting through his shoulder. "Stop! You're hurting me!"

"Put your left hand on the back of your head," Kepford said. "Now."

The man scrabbled at Kepford's forearm with his fingernails, struggling to release himself, but the muscles in the principal's arms corded like steel. "Yield."

"You can't—"

Kepford applied more pressure. "Yield."

With a hiss of pain, Hershel sagged. Resigned to defeat, he placed his left hand on the back of his head. "I'm doing it! I'm doing it!"

"That's better." Kepford turned to Jackson. "You got more cuffs?"

Jackson reached back and handed him a set of flex cuffs. In a few seconds, Kepford restrained and searched the man. Kepford dragged Hershel over to the bar where he'd been sitting moments before.

Keeping one hand on his prisoner, he reached down, picked up his coffee, and drained it in one long swallow. Everyone at the bar stared at Kepford as he set the cup down with a clatter.

He flashed a cheeky grin. "What? It's the apocalypse. Did you think I'd waste coffee?"

Jackson shook his head as he cuffed Greer and hauled him to his feet. "At least you've still got a sense of humor. Thanks for your help."

"Anytime."

The detainees grumbled, nursing their wounds, but their fighting spirits had been broken—for now. They were trouble and Jackson didn't want them anywhere near his county.

"What's the plan?" Kepford's expression was all business, but there was a mischievous glint in his eyes. "Do we get to dump them in the deepest part of Superior?"

"I'll lock them in jail for a night or two, let them blow off steam and sweat for a while. I don't want to waste too much food on them. Then I'll drive them to the edge of the county and let them go. They can hike to Sault Ste. Marie or maybe all the way to Mackinaw City. Maybe by then, they'll have acquired a new attitude."

"Doubt it."

"An undersheriff can dream." Jackson headed for the door, Kepford beside him. They pushed Greer and Hershel ahead of them. "That was an impressive set of moves you did back there. You served?"

Kepford grunted. "Yeah."

"You moonlighting as security?"

"Something like that."

"Interesting side gig for a principal."

Kepford grunted again. Dark stubble bristled across a firm jaw. Fine lines crinkled around his eyes. He looked tough and no-nonsense, but there was a kindness about him, too. It was probably why the students liked him so much.

"Are you going to tell me what you are, officially?"

"Officially? A high school principal."

"Unofficially, then."

"I could, but then I'd have to kill you."

"Oh, so it's like that."

Kepford's mouth twitched. "It's like that."

"You're like Eli. You move like him, act like him. Special Forces? A Tier One Operator?" Jackson guessed.

Kepford gave an enigmatic shrug. Jackson didn't know why he hadn't seen it before. He'd suspected military, but Kepford was more than that. He was a good twenty years older than Eli, but he carried himself like an elite soldier: confident, efficient, and skilled.

Hershel dragged his feet. Kepford shoved him, nearly pitching him to the floor. "I love being a principal, adore working with those kids, their sarcasm, bad jokes, questionable style, everything. But I also have a certain skill set that is applicable here. I may not be a true Yooper, but this is home to me. I realized it's time to stop hiding in plain sight and do some good."

"We could use you," Jackson said, "if you're seriously interested in doing good. The pay is crap. Actually, it's non-existent. And the hours are terrible. We ran out of coffee last week. And donuts."

Kepford didn't hesitate. "I'm head of security here, but I've got some time during the day since school is not exactly in session. Just tell me where to sign."

Jackson steered Greer through the large wooden front doors out into the sunlight, David and Hershel next to him.

Across the parking lot, Faith lay with her legs folded atop the glossy cherry-red BMW. The goat had made herself right at home;

white hairs and muddy hoof prints covered the hood, windshield, and roof. A couple of turds streaked the windshield.

She looked at them with her rectangular pupils and let out a smug bleat. The damn goat was proud of herself.

Greer about choked in disbelief.

"Nice wheels," Kepford drawled. "That yours, man?"

Greer's eyes bulged, veins pulsing on his forehead, cords standing out on his neck. He cursed a blue streak. "My BMW! It's ruined! That's destruction of property! They damn well owe me—!"

Jackson couldn't help himself. He leaned down as he cinched the cuffs tighter and spoke into Greer's ear. "Sorry buddy, we can't control the wildlife."

Kepford looked the sleek BMW over and whistled. Over Greer's enraged blubbering, he quipped, "It feels like he's compensating for something."

"My thoughts exactly." Jackson smiled. It felt good to smile. It had been too long, as if a part of him had already forgotten what joy felt like. Kepford would be a valuable asset. Jackson had a place to stay. He'd rid the county of three troublemakers. And tonight, he'd find Eli. He knew his next move.

All things considered, it had been a productive day.

22

SHILOH EASTON

DAY THIRTY

"What's this fry bread you keep talking about?" Shiloh asked.

Eli leaned over the fire. "It's a Native American dish passed down through a thousand generations. My mother used to make it for me to dip in chili. She'd top it with cinnamon and sugar for a dessert or spread it with thimbleberry jam like toast."

They sat around the Dakota fire pit at Eli's campsite. They'd spent the last few hours setting snares for rabbits and squirrels, then practiced shooting targets with pistols and the crossbow. They'd pinned paper targets to trees and practiced accurate firing while on the move.

Shiloh rubbed the aching muscles in her thighs. Yesterday, he'd made her practice rappelling from the lighthouse a million times. Her muscles were tired and sore, but it was a good sore.

Her stomach growled. "I love thimbleberry jam."

She was hungry for more than sustenance; she craved learning anything and everything Eli could teach her. It fascinated her, all of it, but the hours spent with Eli were also a distraction from her grief, a reprieve from the nightmares.

She leaned forward, resting her elbows on her knees. Her

crossbow was propped against the log Eli used for seating. "How do you make it?"

Eli showed her how he mixed the dough using flour, baking powder, and some salt, along with Crisco and water, then formed the dough into a pancake shape and fried it on a pan over the Dakota fire pit.

While the dough fried, she looked around. Her gaze caught on the shelter behind the boulder. The tent was still erected in the center of the clearing, but he didn't sleep there. Some of the pine boughs had been moved as if he'd been dismantling the shelter.

Her eyes narrowed. "You're moving."

"I never stay in one place long."

"Where are you going?" She kept her voice nonchalant like she didn't give a damn if he left, yet her chest went tight. It was abruptly hard to swallow.

"Not far, and I'll be back soon. Don't worry."

She hid her relief. "Not worried. And I'm not scared."

"It's okay to be scared. Everyone gets scared. It's what you do when you're scared that matters. Action in the face of fear is courage. Without fear, you're just stupid."

"I know a hell of a lot of stupid people."

"I bet you do." The corners of his mouth twitched. "The dough is golden brown, see? Now you flip it."

She did as he instructed. The dough sizzled in the oil as the delicious aroma filled her nostrils. She breathed in and listened to the birds, the small creatures sneaking through the underbrush, squirrels and rabbits, foxes and wolverines, chipmunks, and deer. The river gurgled as a sandhill crane took flight, its great wings beating the air.

"You're moving because Jackson knows where you are. And you don't want anybody to know where you are. Except me."

He looked at her, eyebrows raised.

She pointed across the clearing. "Two sets of footprints. The second set is too big to be mine. And they've got the deep grooves like Jackson's cop boots he wears when he's in uniform. He was here."

"Good observation. You're learning."

She and Cody had tracked rabbits and deer since they were little. Human prints weren't much different. It was about noticing the details. "It's not rocket science."

"I guess not. The bread is ready. Careful, it's hot."

She rolled her eyes as she removed the frying pan from the fire. Using a fork, she shoved a bite of fry bread into her mouth. It was hot and crispy and utterly delicious. Where had this been all her life?

"Good?" Eli asked.

"I've had worse," she mumbled around another bite. She couldn't shove it into her mouth fast enough. It was fluffy bread fried like a doughnut, but not as thick or sweet. It tasted like manna from heaven.

Eli smirked. "I like it, too. I'll keep making it as long as I can find the ingredients."

Shiloh tore the bread in half and handed it to him. For a few minutes, they ate in contented silence, the forest alive around them. Her heartbeat slowed. The anxiety dissipated.

Eli stilled, cocking his head as he listened to something. Shiloh held her breath as she listened to a fox or a raccoon moving through the underbrush to the northwest. She could tell it was small but larger than a squirrel.

"Animal," she said. "Fox, maybe."

After a moment, Eli relaxed. "Yes."

"We could hunt it for supper."

"Next time." Eli rubbed the back of his neck. "There's something I need to do. It might take me away for a while. I don't like it, but it needs to be done."

Shiloh shrugged like she didn't give a flying fart either way. Of course, she did. They both knew it. "It's cool."

"I won't be far, I promise."

She kicked at a stone by her feet. "Whatever."

He finished his food, pulled something out of his pocket, then handed the object to her. It was a small radio. "The sheriff installed repeaters to expand the reach of our radios. This should work within a couple of miles radius. You see anything, sense anything, anything at all out of place or strange or that gives you that unsettled feeling, you contact me." His mouth thinned like he loathed speaking the words aloud. "Then contact Jackson."

She took the radio. "I can take care of myself."

"No one can. Not even me. I need a team, I need backup. No more doing things on your own. No more Rambo."

"Who's Rambo?"

Eli snorted. "Never mind. What I mean is this: a soldier never goes it alone. That lone wolf nonsense is a load of crap. Maybe you get lucky, once, twice, maybe three times, but eventually you'll run out of luck. You need your brothers to have your back."

"And sisters."

"I stand corrected. And sisters. They're your teammates, the ones who will stand by your side no matter what. Leave no man behind."

She crossed her arms and stared him down, defiant. "You, too."

He hesitated a moment, then nodded. "You're right. Me, too."

"Okay, deal."

"Good." He showed her the channel he'd be on, how to call, and how to charge it with the solar battery pack he handed to her. "What's your call sign? You get to pick."

She licked her lips. Out here, with Eli, she felt calm. She felt at peace. The nightmares were far, far away. Whenever Eli was near, the bad memories couldn't touch her. "When I was little, my mom used to tell me a bedtime story about the first wolf who befriended mankind. The wolf protected man and adopted him and his children as his own family. The descendants of that first wolf are dogs. They're still loyal to us and keep us safe. What's wolf in your language?"

He opened his mouth like he was going to say something, then thought better of it. He didn't say anything for a minute. "*Ma'iingan* means wolf."

"That's your call sign. What's mine?"

He studied her, head slightly tilted, black eyes assessing her. She sat up straight, met his gaze, and waited.

"*Waagoshens*," he said after a moment. "It means 'little fox.' You are small but cunning. You outwit those who are bigger and stronger than you are."

She grinned, thoroughly satisfied, and shoved the radio into her jeans pocket next to her lockpick set. "I find that acceptable."

"Shiloh." He was staring at her like he had no idea what to say or do next. He looked incredibly uncomfortable, nervous even, which was weird as heck. Eli Pope never looked nervous or frightened; he was an apex predator, scared of no one and nothing.

She glared back at him. "What?"

"You okay?" he said finally.

"I'm fine."

"You sure?"

She didn't want to tell him about the nightmares or the terror that constricted her lungs when she thought of Boone looming over her, of Cody leaping from the cliff, his body drifting in the cold dark waters. Or that Cody's death had left a gaping hole inside her and she didn't know how to fill it.

She didn't tell him she wished she'd killed Boone with her crossbow. That she'd rather kill a thousand times than lose someone she loved. She'd rather burn down the whole world.

She said, "Like I said, I'm fine."

He watched her the same way Lena did as if he knew better and could see inside her soul to the darkness, because maybe the same darkness lived inside him.

A darkness that looked a lot like grief but also something else.

The nightmares continued to haunt her. A child crying in the night. Dark hair spread across a white pillow. Blood on her mother's cheek, her face. A steady *thump, thump, thump* in the darkness. And a shape, a shadow moving through shadows.

She'd wake in a cold sweat, her memories falling through a black hole the way they'd done that day when she was five, and again when her grandfather was murdered in front of her.

Shiloh squeezed her eyes shut, sucked in a sharp breath. She didn't want to think about any of it. She wanted to forget, to drive it all from her brain. With Eli, she could be someone else; she could become a warrior, not a victim.

Shoving the rest of the fry bread into her mouth, she wiped her hands on her pants as she stood, ready to practice again, to train. More bad guys could appear at any time. She was determined to be ready, to protect Lena and Bear and Ruby and everyone she cared about.

"Shiloh, I..."

"What?"

He looked like he wanted to say something, but it might tear his heart out to do so. It confused her made her anxious. She didn't like it. So she hefted the crossbow and gave him a devilish grin. "You ready to lose again?"

A shadow passed across his features.

"I triple dog dare you."

He rose heavily to his feet. "Alright, kiddo. If nothing else, you're a glutton for punishment. Let's go."

23

ELI POPE

DAY THIRTY-ONE

The wind rushed through Eli's hair. The sun had risen above the horizon, an orange smudge through the clouds. Early morning fog drifted above the water's surface. The lake was liquid glass as the speedboat skimmed across the placid surface, headed toward Grand Island.

Half a mile off the mainland, Grand Island consisted of 14,000 acres of pristine wilderness scattered with cabins, rustic campsites, a visitor's station, and a few homes claimed by fewer than forty residents.

It was also James Sawyer's fortress.

Two armed men flanked Eli, who stood behind the pilot at the helm. Three mercenaries hovered a few feet behind them, hard men with stern faces and flat eyes. They carried HK416 A6 rifles with suppressors attached to eleven-inch barrels. They made no attempt to hide their wicked-looking weapons.

Eli stared straight ahead and said nothing. No one spoke over the roar of the motor.

Back at the marina, Eli had arrived just after dawn and demanded to speak to Sawyer. At first, the mercenaries had refused to give him passage. Finally, one of them had radioed someone, spoken quietly for a minute, then made a motion to Eli to board one of the speedboats bobbing in its slip.

They'd frisked him and stripped him of weapons, including his knife and ankle holster, then ran an RF signal across his body to check for wires. Like the last time Eli had visited Sawyer, the contractors had confiscated his keys, sunglasses, and even his multi-tool.

Anxiety scythed through him as Grand Island grew nearer and nearer. He felt naked, vulnerable, and exposed without his weapons, the way he'd felt every second of his eight years in prison.

He willed his body and his fists to relax, his breathing to even out. He projected a careless calm, a man utterly confident in himself and his purpose.

Jackson had come to him yesterday and asked a thing he had no business asking. They both knew it. And yet, he'd agreed to do it.

He hated being separated from Lena and Shiloh, but this was the way to protect them from far worse and more determined monsters than a couple of hyped-up junkies out for a score.

As the sun burned off the mist, the island showed itself. Veils of mist softened the edges of the northern shoreline. Cliffs reared above their heads, sharp, jagged, and forbidding, the limestone bluffs rising out of the water like great stone castles.

Fog swirled at their bases as if they'd materialized from thin air, from dreams and nightmares, the ghosts of the deep come back to life.

Eli had never taken to the water the way Sawyer had, not like most of the locals who'd grown up on the edge of civilization. The lake was fickle—calm and gentle one day, in a rage the next, pounding the shoreline with startling violence, attempting to shatter boats on the rocks, to drown anyone that dared her waters.

Lake Superior had to be respected, and, like any wild thing, approached with caution.

The pilot cut the engine as they approached the ferry dock at

Williams Landing. A collection of buildings clustered along the shoreline: a visitor's station and a gray shack with a sign that read, "Ferry Service; info, tickets, ice."

The ferry was docked in its slip, laden with crates and pallets of boxes sealed in saran wrap. Men and women were busy loading and unloading supplies into trucks and trailers. Streamlined, teak-decked cruisers and sleek speedboats were anchored along the shore, likely stolen by Sawyer and his men.

Two men jumped onto the dock ahead of him as a couple of guys tied the boat to the pilings. Sawyer strode toward them with long, confident strides, his dirty blonde hair mussed from the wind. He'd been standing on the shore in a tight group of six or seven men, but he broke away from them when he saw Eli. Three armed men followed him.

He met them halfway down the dock and clasped Eli's arm. "I hope this is what I think it is."

Eli pulled away. "Depends on what you think it is."

James Sawyer was lean and muscular, a three-day beard shadowing his square jaw, his cheekbones chiseled as if by the wind itself. His weathered features broke into a grin, but no emotion flickered behind his sea-gray eyes. "You saw the light, my friend. You've decided to join us!"

"I haven't decided anything." He kept his expression impassive. If he were too eager, he'd raise Sawyer's suspicion. Sawyer knew him too well. It was a delicate balancing act, a dangerous game.

Eli knew how to play dangerous games, and how to win them.

Sawyer was nonplussed. "You will. Let me introduce you to a few of my brothers-in-arms."

Eli bristled at the military term used by the likes of Sawyer and his greedy thugs, but he didn't show it. "Sure."

Sawyer jerked his thumb at the man next to him, a big man, bigger than Sawyer, with huge meat-hook hands that made the large automatic he held look like a water pistol. His eyes were dark as flint and as hard, his nose like a hatchet blade set in a broad face. "This is Pierce, my right-hand man."

Pierce stared at him without a flicker of acknowledgment. He oozed former military from his buzzed bowling ball of a head, wide-legged stance, and the way he handled his weapon as if it was an extension of himself. He looked like he could take a grown man apart with his bare hands.

On his right hand, he wore a ring. Eli was close enough to make out the details: the carved snout and fangs of the wolf and the intricate curve of the twin snakes were familiar from the photos Jackson had shown him.

The perpetrator who'd killed Lily Easton and at least seven other girls had left his ring in a grave. He would not be wearing it now. The killer likely was not Pierce.

This fact did not make Eli dislike him any less.

The second guy stepped forward. He was young, mid-twenties, and powerfully built, wearing tan cargo pants, a white tank top that showed off his muscles, with an AR-15 slung across his back. He sported a goatee and wore his thick, shaggy brown hair to his shoulders.

He thrust out his hand. Eli noted the large ring on his finger. "Marcus Dixon. Sawyer's told me a lot about you."

"Strange. I've heard nothing about you."

Dixon gave a good-natured laugh, but Pierce's mouth tightened. The third man didn't react at all. Tall and garishly thin, his features were sunken, the skin of his face pulled tight over his skull.

Though it was early summer, he wore black leather gloves over his long, spindly fingers. A tattoo crawled up the right side of the man's neck: a wolf biting two writhing snakes.

Eli repressed a shudder as a chill touched the back of his neck. The man looked like evil incarnate, like the insatiable, cannibalistic windigo in the flesh. He'd need to keep an eye on this one.

"This is Wes Vaughn. I call him Spider. You see the resemblance. I'm sure you'll get along swimmingly."

Eli had his doubts but kept them to himself.

Sawyer spun on his heel and headed for the parking lot. "I have much to show you."

"I want my weapons returned," Eli said to Sawyer's back.

Without turning, Sawyer waved a dismissive hand. "All in good time."

Sawyer's men stayed close as they walked to a pair of four-by-fours. Sawyer drove, with Pierce in the passenger seat while Dixon sat next to Eli in the back. Vaughn drove the second off-road vehicle with two mercenaries in tow.

Old-growth hardwoods towered around them, the dense canopy shrouding them in shadows. The morning air smelled of pine sap, damp earth, and dead leaves.

Grand Island had served as a nature lover's paradise for hikers, backpackers, kayakers, and cyclists. He'd visited this island dozens of times as a kid, kayaking and hiking, fishing and camping at Freighter View and Gull Point with Jackson.

The roads were gravel or dirt, and trails crisscrossed the island. Eli and Lena used to bike the 23-mile perimeter road that circled the island. The island should have been as familiar to him as the back of his hand, but it wasn't. It was a foreign place, alien and dangerous.

As they drove, he constantly scanned the bluffs, the trees shuddering in the wind, the barren windswept beaches, and the rocky coves, searching for the glint of a scope, the shadowy shape of human predators lying in wait.

He found them. Grand Island was crawling with Sawyer's men, all trained, all armed, all thugs and professional killers. A dangerous bunch.

At the north end of Grand Island, they passed North Light Creek and halted at a section of the island closed to the public. Set amidst a wide clearing along the towering bluffs sat the North Light Lighthouse and a cluster of cabins.

Sawyer leaped from the four-by-four and gestured for Eli to follow him. Vaughn, Dixon, and Pierce fell into step a few feet behind them. Sawyer strode into the center of the clearing. Trees had been cut down, chopped up into firewood, and stacked to allow the wood to season. Several large wind-powered turbines provided electricity.

Down the hill, men and women were constructing greenhouses and more cabins. The workers were younger than forty and fit. Sawyer wanted the strong ones, the tough ones, and he was getting them.

"The gardens and greenhouses we're building over here," Sawyer said, "Chickens are coming. I hate the smell of them, but I love eggs."

"You've got a lot of people here."

"Anyone who comes to work for me gets lodging and food for them and their families. Well water gets pumped via a solar-powered pump and gravity fed to the cabins. We're building turbines for wind power. Low-voltage solar lights are everywhere, and we have plenty of solar and battery-operated lanterns. Plenty of batteries, too."

"You're bringing everything over on boats?"

"What we need and then some." He showed Eli a cluster of shipping containers, each brimming with supplies—pallets of toilet paper, bleach, cereal, peanut butter, light bulbs and seeds, car batteries and coffee.

"You robbed the distribution center."

"We took what was there for the taking. The employees weren't putting themselves on the line. Why get shot for your bosses when the world is ending anyway? We walked in and took what we wanted. The cops didn't arrive for hours if at all, and we were already gone.

"The banks were no different. We have more cash than we know what to do with. You think people would get it already, but most people still accept dollars. Like paper will help them in a month. For now, a loaf of bread is twenty-five bucks. A package of cheese is thirty dollars. And rising rapidly. Gas if you can get it is fifty bucks a gallon, five gallon minimums. And good luck getting home without someone following you and slitting your throat for the fuel in your gas tank. This is only one of our sites. We have several satellite locations and we're growing fast, faster than you can imagine."

"How do you keep people from stealing from you?"

"They won't," Sawyer said in a clipped tone that brooked no argument.

A dog barked. Down the hill, a German Shepherd trotted next to two men wearing tan chest rigs and carrying automatic rifles, patrolling the perimeter. Men were building sniper nests along the sandstone bluffs. Dozens of workers constructed a perimeter fence lined with razor wire.

Sawyer followed Eli's gaze. "I told you. No one is getting on this island unless I say so."

"You're creating your own little fortress."

"No one is getting up these bluffs. If they come from the south, our patrols and our dogs will tear them a new one before they get anywhere near here. Positioned like we are on the peninsula, we can see anyone coming by boat from the north, east, and west and shoot them from above."

"What's your exfil plan if you get attacked?"

"I won't need one, but if I do, I've got this." They rounded the corner of the cabin. A wide circular clearing opened up, with the grass mowed. A gleaming helicopter sat in the center of the clearing.

"Where did you get your hands on that?"

"It's a brave new world, my friend. Anything can be had for the taking. Anything."

Eli raised his brows.

"We're building something great, a new beginning to build upon the ashes of the old."

"Some people aren't ready to give up on the old."

Sawyer made a derisive sound in the back of his throat. "The world was already broken. The few in control got richer while the rest got poorer and poorer no matter how hard they worked. Dangling the American dream in front of people, like if they only worked harder, sacrificed more, and took on more debt, they could achieve it. And here's the joke: few can anymore. That dream has died for ninety-nine percent of people, but no one wants to admit it. Capitalism works but only when the government and corporations running the government aren't corrupt to the core. We are all serfs and slaves. The powers that be wanted it that way, burying us alive with taxes, overbearing laws, and regulations, claiming to protect us while stealing our wealth beneath our noses.

"Don't you see? Mother Nature offered us a giant do-over button. This is the only chance that the peons have to change the status quo. Turn it on its head. Rewrite our history books, and create the myths the next generation will tell about us."

"Is that the tripe you use to brainwash your men? Or do you believe it, too?"

Sawyer laughed. "No bull with you. I always liked that."

They stood looking out over the bluff, the cabins and the Grand Island North Lighthouse behind them. The wind whipped at their hair and clothes. Vaughn, Pierce, and Dixon drifted behind them in silence, hands on their weapons.

Sawyer paused, turning to face Eli. Raised on the lake, Sawyer was never more comfortable than on a boat. He seemed at home here on the island, too, as rugged and wild as the bluffs surrounding him.

He almost seemed boyish, giddily excited. "You're impressed. I knew you would be. Like I told you before, I want you by my side. I'm going to be king of the mountain."

"What mountain?"

"Any of them. All of them." Sawyer spread his arms in a grand gesture. "Everything boils down to resources, who has what and who doesn't. The first person to take control of them is the winner. King of the mountain." He leaned forward, a feral intensity in his gaze. "I'm going to be that king. I am that king."

Eli kept his personal opinions of Sawyer's kingdom building to himself. "Maybe you will. At any rate, I would like my guns back. And my knife. And my multi-tool."

"No way." Pierce had remained silent until now. He stepped forward, his features stony. "You have to earn it just like anybody else. We don't know you from hell. Not going to happen."

Eli said, "I don't need a weapon to kill you."

Pierce's expression darkened, but Sawyer laughed. "Eli Pope is a weapon."

"You've got to be joking. You can't just let him in here like this. He's a security risk—"

"I can do whatever the hell I want."

Vaughn watched the proceedings in silence. His lips were bloodless, his eyes heavily lidded in his skull-like face.

"Sir—" Pierce started to argue, but Sawyer silenced him with a look. The energy shifted, tension heightening. Eli's senses went on high alert. Subtly, he shifted into readiness.

Sawyer dipped his chin at Dixon. It was a shrewd gesture, easily missed, but not by someone like Eli. It was a signal.

Behind him, Dixon shifted into an attack stance.

24

ELI POPE

DAY THIRTY-ONE

Eli adjusted his stance, his adrenaline spiking as he took in multiple threats at once.

A dozen prison-yard fights flashed through his mind. This was no prison fight, not like when he'd faced Darius Sykes in the library. This was a litmus test. No doubt Sawyer's men had zero qualms about killing him, but he could not kill in return or Sawyer would certainly shoot him. Twenty goons would be on him in ten seconds or less.

Dixon and Vaughn fanned out, moving warily, attempting to circle him, weapons drawn. Pierce remained next to Sawyer but looked ready to enter the fray at any moment. Pistols and combat knives were strung to their belts. Two against one was difficult; three against one was nearly impossible.

His heart raced, adrenaline pumping. The edge of the bluff was at his back, a 200-foot drop not five feet behind him. Eli needed to end this quickly. If he let them make the first move, they'd flank or pincer him.

He didn't give them the chance.

Eli lunged at Dixon. Dixon wasn't ready for it. He balked, his weapon rising but his reaction too slow. Eli half ran past him, stepping forward with his right foot before hooking it behind his leg.

Simultaneously, he smashed Dixon's windpipe with the palm of his hand.

Stunned by the blow, Dixon fell backward over Eli's leg. He crashed to the ground. Eli sent two hard kicks to his face, breaking his nose. If he were aiming to kill, he would've stomped the man's throat or skull.

Sensing movement to his right, Eli spun to face Vaughn. Vaughn kicked at his right kneecap, an inch shy of a tendon-snapping blow. Eli gritted his teeth against the pain and dodged aside. Vaughn nailed him with another kick, this time going high.

Eli caught the man's shin, locked his arms, and shoved his leg upward. Vaughn flailed, about to pitch backward. At the last second, Eli dropped his hips, back straight, knees bent. Vaughn's spine and skull hit the ground.

Eli dropped him and brought his heel down on the man's groin. With a groan, Vaughn rolled from his back to his hands and knees. Eli landed a kick to his ribs, then to the side of his head, knocking him unconscious.

Then Dixon was on him again. Back on his feet, blood spurted from his nose and dripped down his chin. A knife glinted in his right hand. He attacked, lunging in and carving at Eli's torso with wide slashing arcs. Eli danced backward, nearly tripping over Vaughn's prone body.

Dixon made a vicious swipe. The tip of the blade sliced into Eli's forearm. Razor blades laced his flesh, the pain making him dizzy.

Dixon started to smile and moved in for another strike. Ignoring the pain, Eli executed a front snap kick into Dixon's stomach. Startled, Dixon stumbled back several steps, edging closer to the cliff. Driving him off-balance, Eli managed to sweep his legs out from beneath him and drop him to the ground.

Dixon rolled onto his stomach to clamber to his feet, but Eli fell on him, forcing him prone and knocking the knife free, which fell and wedged beneath his torso.

Kneeling on Dixon's back, his knees pinning his arms, Eli

seized the man's long hair and used it like reins to smash and scrape his face into the limestone, the knife caught beneath his stomach, utterly useless.

Dixon screamed, caught like an animal in a trap. Vaughn lay unconscious a few feet from the bluff. Rage and violence flowed through Eli's veins. He wanted to kill this man. He restrained himself, exerting incredible control.

Breathing hard, his right hand still wound in Dixon's hair, Eli lifted his head and met Pierce's gaze. "One twist and his neck snaps like a twig."

Pierce raised his pistol and aimed it at Eli's head. His jaw clenched, his eyes radiated fury. "I'm going to kill you, you mother—"

Sawyer shouted, "Enough!"

Sawyer laughed. "Don't kill him, Eli. I think you've made your point quite clearly." He side-eyed Pierce. "He is more than capable."

"Let me have a go at him," Pierce growled.

"I think not. I don't need two of my most talented men killing each other."

Eli released Dixon's hair and rose to his feet. Dixon stood, cursing and wiping dirt and pebbles from his clothes.

Vaughn regained his faculties and sat up, holding his head and groaning. Dixon wiped his bloody nose with the back of his arm, then reached out to help Vaughn up. Vaughn brushed his hand away and stood unsteadily.

Eli shifted his focus between Dixon, Vaughn, and Pierce. The men had been beaten and humiliated, which made them even more dangerous. He hadn't touched Pierce, yet his gut told him Pierce was the one to watch.

Sawyer clapped in approval. "The operators I hired from the Russian and Croatian militaries are highly trained. They do their jobs well. I also have the men I trust, that I've built around me for the last twenty years. They are not as skilled at killing as you are,

Eli, but they can fight, they know their guns and how to shoot. They are hard men, too."

Eli stood with his back to the bluff, shaking from the adrenaline dump, shoulders straight. His pulse roared in his ears. He remained tense, ready for anything. "I have no doubt."

"I don't trust him," Pierce growled.

"You don't have to. I do."

"He's friends with the undersheriff!"

"Not anymore," Eli said evenly, which wasn't a lie. Not even a little. Eli still despised Jackson Cross. He wasn't here for Jackson; he was here to find justice for Lily, but most of all, for Shiloh. If he could help nail the killer of his daughter's mother, then maybe, just maybe he could be worthy to call himself her father.

Sawyer barked out a laugh. "I should think not."

"He's an outsider. We don't know him—"

"I know him. And I say he's good." Sawyer whirled to face Pierce, his eyes flashing. "Are we not good?"

Pierce's mouth thinned. "We're good."

Sawyer looked to Vaughn, then Dixon. "Tell Eli you're good. No hard feelings."

Vaughn glared at Eli and wiped blood from his split lip. "Whatever you say, Sawyer."

Dixon forced a bloody smile. He had not enjoyed being bested, but he would play nice if ordered to. His expression was pained, embarrassed, but he didn't seethe with hatred like Pierce and Vaughn. "Welcome to the island, Pope."

Sawyer slapped Eli on the back. Eli hated it but said nothing. "He's on our side, he's got your backs. Now get yourselves over to med bay before breakfast is over."

Pierce hesitated.

"I said go!"

Pierce spun and stalked back toward the cabins, Vaughn hot on his heels. Dixon limped after him. With growing trepidation, Eli watched them go.

There were a hundred ways to kill a man, dozens of ways to make it look accidental. And there were no cops in sight. Sawyer didn't see it or he didn't care, but Eli sensed it. Pierce and Vaughn would be trouble.

Sawyer looked out across the bluff toward the mainland, his hands behind his back. "Tell me, Eli. Are you with me?"

Eli understood this moment was another test. He'd have only one chance to answer correctly. If he said no, Sawyer would likely allow him to leave on his own recognizance, but he would never be allowed back. It was now or never.

He thought of Shiloh, of Lena, of Lily restless in her grave, and the seven lost girls buried behind Boone's cabin. He thought of a killer let loose in a chaotic, collapsing society, the damage he would do if left unchecked.

He said, "I'm with you."

A flicker of something Eli couldn't read flashed in Sawyer's eyes, something dark and dangerous. "Good."

25

JACKSON CROSS

DAY THIRTY-TWO

Jackson tightened his grip on the steering wheel of the patrol truck. He drove while Devon scrunched in the passenger seat, case files in her lap. They both preferred to drive, but as the undersheriff, Jackson won that battle. Usually.

Jackson and Devon had left Munising that afternoon and headed west along M-28, hugging the coast through Marquette before turning onto US 141 toward the town of Houghton, 140 miles northwest and located on the Keweenaw Peninsula.

They'd stopped in Marquette, the largest city in the U.P, with no success, then Ishpeming and Humboldt, mere dots on the map, before continuing on US 41 toward L'Anse and the tiny towns nestled along Kewanee Bay.

He glanced at Devon out of the corner of his eye. Dark circles smudged her eyes. Her skin was sallow, her features drawn. She looked like she wasn't eating enough. "How are you doing?"

She gave a choked laugh. "How is anyone doing? We should all be on industrial-strength anti-depressants, except pharmacy shelves are gathering dust. How is anyone supposed to deal with something like this?" She waved a hand toward the window at an abandoned SUV on the side of the road. The driver and passenger doors were left open, as if the occupants had been abducted by aliens or had abdicated their own lives.

He had no answer. He couldn't articulate the enormity of what had been lost. No one could. Half the world was in mourning. Humanity was struggling to claim meaning in the devastation, sifting through the ashes of their former lives.

"How are you on food and toiletries?" he asked instead.

"I waited in the FEMA line for three hours like everyone else for a bag of emergency supplies. Sterilizing water is a pain. So are cold sponge baths and meals from cans. I'm over it."

"Lena is working on making a solar oven for cooking. You should talk to her."

"Yesterday, my neighbors brought me some smoked venison. They didn't expect anything in return, either; they just thanked me for keeping them safe."

"Up here, people look out for each other."

Devon looked up from the case files in her lap and watched the empty road ahead of them. "Until their own kids are starving. What then?"

"We're not there yet."

She made a noise in the back of her throat. "And you, boss? You good?"

"I'm fine," he said, though he felt anything but.

They had spent most of the day helping with security for the Alger County FEMA emergency distribution, where several fights had broken out. FEMA had not brought enough of anything.

It took five National Guardsmen and four LEOs to keep the public from rioting. Tensions were high. Jackson saw it in their taut expressions—the fear and helplessness, the doubt and anger.

Most folks who lived in the UP were rugged and relatively self-sufficient, used to harsh winters and isolation. They tended gardens, planted small farms, kept chickens, hunted and fished, but they'd never depended on those hobbies as sole food sources for their families.

It was about more than food—many had run out of the medications that kept them alive.

The FEMA representative could not tell them when the aid truck would return, or whether it would contain the critical supplies the town needed. He couldn't tell them anything about the world outside the Upper Peninsula, either. They were all in the dark. The uncertainty was crushing.

After the aid truck had moved on and the grumbling crowd dispersed, Jackson had written up an incident report between neighbors who'd gotten into a fistfight after John Swanson accused Gus Granger of stealing gasoline from his lawnmower. The week before, Gus had accused John of nicking his new Weber grill and selling it for cash to buy food and fuel.

They were good men, neighbors and friends for two decades, but their eyes shone with a mix of distress and reckless desperation.

Nothing Jackson said placated them. He feared the next time he was called to their properties the repercussions would be more serious than a split lip and bruised egos.

Next, he'd visited Dana Lutz out by the Pictured Rocks Golf Club—the once-pristine golf course now sprouting weeds and overgrown grass. Dana had reported a bad smell emanating from her neighbor's property.

Elmer Dunn was a veteran and excellent hunter, a grizzled loner who owned a handful of rustic cabins he rented out to fellow hunters and fishermen. He was seldom without his faithful bloodhound, Honey, at his side.

With a growing sense of dread, Jackson searched the house, which was clean and uncluttered though heavy with shadows. He heard no barking. That was odd. Honey would have—with a jolt, he remembered.

Two days ago, Moreno and Hasting had responded to a breaking and entering incident in which the thieves had stolen several generators from Dunn's cabins, but not before poisoning Honey with antifreeze.

It was the third case of dog poisonings coupled with thievery in the county that week. They had no clues, no leads. The criminals came and went like ghosts, leaving dead pets and despondent families behind. Jackson made a mental note to warn Lena to watch out for Bear.

Finding nothing in the house, Jackson had moved to the detached garage and workshop at the rear of the property. And there, he found the old man in the woodshed. He had hung himself from the rafters. On the workbench table was a note to bury him next to his beloved Honey.

Crestfallen, Jackson called in the body to Nash, who would take it to the ME's office to join the growing pile of corpses. Guilt and despondency needled him. If they had caught the thieves before they'd struck again, this would not have happened. Elmer Dunn would be alive and as crotchety as ever, with Honey barking at all hours of the night.

Jackson could not be in multiple places at once. He was stretched thin, trying to protect everyone, solve cases, and keep the county and the people he cared about from disintegrating.

With the lack of communication, dwindling resources, and increasing desperation among civilians, law enforcement found itself crippled during the worst possible crisis.

It felt like trying to stop the tide with his bare hands.

As they drove, Devon flipped through the scant case files. Like him, she had them memorized. Still, they pored over the photos and reports again and again, hoping to uncover something, a clue, a piece of elusive evidence, anything they might have overlooked.

Over the last week, in his rapidly dwindling spare time, he'd traversed the eastern side of the peninsula, from Grand Marais to Whitefish Point to Paradise and Newberry. Half the precincts had lost half their manpower. Several were closed. The other half did not have missing persons cases that matched Alger County's victim descriptions.

He caught his first break at Whitefish Point, where tourists visited the Shipwreck Museum and toured the Whitefish Point

Light Station, established in 1849, and where the infamous *SS Edmund Fitzgerald* had sunk in 1975.

At the Chippewa County Sheriff's Department, the deputies were responding to calls, but the administrative assistant had proved immensely helpful. An indomitable woman in her sixties with a halo of white hair shellacked to within an inch of its life, she'd told him in a raspy smoker's voice that she remembered every missing person's case going back thirty years.

For two hours, they'd rifled through files in a musty basement. With a huff of triumph, the woman slapped a dusty file in front of him. Lydia Hughes, age nineteen. She was reported missing by her mother on May 15, 2016. Six years ago. One night she snuck out to party with friends and never returned home. She had a history of opioid abuse, failed stints at rehabs in Marquette and Sault Ste. Marie, and was arrested for shoplifting in 2013 and prostitution in 2015.

Her missing person photo had captured his attention. She was 5'4", 110 pounds soaking wet, with long brunette hair to her waist and an adorable gap between her front teeth.

Lydia Hughes fit their unsub's victim profile. The timeline matched the ME's estimated time of death. Gideon Crawford, the local dentist in Munising, had offered his aid. Normally, they'd use a forensic odontologist to compare antemortem and postmortem records for definitive identification, but they were desperate for whatever help they could get.

Gideon had determined that the distinctive gap, or diastema as he'd termed it, between her maxillary central incisors was consistent with her physical appearance from the photographs, which was enough for tentative identification.

So far, they'd identified four of the seven unknown victims, including the dates and locations where they'd gone missing. A pattern was emerging, a trail of breadcrumbs the killer had left behind.

They still had not found the first victim. That evidence would be gold. If the killer had made a grievous error, it would have been during that first kill. They had to find her.

Jackson pounded the steering wheel in frustration. "This psychopath believed he was scot-free while an innocent man went to prison for his crimes. He thought he had carte blanche to keep killing. He didn't. He doesn't. We *will* get him."

Devon absently chewed her thumbnail. "We will, boss."

She didn't have to list the statistics. Only fifty percent of murderers were caught in the best of times when society functioned, and law enforcement had access to surveillance and top-notch technology.

Only five weeks ago, he would've conducted searches in online databases, checked AFIS and INTERPOL, contacted the FBI, and called county sheriff departments and local precincts across the UP.

That was all gone. The solar flares had erased 150 years of progress in one fell swoop. Now, every step in the case required monumental and time-consuming effort, boots on the ground, blood, sweat, and tears.

It was a crapshoot

And yet, he could not let it go.

Whatever was required of him, he would give it. And he knew that Eli Pope would, too. Even after everything that had gone down between them, Jackson had no doubts.

"Eli is the key," he said with conviction. It was faith that kept him going, sheer force of will. "While he works Sawyer from the inside, we work the case from the outside. Something will break. It has to."

Over the last few days, he'd had sporadic communication with Eli. Luckily, Eli could see the mainland with a good set of binoculars, so Jackson had made use of a cabin perched along the shoreline opposite Grand Island's southernmost point. Using solar-powered lights, Jackson sent Eli messages utilizing colored porch lights, each color sending a specific, prearranged message.

A green light meant to meet at a prearranged spot at 10 p.m.

the next day. A normal white light meant no meeting was needed, and a blue light meant Eli's cover had been blown, get the hell out.

Some nights, Jackson gave the signal, but if it was too risky for Eli, he wouldn't show. Jackson would continue to show up at their designated meeting spot each night until Eli could make the meeting.

So far, so good.

They drove another twenty miles in silence. Other than the abandoned cars, they had not seen a single vehicle on the road. Up here, it wasn't unusual to drive twenty minutes or more without seeing a car headed the opposite direction.

The Upper Peninsula was a wild land empty of people. Yoopers were used to it, preferred it even, though the emptiness could be disconcerting for downstaters, whom Yoopers referred to as "trolls" because they lived below the bridge.

An ominous presence bore down on him, an unnatural stillness. The engine rumbled beneath them. He swerved to avoid a pothole. Michigan was infamous for its boulder-sized potholes. Without maintenance, the roads would be impassable in a few short years, if there were vehicles still able to be driven.

Devon's stomach rumbled.

"I forgot to bring anything to eat, sorry." He was used to grabbing food on the run, nabbing a Gatorade and premade sandwich or frozen burrito at a gas station. Old habits died hard.

"I figured." Careful not to disturb the files in her lap, she reached for the backpack at her feet, unzipped it one-handed, and pulled out two objects wrapped in foil. "I brought dinner."

Jackson smiled. "Let me guess, pasties."

"You're almost smart enough to be a real detective."

He snorted.

"Annalise is an absolute lifesaver." She wasn't that far off. They clung to the few things that remained; it gave them a fragile sense of normalcy that kept them on this side of sanity.

Jackson ate while he drove. The portable meals were perfect to eat on the run. He hadn't been this full in days.

They moved on. Three more police stations, three more futile stops. When the gas tank ticked to empty, they stopped and Jackson refueled with the jerrycans he'd stored in the back of the truck while Devon kept watch.

They'd passed a couple of working gas stations, with handwritten signs stating fuel was seventy bucks a gallon. He hated using so much gas, but he told himself it would be worth it. This trip would be worth it.

Robins and goldfinches chirped. Cicadas buzzed in the overgrown weeds crowding the edges of the road. Not a soul in sight and yet neither felt relaxed. It felt like the trees had eyes, as if they were being watched. Even the familiar forests had gone feral and dangerous.

Trees rose on either side of the barren road: sugar maples, American beech, white and red pine, balsam fir, northern white cedar. They drove by trees, trees, and more trees as they passed through the Baraga State Forest areas and north into the Keweenaw Peninsula toward Houghton.

Gradually, the dense forests gave way to glimpses of civilization. They turned north into the Keweenaw Peninsula, entering Copper Country, so named for the copper mining rush from the 1840s through the 1960s.

Over two hundred and fifty copper mines were scattered across the Keweenaw Peninsula, some boring a mile below the surface. Most were abandoned now. In its heyday, this land had produced ninety percent of the world's copper.

They passed a boarded-up gas station and a bait shop on the corner. The glass in the windows of both businesses had been shattered. "We're already in Hell" had been spray-painted across the front of the sagging bait shop.

Five minutes later, they were in Houghton, population eight thousand and home to Michigan Tech University. The large lift bridge over the Portage River that connected Houghton to Hancock to the north rose ahead of them.

They checked the Sheriff's Office and the local precinct, both located along the Portage River that wound through town.

A young officer manned the front desk of the police station. His Finnish heritage was apparent in his blond hair, square jaw, and blue eyes. Worry lines bracketed the sides of his mouth. The generator ran in the background. Candy wrappers, dirty napkins, and empty bags of mixed nuts littered the messy desk.

"I can't help you," he said. "Whatever it is, we can't help you."

He was twitchy, on edge. He looked on the verge of panic, like the only thing keeping him behind that desk was habit, predictability, a desperate bid at normalcy, and even those conventions were thinning fast. "We've had five suicides. Thirteen drug overdoses. Some of 'em might be suicides, too. And eight murders. We don't have the manpower. We've lost half of our force. Our chief drove all the way to the Soo to ask the state police for aid, but they as much as laughed in our faces. Typical, eh?"

"We're dealing with the same problems," Jackson said.

Devon leaned on the counter and gave him an encouraging smile. "Let us look at your missing persons' files. That's it."

"We only have what's on the server. No access to AFIS for fingerprint analysis—"

"We know." Devon was already headed for the door to the back, circling the reception area, Jackson hot on her heels. "We appreciate the help."

They found two missing person reports within Houghton County within the last fifteen years that matched their criteria. Devon asked to make copies since they still had a bit of fuel in their generator.

Frowning, the officer read the files as he copied them. "You should check in Copper Harbor. My uncle was a sergeant for the Keweenaw Sheriff's Department. They had a missing girl case a long time ago. Like these. He still talks about it occasionally. I think it still haunts him. Maybe you should talk to him."

"Thank you," Devon said. "We will."

The officer's frown deepened. "Take care. It's wild country north of Houghton. Be careful, is all."

Half an hour later, they were back in the truck. The tiny hamlet Copper Harbor was perched on the tip of the Keweenaw Peninsula, still about an hour drive north.

"It's after eight." They wouldn't get back home until long after dark, but Jackson wasn't concerned. He was beyond exhausted, driving forward on sheer adrenaline, but he was concerned for Devon's welfare more than his own. "You too tired to keep going?"

"Did I say that?" A coy smile tugged at her lips. Lately, it had disappeared. He was glad to see the spark was still there.

"One more?" he asked.

They both knew they wouldn't be able to come this far west again. It was now or never.

She glanced down at the new files they'd collected that day, files they fervently hoped contained the clues that would unlock the case. Then she gazed out the windshield at the lonely road in front of them, as if she too were imagining that first victim, one girl lost among hundreds of miles of rugged wilderness, waiting for them to find her.

Devon looked up at him. "One more."

26

JACKSON CROSS

DAY THIRTY-TWO

Devon leaned forward in her seat. Her shoulders went rigid. "What the hell is that?"

Jackson slowed the truck. With his right hand, he unholstered his service pistol and held it low beneath the steering wheel. In the township of Calumet, several buildings had burned to the ground. The police precinct was a broken shell. Black soot crawled up the brick exterior. The roof had collapsed. The stench of burned plastic infused the air. The businesses along Main Street had broken windows and doors torn off their hinges.

A sense of wrongness hung in the air, infused in every molecule of oxygen they inhaled. It was like a film on their skin they couldn't see but could feel, sinking into their pores.

Devon cursed under her breath. "Let's get out of here."

"I couldn't agree more."

They did not turn farther into town but kept driving north along 41. They drove by little shops advertising thirty types of jam, roadside stands that had once sold authentic Finnish or Native American trinkets, and quaint villages.

Despite the devastation they'd just witnessed, it was hard to ignore the stunning beauty up here, this rugged land of green-carpeted hills and steep gorges, rocky streams and waterfalls.

They approached Phoenix, once an old mining town, and halted before the intersection between US 41 and 26. Two Fed-Ex trucks blocked the road at an angle. Concertina wire had been strung on either side of the road along with several vehicles staggered in tactical positions.

Several rifle barrels glinted from various concealed positions. Jackson caught a glimpse of a head here, a shoulder there, crouched forms prepared to open fire.

His pulse quickened, every muscle tensing.

"Slow and careful," Devon murmured.

Jackson rolled down his window and stuck out his badge. "Alger County Sheriff's Department! Don't fire! We're friendlies."

Two figures materialized from behind the delivery trucks and approached with caution. A uniformed female police officer approached the driver's side, her service pistol in the low-ready position. On the right, a scruffy-looking man in a Detroit Red Wings jersey and camouflaged hunting pants hustled up on Devon's side. He carried a shotgun.

Jackson identified himself and Devon. The officer examined their badges. Her nametag read "Miller." She was in her thirties, her brunette hair greasy at the roots as if she hadn't had a good wash in a while. She wore no makeup.

"We can't offer backup or aid," she said briskly. "You'd best turn around and head back the way you came from. No one comes in except for full-time residents. No exceptions. Summer homes don't count. You got to have a picture ID and a Keweenaw County address on your driver's license or you're out."

"We're here on a case," Devon said. "Then we'll be on our way."

Officer Miller stared at her like she'd grown three heads. "A case?"

"A cold case," Jackson said. "We're tracking down a suspected serial killer."

That got her attention. "The Keweenaw County Sheriff's

Department generator ran out three days ago. No one's manning the desk. You won't find anything."

"What happened in Calumet? The precinct was a burned-out shell."

Her expression tightened. "A biker gang from Detroit was up here for a retreat of some kind. It happened four nights ago. They burned down the sheriff's office and used Molotov cocktails to burn the squad cars. Their leader killed the sheriff and declared he was the new mayor. We got him, but not before he and his cronies did considerable damage. You see why we're taking precautions. Alger County should, too. We sure as hell aren't getting back-up from anyone."

"Thanks for the heads up." Jackson felt sick. "We're looking for girls and women who've gone missing in the last decade, maybe longer. Young women with long hair. Troubled backgrounds. Drugs. Runaways."

"We can't help you." A shadow crossed her face. These people were jumpy and on edge. "Frankly, we're focused on protecting our own."

"We came a long way," Jackson said. "We would be incredibly grateful for your help."

Devon leaned across the seat. "An officer in Houghton said we should ask about Sam Caldwell."

Red Wings glanced at Officer Miller over the hood of the truck. "We know Caldwell. He's retired, though."

"Could we talk to him?" Jackson asked. "Then we'll be out of your hair."

Officer Miller gave the slightest nod of her head.

"He lives in Copper Harbor," Red Wings said. "It's another twenty minutes north. If you're dead set on going, we'll send an escort with you."

"We don't need an escort," Devon said.

"Everybody's got a trigger finger these days," Red Wings said. "It's the wild west out here. We're doing our best to protect what we have." He shook his head in disgust. "Can't imagine what it's like in Detroit or Chicago right now."

The seconds ticked by in Jackson's blood. They were running out of time. He was desperate for that critical clue, some breadcrumb that would lead him to a killer in hiding. "We'll take that escort."

27

JACKSON CROSS

DAY THIRTY-TWO

Red Wings escorted them via motorcycle up the peninsula to Copper Harbor via Brockway Mountain Drive, which featured stunning vistas overlooking the hills and coastline.

Copper Harbor was a cute little tourist town nestled on the coast, though everything was closed and shuttered. In between the trees, the water in the harbor shimmered like tinfoil.

Their escort led them to a quiet street, stopping at a two-story home with daffodil-yellow siding and faded blue trim. It could've used a fresh coat of paint, but it was far from derelict.

Jackson and Devon exited the truck and headed for the porch, their service weapons holstered. Down the street, an older couple sat in camping chairs on their front porch, watching the deputies with suspicious eyes.

An aluminum fishing boat sat on a trailer behind a rusty truck. Weeds sprouted shin-high in the overgrown grass. No one wasted fuel on mowing the lawn.

A beagle ran around the side of the house, barking.

"Hey, cutie," Devon said.

"He's trained as an attack dog," said a hoarse male voice. A bulky figure appeared behind the door and nudged the screen door open with the barrel of a shotgun. "He bites. So do I."

Devon straightened. "We'd like your help, Officer Caldwell."

"It's detective, and I'm retired. And Otis and I don't care for strangers on our land."

"Officer Miller sent us." Devon kept both hands visible. So did Jackson. "As did Jimmy Leffler at the Houghton Precinct. He said he was your nephew."

The man scowled. "Did they, now?"

The beagle darted up to Jackson and wriggled his entire body, tail wagging. Jackson bent down and petted the dog's head.

"Otis!" the man ordered. "Down!"

The dog ignored him and continued to blithely lick Jackson's hand. "An attack dog, huh?"

"I said he had training, not that he passed it." The man stepped out onto the porch. In his mid-sixties, a fringe of gray hair circled his balding head. He was heavy-set, a considerable beer belly stretching his faded white T-shirt. He wore sagging black sweatpants and flip-flops. "What d'ya want, eh?"

Jackson scratched behind the dog's ears. "Officer Miller said you might be able to help us with a cold case."

Caldwell stared at them for a long minute, as if examining them, weighing the merits of their souls, or maybe just deciding between abject boredom and the inconvenience they posed to his predictable schedule.

"I suppose you'll be wanting to come inside, eh?" he said with a distinctive Yooper twang.

"Sir." Devon gave him her best earnest, pleading expression. "We came a long way."

"Hurry up then. You're letting the flies in." He turned and hobbled inside.

Without a word, Jackson and Devon followed him. Otis scampered behind them, his toenails scrabbling across the porch.

The man leaned the shotgun against the wall beside the front door and grabbed a cane, then limped into the darkened living room. Outdoorsy magazines were piled on the coffee table. A 'Gone Fishing' sign hung over the plaid sofa.

He settled heavily into a leather armchair across from the sofa. Two oxygen tanks leaned against the wall next to the armchair. "I don't got tea and crumpets, no coffee either. None of that around here for anybody. Find yourself a seat."

They obeyed. Jackson set the files on the coffee table, shoving aside the magazines, while Devon explained the nature of their visit. "Sir, we have some questions—"

"Lemme see what you've got."

Obediently, Devon handed him a file. He flicked on a battery-operated LED camping lantern at his feet and placed it on the coffee table. A circle of yellow light bathed the crime scene photos.

Caldwell took each folder in his ham-sized hands. He looked through each one, read the ME statement, the preliminary autopsy report, and every bit of data they had for each victim. He did not rush.

Jackson resisted the urge to question him, to hurry the process along. Anxiety tugged at his insides. Other than Eli, this grumpy old man was their last best chance.

There was no flicker of recognition. No sudden intake of breath. The former detective worked through photo after photo of the victims in various states of decay and decomposition, most of them not much more than a collection of bones.

With each passing minute, Jackson's heart sank further. The old detective wouldn't be able to help them. They'd come all this way for nothing. Another dead-end, a brick wall, a false trail leading to nowhere.

Caldwell looked up, a line between his heavy brows. "This one."

He set the file on the table and pointed at a photo. It was a close-up of the gold half-heart locket the killer had left with each victim. He flipped through each photo of the locket from each grave they'd excavated. "I know these. This necklace, I've seen it before."

Adrenaline iced Jackson's veins. He sat up straight, notebook in hand. He dared not hope, but he did. "What do you remember?"

Caldwell's expression grew animated. He seemed to lose ten years of age and illness in a heartbeat. "I was the best detective in Copper County, had a clearance rate surpassing seventy percent. When I said I was gonna solve a case, I did it. But this damn case... she was the one who got away. I'll never forget it."

"What can you tell us—" Devon started.

With effort, he heaved himself from the armchair. "Wait right here."

Otis sprang to his feet and trotted after his owner as Caldwell grasped his cane and hobbled from the living room down a darkened hallway. His cane made a steady *thunk, thunk, thunk* on the cracked linoleum.

A minute later, he returned, breathing hard, leaning heavily on the cane, a binder tucked under one arm. He tossed it on the coffee table and sank into the armchair with a groan. From his pants pocket, he pulled a sweat-stained yellow handkerchief and mopped his perspiring brow.

The beagle skittered behind him, a stuffed giraffe in his mouth. It was soggy with saliva and well-chewed. The dog curled up at Caldwell's feet, the stuffed animal beneath his muzzle, and sighed in contentment.

"I made a copy of the murder book. For over a year, I looked through it almost every night. Technically, the case was never upgraded to murder. Hard to prove anything without a body. Her brother and her roommate were both adamant that she hadn't run away. I knew she was dead, felt it—" he thumped his expansive chest "—right here in the ticker."

"Who was she?" Devon asked.

Jackson held his breath.

"Her name was Elice McNeely. Age twenty-one. She disappeared on the night of May eight, two thousand and eight."

Jackson and Devon exchanged an incredulous look. Was it possible? They had found the first victim.

Caldwell shoved a photo at them. It was Elice McNeely's missing person photo, the one the media would've plastered all over the news, put on posters, tacked to telephone poles, and taped to store windows.

Like the others, the young woman was beautiful. Clear skin, defined cheekbones, dark brown eyes set wide apart, straight brown-black hair parted in the center that fell to her mid-back. She was smiling in the photo, but there was something off about her expression, a sort of tightness in her mouth, a distance in her gaze like she was play-acting.

Elice McNeely's frozen smile reminded him of Summer Tabasaw, the Ojibwe girl from Marquette with cigarette burns on her arms. They shared the same haunted look in their eyes. Like they had stared into the void and the void had stared back.

"What can you tell us about her?" Jackson asked. "A troubled past? Any history of drug use?"

"Elice was a foster kid. Her meth-head parents lost custody of her when she was twelve. Only a brother left, and he was worse off than she was. Arrested three times for possession and intent to distribute. He served three years in Baraga Maximum Correctional for grand theft auto. He was a mess, but he loved her, that much was clear to me.

"Elice was a high school dropout. History of drug use. Arrested at sixteen for prostitution. Picked up twice more at seventeen for possession. A damaged kid. A nobody. Who was to say she hadn't run off to Marquette, to the Soo, or further downstate to start a new life? Or dropped off the grid to overdose in a meth house somewhere? But I knew she hadn't."

"Because that's not the girl you saw," Jackson prompted.

Caldwell shrugged. His gaze grew distant as he remembered, his flabby jaw clenched. "I saw a girl who got into a rehab facility and didn't waste the opportunity. One of the few who did the work and got herself cleaned up, for the most part. She got her GED at eighteen after she aged out of the system, then worked as a receptionist for a doctor's office and took night classes at Michigan Technological University in Houghton to earn her ADN, an associate's in nursing. Here was a girl with no parents, no backup plan or safety net, and she was trying, still using, sure, but also trying."

Jackson's respect for the retired detective grew with each passing minute. He hadn't written Elice off as a lost cause or allowed her to slip through the cracks.

"How do you know for certain that she's one of ours?" Devon asked.

Caldwell flipped through the documents and pulled out several photos. He pushed one toward them. Jackson stopped breathing. Devon leaned forward, her eyes bright.

Caldwell thumped a photo with a meaty finger. "That necklace, it was hers."

Devon picked up the photo, and they both stared at it. "She was wearing this when she went missing?"

It was an enlarged photo, a close-up of a half-heart locket glittering on a gold chain at Elice's throat, a replica of the eight victims' lockets. There were seven in the graves, and one on Lily. They were the same size, shape, and color with the same jagged, broken edge where half of the heart had been separated from its missing half.

A chill dripped down his spine like cold water. "Did it contain a lock of her hair?"

"Her roommate, two co-workers, and her brother gave descriptions of the locket. They said she never took it off. According to her roommate, the locket had originally contained her boyfriend's hair, but when they broke up, she put in a lock of her hair, to signify that she didn't need a man in her life to be strong. Her brother said that she was determined to do it on her own."

Devon let out a rush of breath. Jackson's pulse quickened in his throat. They both felt it—a change in the air, instinct raising the hairs on their arms and the backs of their necks.

This was it. This was where this reign of terror and bloodshed had started, in a tiny town at the northernmost point of Michigan, in the wild, rugged middle of absolutely nowhere.

If Elice was indeed the unsub's first victim, then his obsession with the lockets began with her. It had become part of the compulsion. He needed to recreate that rush of the first time, that first girl. She meant the most to him. He knew her. With every murder, he was replicating this first kill, choosing similar victims, repeating the ritual with the lockets, over and over.

"Who reported her missing?" Devon asked.

"Her roommate, Tara Evens, age twenty-four, was a hair stylist at the Aveda Cut and Color here in town. Tara had gone camping in the Porcupine Mountains with a boyfriend for the weekend. When she returned on Sunday night, there was no Elice and no evidence she'd been to the apartment that weekend. There was no sign of forced entry into the apartment. Elice's bed was made; no clothes or toiletries were missing. It appeared that Elice never made it home that Friday.

"No one had seen her since she got off work Friday at 5 p.m. She didn't have a car but got around on a purple moped. It was still parked in the parking lot at the doctor's office. She wasn't captured on any surveillance cameras. She didn't use her credit card. Didn't get on social media or post on Twitter. She simply disappeared somewhere between the office and her apartment. Considering that she didn't take her moped, I worked off the assumption that she was abducted from the parking lot." He paused. "Or she willingly got into the vehicle of someone she knew."

Which complied with Jackson's working theory that the killer knew his first victim.

"Suspects?" Jackson asked. "What about the boyfriend who gave her the locket?"

"We never identified him. The roommate mentioned that Elice had been incredibly secretive about the boyfriend. It had lasted for several months. Going out without telling her roommate where she was going, coming home late."

"Why keep it a secret?" Devon asked.

"The roommate thought it was a married guy, someone Elice was embarrassed to talk about. Elice wouldn't give up his name.

When Elice went to rehab, she started to get her life together. The roommate suspected the secret boyfriend had something to do with the drugs, because when the drugs ended, the late nights and sneaking out seemed to stop, too. Elice told her she'd broken up with the guy, and that he hadn't taken it well. Then Elice started acting weird. She said she thought someone was following her.

"The roommate said she could be dramatic and attention-seeking, but in the weeks before she disappeared, she seemed stressed and agitated. The roommate said she had gotten obsessive about checking the locks. One day, flowers appeared on the kitchen table. Neither girl knew how they'd gotten inside the apartment. Instead of being flattered, Elice seemed shaken, genuinely scared. The roommate blamed herself for not taking it seriously."

Jackson imagined the type of man who might react badly to a woman putting her hair in the locket instead of her ex-boyfriend's. It was exactly the type of slight that a narcissistic sociopath would not tolerate.

His instincts screamed at him that this was the one, this mysterious, menacing ex-boyfriend. Find him, find the killer. "What else did you have on this guy?"

"Nothing. No name, not even a description of a vehicle or him. Whoever he was, he was careful. He was never caught on any security footage around Elice's apartment or outside the doctor's office. The roommate never saw him. Elice didn't keep a diary. Her phone disappeared with her—it was never turned back on, so we couldn't track it. We interviewed and checked everyone she worked with, co-workers, neighbors, and friends. That's where the trail dried up."

Jackson looked through the scant files. "Were you able to go through patient records at the doctor's office? We're looking for a male, likely Caucasian, up to ten years older than her, probably with a history of drug use, possibly married or in a long-term relationship, which he uses for cover. He's intelligent, organized, maintains a steady job, and blends into society fairly well."

Caldwell shook his head wearily. "It never rose to the level of a murder case. I couldn't get the files."

Jackson rubbed his jaw. "It's likely the crime started in that parking lot. Now, we've got a body and a positive identification. We can legally look at patient records to find the identity of the unsub without a warrant and be well within the rules of evidence."

"Could you take us there?" Devon asked. "We've got a working profile of the unsub as long as the doctor still has hard copies of his records at the office."

Caldwell's dull eyes gleamed for a moment. Otis raised his head, the neck of the giraffe nestled in his jaws, his tail thumping. "Dr. Thompson is old school, like me. He'll have the records. The office is closed since nobody's got power, but he'll have a key."

"Can you take us there?"

Caldwell gestured at the oxygen tanks next to his armchair. "I'm not going anywhere, but I can have an officer take you. I've still got influence over there. I'll make it happen."

"Excellent. Thank you. Then we need to cross-reference those names with known meth dealers and users in the area."

"We did," Caldwell said. "Came up with nothing. You're welcome to try again."

"We might see old information in a fresh way with what we know now."

He nodded. "I've got a few contacts for you."

Devon looked down at her notebook, chewing on her thumbnail. "Did you find anything at her apartment?"

"We brushed for fingerprints, her fingerprints, her roommate's, her roommate's boyfriend. There was an unknown set of prints in the bedroom that didn't match anything in the system. We found some red wool fibers on the sheets of her bed that didn't match any article of clothing in Elice's or her roommate's closets. They could have been left by a lover."

Caldwell coughed, a raw, grating sound pulled from deep in his chest, wracking his entire body. He wiped his mouth with the handkerchief, his mood shifting palpably. At his feet, Otis chewed plaintively on the neck of his stuffed giraffe. "Without the body...I never got the break I needed. We circled and circled. She just disappeared."

"Where's the roommate?" Jackson asked. "Could we interview her? Or Elice's brother?"

"The brother died three years ago of a heroin overdose. The roommate moved to Montana to take care of a parent with Alzheimer's last year." Caldwell shrugged. "It's a small town. Word gets around."

A month ago, the distance wouldn't have deterred them. Now, the witness might as well live on another planet. They couldn't reach her.

Caldwell looked at Lily's file and frowned, flicking through the crime scene photos. "The guy you nailed for this one, Eli Pope. I remember hearing about this case. I read about the heart necklace, but the sheriff never released a photo of it or the part about the hair. We had no reason to believe the necklace held any relevance at all."

Heat flooded Jackson's face. "Turned out he didn't do it. I got the wrong guy."

"It's our failures that get us, in the end." Caldwell sank back in the armchair, seeming to deflate. The gleam had left his eyes. He wheezed for a minute. They waited as he struggled to catch his breath. A palpable sense of gloom hung over their heads. Melancholy so thick they could breathe it in. "That's all I've got. All we ever had. He got away from me. With the world going to pot like it is, he'll get away from you, too."

Devon rose to her feet. "Not if we can help it, sir."

Jackson stood as well. "Thank you for your help. We're going to do everything we can to solve Elice's case and catch this guy."

"Take the file. It won't do me good anymore. My investigative days are done." He looked away from them, toward the kitchen, misery swimming in his eyes. The driven detective he once was had disappeared, crushed beneath illness, depression, and resignation.

Jackson took the murder book and folded it under his arm as Devon gathered their case files, photographs, witness statements, and forensic reports. "Sir, are you okay here?"

Caldwell didn't look at her. He stroked his dog's head. "Miller promised to take Otis when I'm gone. That's all I care about anymore. My days were numbered before the crap hit the spinner, now I'm a walking dead man. Three divorces. No kids. I was married to the job. Now my pension is gone. No more checks in the mail, not that I could cash them anyway. I've got COPD, emphysema, and severe systolic heart failure."

"Is there something we could do to help?" Devon asked.

Caldwell waved a dismissive hand toward the shadowed kitchen. Dishes piled in the sink. Flies buzzed through the open window. A dozen medication bottles were clustered on the laminate counter. The pantry was barren. "Took my last beta blocker this morning. It's just a matter of time."

"I'm so sorry," Devon said.

Jackson said nothing. His throat tightened. Because what did you say to a stranger? To a thousand strangers suffering the same fate? Tens of thousands. Millions.

"I didn't ask for your pity," Caldwell said. "Pity yourself. We're all waiting to die. If you haven't figured that out yet, you will soon."

Caldwell didn't bother to stand to see them out. The dog thumped his tail against the threadbare carpet as he stared at them with muddy-brown eyes.

Jackson touched Devon's arm. He couldn't wait to exit this stuffy, claustrophobic house. In truth, all he could think about was the case. Everything had changed. They had new leads to chase down, new questions that desperately needed answering. They'd burned through precious fuel to drive out here, but every drop had been worth it.

"Good luck," Caldwell said to their backs. "You're going to need it."

28

LENA EASTON

DAY THIRTY-THREE

Dusk painted the sky in deepening shades of indigo. Shadows stretched long as bats whirled and dove above the trees, seeking mosquitoes. Dark clouds hung thick and low over the lake, headed their way.

The wind howled across the open waters of the great lake. Gulls squawked and fought over a fish. Lena shivered, quickened her pace, and drew her jacket closer to her body.

The cottage featured a weathervane to determine the wind direction and a barometer to detect air pressure. Steadily rising pressure meant good weather ahead, steady pressure meant no immediate change, while falling pressure meant worsening weather.

When atmospheric pressure dropped suddenly, a storm was on its way. According to the barometer, the approaching storm would be a doozy.

Bear loped ahead of her, nosing the debris and driftwood along the beach tossed above the waterline. His paws traced a path through the sand that was erased by the lapping waves as quickly as it was drawn.

Each morning at dawn and each night at dusk, she patrolled

the property, checked everything, looking for footprints, for any sign of a presence that did not belong.

Even on their land, they were alert and wary. Eli had drilled security protocols into Lena and Shiloh. If they left the property, they checked doors and windows for signs of forced entry before they re-entered the cottage.

Eli had instructed them to clear the grass and foliage around the lighthouse with rakes, but that project was still in progress. He'd had them cart in several wheelbarrows of dirt to cover the dry rocky areas between the beach and the house so that fresh footprints could be easily detected.

After a hard day of work on the property fixing the greenhouse, planting and watering and weeding, collecting and chopping firewood, hauling water, building the springhouse, and repairing odds and ends, Lena looked forward to their nightly walks along the beach.

They'd explored the overgrown paths in the woods and found wild blackberry and raspberry bushes. On the eastern perimeter, Shiloh had discovered a marshy bog where they could collect cranberries in the fall. Lena made a note to learn how to can fruit in preparation for winter.

Usually, Shiloh joined them, but the last few nights, the girl had manned the lighthouse while Lena trained Bear. After Jackson had warned her about the poisoned dogs, she was determined to protect Bear from such a fate.

As they drew near to a lump of deer meat she'd traded with a neighbor for a box of Band-Aids and a baggie of Advil, Bear perked up and ran over to investigate. He circled the meat, sniffing at it before glancing back at Lena, ears pricked in eagerness.

Lena signaled for him to stop. "No, Bear. We don't take food from anywhere but your food bowl inside the house."

His tail drooped in disappointment, but he obeyed. Bear was intelligent, a fast learner, and he loved pleasing Lena. He lived for the accolades and praise she heaped on him when he'd accomplished a mission.

The big Newfie turned his nose up at the meat, albeit with regret, and trotted back to Lena. She sank to one knee in the sand and rubbed him behind his floppy ears, his favorite spot. "Good boy. Good job, Bear. You did so good. The only place you eat is from your food bowl at home, got it?"

They'd been practicing for several days. At first, she'd left food in the front yard in a dog bowl. Once he'd learned to leave the food in the bowl alone, she started leaving treats in different places on the property.

She'd varied the type of treats, from table scraps, steak, a bone, then a turkey leg dipped in anti-freeze. Anti-freeze tasted sweet to dogs and was a common method of poisoning. Afterward, she'd disposed of the food to ensure it didn't accidentally kill the next animal that came sniffing along.

Lena trailed him as he approached the next treat, a Kibble's milk bone. He halted a few feet away and sniffed the air, his tail held straight back.

She waited, ready to give a sharp, "No!" She needed to see what he would do without her presence. She wouldn't be there if someone attempted to poison him.

With a huff, Bear turned away and trotted back to her. He gave her a longsuffering stare, making sure she knew what a sacrifice he'd made to please her.

"I know, I know. I'm terrible for tempting you so cruelly. How about we head back to the cottage before this rain hits? I've got tomato soup cooking, but I bet you're hungry for some delicious Purina dog chow."

She was on her last bag of dog food, but that was a problem for tomorrow. Tonight, she just wanted to snuggle up with Bear and Shiloh and watch the storm roll in.

The timer beeped on her phone. Internet and cell service were long gone, but phones still had a purpose, and she was grateful for her solar charger which also charged her transmitter and the batteries for her pump and glucometer.

Her pump and sensor had to be calibrated every twelve hours, which entailed pricking her finger, using a test strip, and inserting it into her glucometer to read her blood sugar, then loading that number into the pump to calibrate it.

Every seven days she needed to change her infusion set and sensor. Her insurance had only paid for a three-month supply. When they ran out, she'd have to resort to the vials and needles. That familiar panicky feeling rose up, threatening to choke her. Multiple times a night, she awoke in a cold sweat and had to check the mini-fridge to make sure the insulin was there, that the fridge was cold—

Something snagged her attention. A disturbance on the ground. Along the tree line, on the western edge of the property, a footprint was outlined in the mix of sand and pebbles.

She was no tracker, but she and Shiloh had been learning the prints of the creatures who shared this wilderness with them, using one of the books Shiloh had discovered in the lighthouse library.

They'd spotted raccoon, fox, coyote, and porcupine, along with a few moose prints along the north end of the beach. There were black bears out here, too. She hadn't yet seen a cougar or the elusive gray wolf.

She didn't fear wild animals. They didn't kill for sport, not like the human variety.

These prints were human.

Lena drew closer. Her brow knitted as she tugged her hair out of her eyes and studied the footprints. The indentation deepened along the right side into a depression of softened mud. She'd memorized the zigzag print of Eli's boots and the department-issued tread of Jackson's and Devon's shoes. She knew her prints and Shiloh's.

This print was a size thirteen at least, a big man, bigger than either Jackson or Eli.

A shiver zipped up her spine. She crouched and brushed aside strands of beach grass. More prints led up from the direction of the beach. They had not been present this morning. She was certain of it.

Lena rose, whirled around, and pulled the flashlight from her pocket. She shone the light across the black waves and the glittering shoreline, then shifted east, the beam of light bobbing among the trees. There was nothing, no movement.

Lena turned to the lighthouse, a hundred yards northeast of her position. The white tower gleamed against the indigo skyline. Thick clouds smothered the moon. Waves crashed against the shoreline as the lighthouse beam pierced the gathering darkness.

Shiloh's shape appeared in the lantern room, a small shadow backlit against the bright beacon of light sweeping across the land.

Get out, Eli had said. At the first sign of danger, get the hell out, flee to the woods, get the emergency go-bags they'd cached, and go for back-up.

With her free hand, Lena reached for her radio at her hip. She'd warn Shiloh, then call Jackson and Eli. She and Shiloh would flee the property, meet at the rally point, and—

Her heart dropped into her stomach. Her radio wasn't there. Damn it! She'd left it on the kitchen island next to the camping stove when she'd heated the tomato soup.

Swiftly, she lifted her flashlight and flashed it twice, then a break, then two more. It was their signal for *intruder*. A moment later, Shiloh flashed the same signal back. She'd received it and understood. Hopefully, she'd follow the protocol and hightail it to the rally point.

Stuffing the flashlight in her pocket, Lena drew her pistol. Despite the radio mishap, she never left the lighthouse unarmed, not even to let Bear out to do his business. Shiloh, too, carried a pistol along with her crossbow.

Bear's head lifted. His ears pricked. His tail stiffened. The wind blowing off the water had made it difficult for the dog to catch the scent of possible intruders, but he'd caught something.

Bear growled low in his throat. The fur on the back of his spine rose.

Lena froze.

Movement at the lighthouse. Not up in the lantern room, but down below. A shadow darted across the warm glow emanating from the bottom front right window.

Someone was inside the cottage.

Fear shot through her veins. A thousand thoughts slammed through her brain. While she'd been occupied on the eastern side of the property, the intruder must have snuck in on the western end, likely by boat, where an outcropping of limestone protected a tiny cove.

He must have watched long enough to discern her pattern of patrols. He'd watched her leave the cottage, and then he'd moved in under cover of twilight.

Which meant he planned to ambush her when she returned to the cottage. Or he was after Shiloh, not her. Either way, she had to do something, and fast.

If she went to the house, she could be killed or captured. Shiloh might be killed or captured, no matter what she did.

Get out.

Every cell in her body screamed at her to flee. But she could not. Shiloh was inside and Lena would risk hell itself to protect her.

The first droplets of rain struck her head, her cheeks, collected in her eyelashes. She didn't notice. With Bear at her side, Lena ran for the house.

29

SHILOH EASTON

DAY THIRTY-THREE

Shiloh sat cross-legged in the lantern room, binoculars around her neck, her crossbow on the floor beside her, her journal and pencil in her lap.

After she'd spent the morning washing laundry by hand with detergent and water from the rain cisterns, she'd gathered kindling for the woodstove, then helped Lena hang a solar shower, which they'd scavenged from the camping supplies of an empty vacation house on the bluff, from a nearby tree. The black five-gallon bag attracted heat from the sun, warming the water, and gravity did the rest. She'd never appreciated a warm shower so much in her life.

Once she'd finished her morning chores, she cleaned the Fresnel lens, replaced the kerosene in the lamp, dusted and swept and cleaned the glass, and kept her log of boats coming in and out of Grand Harbor.

She ran her fingers over the leather-bound journal, imagining lighthouse keepers of the past journaling the weather, day-to-day activities, and the same record of ships sighted that she now kept, though her log served a different purpose.

Eli had instructed her to keep track of activities on the water, or counter-surveillance as he called it. Any boat she saw, she logged. It was mostly little fishing boats and Sawyer's speedboats and yachts, but occasionally she glimpsed freighters and cargo ships. Most people were out of gas, but maybe the big corporations could still afford fuel.

Several fishing boats had spent the day hauling in chinook, whitefish, bass, and perch. They boasted names like *Kraken, Weekend Dreams, Gone Fishin'*, and *Lady of the Lake*. She had sighted Sawyer's fancy yacht, *Risky Business*, sailing out of the harbor.

Lady of the Lake had sailed back and forth several times along the shoreline. She'd taken photos, but the zoom feature of the phone couldn't take clear close-ups. With her binoculars, she'd watched the three men, dressed in T-shirts and waders, laden with fishing rods and tackle gear. It was a big boat, big enough to hide more than fishing gear.

Next time she saw Eli, she'd show him. He was supposed to come around tomorrow morning for self-defense and gun training. Shiloh could hardly wait.

Every fifteen minutes, she stood and scanned the property with her binoculars. Back and forth, bump up fifteen degrees. Back and forth, shift to the west. Do it all again.

It was tedious, repetitive work. Her neck hurt, her tailbone was sore, her muscles aching from hours of manual labor. She wanted to curl up in her sleeping bag, wearing one of Cody's favorite Star Wars shirts, take a nap while she listened to the rain drumming on the metal roof, and let her dreams take her back to Cody.

But she had grown-up responsibilities. People depended on her. Besides, sleep wasn't safe. Nightmares hounded her, a steady *thump, thump, thump* invading her dreams like her own heart was banging against her ribs, desperate to escape something she couldn't see but could feel, something dark and dangerous and deadly.

Movement snagged her attention. Down on the ground eighty yards to the northwest, at her nine o'clock. White tails flashed. Two tawny, four-legged shadows darted out from the cover of the trees and scampered parallel to the tree line before re-entering the woods at the beach.

Shiloh swiveled the binoculars. The tiny figures of Lena and Bear loped across the edge of the clearing. Above them, storm clouds rolled in thick and dark. The wind thrashed the trees.

Her stomach growled. They were rationing supplies. The garden was producing some cucumbers, lettuce, and zucchini, but it was far from enough food to sustain them. They'd harvested a few ripe tomatoes from the greenhouse, which Lena had turned into tomato soup for dinner. She'd never thought about how much time and effort went into simple meals—

Down on the ground, a flashlight blinked to life. The beam swept the ground, wavering wildly, then angled up toward the lantern room. Two flashes, a break, then two more. *Intruder.*

Shiloh's heart caught in her throat. She retrained the binoculars. Shadows writhed as the wind tore at the trees. One shadow did not move with the others.

A shape that did not belong. A creature upright on two legs, not four. Creeping through the trees, behind Lena and Bear. Bear couldn't smell him because of the wind, the same way he hadn't smelled the deer.

Distant thunder boomed. The air grew darker, thicker.

A shadow stalked Lena in the darkness.

Hands trembling, Shiloh fumbled for the radio and brought it to her lips. "Copy! Is anyone out there? Eli? Jackson, Devon! Anyone! Someone's at the lighthouse. They're after Lena. Come now!"

Shiloh didn't wait for an answer. No time to think, only to act. She catapulted for the stairwell, wrenching open the hatch in the floor and throwing herself down the ladder, then skittered down the first flight of stairs.

She knew what to do. Eli had drilled it into her: race down the spiral staircase, exit the tower, head for the woods, then make it to the rally point and their secret cache.

Eli had helped them pack go-bags. The backpacks were buried

in sealed five-gallon buckets a half-mile away and contained extra food, ammunition, clothing for inclement weather, water purification tablets, first aid kits, and emergency blankets.

From there, she and Lena would get Jackson and—

Something instinctive made her pause on the first landing. Internal warning bells clanged. She strained her ears, her pulse a roar as she held her breath.

Far below her, the door to the tower opened. The dull thud of boots on iron treads echoed off the stone walls.

Terror rooted her sneakers to the floor. *Reykjavík, Iceland. Copenhagen, Denmark.*

Stockholm, Sweden. Desperately, she repeated the capitols and countries that anchored her to reality.

For half a second, her panicked brain tried to convince her that it was a neighbor coming to visit, or Jackson or Devon dropping by, or perhaps Mrs. Grady, the librarian, with more books.

It wasn't.

It was an intruder. And he was headed up the tower, right toward her.

Shiloh was trapped.

30

LENA EASTON

DAY THIRTY-THREE

Lena ran.

Rain spat into her face. The wind whipped at her clothing and snarled her hair.

Her legs were Jell-O, her movements slowed and sluggish, the roaring wind in her face pushing her back, yanking her further from the cottage with every step. Her heart threatened to pound right out of her chest.

Bear remained by her side. She dared not look behind her. She ran harder, her breath torn from her lungs, legs pumping. If Shiloh was hurt, if something happened...

Lena reached the corner of the house. Frantic, she twisted her neck and glanced behind her. Trees swayed. The beach was barely visible. Great gray waves beat against the sand. The rain obscured everything past eighty yards in a haze. The lighthouse beacon swept back and forth, the light blinding her night vision.

Blinking water from her eyes, she crouched against the siding, grasping Bear's fur with her free hand and tugging him to his haunches beside her. She signaled for him to stay on her heels, knowing he would obey.

She couldn't enter through the front or back door; the intruder would anticipate that move. Instead, she crept around the side of the cottage, ducked beneath the kitchen window, skirted the rear door, and circled the white tower of the lighthouse to reach the bedroom windows.

The first bedroom window—hers—was broken. The intruder had entered through the window and used duct tape to stifle the sound of breaking glass. The rain and wind had helped, too. Shiloh might not have heard it, remaining unaware if she hadn't caught Lena's warning.

Lena looked up at the tower, longing to scream Shiloh's name. Sensing her distress, Bear whined. She half-turned and made a motion for the Newfie to be quiet. Bear let out a soft, urgent whine but did not bark.

With her heart in her throat, she approached the window, raised her head, and peered inside. Nothing but shadows. She would have to go in.

Bear couldn't follow her inside. He wasn't an attack dog. Whoever was in the house would shoot him; she was sure of it. Lena signaled for him to sit and stay. She didn't dare speak aloud, not this close to the cottage.

Obediently, he sat, damp tail thumping, his furry features drooping in a sorrowful expression.

Tucking her pistol into her waistband, she gingerly clambered through the window frame and slid across the sill, her jeans snagging on a jagged tooth of glass. The duct tape helped ease her entry. She caught herself on the edge of the dresser next to the window and lowered herself unceremoniously to the carpeted floor.

Rain drummed the roof. Crouching, she strained her ears, blinking to adjust her eyes to the dim interior.

In the reptilian part of her brain, she felt it. The cottage was quiet but the quiet itself was weighted, everything spiked with a single note of wrongness.

The intruder was still in the cottage.

She could feel him.

Lena clutched the pistol with slick, trembling hands. She was no soldier, no cop. Not Eli or Devon or Jackson.

She had no idea what to do. Everything Eli had told her fled her memory. She was pure fear. Fear and desperation mixed with a savage determination to protect Shiloh.

Rising, staying low, she crept across the carpet, pressed herself against the wall beside the bedroom door, and checked the hallway. She looked left, then right. Empty. Dark shadows stretched long; they seemed to grow claws and fangs.

The lantern in the kitchen and hallway provided light, as did the lighthouse beacon sweeping in slow arcs outside the windows.

A scuffling came from the kitchen, then a grunt. A door opening and closing. It was hard to hear over the rain, the wind scouring the corners of the cottage.

Lena entered the hallway, each footfall loud in her ears, positive the intruder could smell her, sense her, hear her. She inhaled the scent of the tomato soup bubbling on the camp stove in the kitchen, such a normal, harmless smell.

The hallway opened to a narrow living room. On the other side, an arched entryway led to the cramped kitchen. The door to the lighthouse tower was in the kitchen, adjacent to the back door.

Nothing moved in the living room. The sofa against the wall, the curtains, the coffee table.

Lena scuttled through the living room, through the archway, entering the kitchen with the gun up. She tried to sweep like Eli had taught her, to take in the room in degrees.

A dark shape reared in front of her.

Blank terror seized her. Panicked, Lena squeezed the trigger. The shot blasted her eardrums.

A figure cursed. Strong hands struck her in the side of the head. Pain exploded behind her eyes. Something hard struck her hand, knocking the pistol from her fingers. It went flying across the linoleum.

She fell back against the island, her spine slamming into the countertop. Struggling to stand, her feet flailed out from beneath her. The air sucked from her lungs. Her limbs froze, refusing to obey.

Move! Her mind screamed. *Move! Do something.*

"There you are." A deep male voice. She caught the glint of the whites of his eyes, glimpsed a broad, bulky body. A face obscured by a black ski mask. "This will teach you a lesson."

Strong arms enveloped her. Thick hands went around her throat, cutting off her breath. She couldn't breathe, couldn't speak or scream.

Bright stars burst in front of her eyes. Dizziness washed over her in waves, her vision wavering. Fear and stress caused her blood sugar to drop precipitously.

Her arms flailed. She clawed at anything within reach. Her fingers found his face, the ski mask. She ripped it off, tried to gouge his eyes, but he reared back out of her reach.

"You'll pay for that, you little whore!" he spat.

Hands tightened around her throat. Pain. Constriction. Darkness. She scrabbled at his thick fingers, scratching and clawing, to no avail. Her windpipe slowly crushed. No oxygen reached her starved lungs.

He had her bent backward, her spine grinding against the countertop. The back of her head banged against granite. He leaned over her, grunting. Thunder rumbled in the distance. Her thoughts grew thick and muddled.

Everything went blurry. Disorienting and fuzzy. She felt herself fading, fading to nothing.

She stretched out her right hand, fumbling, reaching, searching. Her fingertips touched the handle of the cooking pan. With the last of her strength, she gripped the handle and flung the pan upward. The contents splattered her attacker. The entire pan of scalding soup splashed into his face.

With a scream, he released her throat and reared back.

Lena jerked sideways and tucked her chin. Droplets of searing pain splattered her exposed cheeks and throat as she slid off the counter and crumpled to the floor.

Clinging to the last threads of consciousness, she stumbled to her feet. A ring of fire encircled her throat. Scrambling for the pantry, she jammed open the crooked doors.

Behind her, the assailant cursed and flailed, knocking into the counters, plates and cups crashing to the floor. She couldn't see the extent of his burns, but from his screams, she knew it had hurt, and badly.

Where the hell was it? There! The middle of the third shelf, between the cans of chili and the box of half-eaten Cocoa Puffs.

Frantic, she plunged her right hand into the empty Keurig box. Coffee pods were not what she was after. *Come on, come on!* Her fingers closed around the polymer grip.

Not bothering to pull the weapon from the box, she whirled, arms outstretched, palming the grip, her index finger sliding from the trigger guard to the trigger.

She felt rather than saw her attacker lunge at her. Roaring in pain, stampeding like a demented rhinoceros, he plunged across the kitchen.

No time to aim. Lena squeezed the trigger. Then again, unloading three rounds in rapid succession. The cardboard Keurig box tore free of the 357 Magnum revolver.

Not four feet away, he staggered. Her spine pressed against the pantry shelving, she fired again. The assailant sagged to his knees. With a roar of pain, he toppled backward onto the floor.

Lena blinked. Gradually, sound registered. Thunder crashed overhead. Rain pounded the roof. Bear barked frantically. Stuck outside, he raced from the front door to the back and then the front again, desperate to be let in, to help his mistress.

Her breath tore from her chest in painful wheezes. The revolver Eli had given her featured a two-inch barrel and five rounds. She had one round remaining.

Shadows wavered as the lighthouse beam swept over the backyard. Her legs weak and rubbery, Lena forced herself to move, to take a step closer. The revolver aimed at the man who'd attacked her, strangled her.

She felt nauseous, white spots dancing in front of her eyes. Her throat burned with each rasping gasp. Her blood sugar had dropped dangerously low.

Eli's words echoed in her mind: *Don't leave them wounded. Don't give them a chance to kill you or someone you love.*

It went against every fiber of her being to cause harm. Still, she forced herself to spread her feet and square her shoulders. She straightened her arms with the pistol in a firm, two-handed grip, finger twitching on the trigger.

A scream built inside her, pressing hard against her chest, her teeth.

Lena squeezed the trigger one last time.

The man's head thumped against the floor, his eyes rolling into the back of his head. The body jerked, then went still. Dark red liquid leaked from a hole in his sternum.

Lena stood in the center of the darkened kitchen, shaking, chest heaving. The scent of burned flesh scorched her nostrils, gunshots echoing in her ears.

After a moment, she managed to bend and check his pulse. He was dead.

She'd killed someone.

It was self-defense. He'd come here and threatened her and Shiloh. And yet. She had taken a life. A human life. Nausea roiled in her stomach. She took a step, her guts seizing, and vomited all over the linoleum floor.

Her skin had gone cold and clammy, her legs shaky. She was hypoglycemic, her blood sugar crashing. She knew she needed glucose immediately—

Another scream sounded.

It came from above her, from the tower.

Shiloh.

31

SHILOH EASTON

DAY THIRTY-THREE

Shiloh stared over the precipice in sheer terror.

Rain sluiced down her face, plastering her hair to her skull. Wetness clung to her eyelashes, the coppery taste of fear in her mouth.

Trapped at the top of the tower, she'd done the only thing she could—she'd raced back up the stairs to the gallery, yanked open the door, and darted out onto the catwalk.

The wind howled. Lightning flashed. Dense black clouds roiled directly above her, blotting out the moon and stars, pressing down on her like the lid on a boiling kettle. Static electricity singed her skin. Each crash of thunder buzzed in her clenched teeth.

This high up, she was inside the storm.

She circled the catwalk, her back against the stone wall of the lighthouse tower. Inch by inch. Foot by foot. Heart in her throat, one hand on the railing, the grate rickety beneath her feet, like it might detach and tumble eight stories to the rocky ground, taking her with it.

Shiloh was not alone on the catwalk.

The intruder was up here with her.

She was being hunted a hundred feet above the ground, trapped on a catwalk in the middle of a thunderstorm.

She couldn't hear him, couldn't tell how close he was.

He couldn't hear her either, didn't know where she was.

They circled each other, slow and wary. The wind and thunder obscured any sound, but she felt him. The grate beneath her feet thrummed with his heavy footsteps. When he took a step, she took a step.

He knew she was up here. He knew that she knew. They were playing a dangerous game of cat and mouse.

Her jaw clenched, her breath caught between her teeth. She gripped her pistol. He was the mouse; he just didn't know it yet.

Water streamed down her temples and into her eyes. With each step, she strained her ears, heart galloping in her chest, expecting a monster to loom from the darkness, claws outstretched.

A jagged bolt of lightning ripped apart the sky. Her sneakers slipped on the slick grate and almost slid out from underneath her. The terror threatened to paralyze her, made her cold, numb. Blackness reached up with inviting fingers to pull her under.

The catwalk gave a tremor.

He was moving again.

Wiping rainwater from her eyes, she forced herself to move forward around the next curve. The sweeping beam of the Fresnel lens pierced the thick curtains of rain. The world was drawn in smudged shades of charcoal.

Another vibration through the soles of her sneakers. He was moving, but was it toward her or away from her? She paused, listening hard, every sense alert.

Away from her. Maybe.

No time to waffle. Commit to an action and move.

The catwalk creaked beneath her feet. The trees thrashed. The wind plucked twigs and branches and sent them tumbling across the yard far below. The lantern beam swept the darkness, throwing the catwalk into harsh relief.

She reached the rappelling rope. A small object lay next to the guard rail beneath the rectangular window: a rope coiled in a waterproof bag along with a carabiner, gloves, and a harness used in the past for maintenance work on the tower exterior.

The warning clanged in the back of her brain.

A physical presence lurked to her left, not the right. Hoping to trick her, he had switched directions.

No time for the rope. She kept moving, holding her breath, the pistol clutched in both hands as she headed right instead of left, circling back on herself. Rain ran in rivulets down her cheeks like tears.

One step, then another. Heel to toe, trying not to make a sound, to step light as a cat stalking its prey. She would not be the prey. Not today, not ever.

They circled the tower again, engaged in a terrible dance. Soon, he would tire of it. He would barrel around the catwalk and overpower her with sheer speed and size. Unless she managed to shoot him first.

Either way, time was running out.

Terror dug its claws into her brain. Her mind began to slip, her thoughts unraveled as the familiar darkness threatened to swallow her up. *Algiers, Algeria. Luanda, Angola. Porto Novo, Benin.*

Desperately, she recited states and countries, her mind clinging to distant places like flotsam to keep her from drowning. If she went blank now, she would die.

Think! She had to think. Outsmart him or she was dead. He was right behind her. She wouldn't have time to rappel down before he reached her. She had to distract him. Fool him. Wound or kill him first, before he could kill her.

Those were her options. None of them good.

She reached the rappel gear for the second time. The thrum beneath her feet. A glimpse of movement reflected in the watery glass pane.

Shiloh whirled to the left and dropped to one knee. Her kneecap banged the metal grate as she raised the pistol in a two-handed grip.

Lightning split the sky and there he was.

Not five feet in front of her, a figure rounded the curve of the tower. Tall and thin and black-clothed. A black hood covered his head, his features hidden by a ski mask.

He looked less like a man than a monster from myths and fairy tales. Through the rain, something glinted in his right hand—a knife.

Shiloh did not hesitate. She fired once, twice, three times.

The catwalk shook in its moorings. With a startled gasp, the man collapsed to his knees. A bullet struck the stone wall over his head. Fragments sprayed in all directions, a small chunk striking her cheek.

The knife flashed white. It was a bone-handled blade.

She aimed, finger slipping on the wet trigger. The attacker scrambled back behind the cover of the tower before she could fire again.

At least she'd hit him.

He was wounded, dying if she was lucky. This was the best chance she would get. It was time to go.

Shiloh spun and lunged for the rappel bag. With fumbling fingers, she thrust on the gloves, unraveled the rope, and tossed the free end over the side of the lighthouse. She hooked the carabiner into her harness, jammed the figure-eight belay device onto the carabiner, and shoved the pistol inside her tucked shirt so it wouldn't get trapped by the harness.

There was no belayer below her. Eli wasn't there to break her fall. One slip, one mistake, and she'd plummet to her death. Or the monster on the catwalk would lean over the railing and shoot her dead.

Steeling herself, Shiloh gripped the slick guardrail and climbed over the edge. Balanced on the brink of falling. Like Cody.

Time slowed.

The ground was a dizzying blur a hundred feet below her. Her body pelted by wind and rain. Terror an endless scream locked behind her teeth. The darkness dragged her down, down, down.

Cody.

The thought of her brother anchored her, brought her back. He had died for her, jumped to his death to give her a chance to run. He chose his destiny rather than be tortured at the hands of a monster.

She would do the same. *Edinburgh, Scotland. Cardiff, Wales.*

For an instant, her body hung suspended over empty air. Then she dropped.

Shiloh fell backward. Gravity yanked her downward. Vertigo pulled at her.

The wind spun her sideways. Rain spat in her face, she could barely see. She struggled to get her feet beneath her, to lie back and push herself perpendicular to the tower, her feet sliding across the stone as she attempted to kick out.

Her sneakers lost their grip as she bounced against the tower. Pain exploded in her shoulder, her right hip, her thigh. The impact sucked the oxygen from her lungs. She gasped, spinning, unable to right herself.

Twisting in the harness, the rope hissed through the carabiner at an alarming rate. It felt like dying. Her heart seized; her throat closed.

Shiloh dropped further. Falling twenty feet, then thirty. She slid down the face of the tower, harness digging into her waist and thighs. Her right shoulder scraped stone. She floundered for purchase, desperate to kick out, the rope rushing through her gloved fingers.

She managed to throw her right arm behind her back and down to brake, halting her free-fall. Released the rope, dropped twenty feet, right arm behind her back. Jumped off with her feet, pushing out from the tower in controlled drops.

Again. Then again. Three stories, then five.

Finally, Shiloh dropped to the ground.

Her feet hit the earth. Her legs buckled beneath her, her hands shaking as she ripped herself out of the harness and lunged for the tower base, tearing off her gloves as she ran.

Boom!

Thunder or gunshot? She didn't know, couldn't tell—

A large blur bounded out of the rain-drenched darkness. Her heart stopped. Before she could react, it bowled her over. She fell on her backside as a furry form leaped on top of her.

Hot soggy breath struck her face. A warm wet tongue licked her cheeks. Relief washed through her, she was dizzy with it. Alive, she was still alive.

Grabbing the scruff of the Newfie's neck, she clambered weakly to her feet and dragged him back against the base of the tower. "Bear, come! Come on!"

She was down but far from safe.

32

LENA EASTON

DAY THIRTY-THREE

Lena scrambled over the dead body, slipping on puddles of soup and blood, found her M&P wedged beneath the sink counter, and scooped it up as she staggered for the back door.

She burst into the backyard. Rain slashed at her face. The wind battered her. She headed for the tower, half-blinded by dizziness.

Bear stood at the base of the white tower, barking furiously. A small shape clung desperately to the side of the tower.

Lena slid across the grass and mud, blinking hard, desperate to see. Lightning freeze-framed the scene like strobe lighting, the sweeping beam of the beacon like a great seeking eye.

Shiloh was four stories up and rappelling fast. Movement flickered at the top of the tower. A figure on the catwalk leaned over the railing above Shiloh. He'd shoot Shiloh or cut the rope, sending the girl hurtling to her death.

Lena planted her feet, raised her pistol, and fired. Missed. In the dark and the rain, her hands trembling from low blood sugar, it'd be a miracle if she hit him. She fired again. Missed again.

Lightning split the sky into ragged pieces. The figure on the catwalk disappeared, darting back behind the protection of the tower. Though she hadn't hit him, she'd provided cover for Shiloh's escape.

Shiloh kicked off the wall, dropping rapidly.

Her heart thumped in her chest, her mouth bone dry. Fear thrummed through her as she struggled to remain conscious. No time to check her blood sugar, to fix anything. Her legs felt like lead, every step like she was drowning in liquid cement.

She fired again to keep the attacker's head down. Her legs wobbled, her arms weighed a thousand pounds. The muzzle wavered.

Shiloh dropped to the ground, unhooked herself from the rope, and flung herself against the tower. Barking, Bear pounced on her in excitement.

Lena staggered to the base of the tower, near delirium. "Shiloh!"

Bear dashed to her side, his broad withers pressed against her thigh, holding her up. She buried her hand in the wet fur along his spine for support, crossed five yards, and crouched next to Shiloh. "We have to go! We've got to—"

Shiloh's eyes widened. "Behind you!"

A loud crack split the air. Bits of stone and brick exploded from the tower inches above their heads.

Still crouched, Lena spun and raised her weapon. Through the curtain of rain, a third man sprinted toward them, not twenty-five yards away. He held an AR-15 in his hands, the black muzzle pointed right at them.

Adrenaline surged through her veins. Lena fired blindly. The gun went off. Her ears rang. More shots rang out. She blinked the rain from her eyes, straining to see as the beacon swept across the yard. She fired again, aiming at menacing shadows.

"Stop firing!" A short, compact figure ran across the clearing, braids flying, AR-15 rifle against her shoulder. "Get down! Get down! Police!"

Lena lowered the pistol as Devon Harris appeared out of the

rain and darkness. "I shot him. He was coming at you. I got him. You're okay."

Ten yards beyond Devon, a crumpled form lay in the grass.

Lena couldn't muster the energy to nod. Her muscles turned to mush. She sagged, falling back against the tower. The M&P fell from her limp fingers into the mud. She could barely raise her head.

"There's another one up in the tower!" Shiloh shouted.

Devon half-turned from the tower, her rifle against her shoulder, scanning the property. "Moreno and Hasting went after him. They'll get him."

Everything dimmed and pulsed. Cold sweat broke out on her brow. Dizziness rolled through her in waves, her hands clammy, her tongue thick in her mouth.

She gestured feebly for the glucose tabs in her pocket, but her arms wouldn't operate properly. She couldn't seem to sit up, to instruct her muscles to obey.

Shiloh stood over her, hands balled into fists at her sides, wet curtains of hair draping her face. "Lena!"

"What's wrong?" Devon asked. "Was she hit?"

"Her blood sugar is crashing," Shiloh said. "She needs carbs—"

Their voices drifted. Lena couldn't hear them. Bear barked in alarm, sounding far away. Dimly, she felt hot breath and a slick tongue slobbering her face. "I need—I need—"

Shiloh said, "She's going into insulin shock!"

The world faded and Lena couldn't stop it.

33

LENA EASTON

DAY THIRTY-THREE

Lena awoke with a start, her heart pounding.

Devon's soothing voice came from far away. "Hey, Lena. You're safe. You're okay. Everyone's okay."

They were in the cottage living room. Lena lay on the sofa, Devon kneeling beside her. Kerosene lanterns lit the room with a soft glow. A fire glowed in the wood stove, warming the whole cottage. Rain pattered against the darkened windows.

"How are you feeling?" Devon asked.

Lena tried to stand. Dizziness washed through her. Devon took her by the arm and pushed her down, gentle but insistent. "You need to rest."

Shiloh perched on the edge of the coffee table, Lena's bag of diabetic supplies in her lap. "You passed out. I had to give you the emergency glucagon shot."

In the event of a severe hypoglycemic episode like the one she'd just experienced, glucagon triggered the liver to release stored sugar, which raised critically low blood sugar.

It was the only glucagon injection she had.

Lena had gone over instructions with Shiloh and taught her how to read the pump in case something happened and she went into a diabetic coma, either from hypoglycemia or hyperglycemia. A mistake could easily kill her.

She took several deep breaths, steadying herself. The dizziness faded. Checking her pump, she took a couple of glucose tabs to bring her numbers up even further.

"Below 40," Shiloh whispered. "That's how low you were."

Lena swallowed. "Thank you. You did the right thing."

Shiloh rifled through her test strips, medical tape, reservoirs, and sensors, and the boxes of syringes and glucose tablets, her expression tense with worry. "Do you need anything else?"

"I've got some raisins in my bag by the door." While Shiloh scurried to retrieve the bag, Lena glanced at Devon. She spoke in a raspy voice. Every swallow was painful. "There's a dead guy in the kitchen. I killed him. I—I had to."

"Don't worry. It was self-defense. You did what you had to do."

Moreno and three deputies and police officers were working the crime scene in the kitchen, cataloging evidence, speaking in low voices, and writing longhand in notebooks. Hasting and Nash were hunting for the attacker who had escaped, the one who'd gone after Shiloh.

They hadn't caught him yet.

Shiloh brought her the raisins. Lena took them gratefully but found it hurt her throat to swallow, or even chew.

"We need to check you out," Devon said.

"I'm fine."

"You're certainly not. Sit back. Let someone else take care of you for once."

"I'm an EMT—"

"Right now, you're my patient. I've got this." Devon flicked on a penlight and examined her, checking for injuries, tracking her vitals—heart rate, breathing, blood pressure, pupils for bilateral responsiveness, ensuring her skin was pink, and warm and dry, not cold and clammy, including her fingernail beds and lips. Alert and oriented times four.

Her fingers brushed Lena's throat, which made her wince. Red-hot barbed wire encircled her neck.

"Red marks and bruising on the throat. Swelling and mild abrasions. I'll take pictures with my phone, okay? Not much we can do with them at the moment. We're still following procedure where we can."

Lena nodded wearily. She was accustomed to acting as the caretaker, not the patient. It was uncomfortable and disconcerting, though not altogether terrible. "How about my eyes? You see any petechiae?"

"Your left eye. It's bloodshot with small red dots. He got you good."

"I got him better." Violent images flashed through her brain. She blinked them away.

"That you did. You've also got splattered burns on your skin, like our dead guy in there. Might they have anything to do with the liquid spilled across the floor?"

"We plead the fifth," Shiloh said before Lena could answer. "Creative use of soup."

Lena grimaced. "It was going to be dinner. I thought it'd serve a better purpose boiling his skin off. It took a bit off of me, too."

"I haven't eaten all day. Frankly, you smell delicious." Devon gave a tentative half-smile. Her warm brown skin had faded to an ashy hue. "We need to go to the hospital, and get you checked out."

"No."

"It's standard procedure—"

Lena shook her head, then immediately regretted the throb of pain. Her vision had returned, though she was still lightheaded from the insulin crash. "Twenty-four hours. That's the ER wait time. I talked with Dr. Larson yesterday. They're running out of antibiotics and are nearly out of anesthesia medications. FEMA is supposed to be delivering more meds and bandages today, but their last shipment was three days late. It's only a matter of time before the aid trucks stop coming. Dr. Larson told me she procured ketamine from a veterinarian's office for an emergency appendectomy on a nineteen-year-old. I'll just be in the way—"

Devon narrowed her eyes. "I don't care. You know as well as I do that victims can die from bar brawl arm-chokes a couple of hours later when the trachea swells and closes the airway. That's not happening to you. You're going to the hospital for monitoring."

Lena opened her mouth to argue but Devon shushed her with a raised palm. She could be formidable when she wished. "I don't care about the official wait time. We're getting you in."

Lena recognized her stubbornness as equal to her own. Besides, Devon wasn't wrong. Lena would insist on the same for her patients. A patient would need to be intubated if swelling and edema developed.

Devon rose and took Lena's arm. "Let's go. We've delayed long enough."

Shiloh dug her hand into Bear's furry side. "We're coming, too."

They ducked their heads against the rain as Devon helped her to the truck. Lena took the passenger seat while Shiloh and Bear took the back. Bear sat in the middle seat and leaned forward, his head poking between the front seats, panting loudly with a jovial expression like he was ready for the next adventure.

As they drove, Lena turned to Devon. "You okay? I'm not the only one who killed someone today."

Devon gripped the steering wheel. She looked shaky. Her pupils were huge. "Adrenaline dump. It'll pass."

"You saved us, you know."

Devon hesitated. Something shifted in her face, faltered. "I was scared spitless."

"I don't believe it."

"Believe it." Devon tugged her braids back from her face and tucked them behind her ear with one hand. "When I got Shiloh's call, I was at my house. I ran to my car like a bat out of hell. I couldn't get anyone else on the radio, everyone was out of range. I kept trying until I reached a repeater and got ahold of Moreno. He told me to wait for backup, but I knew I couldn't. Running a code 3, a home invasion with folks that I know...

"I about put my foot through the floorboard. I did ninety the whole way. Pushed a hundred a few times. The whole car was shaking. I could barely see out the windshield. The empty roads helped or else I'd probably be wrapped around a tree right now. I felt like I was gonna throw up. I was terrified I was going to wreck the car, terrified I wouldn't get there in time. Terrified."

Lena had entered life-threatening situations before. Usually, she trekked through woods or an urban wilderness looking for a missing person or searched collapsed, unstable buildings for survivors. While dangerous, a tree had never aimed a weapon at her.

Devon had raced in with guns blazing, with no backup and zero intel on what she'd find, how many hostiles she'd face. She'd come in alone, and she'd saved them.

"You ever want to run for sheriff, you've got my vote."

Devon laughed as they pulled into the ER parking lot. It was overflowing. Vehicles were parked along the road and on every square inch of grass.

"I told you they were full. We're not getting in."

Devon took the narrow strip of road reserved for the ambulance and slammed the brakes in front of the ER double doors. "Watch me."

34

LENA EASTON

DAY THIRTY-THREE

Lena sat in the hospital bed, smoothing the crinkly hospital sheets that smelled of bleach, and waited impatiently. Every ten to fifteen minutes, a nurse checked on Lena's oxygen monitor to ensure she was still breathing, but that was about it. The nurse gave her a fun-size pack of peanut M&Ms to raise her blood sugar higher—glancing longingly at the little yellow bag as she did so. Lena still felt weak, cold, and shaky.

As Devon had promised, she'd stormed into the ER, all five foot nothing of her, and demanded a room. And by some miracle, she'd gotten it.

The overhead fluorescent lights in the rooms were switched off to conserve the generator, which rumbled in the background. Battery-operated LED lanterns provided light. The air smelled like sickness scrubbed with antiseptic. Gurneys and cots clogged the hallways outside the doorway as harried nurses and doctors jogged to and fro. Patients crowded every square inch of space, eyes dull with shock and pain.

Shiloh curled up in the plastic chair across the room, Bear at her feet. Dogs weren't allowed, yet somehow Devon had gotten him inside, too.

Jackson barged into the hospital room, looking bedraggled as a half-drowned cat—and as livid. He stomped across the tile floor, dripping rainwater and tracking muddy footprints.

Devon sat up in the chair by the hospital bed. "About time, boss. You stop for a four-course meal on the way?"

"Pasties," Jackson said without missing a beat. "I got one for you and ate both of them."

Devon scowled. "Jerk."

Jackson crossed the room and opened his arms. Shiloh rarely allowed herself to be touched, but she went right to him. He enveloped her in a hug and whispered something in her hair that Lena didn't hear. She nodded and after a moment, stepped back. Only then did Lena see that Shiloh was shaking.

He turned his attention to Lena. His lips thinned, his eyes bloodshot, his hair mussed and plastered to his skull. "I'm so sorry, Lena. I'm sorry I wasn't here."

"It wasn't your fault."

Remorse and fury flared in his gaze. "You could have died. Both of you could've died."

"We didn't," Lena rasped. "We're okay. Shiloh is okay, thanks to Devon."

Jackson flashed Devon a look of gratitude. "Thank you."

"Just doing my job, boss."

Lena looked past him toward the doorway. "Where is Eli? I tried to call him on the radio."

"He's out of range. When he finds out, he's going to kill someone."

"Two hostiles are dead. One got away," Devon said.

Jackson looked pained. "It's me. Eli will kill me, or worse."

She couldn't get thoughts of Eli out of her head. Even in the safety of the hospital, her anxiety wouldn't settle, the knot in her stomach wouldn't untangle. The simple truth was that she felt safer in his presence.

"He hasn't checked in with us in a few days."

Jackson sounded perturbed. Or maybe it was guilt. "I'm not his keeper."

"It's not like him."

"He's fine, I promise," Jackson said, but he wouldn't meet her gaze.

Devon took her notebook out of her jacket pocket. "Did your attacker say anything to you?

"He was too busy trying to strangle me." She closed her eyes. The terrible memories crashed through her brain. It was like watching a jerky movie, the images stuttering, filmy, unclear. It happened so fast.

"He said, 'This will teach you a lesson.' " She rubbed the bridge of her nose. "When I ripped off his mask, he said, 'You'll pay for that.' "

"That's it?"

"That's it. And some names I don't need to repeat."

Devon scribbled in her notebook. "Okay."

Jackson asked Shiloh the same questions.

"He didn't say a word," Shiloh said. "He just came at me. Until I shot him. At least, I think I did. He had a knife, with a bone-white handle."

"We didn't find it. We'll search again in the morning. Maybe we'll get lucky and he dropped it when you shot him."

She stared half-seeing at a spot in the distance, absently rubbing Bear's fur, her eyes glazed. "Maybe."

Jackson touched her arm. "You did good. I'm proud of you."

"I wish I'd killed him."

"You got away with your life. Yours, Lena's, and Bear's. That's victory enough."

She gave a fierce shake of her head. "He's still out there. He could come back. I should have chased him and shot him again and again until he was good and dead."

"We will find him. We'll put an end to this once and for all."

"I wish I'd gutted him with that bone-handled knife. I'd pull out his intestines and tie them around his throat in a bow. See how he likes that."

"Shiloh," Lena said, but she couldn't blame the girl.

Shiloh fisted her hands on her hips. "What? That's what I'd do."

"Law enforcement does things a little differently," Devon said.

Shiloh wrinkled her nose. "That's how Eli does things."

Jackson rolled his eyes. "I have no doubt."

"Who are they?" Lena asked. "What did they want? They weren't thieves. They weren't interested in insulin or anything else. They wanted to hurt us."

"I talked to Hasting on the radio," Jackson said. "The two dead are known associates of James Sawyer. Thomas Peterson did five years of hard time for beating the hell out of a rival in Paradise back in 2010. Eric Collins has been a suspect in several drug-related assaults related to Sawyer. He has a tattoo of a wolf eating twin snakes on his forearm."

Devon narrowed her eyes but said nothing. She and Jackson exchanged a dark look that Lena couldn't read. They knew something they weren't willing to share.

"Sawyer's men?" Lena blinked. The room took too long to come into focus. "That doesn't make sense."

"Doesn't it?" Jackson said. "If he thinks we're getting too close, he's telling us to back off. He left a warning on my parents' back door. That wasn't enough. I didn't listen. So, he sent his goons after you two. He knows we go way back. He knows what you mean to me, what my friends mean to me." Jackson glanced at Shiloh, who had gone to the small window above the non-working air conditioning unit and stared out at the night. "Or maybe his target was Shiloh."

"What are you talking about?"

Jackson stepped closer and lowered his voice. "I believe the real Broken Heart killer is ensconced within Sawyer's group, likely his inner circle, if not Sawyer himself."

The blood drained from her face. "Lily's killer."

"I believe so, and the other victims. Sawyer had a romantic entanglement with Lily. He has the means and opportunity to kill. He's gotten away with murder before."

Lena stiffened. "I know he's a criminal, but he's never threatened me. When Lily was with him, he never hit her like some of the losers she dated. Why would he do this now?"

"Maybe he didn't intend for them to kill you. Maybe he sent them to threaten you. Or, they planned to hurt you but leave you alive to relay a message to me. Back off or else. Then things went sideways when you ripped the mask off the first attacker's face."

Lena nodded, still processing the shock of it all. She felt numb, disconnected, as if she was held to this earth by a string that might snap and she would drift away, higher and higher. Like none of this was quite real.

Someone had tried to kill her tonight. She had killed a man. It was self-defense; she'd done what she had to do to survive. Still, she felt sick to her stomach.

Jackson straightened and stared out the window at the beads of water clinging to the glass pane. The storm had died down, driving north across the lake toward Canada.

Lena touched her throat. It felt like broken glass jabbing into her flesh. "How would Sawyer or his crew know that you suspected them?"

"They wouldn't, unless someone told them. Someone on the inside feeding Sawyer information."

"You mean a cop."

Jackson's features hardened. "I don't know. But I'm going to find out."

Hasting and Moreno appeared in the doorway, wearing trench coats, their hair still wet. Moreno held a radio. "How's the patient?"

"Fine," Lena said. "Did you catch him?"

Moreno gave a grim shake of his head. "He escaped our net. There's no trace of him. He's in the wind."

"The search isn't over," Hasting said. "We're about done at the lighthouse. We had to do all the dirty work ourselves. Don't worry, we won't leave a body in your kitchen. We'll get the corpses carted off to the ME before dawn. You can go back home when you're done here."

"Thank you," Lena said.

Moreno scowled. "Don't know why I'm still doing this. No paycheck. No retirement. I must be doing it for the ladies, fame, and accolades, eh?"

Hasting rolled his eyes. "Definitely not for the ladies."

Moreno gave an exaggerated bow. "It's hard work saving damsels in distress."

"The hard work was done by the time you strolled in, princess," Devon drawled.

Hasting barked out a laugh. Moreno shot him a cross look. "Must be for the fortune, then."

Lena managed a weary smile. "Must be."

A shadow passed behind Jackson's eyes. He looked suddenly older, old and drawn.

Lena repressed a shudder as she glanced at the deputies, at the faces of the men who'd sworn to protect and serve. If Jackson was right, they had a traitor in their midst.

35

ELI POPE

DAY THIRTY-FOUR

Eli stared across the campfire at the men sitting opposite him. The men he ate with, worked with, and slept beside. The men he considered his mortal enemies.

It was his fourth night on Grand Island. Each night was worse than the last. He longed to return to the mainland, to eat dinner with Lena, to shoot the crossbow with Shiloh, to hunt and fish and help them with the springhouse, with the garden, with whatever they needed of him.

He had insisted on his own tiny cabin and Sawyer had generously allowed it. The cabin backed against the west side of the property, near the cliffs. He slept with his clothes on, including his boots, his go-bag at his side.

At night, he did not sleep, nor did he lie in the bed but folded himself into the small closet with louvered doors, the doors cracked, his pistol next to his hand, shoes on. He'd unmade the bed and left a battery-operated lantern switched on in the attached outhouse. If someone breached his room, they'd think he'd left his bed in the middle of the night to use the john.

It would give him a second, maybe two.

One second was all he'd need.

Over the last several days, he'd done his best to insert himself within the organization. He made jokes, volunteered extra sentry shifts, and even took the mess hall clean-up a few times, and, in two days, he'd talked more than he had in eight years.

It wasn't only his voice box that felt rusty. Years of isolation and silence had a way of sinking deep into your pores, your bones. Socializing still seemed unnatural, but he was learning.

As he ate a freshly grilled venison burger slapped between two slabs of homemade sourdough bread, he perused the raucous group around him, studying the men and women and taking mental notes for Jackson.

To his right sat Andy Kade. A Swedish guy in his early twenties, he had a receding hairline and a mousy brown mustache that drooped over his lower lip. He was loud and crass, the jokester of the group who wanted attention however he could get it.

Wes Vaughn hunched next to him, with his wolf tattoo and the slender, black-gloved fingers that reminded Eli of a spider's legs. Sawyer's nickname for him was spot-on. Vaughn kept to himself, a watchful, reserved man who cataloged everything, violence in his eyes.

Pierce, too, was a man built for violence, who enjoyed inflicting pain. Eli watched his back whenever Pierce was in his vicinity. His loathing only grew every moment he was forced to spend in the man's presence.

If Sawyer saw the acrimony between the two men, he blithely ignored it.

Dixon laughed at someone's off-color joke as he stood by the grills, merrily flipping burgers. He didn't appear to resent Eli for beating the crap out of him. Instead, he followed Eli around like an eager puppy, hanging on his every word and begging him to train him in close-quarters combat.

Across the fire and off by himself, Cyrus Lee looked like he didn't belong: ferret-faced, thin and wiry with watery blue eyes and a weak chin. He was a shadow constantly lurking near Sawyer.

Sawyer had said Cyrus was his numbers guy. Eli wasn't sure

what to make of Cyrus or how he'd wormed his way inside Sawyer's empire. He had a ring that he wore on a chain, sometimes over his shirt, sometimes under. He must have done something impressive to earn it.

There were a few women among Sawyer's fighting force, namely Natalia Reyes, who went by the nickname Nyx, the Greek goddess of the night. She was tough, with a crooked smile and buzzed white-blonde hair, a cigarette constantly hanging from one side of her mouth. She wore cargo pants and a tight black tank top, a bandolier of ammo across one shoulder like a Miss America sash.

She was an ace shot but as far as he could tell, she had no ring and wasn't a member of Sawyer's inner circle, a circle which seemed to be diminishing.

Two of Sawyer's men had gone missing the night before last. Sawyer was in a rage over it and had sent several others out to hunt for them. Eli had heard rumblings about an operation gone wrong, but no specifics.

A commotion rose from behind the campfire. Eli shot to his feet and spun, his pistol in his hand as he scanned for threats. Everyone in the circle around the campfire rose with him.

A darkened figure approached from the direction of the cabins, a flashlight beam wavering in circles in front of him. Antoine Toussaint, a former French legionnaire, entered the circle of firelight.

"What is it?" Vaughn asked. In the firelight, he was angular, almost emaciated, the hollow spots beneath his hard eyes like gathering shadows.

Antoine gripped the FAMAS 5.56 x 45mm NATO rifle used in the French Legion Army, which Antoine affectionately called "the bugle" for its distinctive shape. In his thirties, he was powerfully built with a bristling beard and squinty eyes.

He spoke with a faint French accent and had a reputation for reckless boldness in hand-to-hand combat, for the bloodthirsty grin plastered to his face while fighting. He'd happily take on impossible odds; the other men whispered that he was a bit crazy, the kind of man you wanted on your side, not the enemy's.

Tonight, though, Antoine's expression was grim. "We've got trouble."

Five minutes later, Eli stood on the edge of the bluff, the world beyond dissolved into absolute darkness. Heavy clouds obscured the stars. The only light visible from the mainland was Shiloh and Lena's lighthouse. Far below, waves lapped the base of the limestone cliffs.

A group of thirty men and women stood around a man on his knees in the center of the circle. Several kerosene lanterns on the ground provided light.

Antoine jerked his thumb at the slumped, weeping man. "This man assaulted one of our own. A woman named Katerina Crew. They were on kitchen duty, and he struck her and beat her into submission. I caught him in the act and nearly skinned him alive, right then."

Eli gritted his teeth. Anger burned beneath his breastbone. If he'd been the one to catch the culprit, being skinned alive would be the least of his punishment. With the lack of law enforcement presence and the increasing lawlessness, crimes such as these would only get worse.

"Where is the woman?" Sawyer asked.

"Darcy took her to the infirmary."

Sawyer nodded and studied the culprit with an implacable expression.

The man stared at him defiantly. "She was practically offering it to whoever would give her a gun."

"Everyone here already has access to guns."

"You know how they are! She's lying! She was asking for it—"

"Be silent." Sawyer's command shut him up. "Every person here is under my protection. I gave my word. Do you understand what that means? How can I make deals or gain allies or conduct business without that critical layer of trust?"

Sawyer's voice was razor-sharp. He wasn't angry for the same reason as Eli. He saw the act as an insult against his power over his men, and his ability to control and restrain their actions.

Without control, he did not have the power that he so ardently sought.

The man gazed around the circle in growing consternation. He found no friends, no allies. He held little rank or respect. He was either new or low on the totem pole. Eli could see it in the faces of Sawyer's men: their features hardened, lips twisted in disgust, revulsion, irritation, or simply indifference.

"You said we could have anything we wanted!" he cried.

"Incorrect," Sawyer said. "*I* can have anything I want. Not you. Any man of mine exercises self-control. If you cannot choose when and where to release your baser instincts, then you have no business here."

"You gonna kill him?" Nyx asked, fury lacing her voice. "If so, I volunteer."

"Yes," Sawyer said. "We are certainly going to kill him."

They watched him, a silent half-circle of dangerous men and women. They didn't need to brandish weapons or throw insults. They held the power and they knew it.

"No," the man said, half stunned, half panicked. "No! You can't do this! You can't just—you won't get away with it!"

"Everyone here understands that the fabric of civilization is unraveling. The question is, how fast? And what happens if we pull this string or that one? I say, nothing happens. I say no one will miss this piece of trash and certainly not us."

"Come on!" the man screamed. "Let me go! Don't do this!"

The accused attempted to scramble to his feet. Dixon stepped forward and kicked his legs out from under him. He sank to his knees on the hard limestone, then tried to rise, and again Dixon knocked him down.

He wept, great wracking sobs. Spittle and blood splattered the dirt. "Let me leave! I'll just go then. Let me off this damn island. You're crazy! You're all mad!"

Sawyer was unfazed. "I tire of this conversation." He waved a hand at Pierce as he turned and stalked toward the lighthouse, a lantern swinging in his hand. The shadows stretched and contorted across the bluff like a demon shadow growing claws and fangs. "Take care of it."

"No, no, no! Wait—!"

"Let Pope do it," Pierce spoke over the man's cries.

Sawyer swung back around, the first flicker of interest in his eyes. "Of course."

Eli went rigid. He thought he'd passed his litmus test when he'd disarmed Dixon and Vaughn bare-handed, that his previous relationship with Sawyer and his eight years serving hard time would be enough.

It wasn't. Not for Pierce. And Sawyer was willing to humor him.

If Eli did not comply, he would be shot in the head like a dog, perhaps even before the rapist. He could fight off one or two or even four mercenaries, but not fifty, not a hundred.

There was no getting out of this.

Pierce drew his pistol from its holster and held it toward Eli. The wolf ring glinted on his hairy finger. "Do it."

Nyx looked disappointed, like she wanted to kill the rapist herself. Vaughn and Kade were indifferent, while at the back of the crowd, Cyrus looked eager, the firelight flashing in his eyes.

The man rocked on his knees, blubbering and begging. Blood poured from both nostrils and dribbled down his split lips. Snot and tears smeared his cheeks.

Eli felt no pity for him or anyone here, least of all himself.

Jackson had told him in no uncertain terms not to kill anyone. Proving oneself while undercover was a common occurrence, but undercover assets were never sanctioned to kill. No murder. No sexual assaults. No torching churches or government property, nor allowing weapons of mass destruction into the hands of even worse bad guys.

Eli did not concern himself with the laws Jackson followed. He followed his own rules and his internal moral code. Eliminating bad men did not violate his particular ethics.

There were degrees of crime, of sin, of right and wrong. He had no qualms about killing wicked men. The world was in need of rough men willing to stand in the gap. He knew himself; he was that rough man.

It was not a matter of whether he had to do this despicable thing to keep his cover. He wanted to do it. One more predator in the ground; one more innocent victim avenged.

Eli ignored Pierce's outstretched hand and drew his pistol. He pointed it at the center of the kneeling man's skull and squeezed the trigger. Eli shot him between the eyes.

The crack of the weapon's discharge reverberated in the crisp night air. The man slumped sideways. A trickle of blood leaked from the tiny round hole in his skull. Such a small amount of blood for a fatal wound.

Violence took most people by surprise. How fast it was, how merciless.

Eli did not give Pierce a glance or shred of recognition. Sawyer either. He'd done what they wanted and that was enough.

He holstered his pistol and strode across the clearing away from the bluff. The ring of hardened men and women opened for him, and he slipped through them into darkness.

No one followed him. Sawyer did not call out nor would he. Eli had earned this.

There were cold hard truths that he accepted about himself, embraced even. The vast reservoir of fury within him could not be quenched.

Eli had killed a man; he hadn't even bothered to learn his name.

36

JACKSON CROSS

DAY THIRTY-FOUR

"Has Eli found anything?" Devon asked.

Jackson shook his head. "I signaled him last night. We have a meeting tomorrow night if he can make it. He has to be certain it's safe. If Sawyer or any of his men blow his cover, they'll dismember him and throw him into the lake. It doesn't matter how skilled Eli is, he can't take on fifty men, a hundred men, however many Sawyer has now. Hell, he's building an army."

"What do you think he's going to say when he finds out what happened at the lighthouse?" Devon asked.

Jackson's expression flattened. "I think I'll be lucky if he doesn't kill me."

He hadn't told Eli yet. If Eli knew, Jackson wasn't sure if he would go through with the mission, leaving Shiloh and Lena vulnerable without his protection. Or Eli might seek vengeance himself and kill whomever he suspected was responsible.

Jackson was more than tempted to keep that little tidbit from Eli for the time being. Yet, he could not. He owed the truth to the man who had willingly entered the lion's den to find Lily's killer. He owed Eli far more than the truth.

The next time he saw Eli, he would tell him.

They'd spent all day searching for the runaway assailant who'd escaped the lighthouse attack. Other than a few drops of blood on the grass below the tower, they'd found nothing.

He'd disappeared.

It was dark now, after 10 p.m. No streetlights were glowing. The stars were brilliant in the vast night sky.

Jackson had been keeping the case files hidden in his hotel room at the Northwoods Inn. Worried that Underwood or someone else—possibly the leak feeding Sawyer's camp intel—would discover their clandestine investigation if they continued to work at the Sheriff's Office, they sat in the patrol truck in the empty parking lot of the Horseshoe Falls Gift Shop and pored over the case.

Over the last few days, they'd combed through the employee and patient lists they'd gleaned from the Copper Harbor Family Health office where Elice McNeely had worked. Caldwell had pulled a few strings to get them access.

The doctor's office had been like any other: a front desk, sage green carpet, faux-leather seats, enlarged pictures of smiling healthy families hung on the wall, and a side table with fliers advertising various medical devices and medications.

Devon had collected whatever she could find. She'd snatched a blue and yellow flier from a stack and waved one at Jackson. "Ask your doctor if Cialis is right for you," she intoned in a deep infomercial voice.

"That's for Escitalopram, brand name Lexapro, an anti-depressant," Jackson said. "And actually, I think those would be helpful for everyone on the planet right now."

"Why do you always have to be a Debbie Downer?" Devon snapped.

"I dunno, the end of the world, maybe?"

"You're so depressing," she'd said, but she had smiled. Jackson had found himself smiling back. And then they'd gotten back to work.

In the dusty filing cabinets in the basement, they'd discovered three boxes of guest sign-in books dating back to 1998. It would take forever to go through them, but Jackson had read through the early 2000s. The names blurred in his head, haunted his dreams and nightmares: Gordon Lewis, Daniel Philips-Craig, Richard Alonzo, C.L. Jefferson, Paul J. LaVache. The list went on and on.

Caldwell had also given them the names of two cops in the local narcotics unit who'd provided a list of small-time dealers and addicts Elice McNeely might have bought drugs from or got high with back then. They came up with several names but no hits or matches from the doctor's office.

Devon sighed. "I've cross-checked the lists twice. The ones that do overlap don't fit the profile. They're geriatric or the wrong gender, a pimply-faced teenager with asthma desperate to maintain an A-average, a seventy-year-old grandpa with colon cancer turning to street drugs for pain relief."

Jackson had studied the lists, too. Scanned the three dozen names they'd winnowed down by gender, age, and ethnicity again and again: Solomon Pickford, Lucas Dunn, Edwin Hayes, Thomas Bray, D.J. Bitzer, F. Robert Flaherty. No one stood out. Their inability to check the sex offender registry or criminal histories had them hamstrung.

Before they'd left Copper Harbor, they'd stopped at Michigan Tech in Houghton, where Elice had taken classes. No one was on campus. The admin office was locked. With Caldwell's blessing, they'd broken into the library and borrowed several annuals, the college version of a yearbook. They hadn't had a chance to study them yet.

Jackson glanced sideways at Devon. She sat stiff, staring out the windshield. The moon, a sliver of God's fingernail, hung far above them, forever out of reach. No streetlamps shone, no glittering necklaces of small towns strung across the shorelines of the UP. Here and there, the shimmery hint of a campfire or a lantern in a window flickered from the dark.

"You doing okay?"

Her voice was clipped. "I'm fine."

"You shouldn't be out here with me. You should be chained to a desk, seeing a department-ordered shrink, or eating Bonbons on your couch at home."

"First of all, I've never had a Bonbon in my life. Second, the stores are closed even if I wanted one. And third, Underwood says we can't afford it. Between us and the Munising department, we're down five law enforcement officers and three administrative personnel. We need to triple our force and instead, we're losing people like flies."

Jackson's hands tightened on the wheel. His eyes were gritty. He'd barely slept. Lena and Shiloh might have died yesterday. Hell, Devon, too.

He had been up in Grand Marais responding to an armed robbery call when the lighthouse was attacked. Jackson had begged Lena and Shiloh to leave the lighthouse and stay at the Northwoods Inn with him, but they stubbornly refused. The Easton blood ran strong in both of them.

Lena had spent the night in the hospital for observation. They'd barely gotten her in; luckily, they prioritized her case as a first responder. The parking lot was overrun, the hallways crammed with cots and rushing bodies, everyone looking harried, on the verge of a breakdown.

At least Lena was okay. Bruised, but okay.

Worry threatened to consume him on a daily, no, hourly basis. For his town, for the people he cared about, his friends, family, and co-workers.

"You could have been killed, running in balls-to-the-wall by yourself."

"Well, I don't have balls, so you're dead wrong on that count." She tried for humor, but it fell flat.

"I'm serious. You killed someone yesterday. That takes something from you even when you do all the right things, follow protocol, even when it's a good shoot."

"It wasn't a civilian. He was a criminal in the act of assaulting someone. I don't regret it. I'm fine with it. Perfectly fine." Her voice hardened, like she was convincing herself as much as him.

He waited. He already knew this story, at least the official version. As undersheriff, he'd read her file, but she needed to talk it through, and he would listen, when she was ready.

Ten minutes later, staring straight ahead, Devon spoke. "Six months ago, I killed a civilian in the line of duty. My partner and I got a call about an assault in progress. We were the closest patrol car, so we responded. The 911 caller said someone had a knife and was threatening to stab a girl at a party."

She sucked in a tremulous breath. "We pull up. It's not a terrible neighborhood but not great, either. Small houses, overgrown yards, graffiti, and drug deals on every corner. There's a crowd of kids in the front yard, middle-schoolers. They're shouting, yelling, and forming a half-ring around these two kids in the center. They barely notice us. A girl runs out of the house, banging open the screen door, running like a bat out of hell, long braids flying behind her. She turns and she's backing up, her hands up. Then behind her comes another girl. She's swearing and shouting, a knife in her hand. A big knife, a steak knife she'd pulled from the kitchen counter.

"My partner and I are out of the car, shouting, 'Put your weapons down! Police! On your knees!' But these girls, they're not listening, like they're so amped up, so enraged, they can't hear us. It happened so fast. Everything sped up. The girl with the knife charged the other girl. She was going to kill her. I believed she was going to kill her. I acted on instinct, and I fired."

Devon chewed on her thumbnail and looked out the window. "Her name was Jamilah Ferguson. She was in eighth grade. Fourteen years old. She'd taken meth she'd gotten from an older sibling, got high and paranoid, and attacked this girl she thought was moving in on her girlfriend. IA investigated. They ruled it a good shooting, but it didn't matter. The newspaper articles, the social media outcry, the protestors milling outside the precinct. I got hate mail, death threats."

Her lips curled in a bitter smile. "Didn't matter that I was black, too. Maybe the other cops didn't treat me differently, but I felt like they did. I felt like a pariah. It wrecked me. I couldn't sleep. I kept seeing that scene play over and over in my nightmares. I needed to get away. Every city block, every call reminded me of it. I had to get away, far away, where the crimes consist of parking tickets and hunting without permits, and jaywalkers. That's how I ended up here."

"Did you get far enough away?"

"Sometimes the UP feels like another country."

"I'll take that as a resounding yes."

"I thought so, too," Devon said. "Until Shiloh and Cody."

Jackson winced. He recalled closing the handcuffs around Eli's wrists, the Molson Canadian bottle he'd dug out of his trash, the lies he'd told on the witness stand, the guilt that built a permanent home in his chest. "We do things that haunt us. Sometimes, we deserve to be haunted. Sometimes, we don't. The key is to know the difference and let the chaff go."

"I want to fight for something worth fighting for. It's why I became a cop in the first place. Feels like a hundred years ago, but I still feel that way." She rubbed her fingers over the folders in her lap. "If we don't have that, what is there?"

"I know the feeling."

"You keep going. You keep showing up. Why?"

"If not us, then who?" he said simply.

Devon nodded. They were kindred spirits. They drove themselves without mercy, continuing to push, uncover rocks, piece together the evidence, and catch criminals. Monsters seemed to be proliferating at an alarming rate.

"Talk me through the case," Jackson said as they stared into the gathering darkness. "What are you thinking?"

Devon sat up straight. "Here's what we have as far as a timeline. We have identified victims missing from five towns in the UP over a decade and a half period. All were taken in the late spring, mid-April, or during the summer, except for Lily, who was murdered right before Thanksgiving. What does that tell us?"

"Our unsub was working with Boone, so maybe Boone took

the girls when he would have more free time from work, based on the school year schedule."

"Possibly."

Devon looked at the dates again. "There is a four-year span between the first murder and the second. Then a three-year span between the second and third murder. Two killings two years apart, and the last two only a year apart. In the early years, the intervals between the killings, or cooling-off periods, were every three to four years. As the unsub's thirst for violence increased, the cooling-off period accelerated to every two years, then every year. We can extrapolate that if we don't stop him now, he will continue to kill at a faster and faster rate."

"Correct," Jackson said. "What else?"

"Could be a tourist, a backpacker who visits different spots each year. Or he travels for work, spends enough time in each town to identify a target."

"The victims were troubled girls with histories of drug use. How would a random tourist know that? It's one thing to pick a victim based on physical similarities, but these girls could all share the same past. Foster care, abusive parents, runaways, drug and alcohol abuse, arrests and rehab."

Devon nodded. "Maybe the drugs are the connection. Or the homeless shelters, the rehab centers."

"Cross-check the lists of witnesses and associates in each of the identified victim cases with the other victims we have so far. See if any names we recognize show up, or if there's any overlap, especially with Elice McNeely. He might have been her neighbor, her coworker, or a fellow student. But he was close. He had to be. He's there somewhere. We just have to find him."

"On it, boss." Devon hesitated. "Lily is an outlier in several ways. She both fits and doesn't. She was the only one who had kids."

"The unsub may not have known she had children," Jackson said. "Lily didn't look like it, or act like it. She still partied, still had late nights out. When she was at the bar, she didn't talk about them. They were in a separate world."

"She was the oldest one at twenty-six, by five years."

"She could have passed for twenty-one, twenty-two," Jackson said.

"It's possible," Devon said. "Physically, she fits. Slim, dark-haired, young, and beautiful. But why was her body left behind?"

That was the conundrum, one of many. The puzzle pieces fit if you pushed hard enough, but a few jagged edges kept jabbing at him. Unlike the movies, no case is ever tied up with a nice neat bow. Nothing ever fits perfectly. There are always holes, anomalies, little strings left untied.

"Every other case we know of was an abduction, including his first known victim, Elice McNeely. Why not Lily?"

Jackson recalled the case file he'd practically memorized. "There were defensive wounds on her palms and forearms. Maybe she fought back harder than he expected. He got angry, lost control, and killed her there. Before he could remove her from the scene, something interrupted his plans."

"Amos Easton returning home early?" Devon guessed.

"Her father was plastered at the bar until 3 a.m. Tim Brooks confirmed it. According to his statement, he let Amos sleep it off on the hotel sofa. As far as we know, the perpetrator wouldn't have been interrupted. None of the neighbors reported seeing anyone."

"Anyone but Eli," Devon said.

"Anyone but Eli," Jackson said bitterly. "And Shiloh. She was in the house. She might have woken up, come into the bedroom, and interrupted him in the act. He panics and leaves."

"He could have killed Shiloh, but he didn't. Why? Our killer has a conscience?"

"Doubt it," Jackson said.

Devon closed her eyes. "He gets off on killing women, not little kids. Shiloh was a witness, but she wasn't his target. Maybe she interrupted him, surprised or scared him, but he didn't feel the need to eliminate her. Maybe he wore a mask or it was so dark, he didn't think she could identify him. Or because she was so young, he didn't consider that she could tell the police what he looked like."

Jackson grunted. All were possibilities. He should interview Shiloh again. Shiloh might hold the key locked deep in her mind, as she had with Walter Boone. Those memories would be shoved so deep, buried somewhere in the darkness of her subconscious, the brain protecting itself so the child could survive the trauma.

But the girl blacked out in moments of extreme stress, losing pieces of her past, her mind, her very self. Until she was ready, taking her back to the night of her mother's murder might cause further harm.

He'd visited Ruby Carpenter, the traumatized child curled in a fetal ball in that stale, shadowed room, lost in the nightmares of her mind. She was vanishing right in front of them. He'd seen the despair painting Michelle Carpenter's face, the hopelessness.

You could save someone physically, but the mind was a wild, isolated, dangerous thing, as deep, dark, and unknowable as Lake Superior.

The clichéd adage that children were resilient was a crock of rancid feces.

Much as he was desperate to solve this case, to finally put Lily's ghost to rest, he refused to do more damage to Lily's daughter.

Devon gave him a sideways glance. "Shiloh is off the table, isn't she?"

He nodded, his frustration rising. No access to fingerprint analysis. No databases to comb, no network of law enforcement agencies to pool information, to unearth the one scrap of evidence that would blow open the whole case.

The sensation of closing in on a fundamental truth had faded. For every step he took in the right direction, he felt dragged further away. They were swimming against the current, in the dark, absolutely blind.

"What do you think he's doing now?"

Other than Lily and Ruby, the killer had been careful not to take victims from his backyard. Summer Tabasaw was an out-of-towner, and he had known it. He'd buried the bodies here. Boone was here. This was a safe place, familiar grounds.

"He's disguised, like a chameleon. He's not going to stand out like we expect. And he's close. A neighbor, a colleague, a friend—or someone who's simply there, in the background, like a shadow, someone we barely register. I have this feeling that he's no stranger. We know his face. We've seen it before. We've even spoken with him. Maybe he's a part of the investigation, even. Somehow, he's able to keep tabs on the progress of the case. There's a connection with Sawyer. We just have to figure it out."

"We're close, boss. We must be. Otherwise, he wouldn't be scared enough to write you warnings or send goons to attack people close to you."

Jackson grimaced. "Doesn't mean he's worried. He's a sociopath, he gets off on other people's pain and fear. It feels more like this is a game to him. What's the fun in it if you can't play with your dinner?"

"Hell," Devon whispered.

She was quiet for a few minutes. The night pressed in at the windows. Jackson's stomach growled. He was thinking more and more about food: greasy French fries, gooey double cheeseburgers, and delicious seven-layer burritos.

"How long until he strikes again?"

Jackson closed his eyes, saw his nightmares playing out behind his eyelids. "A predator sees an international disaster as an opportunity, fresh hunting grounds with little oversight. If he hasn't already, he will kill again, and soon."

37

JACKSON CROSS

DAY THIRTY-FIVE

"We've got a bear problem," Sheriff Underwood said.

The law enforcement officers seated in the conference room stared blankly at Sheriff Underwood, who scowled back at them, as per his usual. It had become a permanent aspect of his features.

Jackson shifted uncomfortably. "What now?"

Underwood's scowl deepened. "You heard me. Bears. The Luce County sheriff just alerted me. Some fool released the black bears from Oswald's."

Alger County had joined a twice-weekly circuit between the UP counties to share news and information that pertained to law enforcement and community safety issues. They still had a decent supply of gasoline and diesel. When that ran out, they'd be using bicycles and horses.

For a second, the officers blinked back at him.

"Who is Oswald?" Devon asked.

Moreno laughed a big belly laugh that echoed in the stuffy room. Hasting, Hart, and Nash stared at him like he'd grown a second head.

"Oswald's Bear Ranch in Newberry," Jackson said. "It's a sanctuary for bears. The UP has ninety percent of Michigan's black bears. Newberry is forty miles southeast of here, but bears can travel."

Jackson had been to the rescue in elementary school, as had most kids that had grown up anywhere near the ranch. He remembered tossing apples over the chain-link fence to feed the bears and snapping photos with a fuzzy cub.

"They're coming for our picnic baskets," Moreno howled. "Just you wait."

Underwood glared, a vein pulsing in his forehead like he wanted to take off Moreno's head, with his teeth. "What exactly do you find so amusing?"

Moreno shook his head, tears leaking down his cheeks. "Come on! You don't see it? All the crap that's been dumped on us... and now... now we've gotta worry about a pack of ...of giant teddy bears?"

Devon's lips twitched into a smile. "Yogi and Boo Boo are on the hunt."

Moreno leaned back in his chair and threw up his hands. "Exactly! Like fate isn't just screwing with us now."

Underwood shot Moreno a lethal look. "They aren't teddy bears. They'll be hungry, just like we are. They won't be scared of people. They pose a legitimate danger to the community. Remember two summers ago when it was so dry all the berries and crap died on the vine? We had starving 300-pound black bears raiding gardens and bird feeders and garbage cans. This will be worse."

Alexis shook her head. "That's it. We're doomed. We're all going crazy, aren't we? One step at a time."

"Speak for yourself," Moreno said. "I'm completely sane."

"Moreno always did miss a step," Jackson said dryly.

"Now he's missing a whole staircase," Devon quipped.

"I heard that," Moreno shouted. "Y'all better watch your backs, is all I'm saying."

Nervous chuckles spread around the room. Beneath the banter, Jackson felt the tension. Everyone was stressed, tired, and anxious, overworked and underpaid to the Nth degree.

Underwood clapped his hands. "Enough. You idiots act like we aren't facing a crisis, a very real and present danger."

"We know it, Sheriff," Nash said, the grin vanishing from his features.

"Then you'll think this is freaking hilarious. FEMA is threatening to cease emergency supply runs after the attack this morning. The truck was ambushed on 94 outside the entrance to Wagner Falls. The assailants were ready for them. They dropped a tree across the highway and nailed 'em in a pincer move from both sides. Two National Guardsmen were injured, and they got away with the truck and our town's supplies for the next two weeks."

"How many guards did they have with them?" Hasting asked.

"Four."

"Last time, they had eight."

"Budget cuts and staff reductions. They expect the local resources to provide security."

"Which we have been!" Hasting said. "They can't blame us for their failures!"

"They can and they are."

"Budget cuts, my hairy a—" Moreno started but Underwood shot him a withering stare.

Hart shook his head. "The truck was attacked outside of Alger County. It wasn't even our problem."

"It's our problem when the governor says it's our problem."

Jackson stiffened as he watched his colleagues and his friends. A low hum of dread built inside him. Their expressions, mannerisms, and jokes were utterly familiar. He'd known many of them his entire life.

Which one had betrayed Lena and Shiloh? Did he or she realize they'd hopped into bed with a killer?

Was that a shadow behind Moreno's merry gaze? Did Hasting's mouth tighten with guilt whenever he looked Jackson's way? Were Alexis and Nash avoiding him? Why was Hart acting so tense?

Because he was a rat, a mole? Underwood had always disliked Jackson, but enough to betray him?

He just did not know. Just like his family, they felt like strangers, as if any of them could be capable of the worst acts, despicable things, and he wouldn't know it. He'd always prided himself on his gut instincts about a case, but those instincts were failing him. He was too close, too blind. The danger was right beside him, and he couldn't see it.

"At least the FEMA truck for the prison is right on time," Moreno said. "Go figure."

Hasting cursed. "The convicts get fed while the citizens starve. I've got three cans of green beans left at home and these jokers get a four-course meal. What the hell?"

"That's the government for you. Suck it up, buttercup. We need to provide an escort to make sure no one tries to hijack this truck, either. Here's even better news that'll really put a spring in your step. The State is releasing some prisoners."

"Which ones?" Jackson asked.

"They've already got the orders drawn up to release prisoners within six months of completing their sentences. All non-violent offenders are being released on 'probation.' Embezzlement. Arson. Possession and distribution convictions. Racketeering, prostitution. White collar criminals, those sorts."

"When?" Jackson asked.

"The end of the week."

The deputies and cops exchanged uneasy glances. "What the hell does that mean?"

"It means things are bad," Underwood snapped. "The State doesn't want to be responsible for convicts starving to death on their watch."

"People won't be happy—"

"Then don't tell them. They'll figure it out soon enough."

Jackson tensed. "What's next, then? The rapists and child molesters?"

"Alger Correctional has lost half their COs. So has Marquette

Branch Prison. The National Guard has stepped in at Chippewa and Kinross, securing the Soo prisons for public safety. I've heard rumors that downstate and across the country, it's even worse. Staff defecting left and right."

Moreno slid further down in his seat and crossed his beefy arms over his chest. "I feel their plight. Why would they stay if they aren't getting paid? To keep hardened criminals alive while their kids starve? No thanks."

The local prisons had emergency plans in place. Backup generators with multi-day fuel supplies and extra food and water supplies. They would have gone into lock-down mode on day one, inmates confined to their cells so they couldn't gather in groups to challenge the dwindling numbers of correctional officers.

Emergency planning had not taken a crisis of this magnitude or duration into consideration. It had been five weeks with no relief in sight.

"And the violent criminals? What happens to them?" Jackson asked.

"The National Guard will take over the prison systems. The logistics are being worked out now. They'll transport the prisoners from local prisons to select max security locations, likely I-Max." The Ionia Correctional Facility (ICF), also known as "I-Max" after its maximum security housing units, was located in Ionia, a small town in the lower middle of the state, east of Grand Rapids. Underwood rubbed his hands together as if washing his hands of the problem. "The military will take it from there. It'll be out of our hands and good riddance."

Underwood tapped the lectern with impatience. "One other thing, the governor is discussing having the National Guard blockade the bridge."

Everyone knew which bridge he meant. In Michigan, there was only one.

"Why?" Nash asked, bug-eyed.

"Too many trolls escaping the bigger cities and heading north. Like they think they'll find refuge here as if we have endless deer and turkeys for hunting and enough cabins and cottages to shelter an influx of a hundred thousand refugees. We do not. We're having a hard enough time as it is, and it's not even winter yet, eh? Just wait. They have requested the aid of local law enforcement if they need backup at the bridge. Just keep it on your radar."

"They're drip-feeding us one crisis after another," Hasting muttered. "A little at a time, like a frog being boiled alive."

Jackson felt the same way but said nothing.

"Where's our help?" Hart said. "Other than the FEMA drop-offs—and those are freaking fiascos."

"We're Yoopers. We'll make do." Underwood shrugged and transferred his attention to Jackson, staring at him with open dislike. "Cross? Are you with us? You look like death warmed over."

Moreno chuckled again.

"With due respect, we all do," Jackson said evenly.

"Ain't that the truth," Hasting muttered.

He sat straight, but he couldn't deny his gritty eyes, the weariness pulling at his bones, the hunger gnawing at his belly. He wasn't sleeping enough, wasn't eating enough.

When he finally sought sleep in his hotel room, he tossed and turned, consumed with anxiety and dread over the puzzle pieces that wouldn't fit, as well as worry over Eli, Lena, Shiloh, his family, and the precarious fate of Alger County.

He could feel Devon's eyes on him, her concern almost palpable, and Moreno and Hasting, more curious than anything. Underwood narrowed his gaze like he knew what Jackson was up to, where he'd been in his spare time. "Cross, your butt is glued to the eastern roadblock on 28, out by the Pictured Rocks KOA campground. Harris, check in with the Harringtons. Their truck was stolen last night. Someone is breaking into the vacant summer houses along the bluff out on Sandpoint. Hasting and Moreno, take point on that."

Underwood turned to stalk from the conference room.

Alexis stood. "Are we gonna discuss the elephant in the room?"

Underwood paused midstride and glanced back at her. "What?"

"Sawyer."

Underwood stilled. The conference room went silent.

Alexis fisted her hands on her hips. "We all know it was Sawyer who attacked that FEMA truck. And how the hell did he know where and when it would arrive?"

"Good question," Devon muttered under her breath. Several cops and deputies shifted in discomfort, giving each other uneasy glances.

Jackson's suspicions grew stronger. Which one was feeding a criminal organization critical intel? Had one of their own leaked the aid truck's route details to Sawyer? What else could it be?

Alexis said, "This county isn't safe with Sawyer running things like he's some kind of warlord."

"Duly noted. Are you done complaining?"

"We have to do something."

"And what would you have us do? It's like the Mexican police attempting to face down the powerful cartels. Not gonna happen without bigger guns and more soldiers. You wanna take on that island with the folks in this room? That would be suicide. I don't think so."

"You're just going to let him steal everything?" Alexis' voice shook. The blood drained from her face. "Make everyone give him everything they've got just for a bit of propane, fuel, or meds? He's holding life-saving medications hostage. My mom is dying of pancreatic cancer. She's in pain every second of every day. And that psycho is selling the meds that will give her relief. In what world is that okay?"

"No one said it's okay," Hart said in a quiet voice.

"Then why the hell aren't we doing anything about it?"

Underwood's face darkened. "I didn't say we weren't. There's brave, and then there's stupid. We're not going to do stupid."

"We don't have a death wish, Chilton," Hasting said.

"It's our job—"

"We're requesting aid from the state." Underwood cut her off sharply. "I'll update you on a need-to-know basis. Right now, you don't need to know."

No one said aloud what they were all thinking. Everyone knew the state wasn't coming to anyone's aid.

Jackson feared it was too late. Sawyer had been gaining strength in arms and men for years. He had a network of criminals and thugs throughout the UP and beyond. He'd stepped into the power vacuum so quickly and efficiently that no one had time to react, to prepare.

The law enforcement agencies that could have stopped him—the ATF, the FBI, the Michigan State Police, the U.S. Marshals, the Coast Guard—well, they'd never paid much attention to the rural north other than the Soo Locks. They weren't going to start now.

Sawyer had free rein. While people like his own father, the former sheriff, and the current sheriff kowtowed to him, his power would continue to grow. So would the violence.

Anxiety curdled in his gut. With Eli deeply embedded within Sawyer's organization, he had no way to extract his asset if things went sideways. He hadn't heard from Eli in days, didn't even know if he was still alive.

Every night, he gave the signal, and every night, he waited for an hour for Eli to show up at their predesignated location. So far, Eli hadn't made it. Deep down, doubt sprouted. Whether or not he'd made a horrible mistake, whether or not Eli had either been outed, or worse, had double-crossed him.

Alexis flopped back into her chair. "So, we're going to do nothing then. Great, just great."

"Everyone on board?" Underwood ignored her, glaring at each person in the room but taking his time with Jackson. "Everyone know where they're supposed to be?"

Heads nodded wearily around the room.

With a huff, Moreno rose from his seat. "At this point, I'll work for peanuts, like literal peanuts. When are we gonna get—"

"Enough with the whining." Underwood was already striding for the door. "Get the hell out of my hair, Moreno!"

"How about donuts?" Moreno shouted at his back, grinning half-wildly. "I'll take a dozen warm, doughy delights with a creamy icing filling—"

Sheriff Underwood slammed the door behind him.

38

SHILOH EASTON

DAY THIRTY-FIVE

It felt like standing on the edge of the world.

From Shiloh's position on the rocky outcroppings along the western rim of the curve of the beach, there was only the lighthouse between her and the water.

Lake Superior stretched vast and turbulent, the white-frothed waves at the horizon line vanishing into the gray. To the native Ojibwe people, the lake was known as *Gichigamiing*, or the "Great water."

Shiloh had been raised in the trees, in deep shadow-dappled forests, skipping rocks in creeks, climbing towering oaks, touring moss-filmed caves, splashing in swimming holes, searching out waterfalls, smelling rich dank earth, leaves in her hair and burs stuck to her clothes. Hunting, fishing, and exploring were her pastimes.

Though she'd been to the beach a hundred times, this place felt totally and completely different, with a different kind of peace. It was wild and unbridled, with the constant wind and waves, the steady swooping beam of the lighthouse beacon.

The lighthouse had weathered a hundred storms, maybe a thousand. And still, it stood, silent and imposing, whitewashed and strong and immovable. She loved it.

Lena had allowed them to stay. Shiloh had thought for sure that she would force them to leave after what had happened, but she didn't. They would stay.

When she thought of the attack, that crippling panic threatened to choke her, but it never did. She had rappelled down the tower as Eli had taught her. She had fought back.

That's what she would tell Eli when he returned. And he would come when he heard; she knew he would.

Above her head, the beam of light swept back and forth, reflecting off the dark water in a rippling glow. The wind tugged at her hair and pulled at her. She pushed against it and kicked off her shoes, rolled up her pant legs, and waded into the water.

She sucked in her breath at the bracing cold. The waves lapped at her shins, her knees, the spray reaching her thighs. The tide sucked the sand from beneath her toes.

It was mid-June. Summer in the UP didn't hit until July. *Niibin*, Shiloh thought. The Ojibwe word for summer, the way Eli had taught her. *Dagwaagin* meant fall; *biboon* meant winter.

The water remained frigid well into summer, with a chill that would leave you shivering and sometimes aching, deep in your bones. It was why she seldom gave up her dead. The lake had preserved Cody, rocking him in the bosom of the deep until Bear found him and Jackson brought him up from the depths.

Shiloh closed her eyes, missing her brother so much it physically hurt in the center of her chest. It was the kind of hurt that wormed its way behind your heart and lodged there, red and pulsing.

Behind her, Bear lumbered into the water and kicked up more spray. He barked joyously at every wave that came at him. He jumped at some, biting at others like he could eat them, grinning gleefully with his jowls pulled back over his big white teeth. He was the happiest dog in the world.

Shiloh breathed deeply, opened her eyes, and took it all in: the white tower against the gray sky, the white light roaming over endless water, piercing the darkness, guiding the lost home.

The attack hadn't tainted this place. If anything, her affection for it had grown stronger. It didn't matter that she spent hours lugging buckets of lake water to flush the toilets and refill the outdoor shower; collecting rainwater from the cisterns to sterilize for drinking and cooking; gathering firewood for the woodstove; making candles out of Crisco; manning the lighthouse; even weeding the stupid garden.

It was hers, all of it. She was supposed to be here; she and Lena and Bear.

And Eli. She wanted him here, too, in ways she couldn't explain. She felt him out there, somewhere, and waited for him to come back.

Her heart contracted at the wild beauty of it all. Thirteen years old and she had at long last found a place to call home. And she'd be damned if she wasn't willing to fight to the death to keep it.

39

ELI POPE

DAY THIRTY-FIVE

Sawyer grinned at Eli. "We're going back to warlords and fiefdoms. Don't believe me? Look at history. Look at Africa and Syria. It's coming here. The sooner we accept that fact and act accordingly, the better off we'll be."

Eli and Sawyer stood in the center of the gasoline reservoir ten miles outside of Munising. A dozen massive above-ground fuel tanks surrounded them.

Whenever he left his island fortress, Sawyer and his entourage traveled in armored Toyota Land Cruisers. He kept a close-protection detail that included Pierce, Vaughn, Dixon, and several others. They wore AR-15s slung across their chests and looked intimidating as hell.

Eli slapped at a mosquito and shielded his eyes from the blaring sun. Mid-June and the days were finally warming up. It was noon and close to eighty degrees, though the mornings and evenings were still chilly. "How'd you manage to snag this place?"

"We came in with two dozen men with AK47s and RPGs. The staff walked out with their hands on their heads. A few cops showed up and fled with their tails between their legs. That's it, easy as taking candy from a baby. Now it's ours."

"Only for as long as you can keep it."

"We can keep it. The men and women who protect it get plenty for their families. It makes it worth the work. I'd love to go after the natural gas storage fields downstate in Mecosta and Montcalm, Osceola and Newaygo, but a move like that would bring the wrath of the governor down on our heads like a napalm bomb. We're not in a position to take on several companies of National Guard troops, air support, or the U.S. Marshals. Not yet, anyway. For now, we're keeping our activities just low profile enough."

Sawyer pointed to the entrance where a straggly line of three dozen people had formed, carrying jerrycans, wheelbarrows, and carts of supplies. They waited behind the barbed wire fencing and were admitted one at a time by the guards.

At the front of the line, two women sat beneath a tent for shade, with white rectangular tables set up, clipboards and folders scattered across the tables. Behind them stood two delivery trucks, their interiors stacked with crates, bags, and boxes.

Four armed men stood guard beneath the tent. They carried MP5's with collapsible stocks and suppressors slung across their chests, their chest rigs packed with 30-round 9mm magazines. If the intent was to appear intimidating as hell, they were succeeding.

Eli scanned the people in line. Five weeks without power, and they looked bedraggled, exhausted, and hungry. Their clothes were rumpled, their hair greasy, their eyes dull with shock.

Most people couldn't believe this was happening to them, that it was real. They kept waiting to wake up from a nightmare, but they never did.

"You have any riots or fights breaking out?"

"Not much. Security keeps them in line." Sawyer stood like a prince surveying his domain. "We've got plenty for our needs, for our generators and vehicles. Anyone who needs fuel or fill-up for their generators comes here. We're using it as currency. We want beans, Band-Aids, and bullets, the usual."

"You can defend this from local law enforcement, but not the National Guard. Not the state police."

"The staties aren't coming up here. Their hands are full. The rumors coming in from Detroit and Chicago are...apocalyptic."

"That's a big assumption to make."

"Okay, smartass. What do you advise?"

He felt eyes on him, armed men watching him from every direction. Eli caught the glint of rifles, the movement of shadows, a careless cough or grunt. He counted twenty men interspersed throughout the property. He hated the vulnerable feeling, of being this exposed. His fingers twitched at the butt of his pistol on his hip. "You need more men and better weapons."

Sawyer raked a hand through his sun-bleached hair. "We're working on it. I've got a shipment coming in from an arms dealer in Moldova for black market military-grade weapons. Russian weapons. AK47s, RPGs, antipersonnel mines, grenades, and plenty of ammo. We even have DShK machine guns, Russian body armor, and NVGs."

"Russian NVGs are crap," Eli said.

Sawyer shrugged. "They'll beat not having them at all. We've already got MK 3 grenades, Claymores, a couple of Mark 19 auto grenade launchers."

"You're building an army."

"I already have."

Eli grunted. "How'd you get your hands on these black-market weapons?"

"For the last several years, we've been trading drugs for guns, smuggling them into Canada. The weapons black market is growing exponentially up there. Folks don't like it when you take away their rights and freeze their bank accounts. They don't like feeling helpless before a tyrannical leader. So, guns. The market share has grown by three hundred percent in two years."

"And the drugs come from Canada?"

"Some of them. From overseas and suppliers homegrown right here in the UP. The need is insatiable. We can't get enough before it's gone. A lot of people are in pain. We ease their burdens."

Eli kept his opinion to himself and said nothing. He doubted

Sawyer believed his own community-service B.S. He was too smart for that. Someone like Sawyer didn't worry about sleeping at night; you needed a conscience for that.

"And the ship?"

"The cargo ship is called the *Moldova Dream*. It was scheduled to come through the locks two days ago. Dixon's cousin works for a shipping company, and he has access to schedules, invoices, packing lists, certificates of origin, everything. The ship is stuck along with dozens of others, circling the locks. The Soo Locks create their own electricity but don't need electricity to operate—the gates are gravity-fed. But the ships need radio communication and radar to maneuver the channels. Both the lock operators and the captains are effectively blind. They're moving the big boats through with tugboats, but it's a slow, agonizing process. Downstate, they need the supplies. Do you think Lansing is gonna give anything to the UP? Nah. They're abandoning us, just like FEMA is."

"The Soo Locks will be protected by the National Guard."

Called the "Linchpin of the Great Lakes," the Soo Locks were an engineering marvel dating back to the mid-1800s. Freighters over 1000 feet in length could travel the St. Marys River from Duluth, Minnesota into the Atlantic Ocean and beyond.

It was the world's busiest lock system. Over 7000 vessels passed through the Locks every year, hauling eighty-five million tons of cargo. Freighters, barges, tugboats, and sailboats were lifted and lowered the twenty-one-foot drop between Lake Superior and Lake Huron.

Sawyer's eyes gleamed. "Can you imagine the tons of supplies on those ships? Goods tens of thousands of people are hungry for. If only there was a way to get ahold of some of those containers, or all of them. Or gain control of the Locks' hydroelectric power. Whoever controls the Locks would control the flow of all goods and electric power through the UP, through Michigan, Wisconsin, and Illinois."

"The Locks are federal. The government will protect them even if they let the rest of the UP rot."

Sawyer sighed, his eyes dimming. "I suppose you're right, for now. The governor has requested more soldiers, but they haven't arrived yet. Now is the time to strike and capture our supplies before it's too late and the place is swarming."

"How have you been communicating with your man inside?"

"The pony express, by letter sealed in wax. Transported in person, but we're using mopeds instead of ponies."

The hairs on the back of Eli's neck rose. He'd seen Sawyer's hands dozens of times. No ring. "Sealed?"

Sawyer reached for the chain around his neck and pulled it out. He briefly flashed a ring carved with a wolf eating two snakes. "I had seven custom made, one for me and six for my most trusted men."

Sawyer had his ring. It didn't mean he wasn't the killer. It did mean the list of suspects had narrowed down to seven. Eli needed to pass that information on to Jackson ASAP, but he hadn't yet had a chance to escape Sawyer's shadow for more than a minute. "Who else got a ring?"

Sawyer watched him with a sly smile. "You want one, don't you? They have to be earned."

It hit him like an electric jolt. Sawyer admired him. No, more than that—James Sawyer wanted Eli's approval. He needed it.

As much as he would deny it, Sawyer wanted a relationship with Eli. That childish want, that old familiar yearning to belong did not dissipate with adulthood, with responsibilities and broken dreams and cynicism.

Eli tucked that bit of information away. He would use it against Sawyer. It was a weapon. In Jackson, it would engender sympathy, pity, and camaraderie. Jackson's compassion could make him weak when it mattered most but Eli had no such conundrum.

"How do you earn one?" he asked nonchalantly.

Sawyer turned away and kept walking. "All in good time, my friend."

"Who else has one?"

"Jealous?"

"Something like that."

Sawyer just laughed.

Eli knew better than to ask again. He would need to wait and watch. He hadn't been able to meet with Jackson since he'd gone undercover. He'd have to find a way tonight. Who knew when he'd be off-island again?

For several minutes, they walked in silence, maneuvering between the massive fuel tanks. Silently, Eli counted them, made note of patrols and which tanks held snipers in wait on their rooftops.

"Tell me you're in," Sawyer said.

"What's the catch?"

"There is no catch."

"You just happen to have a major shipment of military-grade weapons waiting for you at the Soo? I call B.S."

He slapped Eli on the back. Eli tensed. Sawyer didn't seem to notice. "We had a major shipment ordered for an organized criminal element in Quebec. But now, we're taking it for ourselves. It's the largest shipment we've ever had. It's a game changer."

"You're stealing it."

Sawyer did not confirm nor deny.

"From whom?"

Sawyer gave a nonchalant shrug.

Eli steeled himself. "Tell me who."

"The Côté family."

Eli had heard of them. He'd had run-ins in the prison yard with several members of the Canadian criminal enterprise that had grown a reputation for ruthless savagery over the last several years. A chill ran through him. "You know what you're doing, Sawyer?"

"Absolutely."

"You want us to run this cargo from underneath the noses of the National Guard and the Côté crime syndicate. So, we're clear."

"You know the saying, 'it's not yours unless you can defend it.' With the toys we're about to procure, let the Munising Police Department come. The National Guard. The FBI, the State Police, the crazy Côté family themselves. We'll be ready for them."

"You'll be starting a war."

Sawyer leaned forward, a feral intensity in his gaze. "A war I'll win."

Behind them, someone shouted. Eli spun, pistol in hand.

40

ELI POPE

DAY THIRTY-FIVE

Eli took in the scene in a heartbeat.

Several people waiting in line to barter had gotten into a scuffle. A grizzled old man wearing hunting camo had traded a backpack crammed with canned goods for a couple of jerrycans of fuel, procured from a tank set on a truck bed to the left of the tent.

Eli recognized Johannes Heikkinen, an old-timer, the Finnish owner of a fishing charter in Munising who'd been born and raised here. Johannes had been a friend of his father's, who'd taught Eli poker as a boy. He had also threatened to shoot him with a hunting rifle.

As Johannes exited the fenced area, two people stepped out of the line and accosted him. A short, fat man in flip-flops had punched the old man in the face. A second man with long brown hair tied in a man-bun wrestled one of the jerrycans from Johannes' liver-spotted hands.

Johannes swore at them. He held the remaining jerrycan in one hand. With the other, he withdrew a pistol from beneath his shirt and waved it wildly. "Give it back or I'll shoot you, you thievin' mongrels! They stole my fuel! You saw it! I just traded for it—"

Several of Sawyer's men moved forward to intervene, hands

moving toward holsters. Vaughn slipped on a pair of brass knuckles. The thieves sprinted off as soon as they smelled trouble. The mercenaries didn't bother to chase them—the old man was too old and withered to run. They only needed one scapegoat.

"No weapons. No fights. Those are the rules. You broke them." Sawyer tilted his chin at Vaughn, giving the order. "Now you'll suffer."

Eli's heart rate accelerated. Jackson's rules rushed through his mind. There were circumstances where he was required to break cover, such as if a civilian were about to be murdered. Like right now.

Eli wasn't a monster. He had no desire to see an old man killed, or watch the gun go off and cause collateral damage amid the stunned crowd. Sawyer's mercenaries wouldn't think twice about firing upon innocent people to regain control of the situation.

In his mind's eye, he saw dead kids and weeping mothers. He had to act. There was only one other option. Without a second thought, he took it.

Eli surged forward. He shoved Pierce and Dixon aside and pounced on the old man. Eli punched him in the stomach and pushed him backward until he fell onto his butt in the dirt. He wheezed, the air knocked out of him.

Relentless, Eli seized two handfuls of white hair and hauled him to his feet, grabbed one withered arm, and twisted.

He locked the man's elbow behind him and shoved him stumbling toward the front gates, shouting, "Do not come back! And don't you ever make the mistake of talking to the boss like that! If I see you here again, I'll shoot both your kneecaps and watch you bleed out in the dirt, you got it, gramps?"

Pierce and Dixon stalked hot on his heels. He could feel their gazes on his back like laser beams, seeking weakness. He would not show it to them, could not.

The folks in line watched in stunned silence. A woman pulled out her phone like she was going to video the altercation or call 911. Her teen daughter seized the phone from her and pocketed it before one of Sawyer's thugs could target them, her eyes darting like a hunted animal.

When he reached the road, he spun Johannes around and spit on the old man's stunned face. His thick eyebrows wavered, his mouth open and gasping, blood dripping down his wrinkled cheeks. His watery eyes stared straight into Eli's, bright with judgment and condemnation.

"Get lost, geezer." Eli gave him one last kick and turned back to Sawyer, swiped a bead of sweat from his forehead, then rubbed the blood from his knuckles onto his pant legs. The crowd moved aside, anxious to get out of his way, loathing in their eyes—and fear.

"I'm calling the cops!" a man in line shouted. "You can't treat people this way!"

Pierce sneered. "Go right ahead. See how long it takes them to come, if they do. You'll find out quick enough that you're on your own."

"This isn't right," a woman said. A small child clutched her right hand. She patted her son's head and got out of line. The crate she'd brought for food and supplies remained empty.

A few people followed her but most remained. They looked askance, at the ground, at the sky, at their empty hands, anywhere but at each other—flustered, ashamed, shocked into silence. They were too afraid to speak up and draw Sawyer's wrath upon themselves. Their kids were hungry, too.

Sawyer surveyed the crowd with cold eyes. "Next time, my men won't be so merciful."

Out of the corner of his eye, he saw Kade and Dixon nodding at him, impressed. Vaughn stared at him, impassive, while Pierce looked like steam was about to come out of his ears.

Anger flared through Eli like a slow-burning ember. He forced himself to snuff it out. He'd kept his cover. No one had died; the old man had escaped relatively unscathed. Even better, Kade and Dixon believed he was meaner than they were.

All in all, it was a win. And yet, he felt terrible. His shoulders hunched against the appalled, horrified glares of the townspeople at his back.

"You did good back there. Can't have disorder mucking things up. Disorder leads to chaos. And I'm running a well-oiled machine. The witnesses will tell their family and friends. People aren't stupid. They want something from me, so they'll learn to follow my rules."

"You don't care about rules."

"Everything's up for grabs now. Who gets to make the rules? You? Or me? Sheriff Underwood? Some floozies from Lansing who will never step foot in the UP again? I don't think so. Like I said, if you can't protect it, it's not yours. I can't have my men distracted with petty fights. I need them focused and ready for the bigger threats."

A languid smile slid across Sawyer's face. "We're alike, you and I. Embrace it, Eli. Release that monster inside you. Think what we could do together. What we could accomplish."

"I am thinking about it."

"Of course, you are. You aren't stupid." Sawyer gestured for Eli to follow him. His guards closed into a loose phalanx around them, Pierce taking up the rear. "I want you to go with Pierce to retrieve the weapons cache."

Eli lowered his voice. "Pierce doesn't trust me."

"Pierce will get over it." They headed toward the reservoir entrance. The sun shone bright, the white fuel tanks casting long shadows across weedy, overgrown grass. "You have the tactical skills we need. I've got a few dozen trained mercenaries, and they're good. But you're better. You're from here. You have skin in the game that they don't. You go in, transfer the cargo to our trucks and drive back home. Easy peasy."

Eli snorted.

"It'll be fine," Sawyer said. "We've got drones. We have NVGs. Plate carriers. AR-15s, AK-47s, M4s, and the ammo to go with it."

Eli raised his brows.

"I told you. You're good to go."

"I'm good remaining by your side. You've got threats here to contend with."

Sawyer stared at him for a long moment. "I'm not asking you, Pope."

Refusing would be a mistake. Sawyer would not accept it. "When?"

"Day after tomorrow," Sawyer said. "At dawn."

"How long?" Eli asked.

"One day. Sault Ste. Marie is a 120-mile trip, one way. We've got vehicles, the transport, plenty of fuel. You'll be there and back by evening."

Apprehension wormed inside him. He hated the thought of leaving Lena and Shiloh unprotected. He'd given them as much instruction as he could, but they couldn't hold up under a clear and present danger. A few of Sawyer's trained men would overwhelm their paltry defenses in moments.

He had to trust that they could handle themselves. And that Jackson would watch over them, though he was dubious on that point. He didn't trust Jackson as far as he could throw him.

Jackson would be adamantly against this. He'd say it was too dangerous, the risks too great. Eli didn't care what Jackson thought.

As if reading Eli's thoughts, Sawyer switched subjects. "What are you going to do about Cross?"

Eli kept his expression neutral. "What do you mean?"

Sawyer flashed him a sly look. "Not so long ago, you told me you were going to kill whoever framed you. I gave you that little nugget of intel. It's been a month and Jackson is still walking the earth, breathing rarified air, an irritating thorn in my side."

A dozen conflicting thoughts plowed through Eli's brain. His adrenaline surged as he fought to keep his breathing even.

"Cross betrayed you. If he'd done half that to me, he'd be fish food, another ghost for the lake to claim as her own."

Sawyer's words were nonchalant; he was anything but. If Eli answered the wrong way, he'd raise Sawyer's suspicions. The last thing he needed was Sawyer questioning his loyalties. That way led to a slow and excruciating death.

Besides, he wouldn't put it past Sawyer to kidnap Jackson, gag and duct-tape him, shove a Glock 19 in Eli's hand, and demand Eli kill him then and there.

Yet another test. This time, one he was certain to fail. Or was he?

His heart thudded against his ribs. "Glad you asked. I've been working on a plan. The weapons shipment works perfectly. Soon as we get them and get a bit of training, I was thinking we'd roll on out to the Sheriff's Office in a couple of your armored Land Cruisers, nab Cross, and slaughter every deputy they have while making Cross watch. Especially that perky little female he's so fond of. When we're done, then I'll kill Cross, slowly and painfully, a little gift for eight years of torture in prison. In the end, he'll beg me to put him out of his misery."

Sawyer's gray eyes glinted. He looked like a fat cat who'd just swallowed the canary. He slapped Eli on the back, shook his head, and kept walking. "Damn, son. What have I been telling you? You're the type of psychopath I need by my side."

Eli hadn't needed to fake his hatred. The seething bitterness was all too real. The thought of Jackson getting his comeuppance sent a delicious thrill through his veins. Vengeance had kept him alive in prison, the dark hunger he'd fed through a thousand sleepless nights.

"Cross is mine," Eli growled. "It'll be by my hand."

Sawyer's smile slipped from his face, replaced by a flat watchfulness, like a predator always circling, searching for his next meal. "Go with Pierce and get my weapons, deliver them safely, and he's yours. None of my men will touch him."

Eli nodded. He had the distinct impression he'd just made a deal with the devil. It was not his first, nor would it be his last.

41

JACKSON CROSS

DAY THIRTY-SIX

"I found the locket," Devon said.

It wasn't even 7 a.m., but Devon was wide awake and far too perky for the apocalypse. Jackson, on the other hand, felt like a dead man walking. He hadn't had a full night's rest in a month.

He'd told Devon to meet him in his hotel room at the Northwoods Inn to keep away from prying eyes, though he hadn't expected her at the butt-crack of dawn.

He sat on the edge of the bed, rubbed his eyes, and ran a hand through his rumpled hair. He'd slept in his clothes last night, but Devon didn't seem to notice. These days, most people's clothes were wrinkled and a bit smelly.

He gestured at the files spread across the desk, the files he perused every night, then stored in the vent for safekeeping whenever he left the room. "Tell me."

Devon sank into the chair next to the desk and slapped a slim file on the desk. "Each one is handmade locally by a jeweler in Paradise who sold the lockets in tourist shops throughout the UP. His name is Henry Aalto."

Jackson rubbed his jaw. "He might have said something when the locket was in the news during the Broken Heart Killer case. We could have used some information then."

Devon leaned back in the chair. "He's eighty years old, and I didn't see a TV in his house when I visited, only an ancient desktop computer. He didn't recall hearing about the case when I questioned him."

"Figures. My father was the sheriff then. He kept back some of the information on the locket since we suspected it was the killer's calling card. No picture was released, either. But that's neither here nor there. We need to visit those stores—"

"Already on it. The jeweler gave me the names and locations of the stores, and I spent yesterday visiting ten shops east of Copper Harbor. Most of the stores were shuttered. I had to knock on doors and ask a billion neighbors to locate the store owners and track them down at their residences."

"And?" Jackson asked impatiently. "What did you find?"

"At nine of the ten places, nothing. Nada. Nobody remembered any mass purchases or any suspicious or unusual customers. Then in Eagle River, jackpot."

Jackson stated the obvious. "That's in Keweenaw County. Maybe twenty minutes from Copper Harbor, where Elice went missing."

Devon nodded. "The owner of the Eagle's Nest gift shop recalled a customer who visits every few years and purchases five lockets each time. Always five. And always the same customer. She said it has happened four or five times."

Unable to remain calm, Jackson stood. He was wide awake now. His hands balled into fists at his sides. "Tell me we have a list of customers. Names and addresses. Video surveillance? Anything?"

Devon's expression tightened. "Sorry, boss. The shop used an online database and accounting service. All records were kept on the cloud. When the Internet went, so did the evidence."

"What about a physical description?"

"The store owner doesn't remember much. Male, Caucasian, hair light brown or dark blond. Maybe. She said nothing stood out to her about him. Not large, not small, but average. He wore a baseball cap low over his eyes. She couldn't recall any specific physical details and she couldn't give us an approximate age, either, anywhere from twenty-five to forty. He told her he purchased the lockets for his daughter's birthday parties, that she gave them out as party favors to her friends. The owner thought that was sweet, that he was a wonderful father, which is why she remembered that part."

"So, he could be anybody. Great. How about dates, at least? When was the first time a locket was purchased from that shop?"

Devon shook her head. "She doesn't remember. She guessed fifteen years ago, but she doesn't know for sure. She opened the shop in 2006, so the timing fits."

Jackson cursed in frustration. He wanted to hit something, smash it into smithereens. A month ago, this evidence could have led them straight to the killer. Now, he'd escaped again, slipping between their fingers like sifting sand.

"She did say that the last time he came in was about two and a half months ago. She couldn't remember the exact date, but she thought it was over spring break because her teenage daughter was working the shop with her. She didn't like how he looked at her daughter."

A shiver ran up his spine. "Mid-March. That's when Summer Tabasaw disappeared."

"I found something else." Devon pulled a sheaf of papers from the corner of the desk where she'd scribbled notes in pencil. "According to Caldwell's files, Elice was a patient of the Great Lakes Recovery Center in Hancock, in the Keweenaw Peninsula. Summer Tabasaw and Ruby Carpenter were patients of Great Lakes Recovery Center in Marquette. All the victims had a history of drug abuse."

Jackson closed his eyes. He didn't need to check her file; he'd memorized it. "Lily went to Pathways Substance Abuse Center in 2009 or 2010. It's also in Marquette."

"That's half the victims. I bet we'll find more if we dig."

Jackson nodded. "We need a list of patients, employees, the

victims' medical files, whatever we can get our hands on."

"We'll need a warrant. Those medical files are confidential."

"Then let's get one. There are a few judges in the county still working. You follow the substance abuse lead. I've got a meeting with an old friend."

Devon cocked an eyebrow.

Jackson pointed to the stack of Michigan Tech annuals he'd spent all night poring over. He hadn't fallen asleep until after 4 a.m., and then it was a fitful, restless three hours of nightmares before Devon had knocked on the hotel door. He'd uncovered several familiar names which didn't fit the profile, one of interest.

"I found a photo of someone we know in the 2007 edition. He attended the school the same year as Elice McNeely. He's from Munising and went to the high school with us."

"And?"

"It's Gideon Crawford."

Devon sank back in the office chair and stared at him, eyes wide. "Gideon Crawford, as in Lily Easton's ex-boyfriend?"

"That's the one."

The lurid details had emerged at the trial—how Gideon had been dating Lily, head over heels in love with her by all accounts, but Lily had been sleeping with Eli when he returned on leave.

Lily's affair had broken Gideon's heart; it had humiliated him, too. He'd never recovered.

"How many students attend MTU?" Devon asked.

"The school has an annual enrollment of around 7,000 students. A lot of our kids go there, to Northern Michigan or Lake Superior State in Sault Ste. Marie. Or they head downstate."

"It could be a coincidence, then."

"A coincidence is a coincidence until it's not." Jackson thought of the picture that had snagged his gaze as he'd flipped through the yearbook—Elice McNeely hunched over a lab table, studying a textbook, a younger, much thinner Gideon Crawford at the table beside her, hamming for the camera. "They were lab partners."

Devon's eyebrows shot up to her hairline. "Interesting

development."

"Indeed."

"If he was the secret boyfriend, and he murdered Elice for 'insulting' him by daring to dump him, then he would've done the same to Lily if he'd found out she was cheating. That's motive."

Jackson nodded slowly. Gideon wouldn't be the first jilted boyfriend, or the last, to destroy the one he'd professed to love. Suspicion nipped at him, the old questions rising to the surface: whether Gideon had known about Eli before the murder. Whether he'd been jealous enough, enraged enough to do something about it, to make Lily and Eli pay dearly for their sins.

But could Gideon be a serial killer? Jackson didn't see it. But then, folks seldom saw the evil in their own backyards, the menace in their neighbors, friends, and family members. It was familiarity that blinded us to the truth. He was learning that the hard way, slowly but surely.

"He's the dentist who helped us identify Lydia Hughes using her dental records. You said the killer would try to attach himself to the case somehow."

"That's true," Jackson said. It was a classic tactic among serial killers. He had the sudden sensation of falling.

"And he could have traveled to various dental conventions around the UP." Devon leaned forward, her eyes brightening as if she sensed the same thing he did. "Gideon doesn't have one of Sawyer's rings, does he?"

"Not that I know of, but he knows Sawyer. They're friends from way back, played football together in high school. It's a connection. As soon as I can get out from beneath Underwood's thumb, I'll talk to him. Shake a few trees and see what falls out."

"It's like you suspected, boss," Devon said. "The killer is close. So close, he's in our backyard."

"Maybe." Jackson switched gears. "Anything on the suspect who fled the lighthouse?"

She shook her head. "Moreno and I recanvassed the neighborhood. No one else saw or heard anything. We found no tire tracks, no evidence of a vehicle anywhere near the scene. It appears they arrived by boat, and the surviving suspect fled the same way they'd come."

His frustration built. He felt stymied every way he turned. "Damn it! We need that intel from Eli so we can narrow down our suspects. There's no way we can track down every lead in the middle of a worldwide blackout."

"Half the world," Devon said softly.

"That's true. But the global economy is intricately interconnected. We're interdependent upon each other in ways most people don't comprehend. Remember how the Russian invasion of Ukraine destabilized the global supply chain and drastically increased inflation? And that was a war between two countries, let alone a catastrophe across several continents. The collapse of the American dollar will have worldwide ramifications on financial systems. Think about all the critical import/export cogs grinding to a halt.

"Take medicine for example. I was talking with Dr. Larson at the hospital. She told me that seventy percent of our pharmaceutical drugs are manufactured outside of the U.S., including ninety percent of critical antibiotics like penicillin. Take India, the third-largest pharmaceutical manufacturer in the world. One in three pills in the U.S. and one in four pills in the U.K. are manufactured in India. Australia may have power, but they import ninety percent of their medications. And that's only talking about medicine, let alone the crippled global food chain. China accounts for thirty percent of global manufacturing output, not just medications, but everything—they're as in the dark as we are. The southern hemisphere is facing devastating shortages whether they have electricity or not. They might be better off than us, but no country has escaped unscathed, I know that much."

Devon shuddered. "When you put it that way..."

"Yeah," he said, because what else was there to say? Besides, it was all speculation and rumors. No one knew for certain what was happening outside their isolated bubble.

He hadn't realized how much he would miss the ability to communicate instantly with anyone around the world, up-to-the-minute news delivered to your phone, your tablet, or even your watch.

They were in the dark, both metaphorically and literally. It was a deeply unsettling feeling, like the ground was constantly shifting beneath your feet, unstable as black ice.

He grunted, went to the dresser, and swiped on deodorant, incredibly grateful that the Northwoods Inn had a gravity-fed well and solar-powered showers. Running water kept him feeling human. Funny how the things you once took for granted had quickly become top priorities.

He turned back to Devon. "I need some coffee and I'm ready to go."

"The Gallery Coffee Company ran out of mocha yesterday," Devon said with a morose tone. She was a sugar junkie, unlike Jackson who needed the caffeine to keep him going. "They'll be out of coffee within the week. Unless FEMA delivers more, we're out of luck."

The day was already going downhill. "Figures."

"And Underwood wants a meeting at 8 a.m. We've got another missing person case. Emma Clark reported her son missing last night. Eddie Clark works at the gas station in Chatham. He didn't show up the last three days for work. He has several prior arrests and served three years for attempted sexual assault five years ago."

"I know him," Jackson said. "He's one of the low-life criminals in Sawyer's crew. Eli might know. I'll ask next time we meet."

Devon rose from her chair and pushed her braids over her shoulder. "We've been spending a lot of time on this case. I think Underwood might suspect we're going off-book, boss. You have a plan for that?"

"I'm working on it." Jackson unscrewed the vent and stuffed the case files inside, then screwed the vent back in place. He headed for the door, Devon hot on his heels. "When it rains, it pours."

42

ELI POPE

DAY THIRTY-SEVEN

Anger ran through Eli like an electrical current; he was incandescent with it.

If anyone attempted to touch him, he'd probably electrocute them. Or worse.

The bonfire roared in the center of the clearing along the southern bluff of Grand Island. Several barrels had been cut in half, welded with metal fence posts, and installed with metal grates that served as oversized grills. The smell of grilled venison filled the air.

Frogs trilled and crickets whirred, the night punctuated with raucous laughter. Dixon had wound up the radio and turned up the volume on the emergency station, the only station that wasn't pure static.

The radio announcer spoke of rumors of mass casualties in Europe, starvation, sickness, and disease spreading from contaminated water supplies. There were reports of violent riots in major cities: L.A., NYC, and Miami. FEMA emergency supply trucks were being ambushed en route.

The governor gave a canned speech, beseeching Michiganders to dig in and keep the faith, that despite the dark hour, the light would return. Tellingly, he neglected to say when that miracle might transpire.

Eli barely registered any of it. Only a few hours ago, he'd managed to evade Sawyer's goons to meet with Jackson on the mainland. It had been risky.

He'd told Dixon he was meeting a woman. Dixon had bought it, but Vaughn looked at him like he was a fox he wanted to skin. Vaughn and Pierce both had it in for him.

After he'd provided Jackson with the list of five names of men who owned one of Sawyer's rings, Jackson had sucker punched him.

Reluctantly, Jackson had informed him of the lighthouse attack. How Lena had been forced to kill. How Shiloh had faced an assailant with a knife and then rappelled down the tower as he'd taught her, narrowly escaping with her life.

He'd been able to think of little else since. He needed to leave this place, abandon his mission. Lena and Shiloh needed him. He'd never be able to live with himself if something happened to them. He'd thought they'd be okay; he'd been dead wrong.

He didn't care what Sawyer thought or if he'd try to stop him. Let him try. Eli would destroy anyone and anything that dared get in his way.

This was his moment. Sawyer had traveled to Grand Marais in his newest yacht for a meeting with a couple of enforcers from Paradise in discussions over the acquisition of a new property—a distillery or distribution center or cannabis facility, Eli couldn't care less.

All he needed to do was slip from the bonfire unseen and—

A scrap of conversation reached him, a single word drifting across the circle of flames: *lighthouse*.

Eli tensed but showed no visible signs of a reaction. Slowly, he turned his head and strained his ears to overhear the conversation between Kade and Dixon, not twenty feet to his nine o'clock.

"I'm telling you, man. The cops think it's us," Dixon was saying.

"Why would we go after two women at the lighthouse? We need that beacon to keep working as much as anyone."

Kade leaned in close and lowered his voice. "You sure they think it was Sawyer?"

Dixon shrugged. "According to Sawyer's cop informant, yeah. They're saying it was three assailants and one got away. He had a specialized knife they're searching for. And Peterson and Silvester are still MIA. What do you make of that?"

To Kade's right, a man stiffened, the slight movement drawing Eli's attention. Wes Vaughn was half-turned toward Cyrus Lee, peeling an apple with one hand, popping the sections into his mouth with the other.

Quickly, he shoved something into his pocket and withdrew his hand. That's when Eli saw it. Vaughn usually wore black leather gloves, but the night was downright hot, and Vaughn's hands were bare.

A tan line encircled the bony middle finger on his left hand.

The tan line could be from a wedding ring, but Eli doubted it. Vaughn wasn't married. The tan line was a thick ring of white flesh, from a wide band. It was perfectly sized to the thick, chunky wolf-head rings that Sawyer and his insider cronies wore. And he had the tattoo on his neck to match.

The hairs on the back of Eli's neck stood on end. Was it the same ring that sat in the Sheriff's Office in an evidence box? Was Vaughn the serial killer? He stood casually across from the fire, listening to one of Antoine's stupid jokes. Was this the man who'd strangled multiple women, including Lily?

Dread shivered down his spine. Cold sweat broke out on his brow, his palms clammy. He forced his hands to relax, to keep his fingers from curling into fists when he desperately wished to draw his combat knife and slit Vaughn's throat where he stood.

Despite the rage boiling through him, he had the presence of mind to restrain himself. This was neither the time nor the place to confront Vaughn, not if Eli planned to escape this island with a pulse.

The night was overcast. Heavy clouds obscured the moon as occasional silver patches of starlight flickered across the grass. No one left immediately after supper. They ate and drank and downed beer after beer until nearly everyone not on patrol or dish duty was drunk, everyone but Eli.

He watched, and he waited. His gaze flickered to Wes Vaughn again and again; the man was limping, ever so slightly favoring his right leg.

Dixon came and sat on the log beside him, chattering about a restored 1967 Shelby GT500 he'd found in some rich CEO's garage and stolen for his own. Eli barely heard a word. He kept his suspicious gaze fixated on Vaughn.

An hour later, a lone figure peeled away from the bonfire and strode toward the cabins with an uneven, hunched-shoulder gait. There was no missing his tall, emaciated form. It was Vaughn.

Eli waited a minute, rose to his feet, and made an off-hand comment about answering nature's call. Instead, he hurried to the outhouse, circled behind it, and entered the tree line before doubling back to follow Vaughn.

Beneath the tree canopy, the darkness was near absolute. Eli moved as soundlessly but as quickly as he could, senses alert in case Vaughn attempted to ambush him.

Vaughn visited the outhouse. By the time he shoved open the rickety door and exited, Eli was safely ensconced within the shadows. Staying twenty paces behind Vaughn, Eli fell into lockstep, using his footfalls to obscure his own.

Vaughn stopped.

Eli stopped.

The man stood stock still for twenty seconds. His flashlight beam probed the woods, sweeping left, then right in wide swaths. He half-turned, then hesitated.

Eli did not breathe. If Vaughn caught him, Eli might be able to talk him out of sounding the alarm, but probably not. He could simply kill Vaughn, but a corpse would be even harder to explain away. If he were caught, he was dead.

This was a risk, one he shouldn't take. If he were thinking clearly, he wouldn't. But the anger was blinding him, the thought of this man possibly hurting Lena or Shiloh...

Vaughn started walking again. His boots crunched dead leaves and gravel. In the quiet, his heavy breathing rasped like a saw. His flashlight bobbed ahead.

When Vaughn moved, Eli followed. Against his better judgment, but so help him, he did. Vaughn quickened his step as he reached the cabins. This time, he did not turn around.

Thirty paces ahead, a door slammed. Vaughn froze in the shadows. Heart hammering, Eli froze with him. Footsteps. The sound of a beer tab opening, a grunt, and then the footsteps faded as the person headed back toward the bonfire on the bluff.

Vaughn kept going, his movements stealthy as he crept up to a cabin that was not his. He paused again and glanced to his three o'clock, toward the bonfire.

Eli couldn't see the flickering firelight, but the scent of campfire smoke and roasting hot dogs reached his nostrils. He willed his stomach not to growl. Mosquitos bit him but he dared not slap them away. One landed on his cheek.

Vaughn veered left, bypassing several cabins that sat dark and still. Their occupants were in the mess hall, at the bonfire, or on security duty. The sounds of laughter receded.

Tension wound tighter in his gut. If Vaughn saw him, he'd have to kill him. That would be difficult to explain, plus it'd blow his cover. He wasn't finished here.

Eli flexed his hands and tensed his muscles, preparing himself. If Vaughn was the killer...he wouldn't live long. Eli would make sure of that. Jackson wanted a justice system with courts and judges; Eli's justice consisted of a bullet and a gun.

Half-crouched, he scanned the enclave of cabins set in a semicircle, taking in the dark porches. Soft yellow light glowed from several solar floodlights. Insects buzzed and swarmed within the cones of light. The mosquitos were ravenous.

At his nine o'clock, a shadow flitted at the corner of his vision.

Vaughn threw a cautious glance over his shoulder, flicked off his flashlight, and crept surreptitiously along the side wall of one of the cabins. He edged to the window.

Controlling his breathing to slow his pulse, Eli waited for a thick cloud to drift across the moon. Remaining within the patch of darkness, Eli crouched beside a blue fifty-gallon rain barrel set against the side of the cabin kitty-corner to Vaughn's location.

Soundlessly, he drew his pistol and strained his ears. The screech of a window screen being pried from its frame, another scraping sound, then a dull thump. No other sounds followed. No footfalls of someone approaching. In the distance came a burst of laughter from the bonfire.

Blading his body, leading with the muzzle of his weapon, he crept around the corner of the cabin. The backside of the next cabin inched into view. By now, his night vision had improved. He caught sight of a torso, two legs, and a pair of boots slithering through a jimmied window. The screen leaned against the cabin's exterior wall.

Eli recognized the cluster of birch trees in the clearing to the east. This was Dixon and Kade's cabin. He waited as Vaughn skittered through the window like a spider and disappeared inside the cabin. Then he waited some more, watching. A minute passed, then another. Five minutes later, a scuffling echoed in the still night.

Eli retreated and pressed his spine against the wall, listening. There came a muffled curse, followed by more scuffling, probably Vaughn disgorging himself from the window. He was thin but tall and ungainly.

More scraping as the screen was replaced. Then, footsteps receded.

After another minute, Eli peered around the corner and ensured that Vaughn had indeed vacated the premises. He took a knee and waited five minutes, then ten. Not moving, barely breathing, a shadow among shadows.

After twenty minutes, he glanced at his watch. 10:30 p.m.

Moving stealthily, he waited for another patch of darkness as a cloud covered the moon, then he crossed to the cabin. He circled it, checking for signs of occupancy, and found none. Dixon and Kade were still at the bonfire, utterly plastered.

Eli copied Vaughn's movements, popping out the screen and climbing through the window. He dropped lightly to the floor as the old boards creaked. He tensed, knees bent, pistol held in two hands as he held his breath.

Inside, shadows cloaked everything. He blinked, his eyes making out a twin bed, a dusty dresser cluttered with girlie magazines, a shotgun leaning against the bedroom doorway.

By habit, he cleared the cabin before he searched it. Two narrow bedrooms, a tiny kitchen with a fridge and stove hooked up to propane, and an attached outhouse. Other than the beer cans overflowing in the trashcan, it was neat enough—and empty.

He returned to Kade's bedroom, searched it, and found nothing. In Dixon's bedroom, a leather coat hung over the back of a wooden chair in the corner. He scanned the room, eyes straining in the shadows.

He checked drawers and shelves and pockets and found nothing unusual. In the top drawer of the nightstand, he found a handful of change, a lighter, some crumpled receipts, Chapstick, and a 357 Magnum revolver. He'd seen Dixon with it before.

Had Vaughn left something or had he taken something—

A shimmer on the floor beneath the iron-frame bed. Crouching, he bent down and stared at the object: a fixed-blade bowie knife, the blade six inches long, the handle the smooth carved ivory of bone.

His pulse quickened. Hot anger flushed through his veins. With one hand, he tugged on the leather gloves he kept in his back pocket and gently picked up the knife.

This was the blade Vaughn had used to attack Shiloh. Eli needed no more evidence. Vaughn fit the physical profile. He limped from an unverified injury. Most damning, he sported a tan line from a missing ring. And the knife.

Dixon's rumor had done the dirty work for him. Did Vaughn fear the sheriff would come looking for it? Did he suspect Eli was onto him and had attempted to dump evidence, lay the blame at someone else's feet?

Had Sawyer given the order or had Vaughn acted on his own? That mystery remained to be untangled. Was Vaughn also the serial killer? Or was it Sawyer? Or someone else within the organization? Could it be Pierce, or maybe Kade, or the reclusive, creepy Cyrus? Maybe even the informant cop Sawyer had mentioned a few times.

The missing ring pointed to Vaughn. If Vaughn had killed Lily and the other girls, then he might have gone after Lena and Shiloh as a warning to Jackson, or simply as his next targets.

For that, Eli would kill him. He'd cut him open and bleed out his entrails, watch him suffer the way he'd made those girls suffer.

Unlike Jackson, Eli was not obsessed with the truth. It was vengeance that drove him.

Voices drifted from the darkness.

Eli froze.

Kade's high-pitched laughter echoed outside the cabin, followed by Dixon's low timbre voice, telling another joke. The voices came from the front side of the cabin, from the southwest.

Eli considered taking the knife, but he didn't know about the preservation of fingerprints or chain of evidence. What were the rules now, anyway?

He wanted to take a few photos on his phone, which he kept powered with the solar charger Sawyer had given him, but if any of Sawyer's men saw the pictures, they'd rip his entrails out with a fork and feed his bowels to the crows.

So, he put the knife back and did nothing—for now. He moved for the exit, half-crouched as he crossed the weathered floorboards, checked outside the window, then swiftly climbed out and dropped to the ground. The grass was damp with dew. Cicadas buzzed in the stillness, mosquitoes swarmed his skin.

From the other side of the cabin, the voices grew louder. Eli waited for the squeal of the front door to open, the hinges rusty, the wood warped with age—then he slipped the window screen back in its frame, masking his noise with theirs.

He went still, not breathing, his spine pressed against the rear of the cabin as Dixon and Kade entered through the front door. He detected no alteration in the cadence of their voices or shuffling, drunken footsteps.

The clouds had dissipated; the moon shone bright as quicksilver limning the darkened buildings. Eli moved from shadow to shadow, dropping to one knee at each cabin to check for surveillance.

Instead of heading straight to his cabin, he circled the camp and loped northeast along a trail that led down to the eastern shoreline. Each night, he'd taken to hiking a few miles of the island, establishing an expected pattern of behavior. It allowed him to check the protocols, and make notes of sentry positions, patrols, and security weak points.

His mind whirred with competing emotions—outrage, dread, frustration, and terror. Not for himself, never for himself. In his mind, he pictured the lighthouse, the whitewashed tower silhouetted against the charcoal sky, the beacon shining bright.

He was the lost; the two women in the lighthouse were his home.

He couldn't protect them from afar. That fact nearly killed him. Yet at the same time, he'd uncovered a critical clue. He would not wait for Jackson to investigate. He needed to act.

The convoy to retrieve the weapons cache in Sault Ste. Marie left at dawn. Eli would leave with them.

It was a dangerous mission. He was acutely aware of the risk, the consequences of a misstep, of failure.

Pierce wanted Eli dead. Outside of Sawyer's watchful eye, Pierce would try something. Death by friendly fire was an explanation that Sawyer would have to buy; he'd have no choice. A bullet to the spine would be a simple ambush to engineer.

And yet, this was an opportunity for Eli as well. An opportunity to go after Vaughn without worrying about a hundred of Sawyer's men breathing down the back of his neck. Off-island was his only chance to kill Vaughn without getting killed himself.

It was then, and only then, that he would abandon the island and return to the lighthouse, to Lena and Shiloh. He was, after all, a hunter of men.

Tomorrow, Eli would get answers. Then, he would end Vaughn.

As long as Pierce didn't get to him first.

43

JACKSON CROSS

DAY THIRTY-SEVEN

It was after 10 p.m. before Jackson got off work and headed back to the Northwoods Inn. He'd spent the day tracking down thieves who'd already eaten or sold the merchandise and responded to two overdose deaths, one in Chatham and one at a campground in the Hiawatha National Forest.

Overdoses were becoming more common, as were suicides.

Last night, he'd met with Eli at their designated spot. Jackson had gotten what he wanted. Eli gave him seven names. Six rings, plus Sawyer's.

He and Devon were working on cross-referencing the names from the Elice McNeely file against Sawyer's inner circle. So far, no hits, but they were far from finished.

Jackson had told Eli about the lighthouse attack, he'd had no choice. He'd never seen Eli so enraged. He had the disconcerting feeling that he'd unleashed an attack dog he could not control. He wondered, not for the first time, if Eli could restrain the darkness within himself.

Half a dozen patrons were slumped at the Northwoods Bar. As long as the tap continued to flow, people would show up. The hand-written sign taped to the blank TV screen said: "$40 a glass, cash only."

A man rose from his bar stool as Jackson approached. He moved heavily, swaying on his feet, a glass of amber liquid held unsteadily in his right hand. "Well, if it isn't Eli Pope's best friend."

Jackson halted a few feet away. "Thanks for agreeing to meet with me, Gideon."

"Anything for old friends, eh?" Jackson detected a hint of sarcasm in his voice.

Gideon had played linebacker in high school, and then for Michigan Tech, according to the photos in the 2008 annual. Though much of his muscle had melted to fat, he remained big and intimidating. He was certainly strong enough to hurt someone if he wanted to.

Farther down the bar, another man sat hunched over a Jack Daniels on the rocks. Cyrus Lee watched the scene unfold, a small smile playing on his lips. Jackson suppressed his dislike. According to Eli, Cyrus Lee had one of the rings. He wore it on a chain around his neck under his shirt, which was why Jackson hadn't noticed it before.

They had been sitting together at the bar, Gideon Crawford and Cyrus Lee.

Jackson had memorized the timeline for the night of Lily's murder. Before Eli had visited Lily, he'd been at the Northwoods Bar. Sawyer had been there that night, sitting with Gideon and Lee.

Gideon had no known connection with Sawyer's criminal organization. He didn't have a ring, either, but that didn't mean he wasn't a viable suspect. The coincidences were too great.

"I heard you got Pope off," Gideon said.

"Eli Pope is innocent."

"Just 'cause the law messed up don't mean he's innocent." Gideon's words slurred. "He's still guilty."

"We all thought he was guilty. I did too, believe me. It's not easy to flip that truth on its head. But we must. We owe it to him."

"I don't owe that cheating bastard a damn thing."

Jackson steeled himself. "You don't have to like him, Gideon. That doesn't make him guilty of murder. He didn't do it."

"He has no right to be back here. No right..." Gideon stared into his drink and cursed. He looked up and seemed to realize that folks were staring at him. His reddened face turned scarlet.

"What the hell are you looking at?" he growled at a nearby couple. They quickly glanced away.

Jackson rubbed his forehead, feeling a headache coming on. He gestured to Gideon. "Let's sit down and have a bit of privacy."

Gideon leaned against the bar. "I'm fine right here."

"Suit yourself. I need to ask you a few questions about your time at Michigan Tech."

Gideon swayed. His eyes were dull and bloodshot. "What for?"

"Just verifying a few things for an ongoing investigation. What years did you attend MTU?"

He blinked blearily. "Uh...2007 to 2009. I did my dental prerequisites there since they offered me a damn good scholarship to play for the Division Two Huskies."

"Did you ever come into contact with Elice McNeely?" Jackson knew he had, but he wanted to see Gideon's reaction.

Gideon frowned but answered without hesitation. "Uh... I had a science lab with her, Thursday nights after practice. I mean, it's been a while. I tried to hit on her a few times. She was hot. But real quiet, kept to herself."

"She rejected you?"

"Said she had someone else. I figured as much."

"Did that make you angry?"

He gave a derisive snort. "Why would it? I've had my share of rejections, some more public than others."

Jackson watched his face closely. He didn't see the classic signs of deception in his expression. Gideon was drunk but did not appear to be lying, unless he was very good at it. "Do you remember the necklace she wore?"

"What necklace?" He squinted, confused. "Why are you asking so many questions? I thought that Boone bastard did it. And he's dead. That's what you're saying, isn't it? That it was Boone, not Pope."

"We're tying up a few loose ends."

Gideon gave a disbelieving grunt. "Sure. Whatever you say, man."

"What can you tell me about Elice?"

His eyes cleared then, his posture straightening as wariness entered his gaze, like a deer recognizing the scent of the hunter. "Wait a minute. That's the girl who went missing back then, isn't it? That's why you're asking about her."

"You knew she was missing?"

He shrugged. "Well, sure. Everyone knew. A detective came to our classes and asked around. It wasn't a secret. Most of us thought she'd run away with a boyfriend or something."

A faint scar ran along his collarbone to the right side of his neck. He touched it with his free hand, rubbing the scar tissue almost subconsciously.

Jackson stared at the scar, fighting the urge to recoil. Ugly memories flashed through his head, memories that had nothing to do with Elice McNeely or Lily Easton.

Fifteen years ago, Gideon had been involved in a car accident that had killed his college girlfriend; the same accident that had crippled Astrid. Two vehicles were crushed in a head-on collision on a windy road between Marquette and Munising. It had been pouring rain that night; beer bottles had been found in Gideon's Honda Civic.

After all these years, the details of the accident remained unclear. Gideon had been knocked unconscious; his girlfriend, Allison Grady, was killed instantly. Astrid had refused to speak of it. Either she didn't remember, or the memory was too traumatizing to relive.

The accident had been the tragedy of the decade in Alger County—until Lily's murder. Gideon had never recovered. Though he managed to hold on to his career as a dentist, he'd limped from broken relationship to broken relationship, always with a drink in hand and another on tap.

"I know it was a long time ago, but where were you on the weekend of May 8, 2008?"

Gideon stiffened. His black eyes glinted with anger. "Why? You suspect me, too? I heard you were on a wild goose chase to pin this whole serial murder thing on someone else. Maybe someone you'll later claim is innocent? Which is it, Jackson?"

"Answer the question."

Gideon took a long swig, draining his glass. He looked at Jackson with unbridled resentment. "I only remember because the detective asked me the same thing back then, said he asked everybody he talked to. I was on the chess team, not just a brawny jock. We were pretty good, too. The state tournament was at MSU in Lansing from Thursday through Monday the weekend that girl disappeared. I had nothing to do with any of it."

"Any witnesses I can talk to that can prove it?"

Gideon let out a harsh laugh. "You sure know how to make friends and influence people, don't you? The world is ending, and this is what you're obsessed with? A crime from a million years ago that doesn't matter,"

Jackson could feel eyes on him: folks at the bar, people chatting in the foyer. The place had gone suddenly quiet. "It does matter."

"You're a piece of work, you know that?"

"I'll ask you again. Do you have a legitimate alibi for May 8?"

Gideon glanced over Jackson's shoulder at something—or someone—behind him, maybe at Cyrus. He returned his attention to Jackson, but just barely. "Yeah, Cross, I do. The 2008 annual has a photo of the chess team at the tournament. All of us lined up behind a chessboard with idiotic grins. You'll see the date printed all nice and neat for you, too." He leaned in and exhaled a stale breath into Jackson's face. "Happy now?"

Jackson wasn't happy, not at all. His stomach sank. He *had* seen the photo as he'd flipped through the annual. In his exhaustion, he'd missed the crucial date. Shame pierced him. He hated feeling suspicion toward people he'd known his whole life, hated the way those people looked at him, with betrayal in their eyes.

He offered Gideon his hand. "Sorry about the inconvenience. I appreciate your willingness to clear things up. Thanks for your help."

Gideon didn't bother to take it.

"It's nothing personal, Gideon."

Gideon didn't answer. Years of alcohol abuse had aged him, that and the tragedies he'd endured. He looked tired, defeated. Emotion flared across his features—bitterness, disappointment, disillusionment. Then it was gone.

Expression flat, he turned his back on Jackson and returned to the bar, signaling to the bartender for another drink.

Jackson felt eyes on him again. Cyrus Lee watched him, then tipped back his drink, gulped it down, and slammed his glass on the bar top.

"Good work, Undersheriff," he said with a crooked smile that Jackson couldn't read. Without another word, he slipped from the bar stool and headed for the exit.

Jackson watched him go. He stuck his hands in his pockets, put his head down, and strode for the hallway leading to the hotel rooms. Doubt hounded him, circled and circled in his mind. Fragments of memory, snippets of thoughts, half-remembered dreams. Things hidden from him that he couldn't uncover, no matter how hard he searched.

He couldn't see the big picture. A part of him feared he never would.

44

ELI POPE

DAY THIRTY-EIGHT

The sun rose above the trees, painting the cloudless sky in shades of tangerine-orange and rose-pink.

The spectacular sunrise contrasted sharply with the dread knotting in Eli's gut. He shifted in the front passenger seat of the black Toyota Land Cruiser, hiding his unease. Beside him, Pierce drove.

Their vehicle led the convoy a mile or so behind the scouting vehicle, a Land Cruiser with a two-man team outfitted with thermal NVGs. A drone with a live camera feed zoomed ahead of the convoy to alert them of potential ambushes.

"Can you give me a sitrep?" Eli asked. "Sawyer wasn't exactly forthcoming with details."

Pierce didn't take his eyes off the road. "You'll know what you need to know when you need to know."

"The more intel I have, the better equipped I am to have your back."

"Did I ask you to have my back?"

"Is that how we're playing this?"

"That's how we're playing it, hot shot."

"What crawled up your butt and stayed for breakfast?" Dixon asked from the backseat, then guffawed at his own joke.

In the rearview mirror, Pierce glared at him. "Shut the hell up."

Dixon shut up. The vehicle fell silent, the tension palpable.

Behind him sat Dixon, Antoine, and Vaughn. Wes Vaughn, the man who'd threatened Shiloh and Lena's lives—the man Eli planned to kill today.

Anxiety sparked through him. He pushed it down. He had to stay calm and impassive, had to keep his cover. Revealing an iota of the rage burning in his chest would mean certain death.

Eli had to keep one hundred percent of his focus on the mission. Sawyer had insisted no one knew of the operation, especially not the Côté cartel, whose weapons they planned to brazenly filch.

Eli doubted that, too. Someone always knew.

They'd soon be transporting valuable cargo that criminal organizations would kill to get their hands on. This was a sweet score, worth millions.

The goods would be spread between five medium-sized U-Haul trailer trucks in case they lost one. Two of Sawyer's untrained thugs and at least one trained mercenary manned each U-Haul truck.

Four armored Land Cruisers drove in the front, rear, and middle of the convoy. The Land Cruisers featured push bumpers to shove vehicles out of the way if needed. Up to this point, the highway had remained mostly barren.

From the outside, the vehicles appeared ordinary, but the reinforced, armored frame and ballistic glass promised protection against AK-47 and AR-15 piercing rounds and explosive devices.

The operation might be a cakewalk, or the route could be crawling with bandits and roving marauders. He wasn't taking any chances. He kept his eyes peeled and his weapons close by, alert for enemies from without—and from within.

His position within Sawyer's organization was still perilous. Unlike his years as a Ranger, these brothers-in-arms would eat him alive in a heartbeat. If his cover was compromised, Pierce would take great pleasure in torturing him, then dumping what remained of his corpse in Lake Superior.

He hated to admit it, but he was rattled, unnerved. He'd rather be anywhere than here, a hundred miles from the people who mattered most.

He'd known going in that he'd have to get his hands dirty. Still, procuring high-powered weapons for hardened criminals didn't sit well. It made him antsy and bad-tempered.

Jackson and Lena were rubbing off on him. Damn them.

To steady himself, he turned the VP9 to the side and checked the ejection port. A shiny 115-grain jacketed hollow point winked back at him. The red dot at the rear of the weapon showed him the weapon was charged.

He set the pistol on the seat between his legs for easy access. He did not wear his seatbelt. His battle rifle sat in the footwell, propped against his seat. A Springfield XD-S was nestled in his boot and a fixed blade combat knife hung at his belt.

Before dawn that morning, Sawyer had offered Eli his choice of weapon from his weapons depot. Eli chose a HK417 with a 16-inch barrel, scope, night vision adapter, Harris bipod, and suppressor. Each box magazine carried twenty 7.62x51mm NATO rounds.

Half a dozen loaded magazines were tucked inside his Kevlar tactical vest along with a few M3 offensive concussion hand grenades. For this operation, he preferred the small blast radius, which was good for clearing rooms. Frag grenades had a wide twenty-five-foot blast radius, but they could only be thrown from cover.

They passed a fenced storage facility with a blue roof off to the right, scattered houses with yards bristling with junk—rusting cars, washing machines, kids' toys, a four-wheeler tipped on its side, filmed in moss and weeds.

A minute later, they passed a billboard for the Oswald Bear Ranch in Newberry. Eli saw the exit for Tahquamenon Falls, the famous 200-foot-wide waterfall stained brown from the tannins.

He recalled visiting as a child with his parents before his mother committed suicide. It had been a rare good day.

After a while, exit signs for the shipwreck museum appeared. The museum was located at Whitefish Point, where over 200 shipwrecks littered the treacherous waters, including the infamous *SS Edmund Fitzgerald.*

Dixon began humming the song memorializing the wreck from Gordon Lightfoot.

"Shut the hell up," Pierce growled.

Dixon and Antoine watched the windows. Vaughn stared straight ahead, unblinking. Minutes passed like hours, and then they were entering the city limits of Sault Ste. Marie, population of 14000, the second-most populated city in the UP and home to the Soo Locks.

Though he couldn't see the locks from his position, he imagined the big 700-foot freighters lined up to go from Lake Huron to Lake Superior and vice-versa. It was the third busiest man-made waterway after the Panama and Suez canals. Or, it was. Who knew what was happening now?

They skirted downtown, since Sault Ste. Marie was home to a National Guard Unit, the local cops and sheriff's department, and a U.S. Coast Guard Sector. Dread skittered up the notches of his spine. Danger lay in wait everywhere he looked.

They headed south to the shoreline of the St. Marys River, where they turned right onto a rural drive. Trash bags were piled on the curb along nearly every street, garbage strewn across overgrown yards and sidewalks. He caught the faint whiff of sewage. The city sewer system must have backed up into people's houses.

A minute later, they'd reached a squat brick building encircled by a chain link fence.

"Let's load up and get the hell out of here." Pierce was already out of the Land Cruiser. He looked anxious, his eyes darting everywhere at once. "Dixon and Vaughn, you're checking cargo with me. Pope and Antoine, link up with the security team on Bunson Street. Let's go!"

The first half of the operation went without a hitch. As expected, the goods were already unloaded from the container ship and sat in the vacant paper mill along the St. Marys River. There were hundreds of black-market weapons from Moldova, including Russian-made AKs, Russian AGS-17 grenade launchers, RPGs, landmines, and a plethora of ammunition, packaged neatly in crates packed with Styrofoam.

While a half-dozen mercs worked security and a four-man QRT, or Quick Reaction Team, waited a few blocks south, the rest of Sawyer's crew loaded the dually U-Hauls.

Eli kept his neck on a swivel. His blood buzzed, his skin hot and tingling, every sense on high alert. No threats presented themselves. Didn't mean they were out of the woods yet.

The sun shone bright, the heat oppressive, the air dense with humidity. The street was quiet, too quiet. It was a thick, stifling silence. No lawnmowers, few engine sounds. Blue jays twittered from nearby maple trees. He'd seen few people outside their houses, even in town.

Less than an hour later, the transmitter crackled in his ear. "This is Echo Actual," Pierce said. "Target acquired. Let's roll."

On the way out, they took side roads to avoid driving through Sault Ste. Marie and garnering unwanted attention. They rolled through intersections with dead stoplights, trash and detritus blowing across the road.

They took I-75 South then turned east along M-28, the main highway that cut across the middle of the Upper Peninsula. They passed half a dozen trucks and sedans. Few cars were moving, though several vehicles had run out of gas, abandoned on the shoulder where they'd coughed up their last fumes. Weeds sprang up around the tires, reaching as high as the fenders.

Weapon in hand, Eli scanned left to right and left again. The engines rumbled, tires slapping the pavement. The hot sun beat down through the open window, heat waves rippling the air above the asphalt.

Pierce tightened his grip on the steering wheel, his knuckles white, his profile sharp as a hatchet blade. Eli wiped the sweat from his brow, tense and wary.

The terrain was flat. Rangy meadows interspersed with rows of pine trees and clusters of dense forest. Overgrown underbrush and tall weeds choked both shoulders. There were plenty of places to hide, to wait in ambush for unsuspecting vehicles.

The radio crackled. "Echo Actual, this is Echo Two."

Eli grabbed the radio. Echo Two was the scout team. "Come in, Echo Two."

"We've got a possible FUBAR situation. Images from the drone show a large force behind cover about 300 meters ahead at a choke point. Twenty or so men. Several vehicles. Looks for all hell like a kill zone, Echo Actual."

Eli stiffened, his heart rate spiking as he scanned the terrain ahead, searching for a way out. Before they'd departed for the operation, he'd studied topographical and DNR maps that featured logging roads used for off-roading, ATVs, and snow-mobiling.

He pointed to a breach in the tree line ahead of them. "There's an access road up ahead to the right. We can take it to bypass the choke point."

Pierce grimaced like he loathed taking advice from the likes of Eli.

"We don't have a lot of options, here," Antoine said.

"Fine," Pierce said. "Do it."

"Roger that," Echo Two said. "Headed back your way."

Dixon radioed the rest of the team as Pierce swerved to the right and rumbled onto the dirt access road. Overgrown bushes scraped the sides of the Land Cruiser. The heavy-duty tires bounced and jolted over potholes the size of small swimming pools.

"You think that's them? The Côté family?" Dixon asked.

"Who else would it be?" Vaughn said.

"They don't know we're here," Pierce said. "Can't be them."

"Could be National Guard or a standard police checkpoint."

Antoine looked dubious. "Twenty armed guards? That doesn't sound like a standard checkpoint."

Eli didn't disagree. He tucked his pistol beneath his thigh and hoisted his HK417 through the open window. "Get ready to go loud."

Behind him, Antoine readied the machine gun.

No one spoke. They barely breathed. They kept their eyes peeled for potential threats, for movement in the trees, the glint of a gun barrel, or binoculars. Nothing popped out of the trees to accost them.

After five miles of bumping along the access road, they returned to the highway. The entire convoy paused as the scout team checked the road with the drone.

"Looks clear," Echo Two said.

"Stay alert," Eli said. "If that ambush was meant for us, they won't be deterred so easily."

The scout Land Cruiser retook the lead, while Eli's vehicle brought up the rear. They proceeded with caution. The convoy hadn't gone two miles before a disconcerting sound reached them over the rumble of their engines: a distant *whump-whump-whump.*

"Is that what I think it is?" Antoine asked.

Eli twisted in his seat to look behind him. From the east, two dots appeared above the tree line, larger than birds and flying straight toward them.

"What the living hell!" Pierce said.

With growing dismay, Eli recognized the Huey helicopters. The Bell UH-1 Iroquois was a utility military helicopter most known for its use in Vietnam. Men dressed in dark camo held M2 Browning .50 caliber guns pointed out the open sides of the first chopper.

The blood drained from his face. They had zero air support. No Quick Reaction Team waiting around the corner to offer reinforcements. The choppers zoomed closer. In a minute, they'd be right on top of them. Their weapons swiveled, targeting the convoy.

Antoine cursed.

"Contact!" Eli shouted.

"What the hell!" Dixon said, shocked. "They can't do this. They aren't going to shoot us with those things."

"They can and they will," Eli said.

It was happening, here on American soil. With the government crippled amid a worldwide catastrophe, criminal elements everywhere smelled blood in the water.

Whoever was the boldest, the most violent, would win. To the victor went the spoils. The entire UP, maybe the whole damn state, was up for grabs.

The Côté family wanted their weapons, and they'd do damn well anything to get them back.

The first Huey flew close enough that Eli could make out the pilot and the passenger. The chopper eased to the right as the passenger leaned out the side and aimed an RPG at the convoy. The hostile was seated sideways, legs hanging over the edge, feet on the rails, with the RPG pointed parallel to the chopper so the backblast would exit through the opposite open door.

"Incoming!" Eli shouted into his headset.

The hostile fired the rocket-propelled grenade. A second later, the RPG slammed into the lead vehicle, Echo Two's team. The armored Toyota burst into flames. Black smoke billowed from the shattered windows as glass and metal shards flew everywhere.

"Holy mother of—" Antoine shouted. His words were drowned out by the roar of engines.

Eli glanced in the rearview mirror. A glint appeared on the road behind them. Heat shimmered across the pavement, obscuring his vision. He blinked. A truck crystalized in his vision. He blinked again and two SUVs appeared behind the truck, engines gunning and approaching fast.

Four vehicles. No, five. Then six. Little black sticks poked out from the windows. Before Eli could react, the air exploded with the *rat-a-tat* of automatic gunfire.

45

ELI POPE

DAY THIRTY-EIGHT

"Contact rear!" Antoine yelled.

The former French Legionnaire flipped on the communication headsets attached to their ballistic helmets. Eli and the others did the same. The headsets allowed you to talk to the guy beside you as well as over a closed radio network but filtered sounds like gunfire over a certain decibel level.

A blue SUV outfitted with monster tires roared closer. A dark figure hung out the window and opened fire with an AK-47. Bullets slammed into the back of the Land Cruiser, peppering the windshield and back door.

The armored vehicle rattled but held. For the moment.

Eli swallowed the acid clawing up his throat. The Côté family had known they were coming. They'd planned to destroy the convoy at the choke point. Failing that, they would scorch the earth with fire until every vehicle was a burning pile of wrecked metal.

Chatter burst from Eli's headset.

"Speed up!" Vaughn yelled.

"Go, go, go!" Dixon shouted.

Pierce slammed the gas pedal. Eli jerked against his seat as the convoy accelerated to eighty, then ninety miles an hour.

In the rearview mirror, the pursuing SUV lurched closer. A burst of gunfire hit one of the U-Hauls ahead of them. It swerved dangerously and nearly ran off the road as the driver's panicked curses echoed through his headset.

Sweat ran in rivulets down Eli's spine, adrenaline icing his veins. Time slowed. Sound dimmed. He didn't hear the roaring engines, the throbbing pulse of the helos overhead, the stutter of rapid gunfire.

Shifting to his knees on the front seat, he shoved open the top hatch of the Land Cruiser. The roof had a round hatch approximately eighteen inches wide. When opened, the hatch door faced the front; from the rear, it provided some ballistic protection if someone happened to be shooting at your tail end, which someone was.

Eli stood and braced himself, pushed the HK417 against his shoulder, and released a torrent of firepower. The rounds punched holes in the grill and windshield of the pursuing SUV.

The SUV jerked, tires squealing. Cracks spiderwebbed across the reinforced glass but it didn't shatter. The shooter faltered, then managed to right himself, shooting wildly. Rounds zinged over Eli's head.

Eli fired in steady, controlled bursts. He had no qualms about eliminating bad men. They were criminals, thugs, and killers. If law enforcement or the National Guard showed up, that'd be another story. He had no intention of shooting friendlies, even if those friendlies believed he was the enemy.

More rounds zinged over Eli's head. Wind whipped in his face, his eyes smarting. Eli aimed at the shooter, zeroing in as best he could in a moving vehicle, his finger on the trigger.

Abruptly, the Toyota swerved right. Eli braced himself but too late. He careened sideways, the shot blown as his ribs struck the vehicle's frame. A blast of fiery pain radiated up his left side.

Before he could recover, a 4x4 off-road dune buggy zoomed past the blue SUV, nearly taking off its side mirror as it raced up to the Land Cruiser, attempting to flank it. Two hostiles fired through the open front and sides.

Pierce swerved hard to cut them off. Eli slammed against the opposite side of the hatch, his shots going wide. A razor wire of agony sliced his right arm from his elbow to his wrist.

He clenched his teeth, wincing, and forced his hand to flex. His whole arm throbbed. He was fairly certain it wasn't broken or fractured. At least his fingers still worked. He just needed to hold a battle rifle and squeeze the trigger.

Pierce veered back and forth, attempting to keep the 4x4 dune buggy from passing. At such high speeds, the Land Cruiser shook and bounced. The buggy clipped their right rear fender. A passenger leaned out, a bearded man wearing dark green camo, black war paint striping his face, a submachine gun aimed at Eli's head.

Eli ducked an instant before a dozen rapid-fire rounds slammed into the hatch door. A second later, Eli popped back up, leaned around the hatch, and unleashed a barrage into the bearded man. His body jittered as lead punctured his torso, then toppled from the vehicle and bounced to the asphalt.

One of the Hueys whizzed overhead. A rattle of automatic weapon fire exploded, coming from the Land Cruiser behind them. Eli whipped around, conducting a tactical reload as he moved, the half-spent magazine dropping to the seat below him, his arm throbbing as he slapped in the fresh magazine.

The second U-Haul truck had lost a back tire. Luckily, it was a dually and it kept going with the single tire on the left side. The trailers weren't loaded to capacity, so hopefully it would hold since there was no way to fix it now.

Eli shifted and fired another burst at the windshield of the blue SUV, hitting it with a dozen rounds in rapid succession. Finally, the reinforced glass splintered and caved. Several rounds punched through the windshield and slammed into the driver.

The SUV veered sharply left before spinning out of control. It flipped end over end, spun across the road, and smashed into an oak tree. A thick low-hanging branch pierced the windshield and impaled the passenger through the chest. If he wasn't dead yet, he would be soon.

"Yes!" Dixon shouted with glee.

Eli gritted his teeth and focused on the next threat. The dune buggy raced past the Land Cruiser and headed for the truck ahead of them, attempting to shoot out the tires. Eli spun, faced forward, and raked the buggy with firepower. Rounds nailed the driver and two passengers.

Driverless, the buggy lurched wildly, clipped the rear fender of the trailer, then flipped, skidded across the highway on its roof, and came to rest upside down, smoke pouring from the wrecked engine. One of the passengers had been hurled from the vehicle, thrown several feet into the overgrown grass along the shoulder. He didn't move.

Eli ejected the spent magazine and fumbled for a fresh one from the pouch at his belt. His fingers were tingling; half his hand was numb. Fear sliced through him; he shoved it down. Panic would get him killed quicker than a broken arm.

A thunderous *whomp-whomp-whomp* broke through Eli's concentration. The first helo flew in low and made another pass, coming at the convoy from the west. A deafening explosion shook the ground as one of the Hueys fired another RPG.

The lead U-Haul took the hit. Shrapnel sprayed everywhere, fire and smoke pouring from the wounded vehicle. The U-Haul came to a screeching halt in the center of the highway, half-turned so that it blocked both lanes.

The cacophony of gunfire overwhelmed his senses in a devastating display of power.

The remaining vehicles in the convoy slammed their brakes to avoid a pile-up. Eli swept his rifle in wide arcs, checking for imminent threats. Trapped in the middle of the highway like this, they were sitting ducks.

"I see movement in the truck!" Antoine shouted. "Someone's still alive in there."

Pierce kept driving.

"We've got to help them!" Dixon cried, twisting around in his seat, his face pale.

Antoine shook his head. "We can't just leave them—!"

"We sure can!" Pierce hit the gas. The Land Cruiser's push bumper struck the rear of the trailer, metal squealing in protest as Pierce shoved it aside. The Toyota's squealing tires hit the grass, angling into the ditch along the left shoulder.

Eli bit his tongue hard. American soldiers would never leave one of their own behind, even sacrificing their own lives to do so. Prison had hardened him, but some beliefs remained and went deep to his core.

He had never left a brother behind. Never.

These men weren't his brothers. They were the bad guys. The men he fought for and against were both his enemies. He was living a nightmare like nothing he'd ever experienced. He might die here, with sociopaths the only witnesses to his demise.

"Go!" he shouted.

Pierce edged the Toyota around the burning mass of the lead truck. The rest of the convoy followed. Seconds later, more gunfire exploded.

The vehicle accelerated to ninety miles per hour as they left the burning wreckage in the rearview mirror. Behind them, two motorcycles burst through the roiling clouds of smoke. The motorcycles approached rapidly, separating from the pursuing caravan still blocked by the broken U-Haul.

"More company coming!" Antoine shouted.

The second helicopter, the one armed with the M2 Browning, was a quarter-mile to the west and flying low. It began a shallow bank that would bring it back around in less than thirty seconds.

"Get that chopper!" Pierce screamed.

In the Land Cruiser behind them, Echo Three's team pushed

an M249 Squad Automatic Weapon, commonly known as a SAW, up through the hatch onto a tripod. The SAW aimed for the nearest Huey and barked as it fired 5.56mms at a sustained pace of one hundred rounds a minute at a velocity of 3000 feet a second.

The Huey veered wildly to dodge the incoming fire and surged upward. The SAW ran dry without hitting either bird, but the choppers had been put on alert. Both helicopters flew high and remained out of range, still dangerous but out of play for the moment.

There was no time to breathe a sigh of relief. The lead motorcycle hugged the shoulder, flying alongside the convoy, and drew level with the Land Cruiser. The rider raised a weapon and sprayed the right side of the vehicle.

Eli aimed, squeezed the trigger, and fired. Missed twice. Fired again, and this time nailed him.

The force of the rounds knocked the rider back and threw him off the bike. The motorcycle fell sideways, skidding into the road. The Land Cruiser behind them bounced in the air as it crushed both bike and rider beneath its wheels.

Through his headset, Echo Three cheered.

"Got 'em!" Nyx shouted.

Behind him, Dixon let out a scream. "I'm hit!"

Eli looked down through the hatch. Dixon was slumped in the backseat, clutching at his thigh, which spurted bright red blood. The motorcycle shooter had done damage after all. Several rounds had breached the door and shredded Dixon's right leg.

"Oh, hell!" Antoine muttered frantic curses. "You're okay, man. You'll be okay."

Dixon was far from okay, and Antoine knew it. Eli knew it, too. He motioned at Vaughn. "Take my place!"

Eli sank down from the hatch and squatted on the backseat beside Dixon, pulling a combat tourniquet from his IFAK, or Individual First Aid Kit, from his battle belt.

Dixon screamed in pain as Vaughn took Eli's position and fired bursts at the remaining motorcycle riding their rear end. Pierce jerked the wheel to the left. Vaughn slipped on the blood pooling across the back seat, swearing as he nearly fell into Eli.

"I don't want to die! Don't let me die!" Dixon was just a kid, acne dotted his forehead. The metallic smell of blood mixed with terror filled Eli's nostrils. Panic was catching. Of Sawyer's crew, Dixon was the one Eli hated the least.

"I'm trying. Breathe, just breathe." As swiftly as he could in a moving vehicle, Eli applied the tourniquet to Dixon's thigh above the bullet wounds, turning the wind stick hard until the pulsing blood slowed and then stopped. He secured it in place with the strap.

Dixon had stopped screaming. His skin had gone bone-white. He stared listlessly out the bullet-riddled window.

"Dixon!" Eli said. "Stay with me!"

He knelt on the back seat, Dixon's blood soaking through his pants, and used a pair of trauma shears to cut through the front of Dixon's shirt to check for other injuries. As he tilted Dixon's head to the side, his fingers felt something warm and slick. A bullet had sliced through the ballistic helmet and pierced his skull.

Antoine was busy shooting, but he kept glancing back at Dixon. "Hang on, man," he said. "You're good. Just hang on."

Dixon's lips were tinged blue. His breath was ragged. They were losing him.

"Hand me the grenades!" Vaughn yelled from the hatch. He had a Russian GP-34 under-barrel grenade launcher attached to his AK-47.

With one hand, Eli passed up the canvas bag full of 40-millimeter grenade shells. "That's all we have. Don't waste them!"

A pickup truck roared up from the rear. Vaughn loaded the grenade launcher, aimed unsteadily, and fired. The grenade smashed through the pickup's windshield, bounced into the cab, and promptly exploded. Shrapnel traveling at 3000 feet a second sprayed the occupants.

The pickup careened and spun sideways. It struck a second dune buggy coming up fast; with a screech of metal against metal, the vehicles crashed into each other. Unable to swerve in time, a third pickup truck hit them head-on and a fourth followed. Black clouds of smoke billowed as steam hissed from the jumbled wreck.

Even better luck: the four-car pileup blocked the entire highway. Tall jack pines clustered close to the road on either side. There was no way the trucks or SUVs could get past without physically moving the wreckage out of their path.

Antoine whooped in triumph.

The pile-up had earned them some time and distance, but not much. Their pursuers wouldn't give up that easily. The helos would come back, too.

They'd gotten lucky so far. That luck wouldn't hold.

"We've got to get off the highway!" Eli said.

Dixon moaned and began to seize. He projectile vomited across the back of the front seat before slumping forward, unconscious.

Antoine twisted back around. "Dixon! Is he dying?"

Eli checked his pulse. He was dead.

Eli's heart sank. He hadn't wanted Dixon to die. To stare death in the face was unnerving for any man. It was like looking into the abyss as the abyss looked back.

"He kicked the bucket?" Vaughn asked.

Eli felt lightheaded, sick to his stomach. "Yeah."

Antoine wiped the sweat from his face and cursed. He looked genuinely devastated. "Damn it! Damn it! Damn it!"

"Keep it together back there!" Pierce shouted.

Shouting burst from Eli's headset. "This is Echo Three!" Nyx said. "Our tire is blown. We're screwed!"

Eli twisted and peered through the front seats out through the windshield. Ahead of them, the U-Haul with the blown tire had veered into the oncoming lane, shaking violently. The driver was about to lose control of the truck.

Their pursuers had fallen back, slowed by the pile-up, but they were still coming. The convoy either had to slow down significantly—not an option—or ditch the U-Haul.

"Soon as they lose that tire, they're SOL," Vaughn said, sounding almost gleeful. "Those thugs will put two rounds through the back of their skulls. Not to mention commandeer the U-Haul and take off with our goodies."

"We've got three people in that truck," Antoine said.

Nyx Reyes was one of them. Maybe it made him a chauvinist, but Eli hated the thought of leaving a woman behind, mercenary or not. "If we abandon them, they die."

"Maybe they'll let us go, then." Vaughn gave a careless shrug. "An honorable sacrifice."

Eli clenched his jaw so hard his teeth nearly cracked. There wasn't an honorable cell in Vaughn's spidery body. The man was a sociopath. It took everything in Eli not to punch him in the throat.

"You think they'll turn tail and go home with half the prize?" Pierce gripped the steering wheel, his knuckles white. Tension etched his hard features. "Like hell, they will. The Côté cartel doesn't half-ass anything. They won't be happy 'til they murder every single one of us."

In prison, Eli had interacted with several low-level members of the Quebec-based criminal organization. They were vicious and vengeful, known for their scorched earth policy—cross them, and they killed you and your entire family. "He's not wrong."

"Besides, we can't lose another load," Pierce said. "We need those weapons."

"Then what do you suggest?" Vaughn asked. "I'm sure as hell not dying today."

"You're the super-soldier Sawyer loves so much," Pierce said to Eli, resentment in his voice but fear, too. "Let's see those so-called superior skills put to the test. Or are you as full of B.S. as I think you are?"

Eli wiped the blood staining his hands onto his cargo pants. He tuned out his surroundings—the corpse beside him, Vaughn's depraved smile, the army of thugs in pursuit—and forced his brain to focus, to think.

The Land Cruiser careened past a billboard on the left advertising Oswald's Bear Ranch at the next exit. Eli remembered the sign on the opposite side road on the way in. He closed his eyes, orienting himself, rubbing his bruised forearm, using the pain to sharpen his thoughts.

He opened his eyes. "Less than a mile up ahead is a storage facility. Blue roof, white buildings, fenced with concertina wire. It's a U-Haul rental center. We can get another truck and set up the SAW. With more accurate fire, we can take out those damn helos, then eliminate the hostiles one by one in a ground fight, ambushing them as they pass by."

"That's a terrible idea," Pierce said.

"You want to lose the truck and three good fighters? You're the one who answers to Sawyer. You better decide now. You've got five seconds."

Enraged, Pierce pounded the steering wheel with his massive fists. But he had little choice, and he knew it. "Fine! Radio it in."

"To the left! There it is!" Antoine yelled into his headset. "Go, go, go!"

Ahead of them, the scout vehicle turned into the entrance of Barry's Big Blue Storage. The property was fenced with chain link topped with concertina wire, with a padlocked gate.

The lead vehicle slammed through the gate without slowing. Metal scraped against metal as the gate gave way with a horrible screech and snapped off its hinges. The gate clung to the hood of the Toyota for a good twenty feet before sliding off and clattering across the cracked pavement.

The rest of the convoy followed hot on their heels. The crippled U-Haul hobbled in ahead of them, strips of rubber flapping from the tire rims.

Pierce slammed the brakes. The Land Cruiser jerked to a halt in the center of the parking lot, tires smoking. Long rows of white rectangular buildings lined with cobalt blue garage-style doors surrounded them. Across the weedy parking lot, several U-Haul trucks of various sizes were parked in front of an office building.

They had fifteen minutes tops before their pursuers caught up to them. Or less.

Eli planned to use every precious second to stay alive.

46

ELI POPE

DAY THIRTY-EIGHT

Eli exited the Land Cruiser and scanned the area, weapon up. Most of the unit's garage doors had been pried open, their contents either stolen or scattered along with trash and debris. Lurid graffiti scrawled across the cinderblock walls. The place had been raided.

Eli pointed. "The trucks are over there in the back. Switch out the cargo and get the hell out of here."

Everyone quickly disembarked the vehicles. Nyx dashed across the parking lot, reached the office, and kicked in the door. She reappeared a minute later, shaking her head. "No keys."

"I can get one started," Eli said. "I just need a few minutes."

"This isn't a spring picnic," Pierce said. "Get moving, buttercup."

At Bragg, the instructors had taught Eli a course on stealing vehicles and gas, intended for spec op teams and case agents working in foreign countries. It was disconcerting to use such skills on American soil. It was a feeling he'd have to get used to. "I can hotwire one."

"You boost cars, too?" Pierce raised his thick brows, sounding resentful rather than impressed. "Grand theft auto wasn't on your resume."

"I'm a man of many talents."

Pierce flashed him a look of pure loathing. "So Sawyer claimed."

"What's wrong with your arm?" Nyx asked. "You got nicked?"

"Just a bruise." His forearm throbbed. He held it stiffly at his side. "It's fine. I'm fine."

A dull *whump-whump-whump* reached them. In the distance, a dark speck appeared on the horizon, barely visible. One of the helos was circling, searching for their convoy.

"Maybe you hit the other helo after all," Antoine said.

Eli shook his head. "Not likely. This one is tracking us while the ground element works its way toward our position. The other helo is likely refueling or getting more RPGs. They know where we are, or they will soon. They're going to hit us again."

"Should we just leave the truck and go?" Antoine asked. "Now is our opportunity."

"Not a chance," Pierce said. "We're not leaving that valuable cargo behind. It's worth more than a hundred of you door-kickers."

"That fireworks display back there was impressive," Kade said. "The police will be coming, soon."

Nyx turned in a slow circle, watching the road, her AK-47 pressed against her shoulder, ready for action. "We can't get boxed in. We're too exposed here. I don't like it."

She had a good point. Eli gestured across the parking lot. "There's a field through those trees, about 500 meters to our three o'clock. Take the other trucks there." He turned to Antoine, Kade, Vaughn, and Nyx. "You four load the new U-Haul and fast."

Pierce shot him a hard glance. "You better know what you're doing. If you screw us over, I'll tear off your dick with my fingernails."

"Flattery will get you nowhere," Eli said.

Pierce looked like he wanted to murder him right there. Instead, he reluctantly obeyed. He wanted to live as much as anyone else, and Eli had the most battle experience.

Pierce took the rest of the mercenaries and moved the unharmed Land Cruisers and U-Hauls from the storage facility to the field, which boasted a clear field of fire and a quick exit route if needed.

Eli led the second team to the rear of the property where four midsize U-Haul trucks were parked side by side across from the office.

In modern vehicles, entry points into the fuel tanks featured anti-rollover valves to prevent fuel from leaking in a crash. The valves also acted as anti-theft systems, making most siphon systems worthless.

Of course, you could still punch a hole in the gas tank beneath the vehicle and catch the fuel in a bucket or similar container, which is exactly what the looters had done.

The smell of gasoline reached him as he knelt on the pavement and checked beneath each vehicle. The gas had been siphoned from each one. Without fuel, the trucks were worthless.

Urgency crackled through him. For a millisecond, he considered running, saving his own skin. Sawyer wasn't exactly a model citizen, but the Côté family was far worse. If the cartel got ahold of these weapons—hundreds of people, maybe thousands, would die. The Côté family would be equipped with incredible firepower, outgunning the police, the National Guard, and the Coasties.

Eli could not let that happen. Once the weapons were back in Munising, he could figure out what to do about Sawyer. If the weapons shipment was lost to the Côté family, there was no getting them back.

"What about that truck over there?" Antoine gestured at a vehicle sitting at the end of the row—a dusty navy blue Dodge pick-up, the words "Barry's Big Blue Storage" scrawled in bright yellow letters across the side door. "I think that's a diesel."

Eli could have kissed him. The fuel tank was intact since far fewer vehicles used diesel. He had a feeling that would change rapidly.

Eli grabbed a fist-sized rock and busted the side passenger

window, then unlocked and opened the door. Swiftly, he hotwired the truck, cutting and crossing wires at the bottom of the dash.

Like turning the key to the last position, he completed a circuit with the battery, sending power to the starter. Without a key, the only way to turn it off was to disconnect the battery. That wasn't a problem since they only needed to drive it once.

After a minute, the engine roared to life. The fuel gauge read just over half a tank. Eli didn't let his abject relief show. It was enough fuel to get back to Munising.

He hopped out of the truck. "What are you waiting for? Get loading! Let's go!"

Quickly, the mercenaries worked to unload the goods from the damaged U-Haul into the back of the Dodge. Ten minutes later, they were nearly finished.

The faint sound of engines rumbled in the distance.

"This is Echo Actual. We've got company!" Pierce shouted through their headsets. "They're coming in hot!"

There was no time to react. Sudden gunshots exploded. Rounds pinged the pavement. Chunks of asphalt sprayed the air.

Three meters from where Eli stood, Vaughn jittered and fell to the pavement. He let out an agonized scream.

Adrenaline surging, Eli dove behind the VR-10's armored engine block as everyone ran for cover. Antoine slid in beside him and hunkered down. Kade and Nyx took the other side.

Rounds ripped across the side of the vehicle. Windows splintered. The side panels dented inward from repeated blows.

Antoine cursed. "Holy mother of—"

"Go to the rear and watch for anyone trying to flank us!" Eli shouted at Antoine.

The former Legionnaire obeyed without question. He seized his AK and ran toward one of the storage buildings in a half-crouch as rounds whooshed over his head.

Weapon up, peering around the fender of the Land Cruiser, Eli scanned until he found the source of the onslaught. At his twelve o'clock, three hostiles hunkered between storage buildings at the end of the long, narrow corridor. They crouched on either side of the corridor, using the concrete buildings as cover as they threw down fire.

Eli made a split-second decision. "Get in!"

Taking turns covering each other, they scrambled into the Land Cruiser. Antoine took the wheel as Eli hurled himself into the passenger seat. Kade and Nyx leaped into the backseat.

"We're clear!" Nyx said.

Antoine gunned the engine. The Land Cruiser raced down the corridor, bearing down on the men firing at them. Fifty meters, then twenty-five, then ten. Rounds struck the windshield, grill, and side panels.

Teeth gritted, Eli seized two grenades from his battle pouch, tossed one back to Nyx, and yanked the pin of the other with his left hand.

The armored vehicle drew even with the hostiles. Eli shouted, "Now!"

He flung open the door and dropped a frag grenade. Nyx did the same on the other side.

The grenades bounced and rolled across the concrete. Eli and Nyx slammed their doors shut as Antoine mashed down the accelerator.

As the grenades detonated, their vehicle shot free of the corridor. Behind them, shrapnel exploded, tearing into flesh and bone with lethal force. Chunks of shrapnel punched into the back of the Toyota but didn't penetrate.

Two hostiles writhed on the ground, both gravely injured. The third staggered into the open, screaming and clutching at his belly.

As soon as they were clear of the blasts, Antoine slammed the brakes, threw the vehicle into reverse, and accelerated backward. The rear fender struck one of the hostiles at thirty miles per hour. Antoine kept going, crushing the man against the building.

Eli jerked against the dashboard as a section of the concrete wall caved in behind them. The hostile screamed, his ribs crushed, his internal organs a liquid stew.

"Echo One to Echo Three and Four," Eli said into his headset. "I'm going to drive the compound and root out any more uninvited guests. Keep your heads on a swivel."

"We'll finish tying down the truck," Kade said.

Eli dropped them off at the diesel truck, then climbed into the driver's seat and raced through the complex, searching for any sign of hostiles. The Toyota screeched from building to building, taking the corners so fast the tires screamed in protest.

Other than an empty black SUV one building over, owned by the thugs he'd just eliminated, the facility was clean. He finished the sweep and headed back toward Dixon and the others.

The thumping of rotors filled the air. One of the Hueys flew low and fast over the compound. In the distance, fresh gunfire exploded.

A voice crackled through his headset. "Echo Actual for Echo One."

"Go Echo Actual," Eli said.

"We have a hell of a lot of bad guys approaching!" Pierce shouted. "The other helo is back and just missed us with another damn RPG! We've got approximately thirty men in front of us, and we are taking fire. Our way out is blocked."

"Copy," Eli said. "We're down to four men and one casualty. I'll send Nyx to flank your opposing force. Five minutes or less."

"Don't know if we'll still be here in five!" Pierce sounded unusually rattled, his voice strained. "Hurry the hell up!"

Eli parked next to the Dodge, which the team had finished tying down, and hopped out. Kade and Nyx looked to Eli for direction, their expressions drawn, faces pale. Though they were ex-military, neither had seen combat like this. "What do we do?"

Eli pointed at Nyx. "Take the Dodge and head toward Pierce's position. Flank those jackholes before Pierce starts to cry for his mama."

Antoine glanced at something on the ground behind one of the U-Hauls. "What about Vaughn?"

Even in the stress of battle, Eli had not forgotten about Vaughn. Not for a second.

He glanced at the wounded man, relieved he was still this side of hell.

Vaughn had managed to drag himself behind one of the U-Hauls for concealment. He sagged against the rear dually tire and clutched at his bloody chest, gulping for air as he held a trauma bandage to his gunshot wound. His face was gray.

Competing agendas tore at Eli. He could not let the Canadian cartel lay claim to those weapons. At the same time, he needed Vaughn alive long enough to get answers.

"Pope?" Antoine asked, uncertain. His gaze darted between Eli and Vaughn, clearly reluctant to leave a wounded comrade. "What's the plan?"

"You go," he said. "I'll take care of Vaughn. I've got to stabilize him or he'll bleed out before we get back to base."

Antoine moved for the driver's door of the Dodge, then hesitated. "Pierce would say to leave him."

"Do I look like Pierce? I don't leave men behind. We'll be just behind you. Now go!"

Relieved, Antoine gave a tight nod. He gestured to the others, and they took off for the battle.

Gunfire popped in the distance. The afternoon sun baked the humid air. The birds had startled to stillness.

The scent of gunpowder mingled with coppery blood filled his nostrils as Eli turned to Vaughn.

"Help—help me," Vaughn rasped.

Eli couldn't help the vicious smile spreading across his face. "Oh, I'm planning on it."

47

ELI POPE

DAY THIRTY-EIGHT

Vaughn blinked up at Eli with dull eyes. "I'm...hit."

Eli crouched beside Vaughn, half-facing the wounded man, half-facing his exposed, vulnerable side. He had dragged Vaughn from the open expanse of the parking lot to the nearest storage building and tucked him between the cinder block wall and a rusted metal dumpster. It wasn't ideal but offered decent concealment and cover.

He strained his ears for approaching threats. The sustained gunfire was distant—the bulk of the fighting had moved to the highway. For the moment, they appeared to be alone.

He turned back to Vaughn. This was what he'd been waiting for. This was his moment, his chance. He wouldn't waste it.

"Don't move," Eli ordered.

Eli removed Vaughn's body armor, then with one hand, unsheathed his knife and sliced open Vaughn's shirt. He resisted the urge to slide the blade between Vaughn's ribs. The bullet had entered beneath the man's right arm, just under his armpit where the armor didn't reach. The round must have skimmed along a rib and ricocheted into his chest cavity.

Vaughn sagged against the wall, his bony shoulders hunched inward, his chin lowered as he stared down at his bloody chest in dismay. His torso was sunken, his ribs sticking out in sharp relief against his pasty flesh.

Eli gazed at him with naked revulsion.

"Don't let me die!" Vaughn cried.

"That's entirely up to you."

Vaughn sucked in a ragged breath. The wolf eating the snakes tattoo on his neck bobbed with his frantic swallows. "What the hell does that mean?"

Eli scanned the parking lot behind them, then took a moment to steady his pulse, to calm himself. Rage burned through him. He wanted to harm this man, to make him bleed and scream, to make him feel an ounce of the terror that he had inflicted upon Shiloh. He did nothing to hide his seething hatred. Stay calm, stay steady. Do what needed to be done.

Vaughn would suffer and suffer greatly.

He did not care about right or wrong, only vengeance. But this monster had to live long enough for Eli to get answers, which meant Eli had to save him before he could kill him.

He did a quick scan of the man's body as he reached for his IFAK. With Vaughn's every gurgling breath, the hole made a terrible sucking sound. Foamy pink blood rimmed the edges of the wound.

The bullet had punctured his lung. His lung would likely collapse, followed by shock, coma, and death.

"You've got a sucking chest wound."

"Then do something about it, damn it!"

Eli moved quickly. He had to keep air from going in while still letting air out. He did not have a chest seal in his first-aid kit, so he improvised with the packaging the sterile dressing had come in. He peeled open the packaging, then taped the plastic portion over the wound on three sides with medical tape, creating a makeshift valve to allow air to escape.

Vaughn's breathing eased.

Before Vaughn could get comfortable, Eli grabbed two flex cuffs from a pouch in his battle belt that Jackson had given him earlier. Behind the dumpster were two concrete cylinders about four inches wide and four feet tall, which prevented garbage trucks from accidentally caving in a wall when their hydraulic arms emptied the dumpster and set it back into place.

Eli fastened one of the cuffs around Vaughn's wrist, looped a second one through the first, leaving it open about four inches wide, and raised his arm as he pushed his knee into Vaughn's cadaverous chest.

He howled in pain as he tried to push back, gasping for air. He tried to punch Eli left-handed and landed a glancing blow. Eli absorbed it as he reached down, grabbed Vaughn's other arm, shoved the wrist into the opening, and tightened it.

Vaughn's arms hung above his head, locked around the concrete pole. There would be no surprises from his suspect.

Vaughn's eyes widened with growing horror. "What—what are you doing?"

Eli leaned back on his heels. "We're going to have a conversation, you and I. In the end, if I'm satisfied with your answers, I'll patch you up and we'll get the hell out of here. There's a med center in Newberry that might be open."

There was no way this side of hell that Wes Vaughn was getting out of here alive. Even if the bullet wounds didn't end him, Eli certainly would. But he didn't need to know that yet. Hope was a powerful drug.

Vaughn writhed, jerking at his bindings, trying in vain to escape. He was trapped like a fish on a line, the hook sunk in deep.

"You're not going anywhere. The more you exert yourself, the faster you'll bleed out."

Vaughn moaned. "What the hell are you doing?"

Eli leaned in close and spoke in a low dangerous voice. "I know you attacked the lighthouse. I know you tried to murder a thirteen-year-old girl."

"I don't know what you're talking about—"

Eli pushed his thumb into the bullet wound.

Vaughn's entire body stiffened, muscles straining as he screamed.

"You think dumping that bone-handled knife of yours in Dixon's cabin was going to deflect suspicion? It was a dumb move. Besides, she shot you. It was a graze, but she still got you, didn't she?"

"You've got the wrong man—"

Eli punched Vaughn's left thigh.

Vaughn howled.

Eli gave a menacing smile. "I saw you limping that first day. I knew it was you."

"It happened during the FEMA ambush! I swear!"

"Liar."

"I didn't do it, whatever you're accusing me of. I didn't, man. Your intel is wrong."

"My intel is spot-on."

Vaughn gasped shallow, panting breaths. Greasy sweat dripped down his forehead. Veins stood out across his pinched features. "Who the hell are you?"

"To you, I'm death."

"Pierce was right. You're a spy. You're Cross's patsy. You're a cop or a DEA agent—"

"I'm here for me, for my reasons. Think very carefully before you answer. How and what you say will determine whether you live or die."

Eli pulled a multipurpose tool from his chest rig and tugged the pliers out. He sat the tool on the ground as Vaughn eyed the tool with an expression that was a cross between consternation, dismay, and absolute terror. "What's that for?"

"You know what it's for."

"Screw you."

"You attacked the lighthouse."

"I didn't!"

"I'm not a forgiving man, nor am I a gullible one. Start singing or you will fast lose your usefulness to me."

Vaughn gave a slurred curse.

"You attacked a woman and a child and tried to kill them. Unluckily for you, they fought back."

Vaughn's eyes rolled in his skull, wild, desperate. "No, I—"

"I followed you that night after the bonfire, watched you climb in Dixon's window."

He inhaled ragged gasps. "I...It's hard to breathe..."

Eli watched him intently. He was struggling, gulping at oxygen like a beached fish. One side of his chest appeared larger than the other. The veins on his neck bulged.

"It's called a pneumothorax. Your lung is collapsing."

"Damn you!"

"Admit the truth. Then I'll help you."

Vaughn's eyes widened with stark fear. "I can't...I can't...breathe!"

"You're drowning surrounded by air. How does that feel?" Eli felt nothing but contempt.

Loathing seared Eli to his very bones. It went against every cell in his body to render medical aid to this man. "You ready to squeal like a stuck pig?"

"You'll...kill me anyway."

"You're dead for certain without me."

Vaughn weighed the odds for a fraction of a second. He was human, after all. He wanted to live. He was desperate to live. "Okay," he gasped. "Okay!"

Eli listened to the rate and distance of the gunfire for a moment, alert to footsteps, to movement, then he reached into his IFAK and pulled out a packaged 14-gauge needle.

He ripped off the packaging, placed the needle on the right side of Vaughn's chest, and jammed it into the fifth intercostal space between his ribs, even with the nipple line. There was an audible popping sound.

Vaughn heaved, sucking in air. Within moments, his color improved dramatically.

Eli taped a makeshift valve for decompression over the end of the needle. To have any chance at survival, Vaughn needed a chest tube, an IV, and a surgical team on standby. None of those options were available.

"Start talking."

Vaughn's bloodshot eyes met Eli's, resignation in his gaze. "Yeah, I tossed the knife. So what? I wasn't gonna get caught with it in case the sheriff came sniffing around. My dad gave it to me...I wasn't just going to throw it away...It was safe in Dixon's cabin."

"And you could finger him if and when the sheriff investigated."

Vaughn shrugged as if to say *obviously*.

"You tried to kill a thirteen-year-old girl."

"It didn't start that way, I swear. We were supposed to scare them, put the fear of God into them, into Jackson. Then the bi—" Vaughn caught the flash of rage in Eli's eyes and changed his mind midsentence, "—the paramedic woman, I mean. She ripped the mask off Peterson's face. Then we had to eliminate them. It all went sideways. They weren't supposed to have weapons." Vaughn coughed wetly. "It was...a job. That's it, nothing personal."

It was extremely personal to Eli Pope. He clenched his jaw, fists flexing as he forced himself not to punch the man's teeth into his esophagus.

"Why?"

"None of my business."

"Who sent you?"

Vaughn flinched. He was scared of whoever it was. He should be more scared of Eli.

Eli decided to switch tactics. "Where's your ring?"

"What ring? I don't have—"

"Maybe you killed those other women, too."

Confusion twisted his features. "What the hell! No! That wasn't me."

"You strangled them. You left those broken heart lockets as your call sign, you sick freak. Cross thinks it's you," Eli lied. He hadn't had a chance to inform Jackson about Vaughn's missing ring. "You're in his crosshairs. And now you're in mine."

"No! They caught the guy. Boone. It was Boone!"

"He had a partner."

"Not me!"

"They found your ring in one of the graves."

Eli didn't think Vaughn was capable of losing more color, but he did. His face went fish-belly white. He blinked as if bewildered. "Not...mine."

"Oh yeah? Then where is it?"

A flicker crossed behind his eyes. It was his tell. He was lying. "I don't know... I lost it."

"There's a band of white on your finger. The exact width of the ones Sawyer made custom for his top guys, his brotherhood. You've worn it for a long time, until recently."

"How the hell do you figure that?"

"The tan lines are deep. So are the markings where the band cut into the flesh."

"I lost it."

"Where did you lose it?"

"Nowhere. Around. I don't remember."

Eli leaned back. "Wrong answer."

"I told you—I don't know!"

Eli went on instinct. His gut told him there was more to this. Vaughn was a stone-cold criminal, a murderer, certainly. But it took something else to derive pleasure from torturing women and children, something rotten and twisted, a brokenness deep down in the soul.

His years in Big Army and then as a Ranger had trained him to detect nonverbal cues from the smallest tic or muscle movement, the slightest flicker of the eyes. Eight years in prison dealing with thugs, gangsters, and hardened killers had honed that skill to a razor's edge.

He wasn't certain that Vaughn was the serial killer. If he wasn't, he still knew things. There were secrets locked inside his head that Eli needed to pry out before Vaughn died.

Eli reached for the multi-tool. He flicked open the pliers.

"No, no, no!" Vaughn cried. "You don't have to do this, man!"

Eli hesitated. Jackson's voice echoed inside his head like a warning. Once he began the task of enhanced interrogation, aka torture, there was no going back.

He risked tainting any evidence he uncovered. Vaughn's confession would be worthless in a trial. He was about to commit a felony or worse, but he didn't care. He was committed to the violence required of him.

Jackson would be appalled. But Jackson was not here.

There would be no trial for this waste of oxygen, no courts, no lawyers in Armani suits civilly discussing the intricacies of esoteric laws. Civilized society was a façade that was crumbling by the second.

This was how justice would be served moving forward, how good would win.

Lena flashed through his mind. Again, he hesitated. Lena would not approve, either. He was doing this for her, for Shiloh. Maybe she would hate him for it, but he couldn't stop himself. This was the only way.

Eli let his hatred burn through him, letting his wrath fester until blood was the only thing he craved. This man had hurt Shiloh Easton. There was no pass for that in Eli's world.

For that act alone, Vaughn would die.

48

ELI POPE

DAY THIRTY-EIGHT

Eli seized Vaughn's left thumb and put the end of the pliers around it.

Vaughn squealed and tried to pull his hand away, but he was weak from blood loss and chained to the pillar. "What the hell are you doing—!"

Eli squeezed. He squeezed harder, tighter and tighter as Vaughn struggled. Vaughn heaved for oxygen that wouldn't come. His cry was a raspy squeak. His thin lips had turned blue.

"You asked me who I am. I'm not a cop, so I don't have to play by their rules."

Vaughn made a terrified gurgling sound deep in his throat.

"I can do things to you that no cop, sheriff, or DEA agent could ever dream of, the kind of things that happen to prisoners in dank caves in Afghanistan and prisons in Syria. Do you understand?"

"Stop...please..."

"I'm going to start working on the rest of your fingers. And then I'll move south." Eli gave a cold, merciless smile. "That's right. You know exactly what I'm going to do."

"You can't!" Vaughn cried in desperation. "Don't you dare!"

Eli reached down, undid Vaughn's belt, and opened the top button of his pants. "I'm your worst nightmare."

Vaughn nodded like he believed him, frantic and gasping, his mouth opening and closing like an air-starved fish. "Please! Please!"

Eli removed his hands from the man's crotch. "Talk."

Vaughn sagged against his restraints, panting. Tears ran down his concave cheeks in rivulets. "Whatever I tell you...it can't come from me...he'll kill me."

"Scout's honor," Eli said. "The ring."

"He stole it, okay! It was stolen. That's all. I've been wearing gloves to hide it because Sawyer would get pissed...I've got a sweet deal here, no reason to lose it over something so jacked-up as a dumb ring. Sawyer, he gets weird about loyalty."

Eli nodded like he understood, as if he cared. "When was it stolen?"

"A few weeks ago, after the blood-red skies, after the super-flares hit. Sawyer had moved us to the island. I don't remember the exact day. It was all crazy."

"Before or after law enforcement caught Boone and found his cabin?"

Vaughn wriggled, attempting to sit up, to take in more oxygen, but it wasn't working. Blood puddled the concrete beneath him, seeping outward in an expanding puddle. "I don't know—"

Eli grasped another finger and applied intense pressure.

"After!" Vaughn cried. "I remember hearing about it...when Sawyer heard about that kid he used to let hang around. The kid who drowned, that Boone drove off the cliff—he got pissed like I've never seen him."

"Like how?"

"Dark and furious. Dangerous. Like if you said the wrong thing, he'd shoot you in the head without a second thought. Dixon said that boy was Sawyer's kid."

"Cody. His name was Cody." Eli didn't want to think of Sawyer as a grieving father. "The ring."

"The next day I realized it was gone. I took it off that night and left it on my nightstand...then I went hunting with Dixon and

Kade. The next morning when I came back, it wasn't there...That's it. I swear it!"

Eli considered Vaughn's words, the dilation of his pupils. He appeared to be telling the truth. If the killer had lost his ring while grave-digging, he could have stolen Vaughn's to hide the evidence that pointed to him.

"Who stole it?" Eli asked.

"I don't know."

"That's a lie."

"I said I don't know!"

"You have suspicions."

Vaughn grimaced. His emaciated body quaked. He took shallow, grunting gasps. He was bleeding internally and going into shock. Eli needed him conscious and alive for a bit longer.

"Dixon said six guys have one of the special rings."

"That's right, Sawyer's brotherhood. The ones he trusts the most, the ones who have proven their loyalty."

"I know the six. Pierce, Dixon, Kade, Antoine, Cyrus, and you."

"And Sawyer. He wears his on a chain around his neck, under his clothes...like dog tags."

Eli had noticed the chain. Of course, Sawyer would wish to be included in a brotherhood without actually serving his country, without risking a hair on his head or sacrificing a thing.

Eli put his left hand around Vaughn's throat and attached the pliers to his other thumb. "Who stole your ring?"

Vaughn began hyperventilating. "Don't! You don't have to—"

Eli went to work on the thumb. Vaughn was a slow learner. The man shrieked in pain. He gritted his jaw and scrunched his eyes, arching his back, trying to lean forward though his restraints wouldn't allow it.

Eli switched gears again to keep him off balance. "Who sent you to the lighthouse?"

"No one!" Vaughn's terrified, shifty eyes gave him away. "I told you, it was me. I decided to do it alone."

"For what reason? You have no ties to them, no connection. No reason to go after them. You were sent there. Someone told you to go, someone with sway enough that you obeyed."

"No—"

"Wrong answer."

Vaughn's eyelids fluttered from the pain, the collapsed wound, the shock, the blood loss—pick a number. Eli was losing him.

Eli grasped Vaughn's jaw with his free hand. "Stay with me! Was it Sawyer? Answer me!"

His eyelids fluttered. "Yes...Sawyer."

Vaughn had told Eli what he thought Eli wanted to hear. He had a hunch. He might be wrong, with disastrous consequences. Or he could be right.

"It wasn't Sawyer," he said.

Vaughn blinked. "Sawyer gives the orders...of course, it was."

"Sawyer is many things. He doesn't kill little girls. He has no reason to hurt Lena. And he was pissed as hell when his men went missing. He didn't know."

"You don't know that."

"I do. The same person who gave you the order to attack the lighthouse is the same person who stole your ring, isn't it?"

Eli saw the truth of it in his eyes. His hunch was correct.

Vaughn's lips had turned blue. His skin was cool to the touch and clammy. His pulse weak and thready, his heart rate tachycardic at 160 beats a minute. He was in shock and would lose consciousness within a minute or two.

"Tell me the truth!"

"He told me it was from Sawyer... I had no reason to disbelieve it."

"Give me a name."

"I'm dying—"

"Give me a name!"

Urine soaked Vaughn's pants, mingling with the blood pooling on the cement. He cursed Eli in a weak, trembling voice. His teeth chattered uncontrollably, tears leaking down his gaunt face.

Eli felt no sympathy. He felt nothing but a cold dark rage that burned with unquenchable fire. He did what he needed to do until Vaughn feared him, feared what he would do next more than anything else. He was a conjurer of nightmares, the devil in the flesh.

"A name!" he demanded.

Vaughn's erratic breathing rattled from his chest. His haggard features contorted in extreme agony. He gurgled a word, barely audible.

"A name, damn it!"

Vaughn gave it to him.

This time, Eli believed him. He leaned in close and smiled at Vaughn. It was the smile of the grim reaper, filled with violence. "That was my daughter in the lighthouse."

Vaughn's pupils contracted. "I didn't...I didn't know..."

In the distance, rapid gunfire exploded. The gunfight was heating up. Eli gazed at Vaughn with revulsion. He set down the pliers and picked up his combat knife.

"You...promised..."

"If I had my way, I'd pull out your fingernails and toenails with pliers. I'd cut out your tongue and feed it back to you. Luckily for you, I'm out of time."

With great prejudice, Eli plunged the tactical knife into Vaughn's heaving chest. He twisted hard before pulling it out. He wiped the bloody blade on the man's pant leg.

Vaughn shuddered with death spasms. Eli watched, impassive, as the last light bled from Vaughn's eyes until only darkness reflected back at him.

Eli rose heavily to his feet. As he turned away, he said, "Consider that an act of mercy."

49

ELI POPE

DAY THIRTY-EIGHT

Eli raced across the field to join the battle. Machine gunfire raked the side of the Land Cruiser. Steam billowed from the engine; radiator fluid and oil leaked from a dozen impacts.

The vehicle jolted to a halt as Eli threw open the door and flung himself to the ground, searching for targets through his scope as he crab-crawled across the grass to where Antoine, Kade, and Nyx huddled behind the Dodge pick-up, where the engine block offered decent cover.

"Where's Vaughn?" Antoine shouted.

"Couldn't save him. Too far gone."

It was like dropping into a fighting hole with a nest of vipers. Any one of these mercenaries would as soon put a bullet in his back as wish him a good day.

Maybe except Nyx. And Dixon, but Dixon was dead.

If he wanted to get out of this alive, he'd have to depend on them, and they on him.

Eli peered around the side of the Dodge. The crack of rifle fire filled the air. Gun smoke swirled from the tree line fifty meters north of them, and more gunfire blasted to the south. The team hadn't managed to flank the cartel troops and link up with Pierce as planned.

He squeezed the trigger and fired several rounds at a series of muzzle flashes in the woods across the highway. His first shots went wide. Gritting his teeth in frustration, he reacquired the target and fired again. This time, a figure dropped.

His breathing slowed, his pulse steadying. He was in battle mode, focused on eliminating all threats. He pushed everything else down deep. He did not think of what he'd just learned from Vaughn or the ramifications. He couldn't afford to. A split-second of distraction was the difference between life and death.

To the southeast, Pierce and three mercenaries crouched behind their Land Cruiser, raking the trees across the road with gunfire. Flames engulfed the second Land Cruiser, black smoke billowing skyward. A mercenary slumped against the front right tire, unconscious or dead, blood smearing the side of his skull.

Several cartel members engaged in a fierce firefight with the third Land Cruiser from behind two black SUVs across the highway. Two two-man teams took turns covering each other and firing upon Sawyer's men.

Two hostiles appeared around the corner of one of the U-Haul trucks, firing submachine guns. Puffs of dirt and gravel pocked the ground not five feet from Eli's position. Antoine twisted and cut them both down with his AK, but not before one of them got off a last burst.

With a shriek of pain, Kade tumbled backward. On his back, he dropped his weapon and fumbled at his chest. Eli ducked down and checked him over. Two rounds had punched him right in the solar plexus. Luckily, he wore ceramic plates in his tactical vest. He'd have a hell of a bruise, but his internal organs were still intact.

"You're okay," Eli said over the ringing in his ears. "You're okay."

Dully, Kade nodded, his pupils dilated in shock.

"Man down!" someone yelled into Eli's headset. He didn't know who'd been hit.

Eli spotted two hostiles at his three o'clock. They unleashed a burst of suppressive fire before diving into a shallow depression across the highway, twenty meters northwest of Eli's defensive position.

"Damn, they're getting close!" Nyx cried.

The cartel pushed hard to the right. Here and there among the vehicles and the trees, armed figures popped up, running five to ten meters before dropping down behind cover. At least forty men were advancing. With each sprint, they drew closer and closer.

The cartel moved in packs like marauding hyenas. They were gaining ground faster than they could be eliminated.

Antoine looked east, scanning the trees. "Shooters on both sides of the road!" he shouted over the rat-a-tat of gunfire.

Fear scythed through Eli. They were about to get pinned down. Correction—they were about to be overrun. If Eli and his team didn't move, they wouldn't outlast the next three minutes.

At least the choppers had disappeared. Likely, they'd returned to base to refuel and reload. When those helos re-entered the fight, bringing death and destruction with them, the odds of survival would drop significantly.

The math was crystal clear. Unless something changed quickly, this was it.

Fear threatened to overwhelm him, a terror like he'd never felt. Not for himself, for Shiloh and Lena. He needed to protect them. He hadn't realized how desperately he wanted to live until this moment.

"Get those SAWs up and running!" Eli shouted into his headset.

From his position to the east, Pierce and his team had set up the two SAWs they'd borrowed from one of the U-Haul trucks; Antoine had the third. The SAWs poured 5.56 rounds onto the field. As soon as the first SAW fired the last round from its box, the second SAW opened up while the other crew reloaded.

There were other weapons in the trucks: 81mm mortars and Mark 19 belt-fed grenade launchers, but they were securely packed, and who knew where the ammo was. They'd have to figure something out before the SAWs ran dry.

Nyx did a tactical reload. "We're running low on ammo!"

"We could use one of your bright ideas, super-soldier," Pierce growled over the radio.

Eli eliminated a hostile firing from the trees across the road. He swept his muzzle back and forth. "I'm working on it!"

There were no good options, only scenarios that might buy them a few more minutes if they were lucky. *Think, damn it!* He had to think, or they were all dead.

"This is Echo Four. I'm out!" Kade said.

"Echo Three, I'm on my last magazine," Nyx said.

Ahead to Eli's right, a shallow ditch overgrown with weeds and tall grasses deepened for several hundred meters. Fifty meters beyond that, the ditch crossed behind the cartel's trucks and SUVs.

A seed of an idea sprouted in his mind. To have any chance, they needed to impede the cartel's ability to move and communicate. In the army, one of his survival instructors used to say, if you're trapped, sometimes the only way out is through.

He spoke into his headset. "This is Echo One. There's a ditch that runs diagonally behind the enemy line. Antoine and I are going to crawl to it, bringing a SAW with us. When we get in position, Kade and Nyx will dump smoke using the GP 34s. Make it thick. I want them to buy the ploy that we're going to make a head-on attack. When I give the signal, pour on the firepower like there's no tomorrow. When you do, after about thirty seconds, we're going to open up with the SAW at close range. When you hear it, have everyone head for the Land Cruisers except one of the SAW crews. Keep on them to create panic and confusion."

"I'm listening," Pierce said.

"When you hear us rip into their flank, drive across the field north of their position. The field is still covered with smoke. Almost half of their vehicles are located over there, and they're empty. When you get there, spray the engines with armor-piercing rounds. Use what grenades you have, then get the hell out of there."

This was as good an exfil as they were going to get.

"Copy that, Pope," Pierce said. "Let's do this."

Eli glanced at Antoine, hoping desperately that the mercenary had what it took. Eli had no choice—he had to trust this man with his life. Antoine's face was filmed in soot and dirt, the whites of his eyes visible, fear etching his face.

Scared didn't begin to describe it. Eli was scared, too. His terror didn't matter. They were soldiers. Fear was the thing you ran into, not away from.

"You ready?" he asked.

Antoine didn't hesitate. "Ready."

Eli pointed at the ditch ahead. "Cover me!"

"Copy that."

Rounds tore through asphalt and spit dirt. The boom of gunfire rang in his ears, thrumming in his teeth, pounding in his chest. Trepidation churned in his gut. His heart banged against his ribs, his mouth gritty and dry.

Behind him, Antoine laid down cover fire. Dropping his rifle onto its sling, Eli hefted the heavy SAW onto his back, leaped to his feet, and raced across thirty meters of open ground. Slugs punched the earth to his right.

Eli threw himself into the ditch, slammed to the ground, and rolled onto his chest into a prone firing position, the SAW digging into his stomach and chest. Rocks cut into his forearms, pain radiating up his shoulder, spreading through his ribs like fire.

The depression was slight; hopefully, it would be enough. He raised himself, shouldered the SAW, and immediately scanned for threats.

To the south, at his three o'clock, a hostile fired in his direction. Dirt puffed two meters from his position. Eli twisted, sighted the front window of the truck where the hostile was leaning out, and let several rounds fly.

His first salvo missed. His second didn't. The hostile shuddered and flopped. His shredded body hung from the window. Eli scanned north, searching for more hostiles, then laid down cover fire as Antoine scurried across open pavement and dove into the ditch.

He'd barely landed before his head popped up and he fired a burst southward at a hostile attempting to approach, using the SUVs for cover.

Eli caught the gleam of a rifle barrel peeking out from the front of a truck. Make that two hostiles. They moved like trained operators; in pairs, one covering the other, leapfrogging from vehicle to vehicle. One aimed his rifle at Antoine's protruding head.

"Get down!" he screamed.

Antoine dropped. Eli fired off a short burst over the man's prone form, nailing the first hostile with two shots to the chest and one to the head. The second hostile retreated to cover.

Antoine coughed dirt and ran a trembling hand over the top of his head. "Thanks, man. You had my back there."

"Your back? More like your skull was almost popped like a grape."

"You still have my thanks, brother."

"Don't get sappy on me."

Antoine grunted. "We're probably not getting out of here."

They kept their heads down. They had no air support, no medevac for the wounded. They were overwhelmed by superior numbers. Things were dire and they both knew it.

"The odds are not in our favor."

"I wanted to visit Rome before I croaked. See the Colosseum where the gladiators fought, you know?" Antoine's voice shook. "Damn it!"

An image of Lena flashed through Eli's mind: her smile, that sparkle in her eyes. He needed to make it back, *had* to make it back. To apologize to Lena. To tell Shiloh the truth, come what may. He had too much to do, to say, to make right.

Screw these bastards.

"Your butt is never getting to Rome," Eli said, "but we're going home. Both of us."

"Just another Sunday, right?" Antoine muttered.

Eli choked out a grim laugh. "Tell Pierce to go, and then I'm gonna rock these guys thirty seconds after that. Get ready."

Antoine nodded. "Echo Actual, we're in position."

"GO, GO, GO!"

Smoke grenades arced through the air toward the cartel line. Within seconds, thick white smoke billowed across the road. The rolling smoke swiftly covered an area of over a hundred yards. Deafening gunfire erupted as Pierce's men let loose.

In turn, the cartel increased its rate of fire. Their complete focus turned to the front element. A dozen men stepped out from behind cover as they moved in force toward Pierce's defensive position, just as Eli had hoped they would.

Eli rose up and unleashed the SAW. In this moment, he was a warrior, a death-bringer, an angel of destruction to all who stood in his way.

50

ELI POPE

DAY THIRTY-EIGHT

Eli swung toward the line of trucks and SUVs, firing the SAW. Rounds blasted the road. Chunks of asphalt exploded as bullets stitched across a dozen bodies. Shapes in the smoke jittered and dropped.

Eli and Antoine had effectively flanked the enemy. As the cartel moved toward Pierce's position, Eli and Antoine cut down as many hostiles as possible.

Gunfire from a dozen positions rained down on them. Eli and Antoine flattened themselves. Eli tasted dirt in his mouth. Grass and stones dug into his flesh.

Antoine made short, controlled bursts with his AK, covering their position while Eli reloaded the SAW. They had four more boxes of ammo. Eli switched out his box drum for a fresh one that held 200 rounds of tracers and armor-piercing bullets.

Slugs tore up the bushes behind the ditch. Supersonic rounds cracked the air mere feet over their heads. Antoine cursed a colorful litany of insults.

Eli flipped the belt into place, dropped the feed cover, and re-acquired his target, focusing on the road between Pierce's team and the cartel's position. Once more, the SAW poured 5.56 rounds onto the field, riddling the oncoming enemy line.

He shouted into his headset: "All Echo units, retreat! Get the vehicles moving now!"

Taking advantage of the confusion Eli and Antoine had created, Pierce's team pushed forward. Seconds later, two of the Land Cruisers sprinted across the smoke-covered field.

A dozen hostiles never saw the vehicles until it was too late. The lead Land Cruiser ran into two hazy shapes, cutting them down like traffic cones. Another dropped beneath the third Land Cruiser's tires and was crushed.

Gunfire flew from every direction. In their confusion and panic, the enemy hit each other with friendly fire. Between the thick smoke and gunfire from multiple directions, chaos reigned.

Rounds pinged off the beaten-up Toyotas. Though armored, they were never meant to be used like this, but it sure as hell beat running across an open field without protection. The vehicles rumbled and bounced over uneven ground, dim shapes in the hazy smoke as they reached several of the cartel's parked vehicles and opened fire, barely slowing.

"We're running low!" Antoine said.

Eli laid down a last blast of fire, delivering death with every round. The SAW ran dry. "Time to go!" He gave a half-crazed laugh. "*Si vous voulez*!"

Antoine shot him a shaky grin. "*Merci*!"

And then they were up and running along the ditch, headed back for the Toyota. They could barely see through the thick reddish haze. Antoine leapfrogged Eli, laying down cover fire, rounds impacting all around them.

They dove for cover behind the bullet-riddled Land Cruiser. On his knees behind the armored engine block, Eli did a tactical reload with his last magazine, then dared a glance over the hood. His stomach dropped. The enemy was coming at them from all sides. The other Echo teams had escaped, but it wasn't looking good for Eli and Antoine.

"I think we're trapped, brother," Antoine said.

Eli stiffened. "You hear that?"

"Hear what?" Antoine dropped his last magazine. "I'm out."

The deep growl of engines filtered through the gunfire. The noise grew louder and louder. Screaming sirens split the air.

From the east, half a dozen vehicles burst through the smoke. Several armored personnel carriers raced up to the rear of the cartel. As many patrol cars followed hot on their heels, sirens wailing and lights blazing.

Eli's legs went rubbery with relief. The National Guard had arrived, along with a bevy of law enforcement officers. This was their chance.

"Echo one, Echo one!" Nyx shouted into her headset. "Get the hell out of there!"

More gunfire rang out as the cartel turned and fired on the Guard formation. The chain guns on the M113 personnel carriers raked the cartel's vehicles.

One of the cartel's SUVs burst into a massive fireball. Flames surged thirty feet into the air. Several cartel men fell from the vehicle, screaming, engulfed in flames. The National Guard made short work of them.

Eli let himself feel the first inkling of hope. It was short-lived.

The thrum of helicopter rotors pounded the air. The Hueys headed back for another run, appearing like deadly raptors from above, searching for prey.

One of the helos hovered above a carrier and unleashed an RPG. It streaked through the air and hit the armored carrier squarely on the top where the armor was thin.

With a tremendous boom, it exploded. Fire and smoke belched skyward.

Another carrier burst into flames as multiple RPGs rained down. Explosions shook the ground. A police car burst into flames.

The cartel had professional contractors at their disposal, ex-military trained to kill and experienced in combat zones around the world. The air support with the Hueys gave them a dreadful advantage.

Eli stared in astonished horror. He had never seen anything like it this side of the Atlantic. This was a nightmare scenario from Syria or Afghanistan or Ukraine.

The guardsmen and officers appeared stunned, their reactions sluggish. They hadn't expected such a brazen display of brutality. Most of them had never experienced combat or this scale of violence.

This was a baptism by fire.

Within minutes, the surviving guardsmen and officers had retreated to cover behind the remaining carriers and patrol cars.

The rate of fire was tremendous; rounds pelted the ground, punching through metal, shattering glass, and piercing flesh and bone.

Antoine seized his arm. "We've got to go!"

They catapulted into action. Eli leaped into the Land Cruiser while Antoine sprinted to the Dodge.

Shaken, Eli watched the rapidly retreating scene in the rearview mirror. He couldn't drag his gaze away.

For a terrible instant, he saw the grim stretch of highway as it would look tomorrow—a graveyard of bodies, the ground soaked in blood as crows feasted, shards of glass and spent brass glittering in the indifferent sunlight.

He fled the carnage. Eli hunched forward in the driver's seat, eyes gritty, hands trembling as he gripped the steering wheel, his whole body throbbing.

He'd survived. They had lost five men, including Wes Vaughn. The convoy had escaped with most of the weapons, keeping them out of the hands of the savage Côté family.

And he had a name for Jackson.

Eli tried to tell himself this was a win; instead, despair knotted his stomach.

The air still tasted like death.

51

SHILOH EASTON

DAY FORTY

Forty days after the murders of her grandfather and brother, Shiloh went to Ruby Carpenter's house. She stalked past Mrs. Carpenter, entered Ruby's darkened bedroom, and dragged her up onto her feet and outside to the car by her hair.

Ruby squealed and fought her, arms windmilling weakly, but Shiloh did not care.

"I'm taking her to the lighthouse," she told Ruby's mother, who watched in dull shock, blinking against the sunlight spearing through the open doorway.

Lena sat in the driver's seat of the Tan Turd. Shiloh pushed Ruby into the back seat, ignoring her indignant cries. Before they could depart, Mrs. Carpenter threw open the passenger door and hopped inside. "Whatever is happening, you aren't leaving me behind."

When they reached the lighthouse, Lena parked and got out. "Are you hungry, Michelle? I have a couple of cans of chili I can heat up on the wood stove. And Mrs. Grady brought over some of her homemade bread."

Mrs. Carpenter hesitated, hovering near the vehicle, as if afraid to take her eyes off of her daughter. "I wouldn't want to take your food. I know folks' supplies are running low."

"I'm offering because I want to. Come on in. We've got ginseng tea and honey, too."

Mrs. Carpenter's eyes widened. Her eyes were too big for her face, her cheeks sunken. Shiloh figured she had been giving her meager meals to Ruby.

"The girls will be fine." Lena slung her arm around Mrs. Carpenter's shoulder and steered her toward the cottage.

The women left the girls alone but for Bear, who leaped and frolicked at their feet, sensing an adventure might be underway. He chuffed and nuzzled Ruby's hands while she stood limp next to the van. As if rousing herself from a deep sleep, the girl scratched behind his ears.

"Come with me," Shiloh commanded.

Ruby obeyed. She followed Shiloh meekly, her shoulders bent, head down, feet shuffling. She wore sallow, sweat-stained pajamas that hung from her body like her shoulders were coat-hangers. Shiloh caught a whiff of body odor as they walked across the meadow to the rocky cove. Sedge grass swished their shins as daisies and buttercups nodded in the breeze.

The late afternoon sun shone bright in the empty bowl of the sky, blue as a Crayola crayon. The lake stretched to the horizon. Shiloh led them to the western edge with the tide pools caught among the larger rocks and pointed to a spot of sand.

"Sit down."

Ruby slumped to the ground.

Shiloh sank down beside her. They sat for long minutes without speaking. The shadow of the lighthouse tower stretched across the ground behind them. The tide curved at their feet, wavelets fringed with white froth rolling up and wetting their feet, their bottoms. Neither girl seemed to care.

While Ruby sat staring out at nothing, Shiloh sifted through the sand, searching for her favorite beach stones—Petoskey, agate, igneous volcanic rock, and Yooperlites which glowed under black light.

They sat in her palm like glittering jewels. Cody would have wanted to paint them. He'd liked rock hunting with her; the Yooperlites had always been his favorite.

Shiloh held one out to Ruby. "It's a greenstone," she said as if Ruby didn't know, but of course, she did. She'd grown up here, too. "It's the coolest one I've found."

A glossy, jade-colored rock the size of a robin's egg, the greenstone was round and smooth, clear green with veins of lighter green running through it. Like a marble but natural, formed and polished over time by the pounding pressure of the waves.

"It's for you," she said.

Ruby's fingers closed around it.

"You think about him," Shiloh said. "He's still inside your head."

Ruby went rigid.

She didn't need to say his name. It felt wrong to speak the horror aloud in such a beautiful place. Or maybe that uncomfortable feeling was what they needed, both of them.

Shiloh picked up a piece of beach glass and closed her fist around it. "He put you in the ground. He threw you into that dark hole and sometimes you feel like you're still down there, that you can't climb out, that you never will. But you did, Ruby. You did that. You're in the sun now."

Ruby didn't answer.

"Do you remember how you gnawed the ropes with your teeth? How you made a knot with that rope and beat the trap door for hours and hours without giving up? That's how I heard you. Do you remember?"

Still, Ruby did not respond. Shiloh began to fear that she wouldn't.

"I think you've forgotten," Shiloh said. "Not here—" she pointed at her temple, "But here." She pointed at Ruby's heart.

Ruby dug her feet into the sand. The water rushed up and sucked at their toes. Ruby's toenails hadn't been trimmed in weeks and were too long.

They sat in silence. Shiloh would outwait Ruby. She was

infinitely stubborn. They watched the sand, the waves, the sinking sun setting fire to the sky, rafts of clouds tinged tangerine, scarlet, and watermelon-pink.

The man who had put that fear and devastation in Ruby's eyes was dead. It was a small comfort. There was another one out there. Shiloh could feel him like a demon stalking the shadows, a flesh-eating monster haunting her dreams.

Sometimes, when she closed her eyes, she could sense the things she could no longer remember: snippets, blurred images, flashes of sound. A steady thumping in the middle of the night. A dark shadow moving stealthily through moonlight.

Shiloh stared out at the water, listening and watching, her chest expanding, her heart, her lungs, her fingers, and her toes. Out here was the only place where she felt safe. Here and up in the lighthouse. She knew Ruby felt it, too. She must feel it.

The water darkened to indigo, the frothy tops tinged pink like icing. Gradually, the sky lost its color. Bats soared and swooped above the treetops to the west, chasing mosquitoes.

Faint ribbons of green and purple undulated across the heavens, barely visible to the human eye.

"It's still here," Ruby said finally.

"What is?"

"The aurora."

Shiloh cupped a handful of sand and let it sift between her fingers. "Lena says it's the aftereffects of the solar flares."

Beyond the faint ripples in the atmosphere, thousands of tiny pinpricks of light appeared, a billion twinkling galaxies looking down on them.

"They're still here, too," Shiloh said.

"What do you mean?"

"The stars. They're still here, the same ones that existed yesterday and a hundred years ago and a hundred years from now and tomorrow."

"So what?"

"They're still shining in all this darkness. It doesn't matter how dark the night gets. They're still here. So are we."

Ruby made a noncommittal sound in the back of her throat.

"We aren't going to be better tomorrow. But one day we're going to make it a whole hour without thinking of him or his ugly stupid face. And then two hours, and then an entire day. And that's how it starts."

"How what starts?" Ruby asked in a whisper, her voice like rustling leaves.

"Living," Shiloh said.

After a moment, Ruby slipped her hand into Shiloh's. Her fingers were thin and small and trembling. It felt good. That warmth, that softness that felt like something real.

Shiloh squeezed her hand. Ruby squeezed back.

52

JACKSON CROSS

DAY FORTY

"I've got something." Devon plopped down on Jackson's unmade bed, looked around, and scrunched up her nose in distaste. "You're living in a pigsty, you know."

Jackson shrugged. "I've been busy."

She eyed him, his disheveled clothing, the room in disarray. "I can see that."

It was 7 p.m. after yet another draining day, but Devon looked amped, her eyes bright as new pennies.

"Out with it."

"I was looking into the rehab centers like we talked about, so I visited the Great Lakes place in Marquette. They wouldn't give me access to our victims' files, but I saw something else." She pulled out a familiar blue pamphlet with yellow lettering. "They had these fliers stacked on the reception desk."

A jolt of recognition flared through him. "The same ones were at the Copper Harbor doctor's office."

"Correct. They're for Suma Pharmaceuticals, headquartered here in the UP."

Jackson played the devil's advocate. "That's not so unusual. Suma is well-known around here."

"Right, but it got me thinking. We believe our unsub travels for work, right? A pharmaceutical rep goes around to doctors' offices and promotes his company's meds."

"That would fit."

"I thought so, too. I figured he might work for Suma. Their headquarters in Manistique was closed, no surprise there, so I started knocking on doors until I found someone who could give me the name and address of a Suma employee. I was able to track down an administrator from HR. She took a little convincing, but she wanted to help once I told her about the victims. Without her bosses or legal breathing down her neck, she said she could do whatever she wanted. She had an old list of employees in a desk drawer that she'd used for a volunteer pickleball tournament to boost morale or something like that. It's just a list of names, but it's something."

Jackson looked at the list. He read it once, twice.

He blinked, then blinked again. The familiar name was still there. He'd heard it before, read it before, somewhere. He closed his eyes and wracked his brain.

He opened his eyes. "Where are the sign-in books for the doctor's office? From 2008."

Devon rifled through a box of files, then a second box. Triumphant, she yanked out the dusty blue sign-in book. "Right here."

Jackson thumbed through it, scanning the spidery signatures, page after page. There. He'd found it. He slapped the book on the desk and pointed. "Does that look like the same name?"

She peered at the tiny signature. "C.L. Jefferson."

"C.L. Jefferson is on the employee list for Suma Pharmaceuticals, and his signature is in the Copper Harbor Family Medicine sign-in book several times. The last signature is...April 2008. A month before Elice McNeely goes missing. That places C.L. Jefferson at her workplace."

Devon whistled.

The hairs rose on the back of his neck. He had that feeling, the feeling a hunter gets when he catches the scent of his prey. "That would explain how the unsub met Elice at work without being a patient or employee, and why he slipped through the cracks in the initial investigation back in 2008."

Devon's pupils were huge in the kerosene lamplight. "It's why the local vice cops didn't know her, either. She didn't get drugs from the streets but from this guy. If he worked as a pharmaceutical rep, he'd have lots of samples. They're in recovery and he lures them in with free opioids."

Jackson nodded. "What about his full name? Social security number? Any identification information?"

"Believe me, I asked. That info is part of payroll in their online database, unfortunately. The guy in charge of payroll was out of town when the CMEs hit and never made it back. However, I asked the administrator about the rehab facilities, and if they might have some employee overlap or any connections with the clinics. She said that Suma Pharmaceuticals donates a percentage of medications to drug rehabilitation facilities for a tax break. They've delivered the meds quarterly since 2004. Guess which facilities they donate to?"

"Great Lakes Recovery Centers."

"Correct. The ones in Marquette and Hancock, and Pathways Substance Abuse Center."

"That's it! The clinics are his hunting grounds, the connection between the killer and his victims." He leaned forward, his breath caught in his throat. "Do they have a record of which employee delivered the meds to the clinics?"

Devon stared at him, a fervid gleam in her eyes. "She did."

"C.L. Jefferson."

"Bingo. She said he's been in that position for fifteen years at least, maybe longer. His territory is the entire mid-Peninsula."

His heart shuddered in his chest. An intense excitement drummed through his veins. "It's circumstantial, but it all works. It fits. This could be the guy."

Devon growled in frustration. "Yeah, but we don't even have his first name, just some initials. How are we going to find him? He could be anywhere. If the internet worked, we'd have him already!"

Jackson didn't answer. He stared at the name until his vision blurred. The name Jefferson tugged at his memory, like a thread that needed pulling. It was more than the scribbled signature in the guest registry. It was something else.

He searched his brain but came up with nothing. The knowledge was floating there in the darkness, out of reach. His prey was hiding in plain sight.

There was a knock on the door. Devon and Jackson stiffened. Instinctively, Jackson drew his pistol as he moved toward the door and stood alongside it, out of range. "Identify yourself."

"It's Lori," said a muffled voice from the hallway.

Jackson checked the peephole to verify then opened the door.

Lori smiled up at him, a package in one hand and a plate of sandwiches in the other. "Sorry I'm visiting so late, but I saw the light under the door and figured you were still up. We're all burning the candle at both ends these days."

Lori thrust the package at him. "This is for your mother. Also, someone left something for you at the front desk. No one was manning the desk, so I don't know when it was left, but I thought you'd want it right away."

Jackson took the sealed envelope with his name scrawled on the front. "I do. Thank you."

The skin around Lori's eyes crinkled. "I figured you two hadn't eaten, so I took the liberty of making a couple of peanut butter and honey sandwiches. The honey is fresh from our beehives. It's delicious."

Jackson and Devon thanked her profusely. Once the door closed, Jackson set the plate of sandwiches on the desk and ripped open the envelope. For once, Devon was too amped to eat. She hovered over his shoulder, as eager to see its contents as he was.

Jackson recognized Eli's handwriting, as well as the code they once used as boys, pretending they were spies infiltrating enemy territory.

A single name. The identity of the man who'd ordered the attack on Lena and Shiloh at the lighthouse. Jackson read it again. And again. What sacrifices had Eli made to unearth that name? What risks?

He couldn't think about that now; he had a case to solve. And he was close, so close.

He stared at the name, his mind racing. The letters blurred together.

There was a connection here. A dull but growing awareness, something from his past...

And then it clicked. Like the hammer of a revolver being pulled back.

"What is it?" Devon asked.

For a moment, he raised his head and stared longingly at the unmade bed, the cool sheets already pulled back and waiting, the comfortable pillow. Though he was dead tired, he wouldn't be able to sleep, not tonight.

He headed for the door, the package tucked beneath one arm.

"Where are you going?" Devon asked. "I'll come with you—"

"There's something I need to do."

He had to verify one final thing. This last part, he needed to do himself.

Jackson needed to go home.

53

JACKSON CROSS

DAY FORTY

"Mom," Jackson said. "It's good to see you."

Dolores' whole face brightened at the sight of her son standing on her front porch. She took his arm and guided him into the house, her hand small and frail. "Come in, come in!"

Unlike the rest of the world sliding into decay and disrepair, every inch of the big house sparkled, sterile and dust-free. The sharp scent of bleach stung his nostrils.

Jackson held out the package. "I brought you something."

She looked at the bag and frowned like she half expected a cockroach to crawl out of it. "It's not peanuts, is it? You know Astrid has a very serious allergy—"

"I remember, Mom. It's raw honey from the Northwoods farm along with some sourdough starter. Lori made it special for you. She told me her starter goes back fifty years. This can last forever as long as you feed it and keep it healthy. It just needs a bit of flour and water once a week, and you can keep making bread without needing yeast indefinitely."

Dolores nodded vacantly as if she didn't really understand. "Thank her for me, dear."

He followed her into the expansive kitchen. His chest contracted as he looked her over. She'd gotten thinner in the last two weeks. Too thin. She wore a cashmere sweater though it was the middle of summer, and her linen slacks sagged from her hips.

"You need to eat to keep up your strength."

"I'm not hungry." Dolores gave him an apologetic smile. "Besides, I have to take care of your sister. She needs me, you know."

"Speaking of Astrid, where is she?"

"She's out on the back deck, watching the sunset."

"Her wheelchair is still in the living room."

"She took her cane. I don't think she should, but she insists."

"It's good for her to get some exercise and practice some independence."

Dolores clucked her tongue. "Your sister is a damaged soul, Jackson. She needs constant care and looking after. She never looks after herself, you know."

That was only because she had others to serve at her beck and call, his mother and Cyrus Lee. Horatio, too. They all enabled her helplessness. "I'm well aware."

He glanced through the plate-glass windows to the deck. His sister sat gazing out at the water, her broad back straight, her white-blonde hair burnished by the evening sun. Her cane rested against the arm of the Adirondack chair.

Dolores pulled out a chair at the table. "Sit, dear, I'll make you a sandwich."

"I'm here to help you, Mom. Come sit with me. Rest and relax. Where's dad?"

"He's in a meeting with Sheriff Underwood."

His stomach clenched. "Oh. Do you know what it's about?"

"Your father is a busy, important man. He always has somewhere to be."

His father was supposed to be retired, but Jackson didn't mention that. His mother pulled cups down from the cupboard and busied herself starting the pot boiling on the gas stove. They still had power from the generator, the fuel procured by unsavory means.

"Be careful not to run the power at night, Mom. You don't want to attract thieves and robbers."

"Oh, that's not a problem here, dear. We're completely safe."

"It is a problem, Mom. We aren't safe, that's what I've been trying to tell you. We have to be very careful from now on."

She didn't seem to hear him. Her eyes were bleary. She seemed distant, far away, her answers coming a little too slowly. Was it because her memory was going or because Horatio had overmedicated her?

He clenched his jaw in frustration. Yet another problem to deal with later.

"When can you come for dinner with the family, like it used to be? It's been so long, Jackson. You belong here." She paused in front of a cabinet with empty shelves. She stared at the shelves and blinked rapidly, confused. "Oh, where is the green tea? Your father must have forgotten to purchase more at the store when he went yesterday."

A rush of pity flowed through him. He looked into her watery blue eyes and felt a burst of affection for his mother. He loved her but did not understand her. Why she'd stayed with his stern, hard-nosed father, why she'd chosen to cloak herself with ignorance and denial.

It didn't matter what he told her, what advice he gave, how many times he warned her. If she didn't wish to believe it, she wouldn't. Wouldn't, or couldn't? He wasn't sure.

He patted the seat next to him. "Forget the tea, Mom. Come sit with me."

"Of course, dear." Dolores shuffled across the kitchen and perched on the edge of the chair next to Jackson. "Do you want some lemonade or banana bread? I could make that apple strudel that you love so much."

"I'm good, Mom. Thanks." He swallowed. "I have a few questions for you if you don't mind."

She nodded at him and smiled.

"You mentioned the name Jefferson the other day," he said carefully.

Absently, she touched her hair with a self-conscious gesture. "Did I?"

"It jogged something in my memory. You went to school with an Allison Jefferson, didn't you?"

"That was a long, long time ago."

He nodded, encouraging her. "What can you tell me about the family?"

Her eyes went distant, recalling the past. "Our families used to vacation together on Mackinac Island when we were little. Her great-grandfather built his empire in copper mining over in Copper Harbor. That's where the big money was, that and timber. Allison's family was wealthy and prestigious. Back then, the Jefferson name was known across Keweenaw County."

"You refer to her by her maiden name, not her married name."

"Well, of course. She kept her last name after she was married. It was a bit of a scandal back then. I suppose it made more sense when her husband lost the family fortune gambling on poor investments. It made it easier to leave them behind."

"I remember hearing about that."

"They lost everything, the beach house, the cars, and the big fancy yacht."

"And when was that?"

"Oh, I don't remember. Back in the late 90s, was it? It was quite the fall from grace."

His hands had gone clammy, his heart bucking in his chest. "And the son?"

"They weren't good enough for her, not the husband or the child she'd had with him. She couldn't handle being penniless, the humiliation of losing her status. She didn't just leave her husband, she left that poor boy behind, too. She got a new rich husband somewhere downstate, a whole new life, and she never looked back. I could never do that, Jackson. I would never have abandoned you three."

Her dull eyes welled with tears. He knew she was thinking of his wayward older brother, Garrett, who'd up and left one day, the prodigal son who had never returned.

"It's not right," she whispered in a tremulous voice. "It wasn't right."

He reached across the table and covered her trembling hand with his. "I know, Mom."

"I was a good mother, wasn't I? I tried. I did my best."

"Of course," he said, because it was the answer that she needed.

Dolores blinked slowly as if waking up from a dream. "Why all the questions? You could ask him yourself."

"Oh, I will. I was just figuring out a few things."

But he had already figured it out. The complex convoluted puzzle, the pieces slotting into place, one by one. The picture that formed was a terrible one, but it made sense. It worked.

And finally, he could see.

He shoved back the chair as he stood, then tucked it neatly beneath the table, as she liked it. "I've got to go, but I'll come back this weekend. I'll help you with the garden, okay? We'll build a greenhouse so you can grow food even in winter. It's important, Mom. No more flowers."

She watched him, something bereft and pleading in her eyes. He saw the loneliness then, as deep and wide as Lake Superior. "Did you get what you needed, honey? Did I help?"

Jackson leaned down and kissed her papery cheek. "More than you know."

54

JACKSON CROSS

DAY FORTY-ONE

The two-bedroom, one-bathroom house was located on a quiet street just outside of Christmas. It was a single-story cottage built in the 1950s with beige carpet, beige walls, and orangish oak wood cabinets in the kitchen and bathrooms.

The house belonged to the suspect's grandmother. Luckily for them, their unsub mooched off his grandma and hadn't paid rent in years. Since he was officially a guest and not a renter, they only needed grandma's consent, as long as she had access, which she did. Jackson had gotten keys from her for the house and the shed behind it; no warrant needed.

Underwood would find out eventually, but not today. They searched alone, a state they'd fast grown accustomed to.

There was little décor anywhere. No personal items, no torture chamber hidden in the basement, no trapdoor beneath a faded rug. No secret trove of whips or ropes anywhere in the house. There was not an iota of dust or dirt anywhere.

The house felt sinister in its plainness, its ordinariness, as if you should be able to detect a monster's lair by sight, by scent. There should be a warning, but there wasn't.

They'd been here since dawn. After searching for hours, they'd found nothing.

Disappointment laced Devon's voice. "Damn it!"

Jackson looked out through the kitchen window at the weedy backyard. Fog hung like a dense blanket over everything. A dim square appeared through the mist.

He squinted. "We still have the shed."

The dilapidated shed was shielded by a six-foot rotting wood fence. Vines snaked up the warped and rotting wooden walls. A layer of green moss filmed the roof.

They accessed the padlock with the keys they'd procured from the grandmother. Inside, black mold pocked the drywall. Tools, pipes, wires, and bric-a-brac were scattered everywhere. A lawn mower engine leaned against the stained concrete. A nauseating mix of bleach and motor oil assaulted their nostrils.

"Come on, come on," Devon muttered to herself. They were hungry and tired. Neither of them had slept since last night, pushed to the brink and past it. "Something is here. We just have to find it."

As in the house, they picked through drawers and toolboxes with gloved hands, numbering and photographing items of interest. Jackson painstakingly rifled through bags of trash and combed through storage boxes.

Nothing and more nothing.

A headache pulsed against his skull.

He bent and shone his flashlight beneath a workbench pushed against the far corner. Spider webs glittered in the flashlight beam, along with mouse droppings and tiny rodent skeletons.

His back ached, his knees popping. He started to back out. The sweeping light settled on a smooth section of oil-stained floor swept free of dust, as if something had been pulled across the floor recently.

He squished in further, held his breath.

The beam caught a glint of rusted metal. Far back beneath the workbench, tucked against the wall, sat a metal toolbox.

Kneeling, he groaned and leaned in, a spider skittering across his hand as he dragged it out. Cobwebs clung to his shirt sleeves.

Dust clogged his nostrils. Carefully, he stood and set it atop the workbench.

On closer inspection, it wasn't a toolbox but a rusted fishing tackle box. Jackson lifted the lid and peered inside where there were rows of tiny cubicles filled with various fishing lures. They were expensive things with feathers and rubbery worms and shiny hooks.

Devon set down the wrench set she'd been sorting through. Her shoulders slumped in despair. "I'm finished. We've looked everywhere."

Jackson closed the tackle box and stared at it until his eyes blurred. "We're missing something. I just don't know what it is yet. Damn it!"

"Well, it's not here."

Devon exited the shed. Jackson followed her with legs like lead. He felt heavy, so incredibly heavy.

Another dead end, another trail that led nowhere. It was exhausting, infuriating. He hated this feeling of impotence, of powerlessness, of chasing his tail after another meaningless lead.

Outside, the mist had thickened into a damp, foggy soup. Halfway between the house and the dilapidated shed, Jackson halted.

An eerie feeling rippled through him. The hairs rose on the back of his neck. His subconscious had snagged on something, something his conscious, waking mind hadn't yet noticed...Something out of place.

A disturbance in the force, as Shiloh would say.

"You got something, boss?" Devon asked.

Sometimes it wasn't what was there, but the thing that wasn't. A thing you couldn't see but could feel, that impacted the objects around it like the gravitational pull of a black hole.

"I'm not sure yet." He spun, strode back to the shed, and shoved open the creaking door. In the doorway, he shone the flashlight inside one more time: tools, boxes, trash, the lawnmower. Motes of dust swirled in the cone of light.

He closed his eyes and cataloged the items they'd scoured in the garage, the basement, and the laundry room. They'd gone through everything, missed nothing.

"What is it, boss?" Devon asked behind him.

He opened his eyes. "You see any fishing gear?"

"What?"

"He's got this tackle box full of bright shiny lures but nothing else. No fishing poles, nets, or waders. Nothing. That seem odd to you?"

"Yeah, that seems odd."

Jackson went back to the workbench. He stared at the tackle box. With gloved fingers, he felt the edges of the box. He picked it up and set it back down. Opened it and picked up one of the lures, a feathery thing with a rubber worm.

"These are all brand new, never used. Every single one of them."

"I don't fish. What does that mean?"

"Maybe nothing, I don't know. Why purchase all these lures and never use them? He's got at least forty in here."

Jackson went over the box again with his gloved fingers. Searching, feeling his way toward the thing he needed. He pressed the ridges beneath the lid.

Something clicked.

Jackson removed the false bottom. Beneath the false bottom, something glinted in the shadowy light.

"Devon," Jackson said.

She came up beside him. He could feel the stiffness in her shoulders, the air fairly vibrating with tension. She looked over his shoulder.

Each storage cube held a nest of glittering gold necklaces, their thin, elegant strands twisted together. Attached to each one was a gold half-heart locket.

"Hair," he said in a choked voice. "Is that hair?"

Gingerly, Devon picked up a locket, opened it, and revealed a lock of glossy black hair nestled inside.

His pulse roared in his ears. It felt like being struck in the chest with a sledgehammer. They had searched for this, hunted for it.

At last, they'd found the monster they sought.

Jackson felt himself sway. His mind flashed back eight years to a beautiful, broken girl lying dead in her bed, her long dark hair splayed across the pillow, the necklace glinting, the broken-heart locket that would come to haunt his nightmares.

"They're the same," Devon said.

"It's the other half, the missing half of each broken heart. These are the left-hand pieces of a pair; the right-hand pieces were buried with his victims. These are his trophies."

Devon cursed softly, almost reverently. "It's him. We've got him."

The name was like barbed wire on his tongue. "Cyrus Lee Jefferson."

55

JACKSON CROSS

DAY FORTY-ONE

Jackson thought he'd prepared himself for this, bracing himself like a boxer prepares himself for a punch, for that blow of white-hot pain. He hadn't. Nothing could prepare a person for this.

The truth hadn't been quite real until this moment.

Devon took several photographs with her phone, then pointed. "These are new. They still have the tags from the Eagle River gift shop. He has enough for four more victims."

Jackson shuddered as if a ghost had passed over his grave.

Cyrus Lee Jefferson had stepped foot in his home a hundred times. He'd ingratiated himself with Jackson's father, had dinner with Jackson's family, had kissed Jackson's mother on her wrinkled cheeks, had hovered over Astrid, dutifully serving her every wish and command for years...

He took an unsteady step and sagged against the wall between the weed whacker and a snow shovel hung on hooks. His breath was glass in his throat. "How—how could I not have seen it?"

Devon gave him a concerned look. "You should sit down."

He waved her away. "I'm fine."

"You're not fine."

"It was all there, Devon. I hadn't heard the name Jefferson in years, in decades, except for one time. When I saw the signature in the guest registry, I knew I'd heard that name before, but I couldn't place it. Not until Eli sent the note with his name in code. Then it was like everything just clicked. It was my mother. In passing, she'd called Cyrus a Jefferson.

"His legal name is Cyrus Lee Jefferson. But in Munising, we knew him as Cyrus Lee, his father's last name. We were little kids when all that happened and his mother left. His father used the name Lee, and Jefferson was never mentioned again, as if it was a humiliating secret, and they wanted to bury any memory of her. But when he went off to college and got a job, he used his legal name, of course.

"He must have hated his mother for leaving him, but the family legacy of wealth and power was passed down through her, not his father. He would've gone to Copper Harbor often as a boy before his mother abdicated herself from his life. It makes sense that he would return to a place of familiarity when he took his first victim." He shook his head in despair. "It was there but I didn't see it."

"He's an organized killer, smart and cunning. They blend in. They're chameleons. It's what they do."

"He killed Lily. He could've killed Astrid. Hell, he could've killed Lena, too." He struggled to get enough oxygen. "I missed it—"

Devon's eyes burned with intensity. "Astrid is alive. Lena and Shiloh are okay. He hasn't had a chance to kill again. We're going to take him down before he gets that chance. We found him, and he doesn't know it yet. We have the advantage. We're going to catch him, boss."

He took steadying breaths until his legs could hold him again. "We can't tell anyone, not even Underwood, especially not Underwood. There's a mole in the Sheriff's Office. If Cyrus finds out we're onto him, he'll disappear forever."

"Where is he now?"

"According to Eli's last check-in, he's on the island. He's been ingratiating himself with Sawyer. With Boone gone, he's felt exposed and vulnerable, so he enmeshed himself deeper within Sawyer's inner circle, for protection. He's a survivor if nothing else."

"Like a cockroach," Devon said.

Jackson nodded. Steeling himself, he exited the shed and moved through the overgrown grass. Dimly, he heard Devon on the radio behind him, talking to Moreno.

He felt lightheaded. There was a dull buzzing in his ears.

When he reached the front yard, he turned and looked down the street, empty and silent. No one was out mowing lawns or walking dogs, no children running through sprinklers or riding their bikes. No neighbors chatting, no laughter.

It was midmorning but felt like dusk, the sky low and heavy with dense clouds. The tops of the trees had disappeared. Ribbons of fog snaked between the trunks, slithering along the street, between the houses, swallowing vehicles as it drifted closer, simultaneously beautiful and sinister.

Moreno's truck barreled into the driveway. He hopped from the vehicle, out of breath, his chest heaving, an alarmed look on his face. "They came to his house and there's blood everywhere—"

Jackson shook off the horror threatening to paralyze him. He put a hand on Moreno's shoulder, forcing himself to focus on the here and now. "Breathe, Moreno. Slow down for a second. What happened?"

Moreno was trembling, his hands curling and uncurling into fists. "Hasting. They attacked Hasting."

"Who did?" Devon asked.

"I don't know! He's barely conscious. He's in bad shape."

"We need Lena," Devon said. "I'll get her."

"An ambulance, too," Moreno said. "I radioed Alexis. She's trying to track it down."

Jackson was already moving toward the truck parked in the driveway. "Take the truck, Devon. I'll ride with Moreno."

Panic laced Moreno's voice. "We're running out of time."

Jackson felt that truth slice down deep to the bone.

56

LENA EASTON

DAY FORTY-ONE

Lena stepped through Deputy Randy Hasting's front door and took in the scene with wide eyes. "What happened?"

Hasting's home was a small brick ranch located four miles northwest of Munising, just past Christmas. Devon had picked her up from the lighthouse, along with Shiloh and Bear since she refused to leave them alone.

The front door had been bashed in and hung off its hinges. Inside, broken furniture littered the living room. The glass coffee table had been shattered. Shards of glass winked in the lantern light. Blood splattered the blue and white plaid sofa.

Hasting lay sprawled on his back between the sofa and the shattered coffee table. Jackson and Moreno stood in the living room near Hasting's crumpled body.

"Take Bear to the kitchen," Lena instructed Shiloh.

Jackson pulled a pack of Twizzlers out of his pocket and held them out to Shiloh. "Be careful not to contaminate the crime scene."

Shiloh obeyed without complaint, pulling Bear close to keep him clear of the destroyed living room and snatching the Twizzlers as she stalked past.

"Can you help him?" Moreno's eyes were bloodshot, his skin gray. He looked sick with worry.

"I'll do my best," Lena said. "But you need to get out of my way."

Moreno moved aside. Lena's pulse quickened as she knelt next to Hasting and set down her med kit. She'd gained access to an advanced kit and other supplies via the hospital, though she hadn't transferred her paramedic license. Without the internet, it was a moot point anyway.

She pulled on a pair of nitrile exam gloves and conducted an assessment, asking Hasting basic questions as she worked to ascertain his mental state and check for potential injuries.

His face was bloody and swollen. His lips were split, and ugly purple bruises swelled along his jaw and the side of his temple. Blood crusted his hair and the carpet fibers beneath him.

Lena used a pair of trauma shears from her med kit to cut off his shirt and pants. His ribs were misshapen; black and blue welts marred his flesh.

He'd been beaten to within an inch of his life.

By some miracle, he was still breathing, though barely conscious.

As the officers watched in grave silence, Lena took his vitals—blood pressure, pulse, oxygen levels, respiration rate.

"Don't move," Lena said, though she doubted he could hear her. Quickly, she got a needle into his vein and set up an IV bag of saline fluid, hanging it above Hasting's head on the back of the sofa. "He's tachycardic and his blood pressure is sky high. Devon, help me stabilize his C-spine. Hold his head in this position from behind, just like that. Don't let him move his head, whatever you do."

Devon sprang into action and did as Lena instructed. "Got it."

"Will he be okay?" Moreno repeated.

"I can't answer that right now. I'm trying to stabilize his vitals and keep him from going into shock. He has multiple contusions, probably two or three broken ribs on his right side, and a possible fracture to the left side of his skull. Where's the ambulance?"

"We're working on it," Devon said. "I got ahold of Alexis via the radio. She's working the station tonight. The only ambulance is out of our limited range. Reese went to hunt it down."

Apprehension lanced Lena's chest. "We can't move him without a backboard. It's too dangerous. We need that ambulance."

"Understood," Devon replied, her expression tense.

Hasting groaned. His eyelids fluttered open. He stared up at the ceiling. One of his pupils was not reactive to light. That wasn't a good sign.

"What the hell happened?" Jackson asked Hasting. "Tell us who did this to you."

"Don't strain him," Lena warned.

"No...I want to answer," Hasting said weakly. The IV fluids had bought him a few minutes of lucidity. The cost would be high.

"Who?" Jackson asked again.

"Sawyer."

Jackson raised his brows, startled. "Sawyer came here?"

"Not him...He sent his goons. Pierce and two other guys, mercenaries with Russian accents ... scary as hell. They beat the living crap out of me. The last thing I remember is getting hit in the head with something hard."

"What did he want?" Moreno asked. "To send a message? To let us know that he controls this town, and he can do whatever the hell he wants?"

"Something...like that."

"Sawyer already thinks he has control. He doesn't need to send a message." Something changed in Jackson's voice. "Why would Pierce come here, to your home?"

Hasting sucked in shallow breaths. The room was quiet. Two lanterns on the floor cast eerie shadows over the room, across each of their faces, deepening the purple circles beneath Hasting's eyes, his flesh pale between the ugly bruises.

Lena cleaned the lacerations on his face with sterile water, then daubed on antibiotic cream. She glanced across the room at Jackson. His shoulders were stiff. He stared at something on the wall, his brows lowered, eyes narrowed, with a muscle ticking in his jaw. He was thinking through a problem, figuring out something.

He turned to Hasting. "There's a shiny new yellow Hummer in your driveway, Hasting, yet you drive a beat-up 80s Chevy pickup to work. Two new jet skis in the garage. When Devon and I cleared your house upon arrival, we found a gun safe in your closet, including a box for an expensive Night force sniper scope. That's three grand right there. Kind of pricey for a sheriff's deputy."

"What are you saying?" Devon said.

"I'm asking questions I don't have the answers to."

"No," Moreno said in disbelief. "You're wrong. You've got to be wrong."

Hasting closed his swollen eyes. He lay still as Lena wrapped his head in white gauze.

Moreno loomed over them. "Tell me you have an explanation. Tell me it's not what it looks like."

"Sawyer has a law enforcement officer on his payroll," Jackson said. "He claimed the officer gave him information in exchange for drugs and money. Are you going to tell us you won the lottery? Inherited a mint from your recently passed grandma and forgot to tell us?"

Hasting's nostrils flared. "Nothing, you'll find nothing." His voice cracked, his bloodshot eyes shifting from Jackson to Moreno to a spot on the living room wall behind them.

Lena followed his gaze. A faint outline revealed the spot where a picture frame had hung for many years. The frame had fallen or been knocked to the carpet. Cracked glass spiderwebbed across a photo of a happy family. A younger, thinner Hasting grinned at the camera, his arm around a prettily smiling wife and two little girls.

Jackson had told her about the messy divorce five years ago, the wife taking the kids to Wyoming with a new job and a new surgeon husband.

"We deserve the truth," Moreno said. "Are you really going to spin lies on your deathbed? To us?"

Hasting's tortured gaze flicked to Lena. "Am I dying?"

She didn't want to lie to him. She tried to tell the truth, even when it hurt. He might be a dirty cop, but he was still her patient. She had a responsibility to him, to her role as a paramedic. "I don't have a crystal ball, Randy. I believe you have a depressed skull fracture or possibly a subdural or epidural hematoma. I won't know for sure until we get a CT scan, which I can't do here. Swelling of the brain cuts off access to blood by squeezing shut your blood vessels. You could be hemorrhaging inside your brain. The pressure inside your skull is increasing. You need Osmotic or Loop diuretics and possible surgery to ease the pressure, but I don't have mannitol or any of those drugs and I can't conduct surgery."

A shadow crossed his ravaged face. "Ask me your questions."

"It's true, then," Moreno said.

"Yes," he spat.

The single word echoed in the stillness of the room. Moreno and Devon stared at him, horrified. Jackson looked sick. Lena's chest contracted with pity. She understood their anger mixed with grief. This man, their friend, their peer, had betrayed them and the badge. He was also dying.

"Why?" Jackson whispered.

"How could we have been this stupid?" Moreno's mouth thinned in disgust. "The cop I knew wanted to protect people, to keep his community safe. Once upon a time, you worked hard and had our backs. What the hell happened to you?"

Hasting sucked in a pained breath. "It didn't start that way, I swear. I never meant to hurt anyone. Seven years ago, I met a girl in a bar one night, right after the guys had left. We had a few beers. She was gorgeous and clever, and we hit it off. She thought I was funny and she was interested in me. I thought she was a cop groupie, you know the type. We went back to her apartment before I went home. After that, we met at least once a week. I knew it was wrong but I couldn't stop myself."

He closed his eyes. "After a month, she got me to try my first line of coke. It was stupid. I was stupid. I kept telling myself one more time, but it was addictive. I...I was addicted. One day, she answered the door, but she wasn't alone. As soon as I entered, there was a gun to my head. Two of Sawyer's thugs handcuffed me and she said, 'Nothing personal, just business,' and then walked out. I never saw her again. They spent an hour showing me tapes. She'd recorded me and her, and the coke. They gave me a choice. Work for Sawyer or go to prison and lose my family. It wasn't a choice."

"There's always a choice," Jackson said.

Hasting didn't act as if he'd heard him. "Sawyer wanted information, a little here and there. An inside scoop on cases, investigations, and anything I heard about the DEA. Money came with it, money for a private school, vacations, and an anniversary ring. I tried to quit, tried to say I was out for good, but he took me for a ride on his yacht. He nearly killed me, would've put a bullet in my skull and thrown me overboard without a second thought. My family...they never would've found my body. I told myself I did it for them."

Hasting made a bitter sound in the back of his throat. "The joke was on me. I lost my family anyway."

Moreno's hands balled into fists. "And then what? What else did you do? Did you tell Sawyer's crew about the FEMA supply drop? You did, didn't you?"

Hasting's breathing became shallow and rapid. His heart rate skyrocketed, his skin going clammy.

"Careful," Lena said. "He's on the verge of going into shock."

Jackson took a step closer to Hasting. He stared down at the injured man like he was a bug on his kitchen floor. Lena had never witnessed such coldness in his eyes. When he spoke, his voice was flat, devoid of emotion. "You're the one. You're the snitch who told Sawyer's goons where Lena and Shiloh were staying. That's how they knew about the lighthouse."

57

LENA EASTON

DAY FORTY-ONE

The words sank in slowly and then all at once. Lena rocked back on her heels, stunned. "You? It was you?"

Hasting blinked rapidly as if staving off tears. He had the decency to look ashamed. "Miss Easton, I'm so sorry. I didn't know...I truly didn't know what they would do with that information. I had no idea. Once I found out what happened, that they'd attacked you...I swore I wouldn't help him again. I couldn't live with myself."

Lena's hands trembled as she dabbed the blood leaking from a nasty cut on Hasting's right side between his ribs. Flashes of memory seared her brain—the masked man standing in her kitchen, the nerve-shredding fear, her finger squeezing the trigger.

"But you did help him again," Jackson said.

"When Pierce came, I told him to leave, to get the hell out, that I wouldn't be a part of it anymore. He threatened to out me. I said I didn't care anymore. He threatened to kill me. I'm tired, Jackson. I'm tired of lying, of hiding it, of being the kind of person I'm ashamed to show my kids. I'll never see them again, you know that? How's someone from California gonna get here with this madness going down? I should never have let them go. I shouldn't have been the kind of man that Janet needed to leave."

"Pierce came for a reason," Jackson said evenly. "Help us, Hasting. Make it right."

Hasting's features looked caved in like he was crumpling in on himself. "Pierce wanted to know about Eli Pope."

Lena stopped breathing. "What?"

"Pierce thought that Pope was your informant, Jackson, one of your assets spying on Sawyer. He wanted proof, evidence to take back to Sawyer."

"What did you tell him?"

"I didn't know. I couldn't tell him one way or the other. He finally believed me...but he knew you'd have a file on it. I'm sorry, Jackson. I was delirious, barely conscious. He promised the pain would stop. I wasn't in my right mind."

Fear iced Lena's veins. "What's going on? Is Eli in danger?"

"What did you do?" Jackson asked, razor blades in his voice.

"Pierce forced me to tell him where you were staying, Jackson, at the Northwoods Inn. I...I gave him your room number...I'm sorry—"

Before anyone could respond, Hasting vomited across his chest. He let out a tortured moan that made the hairs on the back of Lena's neck stand on end.

Hasting vomited several times in rapid succession. He convulsed, and his body pitched violently.

"Keep hold of him, Devon!" Lena pushed aside all emotion. It didn't matter how she felt; her patient was dying and she would do everything in her power to save him.

"I can't keep a grip on him!" Devon cried.

Lena made a vain attempt to turn him on his side and maintain his position, but it was no use. It was impossible to keep a good C spine. His arms and legs stiffened, his head and neck arcing backward at a horrible angle. He threw up again. Chunks of vomit spewed across Lena's shirt. His eyes rolled back in his head as he lost consciousness.

She ran through the options in her head. She could do an intubation. She had basic drugs for pain, morphine and midazolam, but not the drugs needed to lower ICP, or increased intracranial pressure. "Without an airlift to a trauma center and a surgical team he won't make it."

"I called Alexis again," Moreno said. "She's out of range. There's no ambulance."

"Keep him alive as long as you can," Jackson said.

Wearily, she rubbed her forehead with the back of her arm. "There's nothing more I can do. He needs a surgeon, stat."

Jackson reached for his radio, stepped into the hallway leading to the bedrooms, and made a call.

Hasting's breath came in labored gasps. He was losing color fast. Lena leaned over him, checking his thready pulse, adjusting the IV bag. He was experiencing Cheyne-Stokes respirations, an abnormal breathing pattern, which was a symptom of end-stage head injuries where the pressure was so great, it physically compressed the brain.

The end was close.

Jackson returned to the living room and clipped his radio to his belt. His face was pale.

"What happened, boss?" Devon asked.

Before he could answer, a seizure gripped Hasting and shook him like a rag doll. His body shuddered. Red-tinged saliva foamed at the corners of his mouth and his eyes rolled into the back of his head. Then he stopped breathing.

For a moment, she considered intubation, attempting to run a full-on code, but with no hope of transport, it was futile.

Everyone stood, silent and stricken, watching helplessly.

Two minutes later, he was dead.

"Is he gone?" Devon asked.

Lena checked for a pulse. "He's gone."

Moreno cursed. Devon stood but didn't move, frozen in place above Hasting's body, her hands balled into fists at her sides.

Lena knelt over Hasting for a moment, her head bowed. She blinked slowly as if coming back to herself, making peace with the deceased patient she hadn't been able to save. He was past this life and its trials; his misdeeds would be buried with him.

She closed his eyelids with her fingers. With methodical movements, she stripped off her bloody gloves and cleaned the vomit from her shirt as best she could. No one spoke as she retrieved the unused antiseptic and gauze and repacked her med kit.

She said, "Where is Eli?"

"I can't tell you—"

Lena rose to her feet. Anger and anguish warred inside her, yet she held her shoulders straight, her chin up, as she faced Jackson with a dignity that belied that terrible bone-deep fear. "Tell me that you didn't put Eli undercover, that he's not on that island right now, surrounded by enemies."

Jackson stiffened. He didn't answer, but he didn't need to. It didn't matter how many lifetimes passed, she could read him like a book.

"You sent him into a nest of vipers."

"I sent him to find Lily's killer," Jackson said, "to catch a serial killer. He felt it was worth the risk. He went in with eyes open, Lena. He knew what he was doing."

Lena's insides felt like broken glass. She couldn't breathe properly, couldn't think straight. Her heart hammered in her chest. She needed to check her blood sugar; she was lightheaded with fear.

Never had she worried for Eli the way she did now. Not during those eight years in prison. Not during the trial. Not the night she'd known for certain that the entire town, the county even, had turned against him.

Jackson reached toward her. "Sawyer likes him. It's possible—"

Enraged, she shook him off. "Sawyer is a predator. He will eliminate any threat to his kingdom, real or perceived. Don't lie to yourself, Jackson. And don't you dare placate me."

Jackson stared back at her. After a moment, he blinked. "You're right. I called Kepford and had him check my room. I hid my files in the vent. Pierce found them—they're gone. Eli's cover has been blown. When they find out, they'll kill him. Sawyer will kill him."

Lena made a sound like a wounded animal. She took a step toward Jackson and jabbed her finger against his chest. "You should have protected him. He's there for you!"

Something shattered in Jackson's expression. "I know."

She saw her pain, fear, and dread reflected back at her. Jackson was worried for Eli, too. But Jackson was an idealist. He would risk everything in pursuit of the truth, of his version of justice, even himself, even his friends.

"You put him in there," Lena said. "You have to get him out. You owe him!" Tears threatened at the corners of her eyes, but she refused to cry. "You owe him."

Before Jackson could answer, Shiloh appeared in the doorway between the kitchen and living room. Bear leaned against her side, the Newfoundland huge next to the tiny girl. She buried one hand in the thick fur of his neck. Her other hand curled into a fist at her side.

She wore her favorite oversized Star Wars T-shirt paired with a ragged pair of cut-off jean shorts, her raven-black hair pulled back in several braids. Scratches and mosquito bites covered her scrawny legs. Lena's throat constricted. She looked so young, young and vulnerable.

Shiloh's gaze flicked to Jackson. "You're going to save him."

"Shiloh—"

She raised her small chin. Her coal-black eyes flashed with fierceness. In that moment, she looked so much like Lily it made Lena's heart ache. "Promise me."

"I promise," Jackson said.

58

JACKSON CROSS

DAY FORTY-ONE

Jackson stood in the shadowed kitchen and drank the last cans of Hasting's lukewarm beer with Devon and Moreno. The scent of blood and vomit wafted through the cramped house.

He tried to put Hasting out of his mind. He wanted to hate him, but there was no hate left in him, at least not for the corrupt deputy. No pity or grief, either. Hasting had paid for his sins with his life.

The walls were closing in, crushing him; his lungs couldn't pull in enough oxygen. He was responsible for this. He was responsible for Eli. Jackson would try to send a signal to Eli via the blue light —get the hell out—but he had the sinking sensation that it was too late.

He feared he'd made Shiloh an impossible promise. He'd betrayed his best friend once; he could not, would not betray him again, even if it killed him.

Moreno rubbed his temples. He looked pale and shaken. "I know what we did to Eli Pope. We are all culpable for jumping to conclusions, for proclaiming him guilty, for corrupting justice. He served his country, then we turned on him. Now you're telling me he's willingly gone into the monster's lair to help us catch a killer. Please tell me at least that it worked."

"It worked," Jackson told Moreno how they'd found Cyrus Lee Jefferson. With the mole uncovered, they needed to bring in officers they trusted. Moreno was one of the good guys. "Cyrus Lee is a killer. And he's on that island with Eli."

Moreno cursed loudly. "Eli will never make it off that island, not unless it's in a body bag. He's probably already dead."

"There's a method to Sawyer's madness. He'll see it as a personal betrayal. And his vengeance will be personal. We have a little time. Not much, but a little."

"Then we better use it wisely," Devon said.

Though they were alone in the house, he lowered his voice. Lena had taken Bear and Shiloh outside to the rusted swing set in the backyard. "I'm going in. I can't ask you to go with me. I don't want you to. I know the risks. I know the odds. I owe it to Eli, whatever happens. I have to do this."

Moreno shook his head. "Sawyer has that island like a fortress. He has sentries, machine guns, a hundred trained men, or more. He's impenetrable. We don't have the weapons or backup. They'll kill us before our boat gets within a hundred meters of the dock—"

"You're not wrong." The dread inside him took shape, with wings and fangs and claws. His mind spun, running a million miles a minute, sifting through possibilities, searching for an option that didn't end in certain death for himself, for his men, or Eli.

"Tell me there's a chance, Jackson," Moreno said. "Tell me we can stage a rescue mission without getting everyone killed. Lena is right. We do owe it to him. All of us."

Jackson looked out Hasting's front window. An insane idea began to form in the back of his mind. The very insanity of it meant it might possibly work. "I know Sawyer. He's predictable if nothing else. We may have a small window of opportunity to save

Eli, and if we're incredibly lucky, to get Cyrus Lee, too. It's a shot in the dark."

"Tell me you have a plan," Moreno said.

"Of course, I have a plan."

"A good plan?"

"I didn't say that."

"But a plan, at least?"

"Definitely."

Devon stared at him. "You're making it up as you go."

He gave a grim shrug. "Is there any other way?"

Precious seconds were slipping by. He was running out of time. The very air felt dense, wrong somehow, the universe holding its breath as everything converged at once, coming to a crucial, pivotal point.

Jackson headed for the door. "Devon, take Lena and the kid home, then you and Moreno meet me at the Northwoods Inn. Moreno, call the homicide in to Alexis. She'll get a tech guy out here and the ME to take care of Hasting. Then gather anyone else you think might be as crazy as we are. Keep Underwood out of it."

"Where are you going?" Devon called after him.

But the screen door had already slammed shut behind him.

59

ELI POPE

DAY FORTY-ONE

The sky darkened like a stain.

A wall of fog rolled in from the north. Electrons sizzled in the air. The hairs on Eli's forearms rose as he watched the gray waves pounding the bluff far below him.

He stood on the southernmost point, facing the mainland, the rest of Grand Island and the compound behind him. A German Shepherd barked incessantly. A brittle gust of wind raked his face. The cold leaked through his skin, a bone-deep chill he couldn't shake.

Eli flexed his fists. Every instinct screamed at him to leave now. To flee this cursed, claustrophobic island while he still could. He did not move. His legs were made of lead.

He had promised himself that he would abandon Sawyer and Grand Island as soon as he returned from the operation two days ago and yet, he hadn't.

Sawyer still had the black-market weapons. And Cyrus Lee was a free man, living and breathing.

Eli had done enough, hadn't he? He had narrowed down the suspect list to a select few, then Vaughn had given him the name of the individual who'd ordered the lighthouse attack behind Sawyer's back. And he'd passed that information on to Jackson.

He was finished, his mission complete.

Or was he? Could he truly walk away and let Jackson have his version of justice? An arrest, handcuffs, and then what?

Eli didn't know for certain whether Cyrus had killed those girls, but he did know that Cyrus had ordered the attack on Lena and Shiloh. For that, he longed to wrap his hands around Cyrus's throat and watch with great pleasure as the life receded from his eyes.

He wanted to kill Cyrus Lee himself.

But as soon as they'd returned to the island, he'd found Sawyer and Cyrus Lee already gone. Apparently, Cyrus had a hidden stash of pharmaceuticals and had taken Sawyer to retrieve it. They were slated to return tonight.

He hesitated, torn. Lena flitted through his mind: her soft smile and those warm intelligent eyes, the way she squared her shoulders in that gentle but insistent way of hers. And Shiloh, his daughter.

A sudden, sharp understanding knifed through him. He could not have both. He could not love his daughter like she deserved and feed on vengeance, allow it to consume him.

Much as his thirst for revenge had kept him going in prison, kept him vigilant and ruthless—it was a thing that would cut him now.

Things were different. He was different. He lived for more than vengeance.

"Pope!" someone shouted behind him.

Eli turned to see Pierce approaching across the bluff. Antoine was beside him, Kade and Nyx trailing a few feet behind. They were armed to the teeth.

Pierce waved in a greeting meant to appear friendly but which radiated menace instead. There was something in his expression—a gleam of eagerness, of triumph—that put Eli on alert.

"We found a rat in our midst," he drawled. "Thought you'd want to know."

"Who is it?"

"Come and see for yourself." Pierce's gaze narrowed. He spoke slowly, as if relishing the words. "The best part is, he's a cop."

Eli fought to keep his expression neutral, to hide his trepidation. "A cop."

It was a feeling, a gut instinct. Everything about this felt like a trap. His mind whirred, his brain on overdrive. Did Pierce know something? Had he guessed the truth?

Pierce shrugged. "A cop or a cop's informant. Same difference. Soon as he returns, Sawyer's going to kill the rat. Or maybe I'll take out the garbage for him."

Eli made his decision in a split second. He knew what Pierce was insinuating, the dangerous game he was playing. They expected him to be scared. Instead, he took the offensive. To have any chance at all, he had to act the part of the lion, not the mouse.

"Enough with the games, Pierce! If you think you know something, spit it out!"

Pierce raised his brows but stood his ground. "What do you think we should do with our little rat?"

Eli made his voice arrogant and contemptuous. "Send a message. Kill this corrupt cop and leave his body as a message for the rest of them. String him up in the center of town. The cops, the sheriff—they don't have the power anymore. We can take out anyone, at any time. They serve us now if they serve at all."

"Is that what you'd do, eh?" Pierce gave a sly grin like he could read Eli's thoughts, his true thoughts. A dark merriment tinged his voice. He took a step closer, his lip curling in naked derision. Not two feet separated them. "You're the rat, Pope. Sawyer knows it, too. We all know it."

Several more of Sawyer's minions fanned out around them, forming a formidable half-circle, caging him in. He was trapped and he knew it.

He had to turn the tables, and fast. To wind up the crazy-brave in one second flat or he was a dead man. He had the sinking feeling it was already too late.

Heart pounding, he surged toward Pierce, his face reddening, hands balled into fists. "If there's an informant, it's you, Pierce! Not me!"

Pierce blinked, startled at Eli's sudden and forceful aggression. "I found the police paperwork in Jackson's hotel room, numbnuts. Not that I have to explain myself to you!"

Eli's voice dripped with scorn. "Cross played you, man. Are you really that stupid? You must be dumber than I thought. Or are you the one working with Cross? Is that why you're trying so hard to frame me and turn the tables?"

The lies he was weaving had to be difficult or impossible to check. He was thinking fast, quick on his feet. "It's amazing how you found exactly what you were hoping to find, isn't it? You've hated me since I got here and took your top dog spot. If you're not working with Jackson, then he played you! Gave you exactly what you wanted to hear."

There was a charge in the air like an electric current. Kade and Antoine exchanged dubious glances. Nyx's hand hovered above her weapon, momentarily uncertain.

"Can't you all see it? He's trying to destroy this place from within!" Eli shouted, incensed. He worked himself up until he believed it himself. "Did anybody search Pierce for a wire, or did you all just go along with a few pieces of paper with zero corroborating evidence?"

"You're a dead man!" Pierce snarled. "I'm gonna kill you!"

"Wait till Sawyer gets back! You're the one who's got some explaining to do!" Eli said, desperate to plant doubt, trying to get someone, anyone, off their game.

This was bigger than his survival. Eli knew Sawyer's defenses, the cartel weapons and their locations. More than his life was on the line. He had to make it out of here alive.

Undeterred, Pierce shook his head as if disappointed in Eli's poor choices. "Hands up, Pope."

Half a dozen goons surrounded him, Ak-47s and submachine guns aimed at his head, his torso, his spine, his heart. Their fingers balanced on the triggers, ready to fire.

His desperate ploy hadn't worked. There was no escape, not through brute force. To survive the night, he'd need to be smarter than them, more cunning. Assuming Pierce didn't turn him into a pincushion right here.

Defeated, Eli raised his hands.

One of the mercenaries stepped in close and patted him down, removing the knife and pistol from his belt and in his boot. Someone kicked his legs out from beneath him and he collapsed to his knees. His arms were dragged roughly behind him. His wrists burned as flex-cuffs cut off his circulation.

Pierce circled around to face him. The barrel of his gun filled Eli's vision, sucking everything inward with the gravitational pull of a black hole. "No one believes a word of the lies you're spouting. It's over for you."

Eli stared unflinching into the barrel. "Sawyer isn't here. You don't say boo without Sawyer's say so. You're just his lapdog. You'll be dog meat when Sawyer returns and the truth comes out!"

"I can do whatever the hell I want!" Pierce yelled, face red, eyes bulging. "I'm going to end you, right now—"

"Pierce," Nyx said with a note of doubt in her voice, a warning. Or maybe Eli hoped that's what he heard. But it was enough. "Sawyer decides, not you."

Pierce clenched his jaw, shaking with indignation, but he maintained his composure. He stepped back and motioned to a man at his left. Antoine's expression revealed zero emotion as he stepped forward, a burlap bag in his hands.

Eli glared up at him. "Guess loyalty only goes so far with you, huh, *brother*?"

Something flashed in Antoine's eyes. Eli couldn't tell whether it was shame, embarrassment, a moment of indecision—or something else. Without a word, Antoine dropped the burlap bag over Eli's head.

Darkness descended. Dusty stale air clogged his nostrils. With every breath, the rough fabric sucked into his mouth. Panic clawed at him, his heart jackhammering in his chest.

Eli sensed someone bending over him, smelled Pierce's sour sweat. Pierce—he assumed it was Pierce—kicked him savagely in the stomach. White-hot pain exploded in his gut and radiated through his ribs.

Groaning, Eli forced himself to straighten, to face whatever came next.

Pierce whispered into his ear: "When I'm done with you, you'll wish you were dead."

60

JACKSON CROSS

DAY FORTY-ONE

"Thank you for coming," Jackson said.

Ten police officers and deputies sat around a conference table in a small building attached to the firing range. The room had no air conditioning and was stifling hot; sweat dripped down their faces. The only light filtered in from two windows.

Jackson had decided to meet at the Munising PD range instead of the Sheriff's Office for three reasons. First, he did not trust Sheriff Underwood. Underwood had the power to shut down this little Hail Mary operation before it got started. Jackson could not let that happen.

Second, they could use whatever time they had to train, prepare, and gear up. Third, meeting at the range provided a plausible explanation if anyone saw them conducting "routine" tactical training.

"Before we do this, you deserve to hear what Devon and I have found," Jackson said. "Walter Boone claimed he had a partner. Some believed he was lying; we didn't. And we were right. His legal name is Cyrus Lee Jefferson, otherwise known to us as Cyrus Lee."

The law enforcement officers gaped at him like deer in the

headlights. Devon sat next to him, her face ashen as she gripped a pencil so hard it nearly broke.

"What the hell?" Alexis said, stunned.

"Someone wise told me that we're often blinded by those closest to us," Jackson said. "The ones we are the most familiar with are the ones we are least likely to see clearly. Cyrus grew up here. We all know him, or know of him."

Methodically, he took them through the investigation, from Boone's confession to Shiloh to the unearthed ring, to their journey west to Copper Harbor and the discovery of the first victim, then tracking down the Suma pharmaceutical connection, and how Eli's Intel had narrowed the suspect list.

"Cyrus Lee Jefferson fits the profile of a sadist killer. He hates women. When he was eight, his father lost the family fortune in a series of bad investments, humiliating his family. Cyrus's mother turned to drinking and pills to numb herself to her reality, including her own son. A year later, she left her husband and son and never contacted them again, as far as we know. He must have experienced that as a deep and traumatizing rejection.

"After his first girlfriend rejected him, he stalked and killed her in 2008. It became a compulsion. Instead of slaking his thirst, it only made him hungrier. He wanted to recreate that first time, to reclaim that ultimate rush of punishing her with violence.

"At some point before he killed his first victim, we believe he met Walter Boone on a dark web chat room. Alexis checked his laptop and was able to decrypt downloaded pictures and videos of the expected type, reams of nasty stuff that'll give you nightmares. She also dug up a couple of saved posts from an incel website.

"Incels are men who consider themselves unable to attract women sexually, and are associated with hostility, aggression, and extreme resentment toward members of the opposite sex. It was here that they discovered they shared the same predilections, the same 'type.' Boone had a rural, off-the-grid cabin, which was just what Cyrus Lee needed. They formed a terrible partnership which got them both what they wanted."

"Why did Boone and Cyrus Lee work together?" Nash asked.

"Boone had a need for sadomasochistic power and control. He got off on torturing his victims for weeks at a time while they were locked in his dungeon. He didn't enjoy the killing part, while Cyrus did. It was a match made in hell. He's certainly not the first serial killer to have a partner."

"A monster," Hart murmured.

"He's human," Devon said, "as human as the rest of us."

Jackson saw it in their faces, the revulsion and horror. That a man like this could walk among them, look like them, talk like them, act like them, and had so easily deceived them all.

"He selected vulnerable women who fit his specific criteria," Jackson continued, "girls without safety nets, most of them runaways or homeless. Most importantly, girls who had succumbed to addictions very much like his mother.

"He beats their faces because he wants to pulverize them, to erase their very identity, everything that makes them human beings, individuals apart from him. He strangles them while they wear the lockets so he can crush the life from them while he looks at it, the ultimate revenge.

"Cyrus Lee Jefferson is cunning, careful, and controlled. Boone was the wildcard. Boone found the last victim on his own, using his connection with his cousin at the school in Munising. Which is why Ruby Carpenter had red hair instead of dark brown or black —she was Boone's choice. That's also why a middle-aged principal is crawling around on an island full of mercenaries, but that's a tale for later."

Jackson's chest burned with regret and self-recrimination. "He kept a girlfriend to give an air of respectability, to solidify his cover within the community. He selected her with care, too. She was crippled, damaged goods, a woman who'd be grateful for any attention from a man. As a bonus, she volunteered at a homeless shelter chock full of troubled teen girls—potential victims. But it was more than that. Like most serial killers, he wanted to keep tabs on the case, insert himself into the investigation, to be in the know.

As the daughter of the former sheriff, the sister of the undersheriff, Astrid gave him access. What better way to keep his pulse on any potential investigations into missing local girls? He ate at our table, listened to our 'shop talk.' I also believe he broke into my room and read the files I would bring home."

Jackson swallowed. "That's how he knew I was still hunting for the killer even after Underwood declared the case closed. He was taunting me with a message painted on my back door and when he sent Vaughn to attack Lena and Shiloh at the lighthouse."

There were somber nods around the conference table. Jackson placed his hands on the table and met the gaze of each of his officers. He knew what he was asking of them, the incredibly high stakes. He asked it anyway.

He said, "Our primary mission is to rescue Eli Pope. We wouldn't have solved this investigation without the evidence Eli found while undercover. We're going to get him back. Our secondary mission is to take Cyrus Lee Jefferson into custody. And this is how we're going to do it."

61

JACKSON CROSS

DAY FORTY-ONE

Jackson's radio crackled with static. "Alpha One, this is Alpha Two."

Devon put down the magazine of the AR-10 she'd been loading and glanced at Jackson, her eyes narrowed. "Who is that?"

Jackson's pulse quickened. This was the call he'd been waiting for. Without answering her, he stepped away from the map of Grand Island spread out on the table, snatched the radio from his belt, and brought it to his lips. "Alpha Two, you're a go. Tell me you have good news."

"I've got eyes on our target right now."

"He's alive?"

David Kepford said, "Affirmative."

Jackson couldn't help it; he breathed an audible sigh of relief. When he could speak again, he asked, "Where is he now?"

"They had him locked in a shed," Kepford said. "When they brought him out, his hands were handcuffed behind his back. He's sporting two black eyes and most likely a broken nose. His shirt is stained with blood. He looks like death warmed over, but he's still breathing."

"Walking without help?"

"Yes. They shoved him a few times, but he's upright."

Jackson swallowed back the surge of emotion. Guilt washed over him, mingled with relief. He couldn't afford to allow feelings to cloud his judgment.

Eli was still alive. That's what he needed to focus on. Anything else could come later.

"Do you know where they're taking him?" Jackson had a guess, but he needed confirmation.

"The ferry dock at Williams Landing. I was able to follow them without being detected. There are fifteen armed men standing around on the dock. They're smoking and wearing plated body armor. A few appear to be Russians, Eastern European, at any rate. They're carrying submachine guns. My Russian's a bit rusty, but one of them said something about Pope being fish food."

"Did you see them take Eli onboard one of the boats?"

"Negative. I couldn't move fast enough to remain undetected. But they're gearing up to leave soon. Several men are refueling Sawyer's yacht. They're adding diesel preservatives and they've got a generator with a pump and hose going to the boat's fuel tanks. If I were a betting man, I'd bet good money your man is on board."

"Today, I am a betting man. I've got no choice."

"Roger," Kepford said. "I've overheard snatches of conversation. Sawyer wants to 'entertain him' on the yacht before dumping him overboard."

Jackson had suspected as much. "Sawyer has a particular way of doing things. He always has. He thinks it gives him flair. It makes him predictable. Have you seen Sawyer yet?"

"That's a negative."

"Let me know when they leave. We've got eyes on the boat, albeit from a distance."

"Roger that. Out."

Jackson holstered his radio and turned to face his team. Across the table covered in maps and weapons, Devon stared at him wide-eyed. Her mouth hung open.

Moreno stood beside her. His slack face had lost its color. "Was that the high school principal on the line? You sent a teacher to infiltrate Sawyer's fortified island? Please tell me I'm hallucinating."

"Yes, but not just a teacher, a former Marine."

After returning to the Northwoods Inn that morning, Jackson had searched his hotel room from top to bottom. The screws holding the vent in place had been loosened. As Kepford had confirmed over the radio, his case files were missing.

At 7:30 a.m., Pierce had entered the Inn unmolested, managing to sneak past the security team on patrol. The nineteen-year-old in charge of that sector had fallen asleep from exhaustion.

Pierce had accosted a maid in one of the isolated hallways and had stolen the universal key. The old lodge still used physical keys and hadn't upgraded to electronic key cards.

As if to mock him, Pierce had left the keys lying in the middle of Jackson's unmade bed.

Jackson had tamped down his fury and channeled it into action. He had a hunch and a prayer he desperately hoped would pan out.

And so, he'd sought out David Kepford. He'd found him on the other side of the Northwoods sprawling property, constructing a sniper hide inside the trees lining the long gravel drive.

It was mid-morning. The hot sun beat down on his head and shoulders. Black flies and mosquitoes buzzed around them. In the distance, goats bleated and chickens squawked.

Two-man security teams patrolled the perimeter of the property, shotguns slung over their shoulders. For the most part, they were regular people: teenagers, bankers, farmers, mothers and fathers, people coming together to protect what they loved. As head of security, Kepford had his work cut out for him.

Kepford swatted at a fly as he hooked his hammer to his belt and shielded his eyes. Beneath his faded Detroit Redwings shirt, the imprint of a pistol bulged.

"What can I do for you, Undersheriff?"

Jackson handed him a lukewarm water bottle. "I'm hoping you can help me with a problem."

As he explained their predicament, Kepford drained the water, then crossed his arms over his broad chest, leaned against a tall birch tree, and grinned. "Sounds risky as hell."

Jackson eyed him warily. "I have a feeling you've done stuff like this before."

"It just so happens that in another life, I graduated from the 3rd Marine Division Scout Sniper School on Ford Island in Hawaii."

Jackson raised his eyebrows. "You were a sniper in the Marines?"

"Nah. I just attended the training. All sorts of folks graduate from sniper school: SEAL Team One, the 25th Infantry Division, any of the three-letter federal agencies."

"What exactly did you do before you were a high school principal?"

Kepford's eyes crinkled with merriment, like he was enjoying this conversation. "As I said before, I could tell you, but then I'd have to kill you."

Jackson rolled his eyes. "Sure."

Kepford belted out a hearty laugh. "I do what needs to be done. It sounds like you need a man inside, someone to infiltrate the island and gather critical intel. First and foremost, to determine if your asset is even alive."

Jackson held Kepford's gaze. "That's correct."

"I can tell you this much, if you lead a team in blind, you'll lose everyone. You have no idea what you're walking into."

"I know. But I can't just leave him to die. I'm the one who sent him into that viper's nest. I can't stand here and allow a serial killer to escape, either. If he gets away now, we'll never catch him. In this chaos, he'll be free to kill and keep killing."

"Any chance your department has access to a Predator drone?"

Jackson snorted.

Kepford's grin widened. "I had to ask. Anyway, I'll do it. I can get you the intel to make an informed decision."

Jackson's heart stuttered with hope. "Are you sure?"

"Isn't that why you came to me?"

Jackson couldn't deny it. "I know the odds aren't good."

"It's gonna suck without a drone, but I've done reconnaissance and surveillance hides. This is a job for two, but I'll manage. Besides, I've got a better chance as one man without you guys stomping around, making a ruckus, and getting yourselves shot. It's a high-risk assignment, but compared to working undercover in Sawyer's group, it'll be easy-peasy."

One man creeping around on an island crawling with Russian mercenaries and ex-military contractors was incredibly dangerous. Guilt wormed its way inside him, but he couldn't stop now.

Kepford looked almost giddy, as if it were possible to get excited at the thought of capture, dismemberment, and death. "Once upon a time, I used to live for this kind of crazy. Why do you think I'm volunteering?"

"I shouldn't be asking you to do this."

Kepford straightened his shoulders. The smile dropped from his face. "Listen, you've got a former Ranger on that island who served his country well. He got the short end of the stick, and yet he's willing to put himself out there to do something good in the world. I respect the hell out of that."

"Still—"

"Don't get your panties in a wad, Undersheriff. Look, I didn't know this killer's other victims, but I know Ruby Carpenter. I know Shiloh Easton. They're my students. And Boone hunted in *my* school, right under my nose. I've gotta live with that, now. I'm not doing this for you. I'm doing it for Eli Pope, for those girls, and for me."

Jackson nodded. He understood.

Kepford pulled something from beneath his Red Wings jersey. It was a gold medal on a chain. "This is a Saint Michael's medal. My grandmother gave it to me the day I joined the Marines. It's a symbol of perseverance of good against evil. Saint Michael protects warriors fighting the good fight. I've made it this far with him watching over me." He patted Jackson's shoulder like he was the one who needed comfort. "Don't worry, I'll be fine."

Jackson had needed more than a little luck. And he'd gotten it in the form of a high school principal with a secret past. If only that luck would hold out a little longer.

Seven hours ago, Kepford had slipped from the mainland. The last time Jackson had seen him, he'd transformed himself into something unrecognizable, wearing a ghillie suit with his face painted with mud and charcoal.

It had taken him this long to make contact.

Now, Jackson stood in front of Devon, Moreno, and Jim Hart, along with half a dozen of the deputies and Munising Police officers he'd cobbled together, including Danny Ellison and Charles Payne.

"This is good news, people," he said. "Or as good as we're going to get. Instead of facing a hundred armed mercenaries hunkered down on a heavily defended island, we'll only have to deal with twenty or so. That's the plan, anyway."

Nash looked more pale than usual. He muttered something about best laid plans going awry.

"No plan survives contact with the enemy. That's a given." Moreno leaned forward, his expression tense. He gripped his AR 10 with white-knuckled fingers. A dozen filled magazines were stacked on the table in front of him. "We can overtake them on the yacht. It's our best shot."

"It is," Jackson said.

"Then what the hell are we waiting for?" Moreno asked. "Why are we still here? Kepford got us the intel. Every second we delay is a second we risk this whole thing blowing up in our faces. Let's blow this joint."

Since Hasting had died, Moreno was a different man. Gone were the jokes and the sarcasm. He was a man possessed.

Jackson held up a hand. "Hold up, cowboy. They haven't left the wharf yet. It needs to be a good distance from the island before we hit it."

Moreno scowled. "While we're messing around, Eli could be tortured or killed."

"I'm aware of the risks," Jackson said with a calm he didn't feel. "If we don't do it like this, Sawyer's QRF team will be swarming our butts within minutes. We have to wait or we'll end up fighting a hundred men. Exactly the scenario we don't want."

Moreno leaned back in his seat, clearly unhappy. "Fine."

Jackson tapped the maps laid out on the table. He'd drawn a diagram of Sawyer's yacht, including possible locations that Eli might be kept, as well as the locations of the engine and turbines. Luckily, he'd been on the boat himself. "It's time to load ammo, gear up, and get to the boats."

He looked around at his team. Every one of them had volunteered to put their lives on the line for this ad hoc, near-suicide mission. He'd said it before but felt the need to say it again. "Tonight is liable to be the fight of our lives. Anybody who wants to leave, now is the time. No one will fault you or hold it against you."

No one made a move to leave. No one even twitched a muscle.

Moreno said. "I always did want to go down in a blaze of glory."

Hart hooked his thumb at Moreno. "If he's in, so am I."

Devon gave Jackson a grim smile. "We're with you, boss, all the way."

62

SHILOH EASTON

DAY FORTY-ONE

Eli was in trouble.

From the lantern room, Shiloh watched through powerful binoculars as evening descended like a soft indigo blanket over Grand Island. Thick rafts of clouds obscured the sunset. The lighthouse beam swept across the waterline, its light penetrating deep into the twilight.

From her perch at the top of the lighthouse, Shiloh had a spectacular view of the coast curving to either side of her. The base of Grand Island arose out of the water a half-mile distant.

Luckily, she'd charged her iPhone with the solar charger before the clouds had rolled in this afternoon. She nodded her head to her downloaded music, Imagine Dragon's *Bones* on repeat as she scanned the ferry dock at Williams Landing, where several boats bobbed like tiny toys.

Her pistol lay on the floor next to her feet, fully loaded. The crossbow leaned against the glass wall across from her. Her weapons never left her side. She had the radio, fully charged and ready to go.

Bear had finally worked up the courage to climb the spiral staircase, though he'd whined his complaints the entire way, an aggrieved look on his shaggy features, but he'd made it. Lena and

Bear had kept watch in the lantern room with her for most of the day.

Well, the Newfie had flopped on his side and snored, his big head lolling across Shiloh's legs while the humans remained alert and watchful.

Around 7 p.m., Lena had descended the winding spiral staircase to cook some stew on the camping stove. Shiloh had barely eaten all day. Worry twisted her stomach in knots. She didn't want to waste time eating, but Lena had insisted.

She wriggled her butt on the wooden floor, trying not to disturb Bear's snores. She had to pee. It didn't matter. She refused to abandon her post for even a second.

"Come on, come on." Again, she panned the shoreline with the binoculars. The bluffs rose steeply, limestone cliffs carpeted with thick pine trees. Tendrils of mist snaked across the dark water like sinuous fingers, stretching longer and longer. Apprehension sprouted in her gut.

If the fog got much worse, she'd lose sight of the docks—and the boats—completely.

Shiloh needed to help Eli, to help Jackson save him, the way they'd saved her from Boone.

She couldn't see them from her position, but Jackson had a team of law enforcement officers at the marina, waiting on her signal. Every cell in her body longed to be down there with them, to go into battle, to fight like a warrior.

She hated being a kid, hated the sensation of helplessness. If she had a snowball's chance in hell of getting away with it, she'd stowaway in one of the attack boats, but Jackson would sniff her out for sure. Lena, too.

Eli was out there. Eli was the *Ma'iingan,* the wolf. He was the hunter, not the hunted. No one was supposed to be able to hurt him.

But deep down, in that dark place where terror coiled like a viper waiting to strike, she knew that wasn't true.

She told herself that Jackson was going to save him. All she could do was pray useless prayers and make impossible wishes. Maybe that was all that anyone could do.

The fog thickened. Five more minutes, and the dock would disappear, the boats swallowed in the mist like they'd never existed in the first place.

"Come on," she muttered. "Let's go, you stupid, slimy, dumb piece of—"

Movement caught her eye. Swiftly, she zeroed in on the ferry dock through the glass and squinted. Tiny figures moved down on the dock, too small to make out any details. They were dark stick figures against a stifling gray soup.

A moment later, the biggest boat began to move.

Her breath hitched in her throat. The black flag flapped in the breeze. *Risky Business* was scrawled in gold script across its rear end. Sawyer's yacht was easily recognizable, even from this distance, even through the gathering fog.

Shiloh seized the radio.

63

LENA EASTON

DAY FORTY-ONE

Lena couldn't sleep. Not with Eli and Jackson out there, in danger. She tossed and turned for hours, plagued by fears, tormented by what-ifs.

At 3 a.m. she sat up straight in bed, her pulse racing, ribs tight like someone had been pressing down on her chest. She'd broken out in a cold sweat. It was the nightmares again: intruders invading the house, Lena pointing a gun but unable to fire; Shiloh stolen by shadows, always out of her reach; the fridge failing, destroying her insulin.

Compulsively, she rose in the dark and checked the mini-fridge she kept in her bedroom, and made sure it was running, the vials still cold. It was a fear that never left her, a constant anxiety beneath the surface of things. The Frio cooling packs were still good; she'd immersed them in water yesterday. Still, she checked, just to make sure.

She needed to check the springhouse, too, where she'd stored half the vials. It didn't matter that it was the middle of the night. That panicky anxiety was rising in her chest, she had to check.

The numbers on her pump were running high; stress always spiked her blood sugar. She bolused herself on the way out. As she exited the cottage, the wind nearly knocked her sideways.

Lena padded soundlessly across the grass, flashlight in one hand, her M&P in the other. The night was dark and starless. The lighthouse beacon struggled to pierce the thick veil of fog that cloaked the world.

She was halfway to the creek when a terrible sound broke the stillness.

A terrible cry. A woman or child's scream.

Fear shot through her. Weapon drawn, she spun and scanned the yard, the trees, the beach.

The fog wrapped the point in a thick blanket. It was impossible to see more than a hundred feet in any direction.

Where was it coming from? Shiloh was safe inside, up in the tower, the big Newfie snoring at her side. Was it one of the neighbors, or—

The sound came again, a high-pitched, mournful shriek. It was the dying scream of an animal. It sounded so human—scared, lonely, in pain. A cry in the darkness.

Something appeared through the fog. An enormous, lumbering shape. She squinted, weapon up, hands clammy as her finger slid to the trigger.

And there it was. A giant black bear ambled across the yard, headed straight toward her.

Her brain took in the details in a fraction of a second: the coarse black fur, the heavy muscular body, the tiny eyes peering at her, as startled to see her as she was to see it.

Its jaws were painted black with blood, a small, red-furred creature limp in its mouth. It was a fox. In its death throes, the fox had made the almost-human screams.

The black bear halted. It stared at her. She stared at the bear. They faced each other, not thirty feet apart.

If it charged, she was in trouble. She'd be able to fire off a few rounds, but the 9mm pistol wouldn't be enough to take down a 500-pound animal before it reached her.

It reared onto his hind legs, taller than she was, and sniffed the air. The pungent odor hit her nostrils: dank and sour, the taste of blood strong in her mouth. It snuffled, swinging its massive head back and forth, snout in the air as it chugged heavy breaths.

Lena didn't move, she didn't even breathe. For a long minute, she stood, the wind whipping her hair, her clothes. She couldn't tell if it felt threatened or curious, if it wanted to eat her or was as startled as she was.

The Sheriff's Office had put out a warning about the black bears let loose from Oswald's Ranch down in Newberry. Was this one of those bears, or one of the wild ones who roamed the Upper Peninsula, along with the reclusive gray wolf?

Did it feel lost, returned so abruptly to the wilderness? Or had it found home at long last? Whatever it was thinking, it did not seem frightened of her.

The black bear was beautiful up close, dangerous but captivating. She couldn't take her eyes off it. It was a reminder that up here, humans weren't necessarily at the top of the food chain.

She didn't want to kill such a regal creature, loathed the thought of squeezing the trigger, but she understood one thing about herself: she would do it if she had to. To protect herself and her family. She'd done it before and she would do it again, as many times as were required.

"Go," she whispered. "Just go."

Finally, the big bear dropped to all fours, the dead fox still in its jaws. It turned from her and loped along the edge of the tree line, grunting and chuffing until it disappeared, swallowed by the fog.

Arms trembling with relief, Lena lowered her pistol. Her face was wet. She hadn't noticed the tears streaming down her cheeks. She wasn't sure what she was weeping for, the lost world or her own damaged heart.

It felt like a sign, a portent. An omen for good, or for evil, she did not know.

A weightless, unmoored feeling expanded within her ribcage. The more she knew, the less she understood. This universe, after all, was as unknowable as the human heart. She knew only that she was alive and breathing, and that was a precious thing.

She hadn't prayed much, hadn't been raised in church, but she believed in something larger than herself, in the purpose of things. There had to be a reason for all of this. There was beauty to be found even here, even now. She prayed, harder than she ever had, for Eli, for Jackson, for all of them.

64

JACKSON CROSS

DAY FORTY-ONE

Jackson stood at the helm of a white cigar boat with green racing stripes emblazoned across the sides. A second cigar boat, this one red with orange racing stripes, cut through the dark water a dozen yards to their left.

The cigar boats were long and thin and resembled the shape of a cigar. Their aerodynamic shape made them extremely fast, reaching speeds above ninety miles an hour, like a bullet skimming across the water.

They were ridiculously expensive. Left at the marina, Jackson had borrowed them.

He'd gladly sacrifice every boat in the UP to get Eli back and keep his deputies alive.

The cigar boats rocketed northward, slicing through the fog as they headed deep into the lake, their wakes leaving a double V of white water. They were trailed by two open console boats with emergency water rescue Rigid Hull Inflatable Boats, or RHIBs, in tow.

That afternoon, the fog had rolled in thick and dark, whipping the waves into a foaming frenzy. It was not an unusual occurrence for Lake Superior, infamous for her mercurial moods.

The chilly air slapped at his face, sweat trickled down the back of his collar. A palpable sense of wrongness worried at his thoughts, thickened in his throat, made it difficult to breathe.

To his left, Devon stood tense and silent, scanning the bucking waves, bracing her feet to keep her balance as the cigar boat bounced over the swells, sprays of freezing water splashing them.

The law enforcement officers wore tactical vests over their uniforms. At their feet lay duffle bags with extra weapons, dozens of loaded magazines, plenty of ammo, and flash bang and smoke grenades. They'd brought drop nets, rope, and sport water drones.

For the operation, Jackson had managed to gather a ten-man team. Jackson, Devon, Moreno, and Hart, the former marine, in one cigar boat, with Baker, Flores, the rookie Nash, Alexis, and Charlie Payne split between the two remaining boats.

Twenty minutes ago, Shiloh had radioed him. "I can see the big boat! It's leaving the wharf now. Over."

"Good job. Are any of the other boats leaving with it?"

A pause as Jackson held his breath, then Shiloh said, "No. Nope. Negative. Did I say that right? The other boats are still docked. The big one left by itself. Over."

"Perfect. You did great, Shiloh."

"Remember what you promised me."

"I remember. Out."

Jackson couldn't think about promises that they both knew he might not be able to keep. He keyed his mic again and radioed Kepford. Again, there was no answer. "Damn it!"

Devon stepped closer, her legs wobbly. She wore a tactical vest and carried an M4 on a sling around her neck. "What is it? You look worried."

"I haven't heard from Kepford in over an hour."

"Maybe he's in a spot where he can't communicate."

"Let's hope so." Jackson glanced at her out of the corner of his eye. "You okay?"

"Fine and dandy." Devon had been an inner-city street cop—she was tough as nails, but she had little experience with boats or open water, and it showed in her unsteady gait. She looked green around the gills. "I'll be fine. How long until we intercept the yacht?"

Jackson glanced at the radar screen. "We're about fifteen miles out."

"How can you tell?"

"This is 4kw radar. It has a range of about forty-eight miles. See that dot? We're here. That's Sawyer's boat right there."

"It feels like we're going way too slow."

Jackson felt it, too. The tension and dread, the fear spreading like a fungus. "We've got to let him get far enough from the island before we close the distance. We need to cut him off from escape and rescue. Right now, he's cruising at about eighteen knots. That yacht's max speed is about twenty-five knots. Our slowest boat is twice as fast. We'll start speeding up soon."

Devon chewed on her thumbnail. "Isn't waiting this long too risky? Sawyer could stop anywhere and put a bullet in the back of Eli's head. It could be done already."

He pointed to the radar again. "It's possible, but I don't think so. Sawyer has a favorite spot. The rumored location is somewhere around here. That's where we'll intercept him."

Slowly but surely, they closed the distance. Jackson gestured for one of the deputies to take the helm as he and Devon moved to the bow of the cigar boat. Jackson unstrapped his AR-15 and held it against his chest.

Condensation beaded his hair, his body slick with sweat. The world dwindled, the fog closing in like they were being swallowed by an enormous unseen enemy.

Lily Easton's killer waited for him. And Eli, the friend he'd put at risk, whose allegiance he still questioned. He was not unaware that this whole setup might be a trap, that Eli might have absconded to Sawyer's side. It had happened before with undercover agents.

After everything that had been done to him, that Jackson himself had done to him, would it surprise anyone?

Despite his misgivings, his doubt, his fear, he forged ahead. He still believed.

Forty minutes later, they had closed the gap to less than 500 yards.

"One Victor One to all Victor units," Jackson spoke into his mic. Everyone had headset radios and each boat had NVGs, or night vision goggles, for the helmsmen as twilight descended. "Keep your lights off. No smoking, no talking on deck. In approximately two minutes, we're going to start moving toward them. Keep sight of the orange cigar boat, and we will lead you in."

Victor Two said, "Target moving at nineteen knots, at a bearing of 260. Over."

"Remember, do not shoot up the yacht. Our target is onboard, and our goal is to keep him alive. Out."

Everyone tensed, nerves raw and senses on high alert as they drew closer. Jackson strained his eyes, searching for a shape, a shadow, or an outline in the swirling gray nothing.

Fog rolled in dense curtains. It absorbed sound and shape and color. Everything had transformed into shades of gray, utterly monochromatic, as if all warmth and sunlight had been leached from the earth and would never return. This was all there was, all there ever would be.

The hulking shape of the *Risky Business* reared out of the mist like a ghost ship.

65

ELI POPE

DAY FORTY-ONE

Eli's wrist was bruised and bloody. Hell, his whole body was bruised and bloody. He slumped against the bulkhead, his right hand handcuffed to the front leg of a steel table bolted to the floor.

He was locked inside a small square room approximately eight feet by ten feet, a safe room located below deck on Sawyer's yacht. Blank security monitors lined one wall along with comms equipment.

The steady rumble of the engine threatened to lull him into an exhausted stupor. His ribs ached; one was likely cracked. His skull pulsed with pain like he'd been struck in the back of the head with a pickaxe.

Pierce and his crew had beaten him into unconsciousness, locked him in a shed, and then dragged him onboard. They'd removed the hood and shackled him to the table before locking the steel hatch and leaving him alone with his suffering.

He didn't know how much time had passed or what day it was. It might have been minutes or hours. Time stretched and folded in on itself. Pain was his constant companion. Harsh white light blared into his eyes.

He'd spent considerable time attempting to extricate his wrist from the metal handcuffs, to move, bend, or break the table leg, but it was no use. He was caught like a chained dog.

Memories of prison scythed through his mind: the nightmares, the familiar stench of sweat and terror. Fear stuck in his throat like a hook.

He did not want to die like this, trapped and caged within four gray walls.

The dull thud of footsteps pounded down the ladder outside the steel hatch. The deadbolt clicked and the hatch swung open.

Eli raised his head as Sawyer, Pierce, Cyrus Lee, and Kade crammed into the cramped space. His right hand reached instinctively for a weapon, but the handcuff jerked him up short. The raw skin encircling his wrist burned.

Cyrus Lee laughed. The sound echoed tinnily in the small space.

Eli eyed the four men, watching their hands, their faces, their eyes. Kade stood to Sawyer's left, a big brute of a man who loomed large in the cramped safe room. He cradled a submachine gun in his arms.

Cyrus hung to the right, a little behind the others, a satisfied smirk on his face. He took a casual swig from a beer bottle, like he was here for a party.

Behind Pierce, Sawyer's face betrayed no emotion. His eyes were gray and emotionless. He held a manila file folder in both hands, his whitened knuckles his only tell.

"This a social call?" Eli said. "Unfortunately, I'm out of girl scout cookies. Come back another time."

Pierce stepped forward and dropped the top section of a ghillie suit along with a small gold medal on the table. "Any idea who this belongs to?"

"Nope."

"Look closer."

He blinked rapidly to clear his vision and his mind. The ghillie suit was not his. Blood splattered the burlap fabric and bits of leaves and twigs woven into the suit. He'd never seen the medal before.

"Still nope."

"It's a Saint Michael's medal," Pierce said. "It's a Catholic thing. But then, you know that."

Eli gave a pained shrug. "Does it belong to a friend of yours?"

"A friend of *yours*," Pierce spat.

"I have no friends," Eli said.

Kade smirked. "Truer words have never been spoken."

"Talk or you die," Sawyer said evenly. "Frankly, I'm tired of your games."

Eli knew death waited for him whichever way this played out. "I wouldn't tell you even if I knew, which I don't."

Kade's big shiny face reddened with anger. "I had a small roving patrol at the edge of the cabins. He was spying on us. He managed to kill three of my men and almost made it to the tree line and got away. He was your partner. You were working together to spy on us."

Eli masked his surprise. Jackson hadn't mentioned a second asset on Grand Island. Eli had been utterly alone. "I have no idea what you're talking about."

"Cross had eyes and ears on our island," Kade said. "You were working for him, and so was this POS. One of my Legionnaires emptied a twenty-round magazine into his back. He's dead, just like you'll be soon."

"You're mistaken—"

Sawyer slapped the file folder on the steel table next to the crumpled ghillie suit. "Stop lying! We have the proof right here. I've read every sentence, every dotted 'I' and crossed 'T.' Your handler takes thorough notes. He thought he was being clever by hiding the files in a vent in his hotel room, but Pierce found it. Imagine how surprised we were to discover what you've been up to."

Eli gritted his teeth against a fresh wave of pain. His ribs felt like he'd been kicked by a horse. He breathed deeply, controlling his oxygen, his stress levels. "I guess you already know everything then, don't you?"

"Start talking, and maybe this will go easier for you." Pierce picked up the medal by the chain and dangled it in front of Eli's face. "Tell us who the spy is and what he was doing on the island."

"Sightseeing?"

"You're only making this worse for yourself."

"Practicing nude yoga."

"Your choice, jackhole." Pierce angled a kick at Eli's ribs.

Pain racked his entire body. Wetness blurred his eyes. He gasped, sucking in oxygen, willing the fire in his side to lessen. It didn't.

Pierce leaned in close. "Or maybe he came for you, to get you out. Cross figured out you'd been compromised, and they staged a rescue mission."

Eli choked out a genuine laugh of disbelief. "I have no idea who that belongs to, who he was, or why he was there. But I can tell you one thing, he wasn't there for me. No one's coming for me."

Sawyer's weathered skin paled beneath the harsh fluorescent light, his mouth a thin bloodless line. "You're a damn fool, Eli. You betrayed me. And for what? For people who framed you? Who sent you to prison? For the Rangers? The same people who handed you over to the Alger County Sheriff's Office and the State of Michigan without a second thought? For the town that turned on you and still hates you, even though they know you're innocent? No one cares about you. They've thrown you to the wolves."

Eli winced. "I'm well aware."

Sawyer stared at him for a long moment without speaking. Shadows swam behind his dark eyes, like a shark swimming in the deep. For a second, emotion flickered: disappointment, bitterness, bewilderment. "Why? Tell me why."

Eli kept his gaze on Sawyer, though he sensed Cyrus Lee's malignant presence with every cell in his body. Should he tell

Sawyer his suspicions? He couldn't predict how Sawyer would react. If Sawyer let Cyrus Lee escape, he'd never be found.

He said nothing.

Tendons stood out on Sawyer's neck. "I was the one who gave a crap about you. The only one! I brought you in, gave you a home, a brotherhood. And you spit in my face."

"Some brotherhood." Eli kept his voice steady, but his anger ran deep. He'd buried his revulsion for days. His self-control had reached its breaking point. He was dead anyway. "You traffic drugs, addiction, and death. You trade weapons with terrorist groups and gangs who gun down innocents. I would never join you, Sawyer. I would never be a willing participant in the destruction you deal. I'd rather die."

"We're on the same page, then," Pierce muttered.

"If I don't do it, someone will take my place tomorrow, someone even worse than me. Don't you get that? The demand is there. We're only giving the people what they want. You could have replaced Vaughn, you know? Stood at my side, my most trusted advisor. We could have ruled like kings! I gave you that chance, the opportunity of a lifetime. You're a damn fool to throw it all away."

"Guess I'm a fool."

Sawyer shook his head as if immensely disappointed. "You're a bigger fool because you don't know who you are. Even if I let you walk out of here alive, they will never accept you. Never. They will hate and despise and fear you every single day of the rest of your miserable life. You will be alone forever, utterly alone. You aren't like them. You aren't one of the sheep. You're a wolf. You're one of us. We're the same."

Eli fought to keep his expression neutral, to shield his true emotions. Sawyer's words struck close to home, arrows piercing straight into his deepest fears and darkest desires.

And Sawyer knew it.

"I will never be like you," he forced out.

"You're right." Sawyer shook his head again, this time with disgust. "You're a fool and now you're a dead fool."

"Do you know what's going to happen next?" Pierce asked.

"You untie me, apologize for the inconvenience, and we sit down with tea and crumpets?" Eli deadpanned. "Or better yet, why don't you jump in the lake and drown to save me the trouble of killing you with my bare hands."

Cyrus Lee laughed with a high-pitched, nasal sound.

Pierce shot him a furious glare. "Why the hell are you even here? You're just a paper pusher."

Cyrus took another swig of beer and dropped his gaze, appropriately cowed. A look of pure hatred flashed in his eyes and then was gone.

"Both of you shut up." Sawyer leaned down until his face was inches from Eli's. His eyes were cold burning ice, merciless. No warmth. No human emotion at all. "I'm going to take a pair of pliers and remove your fingernails one by one, then your fingers. Then I'm going to cut off your balls and stuff them in your mouth to stifle your screams. Then and only then will I wrap your body in chains and dump you overboard while you're still breathing. The fish will start eating the stumps of your fingers while you're sinking. You'll be lost to the lake and no one will ever find your mutilated body. No one will even look. No one will miss you or think about you ever again. You'll just be gone—"

The yacht shifted hard to port. Eli slid sideways, the handcuff jerking his wrist and cutting into raw flesh. Stinging pain flared from the tips of his fingers to his elbow joint.

Kade stumbled backward. Cyrus slid sideways, liquid sloshing over his hands. Pierce threw out his hand to stabilize himself against the bulkhead. "What the hell—"

Over the growl of the engines came the distant rat-a-tat of gunfire.

Sawyer's radio crackled to life. "Sir, a cigar boat just blew by and fired an automatic weapon at the fantail!"

Sawyer seized the edge of the table, welded to the floor for stability, as the yacht pitched again. Cyrus Lee's shoulder slammed into the bulkhead. He dropped his beer bottle and let out a grunt of pain as the bottle rolled across the deck.

More gunfire, louder and closer as Sawyer's men returned fire on the top deck with submachine guns. Sawyer spun toward the hatch, reaching for the pistol at his hip. "Send someone to guard Pope. He's not going anywhere. Let's go!"

Sawyer and his men rushed out of the safe room and headed topside. The hatch slammed shut, leaving Eli alone to contemplate his impending doom.

66

JACKSON CROSS

DAY FORTY-ONE

Jackson spoke into his mic: "Victor One to all Victor units. Two minutes from my mark, start your attack. Send the rafts to foul the propellers with the nets. The cigar boats will attack the fantail. As soon as we open fire, cut the rafts loose. Victor Five and Six will head for the bow to dump the special cargo. Do not board until we slow or stop the yacht."

"Copy that, Victor One," came the replies from the center consoles and the RHIBs.

It felt like his guts had been dumped into a blender and set on "puree." Fear touched the back of his neck with cold fingers as the yacht loomed closer and closer, rearing above their heads in the gloom, sharp and jagged and forbidding.

The boats closed in. Four hundred yards. Three-fifty. Three hundred. Time to go loud. Jackson pressed the mic again. "Now! Now! Now!"

The green cigar boat went full throttle. White sprays of water jetted high in the air as it screamed toward its target. Deputies opened fire with their battle weapons, aiming for the engine section of the fantail.

Tracer fire sprayed from the AR-10s, arcing like bright flares through the night. Rounds pinged the hull of the *Risky Business*, ripping through the aluminum composite. The sounds of battle were deafening. Smoke and fog swirled in the darkness, obscuring their vision even with NVGs.

The orange cigar boat followed the lead of the first boat. The tracers shot across the sky like fountains of red light arcing toward the boat's stern. Thunderous cracks and booms shook the air, loud as a fireworks display on the Fourth of July.

Like the Northern lights that had captivated the world even as the solar storms laid waste to power grids across several continents, it was spectacular but utterly devastating.

The first tracer rounds struck the stern of the yacht. Shouts and screams echoed above the growl of the engines and the boom of submachine gunfire. A dozen armed men rushed to the port-side gunwale and opened fire with AK-47s, aiming for the cigar boats and center consoles swerving alongside the yacht.

The small boats were agile and quick and nearly invisible in the dark and fog. They rocketed past the yacht, spraying water and shooting death at seventy miles an hour, then swept around for another pass, weaving in and out of the fog, appearing and disappearing with startling dexterity.

As the first center console made another pass, Sawyer's men unleashed a salvo of firepower. Rounds peppered the boat's windshield, knocking the glass from its frame as the deputies dropped to the deck, seeking cover behind the gunwales.

Gunfire raked the hull. A Munising police officer screamed and toppled backward into the water. A deputy on his knees sprayed half his magazine at the fantail before zooming past.

The orange cigar boat made a run on the port side of the *Risky Business* as deputies emptied rounds into the fantail from the starboard.

A bright flash streaked across the sky. A loud whoosh screamed overhead.

"Incoming! Get down!" Jackson screamed into his headset.

The orange cigar boat careened hard to starboard to dodge the attack. The RPG skimmed across the helm but hit the driver—

police officer Charles Payne—throwing him twenty feet from the boat before exploding.

The blast threw up a great spray of water. Huge waves rolled outward from the impact.

Without a driver, the cigar boat swung wildly as one of the deputies leaped from the stern, scrambled into the cockpit seat, and struggled to get the boat under control.

Jackson turned from the carnage, sickened. They'd already lost two men. A few direct hits from those RPGs and this battle would be over before it started.

They had to move fast, get in close and disable the yacht to board it. It was their best and only chance.

"We're going to ram the port fantail!" Jackson yelled into his headset as he raised his AR-15, braced it against his shoulder, and opened fire, hoping desperately that Eli was stowed safely below deck. "One Victor Four, this is Victor One."

"Go Victor One," Alexis said from the first center console.

"On your next pass, light up the starboard middle section with all the firepower you can. That RPG was fired from behind the middle lifeboat. Soon as you hit them, we're gonna ram the port fantail and board!"

"Copy that."

"One Victor for Five and Six. You guys ready?"

"We're ready!" Nash shouted back.

"Drop the packages, now!"

The two RHIBs dropped free from behind the center consoles, Nash manning one, Jim Hart the other. The inflatable craft maneuvered in front of the bow of the *Risky Business*, then Nash and Hart threw drop nets into the water.

Each net expanded to twelve feet across and sank with weights attached to each end. Lines attached to the nets provided tension and directed the nets beneath the yacht. Two underwater drones dragged the net beneath the hull and toward the propellers. It was simple yet lethally effective.

"Packages deployed!" Nash shouted into his headset.

The engines of the *Risky Business* made a horrific grinding noise as the nets caught in the propellers. The yacht jerked and slowed to less than five knots. It lost considerable power and listed slightly port side.

Jackson couldn't keep the grim smile from his face. The improvised weapons had turned out brilliantly. He glanced at Moreno at the helm of the cigar boat and nodded.

"Let's get this party started!" Moreno gave a half-crazed laugh as he opened the throttle and headed for the fantail along the stern. Jackson and Devon braced themselves, shooting at the upper decks to provide cover fire for Moreno's maneuver.

The boat bounced on the waves. Jackson's rifle juddered. It was impossible to sight targets accurately. It was spray and pray. As inaccurate as their shots were, the continuous gunfire kept the enemies' heads down.

The bow of the green cigar boat rammed the stern's hull at ten knots an hour, fast enough to do damage but not destroy the boat or hurl its passengers into the seething waves. Fiberglass scraped against fiberglass as a section of the yacht's hull collapsed inward.

The yacht bucked in the water as the smaller craft violently rammed the aft end. The tangled propellers were crushed. Smoke billowed upward as steam hissed through the cracked shell.

"Reverse!" Jackson cried.

"I'm working on it!" Moreno shouted.

Sawyer's men recovered quickly. As Moreno worked on reversing the console and freeing it from the wrecked aft section of the yacht, half a dozen mercenaries leaned over the upper deck railing and opened fire.

Rounds struck the cigar boat's hull, tore through the fabric awning, and slapped the water. Jackson and Devon dropped to their knees and returned fire. A round zinged past Jackson's head and impacted a foot away. Heat singed his cheek.

The orange cigar boat zoomed along the starboard side, shooting at the top deck with suppressive fire to give Jackson's team cover. Several windows in the upper deck shattered, raining glass upon the enemy and forcing the shooters to seek cover.

A figure popped up and hurled something over the side of the gunwale. In the glow of muzzle flashes and tracer fire, Jackson glimpsed a small object hurtling through the night.

It dropped to the deck of the orange cigar boat.

Fear turned his insides to liquid. "Grenade—!"

Too late. The grenade bounced across the deck and rolled against the seats of the bow where two officers stood. They had no time to react. The frag grenade exploded with a *whoomp*.

The 2.5-inch steel sphere contained six ounces of high explosives. It burst into a thousand lethal fragments that hurled high-velocity shrapnel into anything within fifteen meters. The shrapnel peppered the officers' arms and legs and shredded their body armor.

Both men fell backward and toppled over the side. The third police officer manning the throttle had collapsed into a fetal position behind the helm.

Jackson couldn't tell if the officer had been injured or killed. Horrified, he cursed. He'd never lost a man before. Now, three were likely dead. "Victor One to Victor Four, are you hurt? What's your status?"

"This is Victor Four," Alexis said finally. "I'm okay, taking the helm now."

Jackson hid his abject relief as he ordered Alexis and the center consoles to engage, keeping as many combatants occupied as possible. "Victor Five, use the radar to watch for Sawyer's QRF team. They will be coming."

"Copy that, Victor One," Nash said.

Moreno had worked the bow of the cigar boat free and pulled up alongside the stern of the yacht next to the boarding ladder. "That fantail is starting to smoke. Let's get our target and get the hell out of Dodge before Dodge sinks!"

"Roger that!" Devon said.

Jackson shouldered his rifle and scrambled up the boarding

ladder. He slipped twice on the slick rungs, his body vibrating with adrenaline. Clinging to the side of the yacht like a barnacle, he was exposed and vulnerable. The knowledge offered little comfort.

Moreno slithered up right behind him with Devon on his tail. One of the RHIBs motored in close while Hart seized the ladder and clambered onboard with them.

A round pinged next to Jackson's face. Two more followed in rapid succession. He pressed himself against the ladder and climbed faster. More rounds boomed over his head as he swung himself over the railing and landed boots first on the slick deck.

The *Risky Business* was crippled and taking on water. They still had to contend with fifteen or more armed hostiles. Eli was somewhere onboard, as was Lily's killer.

"Victor One to Victor all," Jackson whispered. "We're on the boat."

67

ELI POPE

DAY FORTY-ONE

The instant the hatch closed behind Sawyer, Eli lunged for the manila folder. It slid across the table. He missed, and it slipped out of reach. He strained for the folder, his shackled wrist throbbing, tendon and bone stretching, the metal cutting deep.

The folder teetered on the lip of the table.

Come on, come on! He stretched farther than he thought possible, every muscle aching in protest. The folder wavered, balanced precariously, about to fall off the table and out of reach.

Just a bit farther. His ribs burned and his thighs were on fire. Above him on the upper decks, automatic weapons blasted. The yacht swayed.

The folder slid backward half an inch. His fingertips touched the corner. He managed to pull it back his way as the floor rocked beneath him.

Eli sank to his butt, the prize in hand. Back against the bulkhead, he thumbed it open, holding it awkwardly with one hand shackled to the table leg. He held his breath in anticipation.

Inside the folder were several print-outs and sheaves of documents held together by paperclips. Relief flared through him. Those paperclips were the best sight he'd seen since he'd gone undercover. Utterly benign objects, but in his skilled hands, they meant the difference between life and death.

Taking one gingerly between his fingers, he bent the thin metal, then inserted one end into the handcuff key slot. Escaping cuffs was a common game played at the bar when he was stationed at Fort Bragg. He'd done this very thing dozens of times, albeit with less riding on the line.

Pushing down, he utilized a twisting motion for about forty-five seconds. The cuff unlocked with a click.

Rubbing his sore wrist, he quickly glanced around the safe room. It was mostly empty but for the steel table, the blank camera screens screwed high on the wall, and a sturdy gun safe in the opposite corner. He examined it quickly; he couldn't get it open without some serious tools.

A wave of dizziness rushed through him. He staggered as the teak floor rocked. Stars burst behind his eyes. He had no idea when he'd last had food or water. Close to a day. His gaze locked on the object that had rolled across the floor and now rested against the side of the gun safe.

The glass beer bottle had a familiar label. Molson Canadian, his favorite. In true Ranger form, he ignored the gunfight raging outside, picked up the bottle and drained it in several swallows.

Footsteps sounded above him.

Eli flipped the bottle, gripped it by the neck, and smashed the end against the tabletop. Drops of dark liquid spilled and puddled on the teak floor. Molson beer was truly the nectar of the gods. Eli gave the wasted beer a mournful look.

The footsteps pounded down the ladder, closer now.

Swiftly Eli moved to the side of the door and bladed his body, the beer bottle gripped in his right hand. Adrenaline surged through his veins, dulling the pain in his ribs.

The door opened and a man stepped through. The hostile expected Eli to be bound to the table across the room; that's where he focused his attention. He never saw his attacker.

Grasping the broken beer bottle by the neck, Eli seized the

attacker's shoulder and yanked hard as he simultaneously thrust the jagged ends into the side of his neck and pierced his carotid artery. Bright arterial blood spurted across the room.

Eli took the man to the ground. His head bounced against the teak deck, stunning him for an instant. Eli knelt on his chest and smashed his fists into the man's damaged windpipe until his body went limp.

Breathing hard, Eli sank back and looked over the assailant for the first time. Male, late teens, peach fuzz dusting his chin and upper lip. He wore khakis and a white button-up shirt drenched red.

Eli searched the body for a weapon and found nothing, not even a pocketknife. The corpse held a bottle of water in his right hand.

He was a member of the wait staff, a non-combatant. The kid had brought the prisoner water, an act of grace that Sawyer surely hadn't sanctioned.

In return for his kindness, Eli killed him.

Aghast, Eli turned his head and vomited. *You're a wolf.* Sawyer's words echoed inside his skull. *You're one of us.*

Eli rose from the corpse of the boy on leaden legs. He wiped his bloody fingers on his pants and gave one last glance at the crumpled form, willing the tremor in his hands to stop. It didn't.

If Eli had had a crystal ball or could see through walls, if he'd had a second to think rather than acting to save his life...Even if he'd tried to knock the kid out or gag him, he might have screamed out a warning. Eli had done what he had to do with the intel he had at the time.

Justifying the kill didn't make him feel better. There was nothing he could do, much as it horrified him.

Turning back to the safe room, Eli scanned the empty table, then the deck. He bent and scooped up the St. Michael's medal and slipped it over his head beneath his shirt. The cold metal settled on his bare chest next to his dog tags.

Pierce wasn't the only one who wanted answers. He too wanted to know who'd given his life for a recon mission somehow connected to him. Who would sacrifice himself for Eli? It didn't make sense.

Pausing, he listened at the hatch before exiting the safe room cautiously and scanning the salon ahead of him. Curved leather sofas hugged the bulkheads. On the opposite bulkhead next to a built-in mahogany bar sat a beverage fridge filled with wine. Leaning against the bar to the left was a haphazard pile of fishing supplies: a tackle box, fishing rods, and a pile of nets.

A glint caught his eye. Hidden in the tangle of nets was a metallic object. He squatted, moved the nets aside, and hefted a gaff hook. Weighing about three pounds, it was two feet long with a wooden handle and a wicked meat hook protruding from the business end.

He traded the beer bottle for the hook.

Eli froze and strained his ears. Two sets of boots above him. Two hostiles hurried down the narrow companionway ladder toward the salon.

The first attacker hurtled into the salon, leading with the muzzle of his AK-47.

Eli moved like lightning. He burst from the right and swung the gaff at the hostile's face. The man screamed and dropped his weapon, flailing desperately as the rifle went flying across the deck.

Eli jerked at the gaff to free it for another strike, but it was stuck fast. The second hostile pushed into his partner, attempting to shove his body out of the way to get a clear shot at Eli with his suppressed pistol.

Dropping to a crouch, Eli pushed the first attacker into the second and shoved them against the bulkhead in the narrow hallway, pinning the second man's weapon to his chest.

Cursing, the second attacker struggled to free his smashed right arm and his weapon with it. Eli sensed his left hand reaching for something at his belt—a fixed blade.

He dropped his weight and fell backward to the deck, but not before grabbing the HK45 pistol from the man's grasp. Fumbling for a better grip as he rolled onto his back, he brought the weapon up and around.

As the hostile fell on him with the knife, Eli's finger found the trigger. He punched the suppressor against the man's chin and fired a single .45 caliber round. The bullet slammed through the bottom of his chin, up through the roof of his mouth, and into his brain.

The man collapsed on top of Eli. The tip of the knife glanced off Eli's breastbone before falling harmlessly to the deck. Eli heaved the dead weight aside, snatched the knife, and clambered to his feet, gasping for oxygen.

Two bodies lay crumpled at the bottom of the ladder. After ensuring they were indeed deceased, Eli shoved the HK45 threaded with a suppressor into his waistband and retrieved the first attacker's AK-47.

He stripped the dead mercenaries of their spare magazines, a chest rig, and plate carriers. Fully armed, he moved to the companionway to ascend to the upper decks. Streaks of blood smeared the mahogany steps. Eli crept up the ladder, weapon at the ready.

His heart pounded in his chest. He willed his breathing to slow, his pulse to steady.

He entered the upper salon, swinging left then right, then crept up the last ladder and reached the main deck. Outside, night had fallen, a stifling darkness sans stars or moonlight.

The glow of the red emergency lights provided the only light. Here and there, muzzle flashes sparked.

Two men in full tactical gear stood ten feet to his nine o'clock, facing away from him.

The closest man took a knee and shouldered a three-foot long tube, aiming at something in the water, out of Eli's sight line. The RPG rocket launcher had a sighting range of 500 meters with a velocity of 117 meters per second. At full speed, it could penetrate eleven inches of steel.

Eli raised his sights, steadied his breathing, and exhaled. As the gunner aimed the RPG at a target off the stern, Eli sent two double taps to the back of their heads below their helmets, severing their brain stems.

The men dropped, dead on impact. The rocket launcher tumbled forward and the RPG slipped harmlessly over the gunwale into the water two stories below.

Eli crouched behind the bulkhead of the companionway, expecting return fire, but there was none. After a moment, he clambered unceremoniously across the bodies and made his way along the deck, staying low and out of sight behind the gunwale.

He didn't care who they were fighting. He might go down with this ship, but not without exacting his pound of flesh.

Quick and silent as a shadow, Eli moved for the cockpit of the *Risky Business*.

68

JACKSON CROSS

DAY FORTY-ONE

Jackson and his team crept toward the bow along the upper deck, crouching as they moved in a leapfrog formation from cover to cover, behind the corners of bulkheads, lifeboats, and large metal crates likely packed with stolen weapons.

Pressed against the bulkhead wall of the *Risky Business*, Jackson brought the twelve-gauge shotgun with breaching rounds to his shoulder and aimed at the hinges of the aft port side deck hatch.

Along the stock, Moreno had written in black sharpie marker: "Keys to the kingdom."

"On one, we go in," Jackson said into his headset.

Moreno stood to the right, ready to pull the door open as soon as it was breached, while Devon and Hart hugged the left bulkhead, Hart ready to throw a smoke grenade to obscure their entry as soon as the hatch blew.

Jackson nodded to Devon.

"Three, two, one!" Devon yelled.

Jackson squeezed the trigger in rapid succession. *Boom! Boom! Boom!*

The hinges disintegrated from the breaching rounds. The hatch hit the deck, splintering into pieces. Hart stepped forward and hurled the smoke grenades. The canisters rolled across the deck, releasing billowing clouds of white smoke.

Jackson took the lead, switching out the shotgun for his AR-15, sweeping left and right as he entered the narrow hallway and moved deeper into the yacht, heading for the cockpit. Hart and Devon followed with Moreno taking the rear and watching their six.

Less than twenty feet from the cockpit, the first rounds struck the bulkhead two feet above Jackson's head. He fired wildly, seeing nothing but smoke and darkness ahead. A second round zipped past his shoulder.

Behind him, Hart gave a pained grunt. "I'm hit!"

"Take cover! Contact ahead!" Jackson dropped his shoulder and flung himself through the hatch to his left, entering a small cabin bedroom lined with bunk beds along the far bulkhead.

With one hand, he kept firing around the corner while with his left hand he seized Hart by his chest rig and dragged him into the room beside him. Simultaneously, Devon and Moreno hurled themselves through a hatch across the hall.

Jackson dragged a large metal box for storing weapons to the doorway and crouched behind it for partial cover, edging himself around the hatch to return fire and keep Sawyer's men from pouring down the funnel of the hallway and overwhelming them.

"Talk to me, Hart! You still alive over there?"

Hart groaned. "A bullet nailed me in the chest. It got the plate carrier, I think. I hurt too much to be dead. Feels like a giant just punched me in the solar plexus."

"Sounds about right."

Heavy fire traded back and forth between law enforcement and Sawyer's men. Men stuck their AKs and ARs into the doorways without aiming, shooting till their magazines ran dry. Casings from spent cartridges poured onto the deck floor, rolling back and forth as the stalled yacht rocked with the waves. The air reeked of gunpowder, gun oil, and iron from the blood of the dead.

Hart pulled himself into position along the opposite side of the hatch, a 9mm pistol gripped in both hands. "Ouch! Damn, that hurts."

"Stop moving, Hart!" Jackson commanded.

Hart ignored him. "Somebody's gotta keep your butt alive."

Jackson grimaced as he fired several more rounds. "Have it your way. Cover me while I reload."

"Copy that."

A round struck the bulkhead. Wood splinters and chunks of fiberglass peppered his face as a shard of shrapnel lodged into his neck. He touched his skin with his left hand and felt blood. He didn't feel any pain; that would come later.

At least Sawyer's men weren't throwing frag grenades. The grenades exploded shrapnel for thirty yards in every direction and were meant to be thrown from hard cover, which the yacht was certainly not.

"Five Victor to One Victor, what's your status?" Nash asked over the radio. He had remained on the water, manning one of the center console boats.

"We're blocked in the hallway along the port deck hall, receiving heavy fire. Do you have more flash bangs?"

"A stinger missile would be helpful," Moreno muttered.

"That's a negative on both counts, Victor One," Nash said. "The yacht looks like it's sinking. I don't know how much time you've got. Sawyer likely got off an SOS to the island, so his quick response team will be inbound with boats or even a helo. You've got to get out of there!"

"I've got one more flash bang," Devon said. "I'll make it count. We've got to push down this hallway or they'll bleed us out of ammo. We're almost to the cockpit. Let's do this."

Jackson glanced down at his dwindling ammunition. He was down to two magazines for the AR-15 and a half mag in his 9mm pistol. Devon was right.

They attacked now or they died here.

He said, "Roger that."

69

ELI POPE

DAY FORTY-ONE

The yacht was sinking. Smoke billowed skyward, tinged red as flames licked the portside gunwale. Half a dozen corpses in tactical gear littered the decks.

In a crouch, Eli approached the cockpit along the portside outer deck. Dressed in borrowed gear from said corpses, with a helmet and night vision goggles over his eyes, he could pass for one of Sawyer's goons.

Hidden behind the gunwale, he was close enough to hear conversation. Close enough to put a bullet in a few skulls, too. His finger twitched on the trigger guard.

Ahead of him, several men crowded into the opulent mahogany-lined cockpit. Pierce, Kade, Cyrus Lee, and Antoine stood near the helm while Sawyer sat in the captain's seat and glared at the bank of controls, radar screens, and communication equipment.

Two Russian mercs with big barrel chests and bulging arms cradled submachine guns and faced the starboard outer deck. Their attention was focused aft, where intermittent gunfire blasted. On the starboard side, several speedboats made passes, aiming machine gunfire at the stern.

"We've gotta get back to the island." Kade sounded rattled. He was packing a bloody wound in his shoulder, teeth clenched against the pain. "I need a doctor."

Cyrus Lee shot him a derisive look. "In case you haven't noticed, we aren't going anywhere. We're dead in the water."

Pierce reloaded AK magazines from a box of ammo beside him. "Relax, you pansies. I called in the QRF team, but it's gonna take them time to get here. Thirty-five minutes out. We just gotta hold our position until then."

"What about those deputies who made it on board?" Antoine asked. "They keep getting closer."

Eli strained his ears, sure he hadn't heard right. Deputies? What deputies?

"We have a plan for them," Sawyer said dismissively.

Antoine shifted from foot to foot, his expression tense. "You going to kill them? More cops?"

"Relax, man." Sawyer gestured to the Russian mercenaries at the hatch. "Let them think they'll make it to the cockpit. We've got a little surprise in store. The RPK machine guns will take care of them."

The Russian mercs had set up the wicked-looking guns side by side, facing toward the aft deck. With two weapons, one could continuously fire while the other reloaded or changed barrels. The big guns would obliterate whoever tried to breach the aft hatch.

Pierce smiled as he slapped in a magazine. "Cross won't even know what hit him."

Eli blinked, certain he'd heard incorrectly. He hadn't.

This wasn't the work of the Côté family or a random gang. It was Jackson who had brazenly attacked the *Risky Business*.

Jackson who'd come...for what? Surely not to save Eli. That made not a lick of sense. Eli did not understand what was happening here.

He knew one thing: if Jackson was approaching from the aft deck, he and his team were about to get shredded. Adrenaline iced Eli's veins, his hands clammy. If he was going to act, it had to be now.

Sawyer turned and glowered at Kade. "Where the hell are the men I sent after Pope? Go get him. It's time for him to die—"

"Too late, jackhole," Eli said in a loud voice. "I'm already here."

Startled, Cyrus Lee gaped at him. Pierce and Antoine spun toward him, weapons rising. Eli was in position, squatted behind the corner bulkhead, his AK aimed at Sawyer's head. "I've got a bead right between your eyes, Sawyer. One wrong move and your boss will lose his head. Your choice."

The men froze, hesitating, their gazes flicking between Eli and Sawyer. No one moved. The yacht rocked beneath their feet.

"Take your hands off the PKs, right now," Eli ordered. "Sawyer, tell your men to cease firing on the deputies and to back away from those machine guns. Now!"

Sawyer's Adam's apple bobbed in his throat, his only tell that he felt anything at all, let alone fear. His gaze met Eli's across the cockpit. Eli knew Sawyer saw zero doubt or hesitation in his eyes. Eli would shoot him dead in a heartbeat, and Sawyer knew it.

"Do what he says," Sawyer said between gritted teeth.

"But—" Pierce started.

"Do it!" Sawyer bellowed. "Stop firing!"

Shouted orders in Russian and English went up and down the boat. The mercenaries ceased firing. The other side followed suit. Within seconds, the barrage of gunfire fell silent.

An eerie quiet descended. The yacht's injured engines groaned as waves slapped the hull.

Eli kept his weapon trained on Sawyer's skull. A half-dozen pairs of eyes locked onto him, AKs and ARs aimed at his head. Tension crackled through the air.

Footsteps approached from the aft deck. "This is the Alger County Undersheriff!" Jackson's familiar voice shouted from the hallway. "Hold your fire!"

Half of Sawyer's men spun and aimed their weapons at the law enforcement officers. The other half kept their guns on Eli. The officers looked across the cockpit at Sawyer's men. Sawyer's men looked across at Jackson's men.

Sawyer took in the new development without a change in expression. "Well, this is quite the twist."

"Do not move, Sawyer!" Jackson said.

"Wouldn't dream of it."

Jackson stepped forward, the stock of his AR-15 pressed against his cheek. Beads of sweat rolled down his forehead, a muscle jumping at his jaw. "Weapons down! Now!"

"Looks like we're at an impasse here, Cross," Sawyer said. "I've got guns on your men. You've got guns on me. I've got more guns on you. Maybe you kill me, maybe you don't. But for sure, you're dead, and your friends."

"Lower your weapons. I won't warn you again."

"You're trespassing on my boat, Cross. You have no warrant. You can't be here."

"You assaulted and kidnapped one of my deputies."

Sawyer lifted his brows in a facsimile of surprise. "I'm sure I haven't the faintest idea what you're talking about."

"I deputized Eli. He's my asset, my agent."

"Huh," Sawyer said.

Eli's body thrummed with tension, his nerves raw, his finger jumpy on the trigger. Anyone even flinched, and he would open fire.

"Your beautiful yacht is wrecked," Jackson said. "A third of your troops are corpses lying all over your pretty teak deck. You know it's time to cut and run. And you can. I'm not here for you."

"Then what the hell are you here for?"

"I'm here to bring Eli home. We're leaving. And you're going to let us."

The ground seemed to fall away beneath Eli's feet. He felt shaken, disoriented. Jackson should never have risked so much to rescue him. And yet, here he was.

And he wasn't alone. Half the county's law enforcement officers were with him. They'd come for him, for Eli.

It made no sense.

Sawyer half-turned his head to Eli and lowered his voice.

"Why the hell are you fighting for the man who betrayed you? Help us kill them and all will be forgiven."

Pierce looked like he was going to stroke out from suppressed rage. The tendons on his neck stuck out like cords, his fists clenched around his lowered weapon. "Sawyer, you can't possibly—"

Sawyer ignored him. "It's not too late, Pope. Help us and I'll forgive your transgressions. In a year, we could run the whole state. Think about it. Don't die for the man who locked you in a cage. Be smart. You've always been smart."

Eli thought of the young man below deck in the wait staff uniform, dead. He could feel his dog tags beneath his T-shirt, the St. Michael's medal. He thought of the mysterious man who'd died for him.

There were degrees. Things he could live with and things he could not.

Maybe he and Jackson were more alike than he wanted to admit. Damn it all to hell.

"You're a snake oil salesman, Sawyer," Eli said. "You don't believe your own spiel. I certainly don't."

Sawyer smiled a shark's smile. His eyes glittered in the red emergency lights. "I should have listened to Pierce and killed you on the island. A bullet to the back of your head would've ended this. I had a moment of weakness, of sentimentality, thinking you owed me something. An explanation. An apology." He gave a hard laugh. "Trust me, I will not make that mistake again."

His mind cycled through the possibilities. It was a calculated risk but one he had to make. "I'm not your rat. At least, not the rat you think I am. I wasn't sent here for you, Sawyer."

Sawyer's features remained expressionless. "Then why, pray tell, are you here?"

Jackson spoke loud and clear. "For Cyrus Lee. Or more accurately, Cyrus Lee Jefferson."

Cyrus Lee's head jerked up, his nostrils flaring like a wild animal scenting danger.

"What are you talking about?" Sawyer said.

"He's a serial killer," Jackson said, confirming Eli's suspicions. "He's been killing women for years."

Sawyer blinked. "What?"

Cyrus's mouth flattened to a bloodless line. Something dark flickered behind his eyes. "Liar! You're crazy!"

Eli licked his lips. His mouth was bone dry. "My objective was to find out which of your men was missing the ring that Jackson found in one of the victim's grave."

"You killed Vaughn," Pierce said accusingly. "I knew it!"

"He got exactly what he deserved," Eli said. "Before he died, he told me Cyrus Lee sent him after Shiloh and Lena. Cyrus told him the order was from you, so he didn't question it."

"I gave no such order." Sawyer's eyes darkened. "My men do nothing without my approval."

"Cyrus Lee did," Eli said. "More than that, he murdered Lily Easton, the mother of Cody Easton, your dead son."

70

ELI POPE

DAY FORTY-ONE

Sawyer looked shaken, undone in a way Eli had never seen him. "The sheriff said it was Boone."

"Walter Boone had a partner," Jackson said. "It's Cyrus. Or more accurately, his legal name: Cyrus Lee Jefferson."

Cyrus bared his teeth like a cornered jackal. "He's trying to get under your skin! He's trying to save himself. He's the one whose been ratting you out to Jackson! You know me! You've known me your whole life."

But Sawyer watched him, eyes narrowed.

Jackson turned to Sawyer. "Have your men lower their weapons. I'm going to do the same with my men. I'll explain everything."

"Don't listen to him, it's a trap—" Pierce whined, but Sawyer ordered his men to lower their weapons. Jackson's team did the same.

The two sides stood, facing off.

Eli could feel the weight of his weapon growing heavier by the minute, his muscles straining, heart hammering, adrenaline icing his veins. Tunnel vision hit him, the front sight post clear even as the rest of the world blurred, faded, threatened to disappear.

Meeting Sawyer's gaze, Jackson began to talk. He explained it all. Their suspicions, the evidence, and how they'd followed the crumbs to Cyrus Lee Jefferson. With one hand, he pulled out his phone and held it toward Sawyer, flipping through several photos.

Eli didn't dare take his gaze off Sawyer to look himself, but he could see by Sawyer's reaction that they were more than convincing.

Antoine's mouth twisted in revulsion. "Is this true?"

"Of course not!" Cyrus began to laugh, a high, reedy sound like a hyena. It chilled Eli to the bone. "You can't prove anything!"

"Jackson just did." Eli spoke to Sawyer because Sawyer was the one who decided who lived or died tonight. "He sent two of your men to hurt Lena and Shiloh. He stole Vaughn's ring because he lost his own burying the body of a dead girl he'd murdered, one of at least seven."

"You're lying—!" Cyrus screeched.

"Give me your ring," Sawyer said in a steely voice.

"Come on, Sawyer! You can't give credence to anything he's saying. Even the sheriff thinks Jackson is nuts. And now he's got Pope drinking the Kool-Aid, too. You can't think—"

"I said give me your ring."

Cyrus took a step backward. His spine pressed against the control console, his left elbow banging against the steering wheel. His face paled, his pupils constricted to two dark pinpricks. His right hand instinctively curled at his chest, where the ring hung on a chain beneath his shirt.

Sawyer flicked his hand, the barest hint of a movement. Antoine and Kade surged forward. Before Cyrus could react, they seized his arms. Antoine forcibly removed the ring from the chain as he writhed and cursed in protest, then stepped back and handed it to Sawyer.

Veils of mist pressed against the shattered windows of the yacht. They floated in an eerie murk, the deck beginning to tilt, to sink as smoke snaked between their legs, drifting up from the aft deck.

Devon looked at Jackson with wide eyes. "Boss we need to get off this boat."

"This tin can is starting to crumple!" Moreno yelled from down the hallway.

"We're almost done here," Jackson said.

Kade loomed over Cyrus, his hands fisted. Cyrus recoiled, cringing like the coward he was, no match for the stronger man. Sawyer palmed the ring and stared down at it. Everyone watched, silent, as Sawyer stiffened. His eyes flashed with shadows beneath dark water. "This isn't yours."

"Of course, it is. How could it not—"

"Vaughn was tall but thin. You're a small man. His ring fits you well enough. I had each ring made custom. The design is intricate, the metal expertly crafted by a true artist. Each one cost me a small fortune. Down here in the right hand corner, the snake's tail forms an 'S' for Vaughn's nickname, Spider. On yours, the snake's tail curls into a 'C'. Where is your ring, Cyrus? Was it buried with a dead girl like Cross claims?"

Cyrus's mouth went slack. "It's not what it looks like."

Sawyer took a step toward him. Menace radiated from every pore. "It looks very bad for you, my friend."

Cyrus threw up his hands. His pinched, ferret-face contorted, his eyes flitting wildly back and forth, searching for an escape route, but there was none. He was trapped inside the cockpit, surrounded by men with guns. "I just misplaced the ring, that's all—"

"Are you the reason Cody is dead? That *Lily* is dead?"

Cyrus shook his head, terror in his eyes. "No—!"

Livid, Sawyer's jaw muscles bulged. But there was something else in his face, something more than anger. It was grief. Grief for a child he'd never claimed as his own.

Jackson said, "We have the necklaces, your calling cards. And we found Elice McNeely."

At the mention of Elice's name, Cyrus Lee's pupils retracted to pinpricks. He muttered something that sounded a lot like, "Stupid whore."

A distant explosion sounded from below the deck. The waves pounded the hull as the boat listed port side. The air smelled singed, of things burning.

Cyrus licked his lips. "You think you're so smart. You're not, Cross. You're not half as smart as you think you are."

"What the hell happened to the ring, Cyrus?" Sawyer demanded.

Eli saw it then. The transformation. Cyrus curled his lip, revealing his small pointy teeth like a badger showing its fangs, feral and savage. He was a cornered animal and he knew it. The only way out was to chew off his own limb.

Though it wasn't fear in his face, Eli realized. It was indignation. Arrogance and disdain.

"I looked for it!" Cyrus Lee snarled. "It gave me a blister, so I took it off. I went back and dug that damn body back up, crawling with maggots, bloated and revolting. There was no ring. I looked! It wasn't there! I don't make mistakes!"

"It was there." A fervid intensity glinted in Jackson's eyes. "You didn't look hard enough. The ring was beneath Summer Tabasaw's body. As if she were hiding it from you, waiting for us to find it, to let it lead us right to you."

Cyrus Lee's mouth twisted with a horrible, rapacious glee. "All those years I got away with it! All those girls! You people had no idea. You were so stupid, stupid, stupid!"

Sawyer looked stunned. "You did it. You killed them."

"Those girls were trash. I did the world a favor. All those missing posters and no one ever looked closely for any of them. They were throw-aways. Whores and sluts, all of them. They were asking for it. They *wanted* it!"

The mask slipped completely, then. In the eerie red light, his skin was pulled so tight over his bones that it was like looking at a skull. A smiling mouth. A cut-out for two eyes.

He looked like a caricature, an approximation of a human being. There was no soul behind his eyes. Nothing but a howling darkness.

71

ELI POPE

DAY FORTY-ONE

Sawyer flipped his pistol and punched Cyrus in the face. His neck snapped back. Bright red blood bubbled down his chin and dripped onto the mahogany.

"You sick, twisted freak!" Sawyer spat.

"Holy hell," Kade said. The Russian mercenaries kept their faces impassive, but Antoine looked stunned, sickened. Pierce stared at Cyrus with repugnance, like something slimy and rotting he'd discovered on the bottom of his shoe.

Cyrus tried to wrench free of Kade and Antoine's grasp, but it was useless. His features contorted, his eyes bulging with rage and hatred as he glared up at Jackson. "I could have killed your sister a thousand times. You know how many times I put my hands around Astrid's long white throat? How I imagined how I would strangle the life out of her at the breakfast table, right across from your dumb smug face?"

"Shut up!" Jackson trembled with anger, the whites of his eyes showing. "Don't you dare say her name!"

"You're blind. You've always been blind, Cross." Cyrus sneered. Blood oozed between his split lips. Two of his teeth were missing. "Poor Astrid, always the victim. She was so very helpful to me. Thank her for me, would you?"

Eli's gut churned with revulsion. "Let me kill him."

"No," Sawyer said.

"No one is killing anyone," Jackson said.

"Sawyer—" Cyrus said, gratitude in his voice, his shoulders sagging in relief. "I owe you, man—"

Sawyer squatted before Cyrus. His hand shot out like a snake. He seized the man's throat and began to squeeze. "I invited you into my brotherhood. I trusted you, gave you everything. What do you think I'm going to do to you? How do you think I'm going to make you suffer? Because you will. Suffer."

Sawyer tightened his grip. Cyrus writhed, his feet scraping the deck, but he was caught fast. He clawed uselessly at Sawyer's fingers, retching and gasping, spittle bubbling from his lips.

Jackson took a step forward. "Sawyer, don't do it—"

"This is my business." Sawyer looked up at Jackson, his eyes burning. "My kingdom."

Jackson's finger tightened on the trigger. "Release him! That's an order!"

Cyrus Lee's face had gone reddish purple. His tongue was sticking out. Finally, Sawyer released him and stood. Cyrus slumped, gagging and gasping for oxygen. He turned his head and vomited on Kade's shoes.

There was no give in Jackson's voice. He was rock steady. "Here is what is going to happen. We are going to leave. We're taking Eli with us, and Cyrus Lee Jefferson. You will let us go, and in exchange, we won't arrest you. Your men will come to tow your yacht back to your island, and you will be free to fight another day. But not today."

"Cyrus is mine," Sawyer said.

Jackson shook his head. "I can't just leave a suspect—"

"That's the deal. I'll capitulate to you, Cross. I respect a man when he deserves it. You figured it out. You exposed the killer in my organization. For that, I owe you. Whatever you think of me, I do not abide child-killers. I am not that kind of monster. This scumbag conspired with Boone, the man who murdered my..."

Sawyer's features hardened. Shifting emotions crossed his face—grief, remorse, regret. They were gone so swiftly they might never have existed. "...My son."

Cyrus writhed, a feverish, desperate sheen in his eyes. "Sawyer, we can work this out! I got you the pills, didn't I? Just like I promised. A whole shipment. I still have value to you—"

Sawyer spun and slammed his fist into Cyrus Lee's temple. His brain bounced in his skull, his eyes rolling back in his head. Sawyer didn't let up until Cyrus sagged, broken, his eyes swollen shut, his nose shattered, his face a grotesque mess.

"Stop, Sawyer!" Jackson said. "Let the justice system deal with him—"

"What justice system?" Sawyer looked across the cockpit at Jackson, breathing hard, his mussed hair in his eyes, looking more human in his pain than Eli had ever seen him. "There is no justice but this, right here, right now."

The deck tilted precipitously. Tendrils of smoke snaked inside the cockpit and thickened at their feet. The stench singed Eli's nostrils and stung his throat. He coughed violently. It was getting harder to breathe. His weapon weighed a million pounds.

"Time to go, boss!" Devon shouted.

Sawyer said, "My men are coming for you. If they catch sight of your boats, our deal is off. They'll kill every one of you."

Jackson glanced from Sawyer to Eli to Pierce, his features strained. He looked like a man about to fall to pieces. "I can't let you do this."

"This animal took what is mine. These crimes against my flesh and blood will not go unavenged. You have a choice. Your men don't have to die with him. But Cyrus Lee will die, and by my hand."

Sawyer was a lot of things—a criminal, a murderer, narcissistic and opportunistic—he was also complicated. He hadn't publicly claimed Cody, but he'd cared for his son, and had clearly grieved for what he'd lost.

The past never died. It was always present, informing the here and now, directing the future, the ghosts they thought they'd left behind still haunted them all.

"Let Sawyer have him, Jackson," Eli said.

Jackson shook his head but faltered, torn by indecision. Eli knew that Jackson was thinking of his men now, of getting them out alive.

"Boss!" Devon shouted. "Hart is losing blood. The yacht is on fire and sinking. Let's go!"

Nash's tense voice came through their headsets. "Victor Five to Victor all, we've got company on the radar. Five minutes, tops."

Eli knew that Jackson wanted due process, the rule of law, but sometimes the win was walking away alive. If he wouldn't go on his own, Eli would force his hand.

His AK-47 trained on Sawyer, Eli rose and crossed the slanting cockpit deck. Several guns followed his movements as Eli sidestepped the bulkhead and walked to Jackson's side. "I'll cover you. Devon, make him go while you still can. Go, go, go!"

Devon took hold of Jackson's arm, and with her pistol aimed at Pierce, she dragged him backward toward the outer deck that led to the aft ladder, where they could exfil to their boats.

Reluctantly, as if he hated himself for it, Jackson went.

Eli backed out of the cockpit, his weapon up and swiveling, alert for any sign of aggression. Sawyer's men watched him go, fear on their faces. Smoke filled the cockpit in a reddish haze. Antoine bent in a coughing fit. Kade wiped fiercely at his weeping eyes.

Sawyer stood over Cyrus Lee's crumpled form. He looked up and met Eli's gaze. "Pope."

Eli paused, muscles straining as he held his weapon on Sawyer. The deck tilted with a sound like metal tearing itself apart. Every cell in his body ached, his ribs burned, smoke stinging his eyes, clogging his throat.

"Next time I see you, I will kill you." Sawyer's voice was flat. He was the shark again, cold and calculating. "Get the hell off my boat."

72

ELI POPE

DAY FORTY-ONE

Rain poured in sheets, battering the porch roof, dripping down the windows, soaking the parched ground. Rainwater plastered Eli's hair to his forehead; his clothes were drenched. He hobbled to the front door and knocked.

A moment later, the door opened. Lena stood there wearing faded striped pajama bottoms, her black rectangular insulin pump attached to her belly protruding beneath her white tank top. Her hair fell mussed across her shoulders. She wore not a stitch of makeup, her face pale and drained.

She was the most beautiful woman he'd ever seen.

Lena took a step back, her eyes widening as she took him in, bedraggled on her front porch, sopping wet, stinking, bloody and bruised.

What a sight he must be, like a starved stray dog.

"Eli," she breathed.

Embarrassment heated his cheeks. "I'll go. I shouldn't have come. I—"

Tears sprang into her eyes. He had no idea why she was crying, no clue what to say, how to fix this, whatever this was.

"Jackson did it," she said. "He brought you back."

"He shouldn't have."

"He should have," she said with all the confidence and certainty in the world. "I had faith in him, in you."

"Three police officers lost their lives and Jim Hart took a bullet to the shoulder. A former Marine infiltrated Sawyer's island just to find me, to help me. He...he died, too."

Her face fell. "I'm so sorry, Eli."

Bear pushed through the doorway at Lena's side, sniffed him and whuffed in greeting, tail wagging, nosing at his pockets in search of a treat.

"Sorry, boy, I've got nothing tonight."

Bear licked his hand in forgiveness.

"I don't know why I'm here...I thought...I wanted..." He couldn't say aloud what he wanted, how he had counted down the days and hours and minutes until he could get back here, to this little cottage, to the lighthouse. How Lena's smile had kept him going during those sleepless, nerve-wracking nights on Grand Island.

"Are you okay?" he asked. It felt like years since he'd last seen her. So much had happened. He had a lifetime of things to say and was suddenly tongue-tied.

"I'm not the one who was kidnapped by a sociopath and almost killed."

He tried for a grim smile but fell short. "And Shiloh? Is she okay?"

"Shiloh is sleeping. She tried to stay up until she knew you were safe, but she dozed off in the lantern room around 3 a.m. I put a blanket on her." Her smile lit her entire face. "I can wake her, she'll be thrilled to see you—"

"Let her sleep. She needs it."

Lena dropped her gaze and scanned his body, her eyes snagging on his bruises, the blood staining his shirt. Her brow knit in concern. "You're hurt."

His body ached all over. "I'm fine."

"I call B.S. That macho attitude will get you killed, Eli. An infected cut can turn into gangrene, and we can't call 911 anymore when something goes wrong. I have my first-in bag in the cottage. Come in."

The thought of her hands on him made his cheeks burn. "I've got my IFAK. I know how to patch myself up. I've done it before."

Lena opened the door wide and stepped aside, beckoning for him to enter. Bear gazed up at him expectantly, tongue lolling.

Eli didn't move.

She gave him a look that made his heart stutter. "I'm not asking, Eli."

He cleared his throat, sheepish. He never could resist Lena. Obediently, he followed her inside, squishing past Bear. The Newfoundland practically filled the doorway.

Lena frowned at his noticeable limp and gestured for him to sit at the wooden chair in the little kitchen. A kerosene lantern hung on the wall cast a warm glow across her face.

Bear followed close at her heels as she moved about, then set her bag on the table next to her insulin paraphernalia and dug out iodine, bandages, and gauze. She made Eli remove his shirt. It wasn't anything she hadn't seen before, and yet he felt strangely embarrassed, but Lena was in EMT mode: brisk, efficient, professional.

She took something from the counter, then knelt beside him and got to work.

"What's that?" he asked.

She hefted the amber jar. "Raw honey."

He made a face. "Are we making tea?"

"For your information, honey has been used to treat burns and mild injuries for thousands of years. It's an excellent natural antibacterial and antiseptic. The hydrophilic properties keep the skin at the right moisture level for optimal healing."

"Whatever you say, doc," Eli said.

"I'm not a doctor. I just play one at work," Lena quipped. He'd heard her say it before, a corny line paramedics loved to use on unsuspecting victims.

Eli rolled his eyes.

Lena applied a few drops of iodine to a sterile cloth and used it to disinfect and clean Eli's skin. Then she daubed the raw honey on Eli's many cuts and scrapes before covering them with gauze.

Her hands felt like butterflies on his skin. He barely felt the pain, his chest and neck growing hot. For a few minutes, she worked in silence, the pattering rain and the dog's panting breaths the only sounds. The antiseptic worked with a cleansing burn.

Bear sat on his haunches, head tilted and ears pricked like he couldn't quite figure out why they'd put honey on someone's chest instead of in their mouth, where it clearly belonged.

Eli gave him a commiserating look. "I don't get it either, boy."

The Newfie plopped down on the linoleum, rested his big head on his paws, and watched them with his soulful brown eyes. His tail made a rhythmic thump on the floor.

"Seriously, though," Lena said. "I've been reading the homesteading and natural remedies books that Shiloh got from the library. They're quite enlightening. I got these iodine bottles right off the pharmacy shelves. Iodine has been used for a hundred and fifty years as a disinfectant. It has antimicrobial and antiseptic properties to prevent infection. We're going to have to learn naturopathic treatments from here on out."

Lena leaned back when she'd finished, stealing a dollop of honey and sucking it off her finger. "Good news. I think you'll live."

"Thank you."

She looked up at him, her eyes dark and glinting. "Where are you sleeping tonight?"

"Ah..." He'd planned to return to the hide he'd built, though the damp night would be miserable. He'd endured misery plenty of times before.

"Absolutely not," she said as if reading his mind.

He stared at her, startled.

"Shiloh found your secret hideout."

Damn, but that girl was good. He couldn't help it, he nearly burst with pride. The hide was well hidden. Trained soldiers could have walked six inches from it and had no idea it existed.

"It's not called a secret hideout."

"I don't care what it's called. You were spying on us."

"Protecting you."

"Some might call that stalking."

"Would you have let me stay?"

Her lips twitched. "Of course not."

"I did what I had to do. It wasn't enough. I didn't want to go undercover for Jackson. I hated the thought of leaving Shiloh, but I thought that finding the killer would protect her, too. If I had known what was going to happen, I never would have left."

"You caught him." It wasn't a question. Her eyes were intent, her features taut.

Eli nodded wearily. "It's over. He's dead."

She took that in. He saw her grief, the years of loss, then something fell away, a release like an unclenched fist. "Did you kill him?"

"Sawyer wanted the honor."

Her jaw worked as she thought it over, then after a moment, gave a grave nod. "Okay," she said. "Okay."

"A man died for me. The principal of the high school, he was a former marine. I don't understand it. I didn't even know him." He shook his head, as bewildered as the first time he'd heard David Kepford's name. He touched the Saint Michael's medallion beneath his shirt, next to his dog tags. "I didn't deserve it."

"You're a good man whether you see it in yourself or not, Eli. You deserve to be saved."

He didn't say anything. His throat was too tight, his eyes stinging.

"I see it in you," she said, "even if you don't yet."

After a minute, he nodded.

"Tell me what happened," she said.

"It's a long story."

"I'm not going anywhere. You aren't either."

"What do you mean?"

She blushed a little. "There's the assistant's cabin on the property. If I know you, you're planning to go right back to your hide-out, out in the cold and rain with the bugs and no bathroom. Tell me I'm wrong."

"You're not wrong," he admitted.

She laughed, that high clear sound like water rippling over smooth stones that he adored.

Still kneeling, she looked up at him as she brushed an unruly strand of hair behind her ear. "You aren't staying out in the cold. I'd never treat a dog that way, let alone a person. If you won't go home, then stay in the cabin."

The lantern light wavered and flickered. Outside, the rain drummed against the roof and wept down the windowpanes like tears. Hours ago, he thought he'd never see this place again, never see Lena or feel her presence, never get a chance to undo all his wrongs.

He wanted to kiss her. Longed to take her face between his palms and kiss her like no one had ever been kissed before.

Doubt gripped him. If he accidentally scared her away, he would lose this fledgling friendship that he treasured. He couldn't risk it.

He said, "I don't want to intrude."

"You're Shiloh's father. She needs you." Lena finished bandaging his arm, then stood and touched his shoulder, her fingers light as a butterfly. "You did a good thing, a brave thing. The town won't forget it. They owe you." She gave a wan smile. "They'll start to see you the way I see you."

He didn't dare ask how she saw him.

"It's settled, then. You're staying."

Eli didn't argue with her. He didn't want to, anyway.

She peered into his eyes, concern reflected in her own. She put her hand on his, which rested on his knee. "Are you truly okay?"

Emotion vibrated along an invisible thread between them. After all this time, after all these years apart, the heartbreak and pain, it was still there, that thing that connected them, yesterday and today and forever.

He looked down at her small pale hand over his own. She knew that he was looking, that he was aware, they were both suddenly aware—but she did not pull away.

"We will get through this," she said. "We will."

He believed her.

73

JACKSON CROSS

DAY FORTY-EIGHT

They put Cody to rest on a Tuesday morning, a week after the attack on Sawyer's yacht.

The ME had released the body after the autopsy, and in the end, there was no good reason not to grant Shiloh's request. The two funeral homes still in operation within the county were backlogged by the dozens, if not hundreds.

With no way to refrigerate the bodies, people were digging graves for their loved ones in their backyards. The Sheriff's Office had released a notice to keep corpses—human and animal—a safe distance from potable water to prevent contamination.

There would be more funerals. Jim Hart and another injured officer had survived, but two police officers had been killed, including Charles Payne. David Kepford's body had not been recovered from Grand Island, but he was presumed dead.

A pang struck Jackson's chest when he thought of the principal and his honorable sacrifice.

Yes, there would be more funerals, but today was reserved for Cody Easton.

Lena, Jackson, Devon, Eli, and Shiloh stood on an isolated section of the beach a few miles west of Christmas. Mrs. Carpenter and her daughter Ruby had wanted to attend, but Shiloh hadn't wanted anyone else. They honored her wishes.

Cody had loved the water. It had been his salvation the way the woods were Shiloh's. She wanted him at peace in death in a way he'd been denied in life. They had helped Shiloh build the pyre, but Shiloh had done most of the work herself.

The girl poured gasoline on the branches, lit it with a lighter, and then Jackson and Devon pushed the boat out into the water.

The tide took the tiny fishing boat named *Little Neptune*, the boat Sawyer had given to Cody, deeper into the lake. Flames burst to life. The dry twigs crackled. Pine boughs sent billowing smoke skyward.

Shiloh stepped back and watched in silence. She had not wanted a service, no sweet words spoken or songs sung, she said Cody would have hated it, and so they followed her lead.

Rituals and rites of passage had mattered to humankind for thousands of years and would matter still. It was how they kept themselves human—reminding them that heartbreak and hope existed, side by side.

Jackson squeezed Lena's shoulder as she leaned into him and wiped her eyes. Sensing the melancholy mood of the humans, Bear slumped beside her, head drooping forlornly, ears down, tail rhythmically thumping the sand.

Lena looked up at Jackson with a weary smile. "You did good, Jackson."

"Eli was the one—"

"But you figured it out." She squeezed his hand.

Instead of feeling triumphant, he felt drained, dispirited, and more than a little lost. He still had questions. There were loose threads, pieces that didn't quite fit.

He had been in law enforcement long enough to understand that some questions would never be answered, some pieces of the puzzle lost forever, like what drove a person like Cyrus to kill, to enjoy it, relish it, crave it. What could twist a human being to such depraved depths?

The facts were scarce, they had only a bare-bones account. The fundamental truth, the raw *why* of it, would remain a perplexing enigma. Cyrus would certainly never have revealed it.

Still, the case was closed. Cyrus Lee Jefferson was dead.

Never one for subtlety, Sawyer had sent Jackson a package via a bicycle courier; inside a velvet-lined box lay Cyrus Lee's finger, the stolen ring with the etched wolf and writhing snakes still attached above the severed knuckle.

Jackson said, "Somehow, it still doesn't feel like enough."

"It's enough for me," Lena said softly.

"Things are getting worse."

She gave his hand another squeeze before letting go. "I know that, too."

Jackson glanced across the beach where Eli stood apart from the rest of the group. He skipped stones in the water, kicking at flat pebbles to find more good rocks. He wore his rifle slung across his back, his gaze constantly scanning, always alert.

Shiloh approached them. Lena flashed Jackson a knowing smile and departed to chat with Devon, who was sitting in the sand near the shoreline. At her side, Bear whined plaintively, and she motioned for him to get up. "Oh, go on, I know you want to play."

Bear was more than happy to oblige. He trotted toward the water, kicking up sand in all directions with his dirty paws.

Shiloh stood beside Jackson and they watched the little boat drift farther and farther out into the vast lake. The sun burned bright overhead. Black flies buzzed around them, Shiloh waved them away.

The *Little Neptune* grew smaller and smaller.

Jackson mopped sweat from his neck with a handkerchief and shoved it into his pocket. He pulled out a half-melted Twix bar he'd been saving and handed it to her. "It's not a Snickers bar, but—"

She grabbed it from him greedily, unwrapped it, and scarfed it down in two bites. "I'd kill for chocolate. That's not a confession."

He smiled. "I heard you're starting a garden."

"Hmmph. Everything dies. The bugs are eating my tomato plants. Rabbits keep getting the lettuce. I'm a fighter, not a damn gardener, but Lena's making me do it."

"Even warriors need to eat."

She wiped her fingers on her overalls. "Yeah well, in the old days the warriors had the food made for them."

"By the women," Jackson reminded her gently. "Maybe it's better that we aren't living back then, eh?"

She scowled at him, then folded her arms over her scrawny chest and thought about it for a second. "Fine. Whatever."

"And the lighthouse?"

"Lena says that when you take something, like a life, then you need to give something back. Lena heals people. I make sure the lighthouse guides sailors home."

A trade line had started up along the coast, fishermen loading up supplies and running up and down Superior, stopping at local harbors to trade for goods in each town. Trade was critical to the survival of the UP—it needed to be protected.

"She's right," Jackson said. "It's important."

Shiloh rolled her eyes but there was no bite to it. It was clear that she loved the lighthouse, that she took her responsibilities seriously. He understood the importance of a mission, a purpose. And he understood why Lena had insisted on staying.

Shiloh slapped at a mosquito that landed on her arm. "Eli told me what happened."

"He told you everything?"

"He said I deserved to know."

"You do."

"He said the man who did it won't ever hurt anybody again."

"He's right."

Shiloh kept her face straight ahead, but he could feel her studying him out of the corner of her eye, appraising him. "Do you think Cody is at peace now?"

"I do."

"Do you think my mother is at peace?"

"I hope so."

"I'm remembering."

He gave a start. "What?"

"In my nightmares." Her small hands were clenched into fists at her sides. She turned her head and stared at him with those hard unblinking eyes. "The memory is locked in my head. It has to be there, right? Like it was with Cody. It went away, but it came back."

"This is different," he said with caution, though he couldn't deny the leap in his pulse. "You had barely turned five. It's been eight years. A child's memory is—"

Her mouth thinned. "Unreliable?"

He winced at her choice of words. "A challenge."

She closed her eyes and tilted her face up to the sun, eyelashes brushing her tan cheeks. The heat beat down on them, the mosquitos and black flies buzzing, the breeze brushing tendrils of raven-black hair across her elfin face. An arrow was tucked into the messy bun she'd tied back with a rawhide string. "I see things in my dreams. Hear things. I want to remember."

"It'll be frightening. And painful. It will be incredibly hard."

"I'm not scared of hard."

"No, no you aren't."

"I need to know."

Jackson nodded. He recognized that need in himself, that same obsessive compulsion to understand, to uncover the *why* and *how*, to seek the truth to its bitter end.

"Will you help me?"

He hadn't wanted to push her, but if she was ready, then he would help her in any way that he could. "I will."

"Good."

Cody's pyre faded into a distant speck on the horizon. As it diminished, Shiloh seemed to lighten, to grow taller, her narrow shoulders straightening like a tremendous burden had been lifted.

Bear bounded up to them, soaking wet, covered in sand, and

shook himself. Water sprayed everywhere. With a startled shout, Jackson tried and failed to leap out of the way.

Shiloh grinned. "Next time, even closer to Jackson. He smells like he needs a bath."

"I'm not the one with leaves and pine sap stuck in my hair. Is that an arrow?"

Shiloh's grin widened. "It's in my blood. Mom always said I was half Ojibwe."

Jackson raised his brows but said nothing. He'd long suspected a certain truth but had never voiced the question. Maybe it was time to ask, to seek an answer that would lead to something good for a change.

Bear nosed Shiloh's hand and then dashed back into the water, barking joyously, his floppy ears streaming. Shiloh ran after him. Girl and dog plunged into the waves, happy together.

Jackson smacked at mosquitos—they were relentless, and he was nearly out of bug spray, damn it—and strode across the sand to a long section of driftwood. He sat down, removed his shoes and socks, and dug his toes in the sand.

The sun beat down on his head, warming his face, his neck. He closed his eyes and the dark memories rushed in, Cyrus Lee Jefferson's snarling face, his empty glinting eyes. He tried to push them out. It didn't work.

A shadow fell across him. He glanced up and shielded his eyes, startled. "Eli."

Eli said nothing as he scanned the beach behind them, then east and west. He perched on the edge of the beached log as if ready to flee at the slightest provocation.

They sat not two feet apart. The waves lapped the beach. The land curved green and hilly to the east. They watched Shiloh and Bear jump in the sparkling waves, Lena and Devon with their pants rolled up, wading to their knees in a shallow cove.

Jackson recalled a thousand summer days like this. His throat went tight. He was afraid to speak in case he ruined the moment. The two men had barely spoken since the rescue mission.

"Something's bothering you," Eli said.

"Why do you say that?"

"I still know you. We don't change that much."

Jackson grunted. "I suppose that's true."

"What is it?"

Jackson hesitated before answering. "I did the same thing as I did to you. I short-circuited the system. Trashed due process, the rule of law for my purposes."

He had allowed Sawyer to kill a man. He'd known it would happen and he'd walked away.

True, it was to save his life and the lives of his team, including Eli. That didn't mean it sat right with him. It didn't. It never would, like a splinter that worked its way deep beneath the skin.

"Right and wrong isn't always about the law," Eli said in a low voice. "You did the right thing. You got me out. You saved the rest of your officers. Cyrus Lee got his justice. It might not be the justice you would've chosen, but it is justice, nonetheless."

Eli was right. Jackson knew he was, much as he hated it. There were things a man had to live with, choices he regretted, truths he would chase after forever, yet never comprehend.

Jackson would have to console himself with the fact that Cyrus Lee Jefferson would never hurt another victim again. It would have to be enough. He'd make it enough.

In the end, he had to try to live with the scars.

He should have felt at peace. Yet the nightmares hadn't lessened; if anything, they'd intensified. He couldn't rest, not with the way of the world.

More trouble was brewing. Rumors were swirling that the Côté cartel was amassing in the east. They'd gained control of the northeastern half of Canada and were threatening to cross the International Bridge and take Sault Ste. Marie. The crime family was seeking a shipment of stolen weapons and wouldn't stop until they'd retrieved them.

Sheriff Underwood was furious with Jackson for undermining

his authority and directly disobeying his orders. So far, he'd been able to avoid a confrontation, but it wouldn't be long.

A reckoning was coming.

Jackson sat, rubbing his jaw, worrying about tomorrow's problems, Eli quiet beside him. It was a familiar feeling, comfortable even, after so long.

After a time, Eli asked, "You thirsty?"

"Depends on what you're offering."

Eli snorted. He shrugged off his rucksack, pushed it down between his feet, resting the rifle against the driftwood, and reached into his rucksack. He pulled out two beer bottles. "It's lukewarm at best."

"You expect me to drink this crap?" Jackson could barely get the words out around the lump in his throat. "I see your poor taste hasn't evolved in eight years."

"I've been saving them for a special occasion. And then I thought, what the hell? Piss poor company deserves a piss poor beer."

Eli took one for him and held out the other to Jackson. Jackson willed his hand not to tremble as he reached for the Molson Canadian.

His vision went suddenly blurry. He blinked several times and cleared his throat. Must be the sand getting in his eyes. "Eli, I—"

"Shut up and drink."

Jackson drank. They sat like that for a good thirty minutes. Slapping mosquitoes, baking in the shade, drinking beer like it was any normal day, like this could someday be normal again, the two of them, together. Something that felt a lot like hope grew wings and fluttered in his chest.

The sun had begun its descent across the sky when Devon strode across the beach toward them. Her features were drawn, her expression somber. She held the radio in one hand.

Jackson and Eli turned to face her.

"What is it?" Jackson asked.

She glanced from Jackson to Eli and back to Jackson as if

dreading what she had to say next. "The prisoner escort. The bus that was supposed to transfer the tier three convicts from Alger Correctional to I-Max downstate. I just heard from Moreno that the bus never made it to the bridge, didn't even make it thirty miles. They found it on M-28 before the cross-section with 78, in Seney Township."

Jackson tensed. "Found it how?"

"Overturned off the side of the road, on fire, the fuel siphoned. It appears they were ambushed. Someone on the outside knew when and where the transport bus would be. The COs are dead. Two dead convicts on board, but the rest escaped."

It felt like the oxygen had been sucked from the air. Jackson couldn't breathe. "How many?"

"Twenty-two maximum security convicts. They may not come here, boss. They could head south and try to cross the Big Mac to get downstate or the International Bridge to cross into Canada."

"They'll come here," Eli said. "Munising is still the closest town. We have food, shelter, transportation, and everything they need. Plus, a lot of them will know this area. They'll go where they're comfortable, to familiar territory. Predators always do." His voice was strained. "Tell me Darius Sykes wasn't on that transport."

"I've seen the list. Darius Sykes is on it."

Eli rose to his feet, his expression stricken.

"Eli," Jackson said as if to give assurance, but there was no assurance to give.

"Sykes said he would get out. He promised he would hunt down every person I loved and slit their throats in front of me." There was real fear in Eli's eyes. He looked at Jackson like he was drowning. "He's coming for Shiloh. For Lena, for all of us."

74

JACKSON CROSS

DAY FIFTY

"We have a problem," Devon said.

Jackson looked up from the breaking and entering case he'd received that morning. He had a growing stack of files two feet high on both sides of his desk. "What is it?"

Devon held a case folder in both hands so tightly that her knuckles had turned gray. Her face was ashen. "I was going through the files one last time. I guess I'm a bit OCD."

"That's why I like you."

She shook her head, her eyes glassy with exhaustion. "I went down to the basement and looked through the old files from that week, the week of Lily's murder. I don't know why. Something was bothering me."

He sensed it in her voice, the thing that was coming. A terrible dread settled like a stone in the pit of his stomach. He stared at her, bracing himself.

"I found something."

"Spit it out, Devon."

"Cyrus Lee had an alibi for Lily's murder."

The room tilted. He felt the solid ground sliding away from him. "No. That makes no sense."

"Here." She pushed a file across his desk, opened it, and

punched her finger at a series of photographs taken as stills from a surveillance camera. They were time and date-stamped. "Cyrus Lee was in Munising the night of Lily's murder—at first. He was at the Northwoods bar with Gideon Crawford and Tim Brooks at the same time as Eli Pope."

"Small town on a Saturday night," Jackson said, scrambling desperately for something, for anything, to hold onto. He had the sensation of falling, of plummeting into nothingness.

"Eli left at 9:36 p.m. to go to Lily's house. Cyrus left shortly after and drove to the Blue Lumberjack Tavern in Marais to play in a pool tournament. According to the bar's footage, he arrived at 10:12 p.m. He was on-screen until the bar closed at 1 a.m., but he was there for another two hours afterward, until well after 3 a.m. When he won, two sour contestants accused him of cheating. There was an altercation. Cyrus isn't the type to win in a bar fight. He tried to flee but they chased him down and laid into him. Charges were filed, but then dropped a couple of days later."

Jackson sank back into his office chair. His shoulders hunched inward as if warding off a blow he hadn't seen coming. But he had seen it coming, hadn't he? Somewhere down deep. What he'd missed, the anomalies he'd overlooked, the empty spaces in the puzzle.

"I have Lily's file memorized. That's not in there."

"This isn't from Lily's case file. It's a drunk and disorderly arrest. Cyrus was only mentioned in Lily's case as a witness confirming Eli's presence at the Northwoods Bar that night. That's all. He was never a suspect, never provided an alibi. There was no reason to."

"He was arrested? Why wasn't that on his rap sheet? We looked at that—"

"He wasn't arrested. He was the victim, not the perpetrator. During the window of Lily's murder, Cyrus Lee Jefferson was thirty miles away, getting the crap beaten out of him."

Jackson struggled to breathe. It felt like a thousand-pound

monster was sitting on his chest. "Who—who was the arresting officer?"

Devon hesitated. "The sheriff at the time. Horatio Cross."

Something wriggling and slimy oozed inside him. Cold despair iced his chest. They'd come so close, had come so far. They'd caught a serial killer, of that he had no doubt. They'd matched his whereabouts with the locations and dates of each of the missing girls they'd identified. They'd tracked down the lockets. In the end, Cyrus admitted to what he'd done.

But had he, truly? Had he claimed he'd killed Lily?

No, he had not.

Devon chewed on her thumbnail. She'd bitten the nail to the quick, a single droplet of blood dribbling down her thumb. She watched him in alarm. "What does this mean, boss?"

Jackson rubbed his bloodshot eyes. "It means...it's not over."

"I don't understand. How would a copycat know about the lockets? None of the bodies had been discovered before Lily was killed."

Jackson had no answer to that question. He hadn't a clue. It made no sense. Cyrus had been a careful, calculated, organized killer, whereas Lily's death had been messy, chaotic, and rage-driven, the work of a disorganized killer.

A second killer who'd cloaked himself in the M.O. of a serial killer to avoid detection. It was possible. But how could anyone have known his Modus Operandi?

Cyrus Lee Jefferson's cryptic last words replayed in his mind, taunting him. *You're blind. You've always been blind.*

"I don't know," Jackson whispered brokenly. "I don't know if I have what it takes."

Devon rounded the desk and stood beside him. The night pressed against the windows. Shadows from the kerosene lanterns bobbed and flickered across the walls. There were no sounds but their shallow breathing.

Devon put her hand on his shoulder. Her palm was warm and

firm. "You're not going to give up, boss. That's not who you are. You'll catch him, if it's the last thing you do."

He looked up at her, shell-shocked. Lily's ghost cried out to him. He could not rest, would not rest. His soul would never be at peace as long as she haunted him, day and night, in his waking hours and his nightmares. She would always haunt him.

How far would he have to go? How much of himself would he have to give? What sacrifices would be demanded of him, of all of them, before the end?

He did not know. He knew only that the world was burning, and he was about to walk into the fire.

AUTHOR'S NOTE

Thank you for reading the second book in the *Lost Light* series, *The Dark We Seek.*

Writing this book was a difficult but awarding journey. This series is the first time I've combined a survival story with a murder mystery.

Not only was it the longest manuscript I've written by almost 100 pages, I wrote it while ill with Hashimoto's Disease, an autoimmune disease where the immune system attacks the thyroid, slowly destroying it over time.

I believe in treasuring the good things even through difficult times. If we wait until everything is perfect before we start truly enjoying life, we will never find happiness or peace.

As I was finishing *The Dark We Seek*, I was able to travel to visit the Upper Peninsula. We drove nine hours to Copper Harbor to see the Northern Lights!

It was my first time, and let me say, it's as spectacular as I'd imagined. It was a precious gift to watch the auroras while writing a series about the geomagnetic storms that spark such gorgeous light shows.

While beautiful, they're also a reminder that the sun is immensely powerful. One day, a massive solar flare might bring more than colorful skies. I hope not, but it's always a good idea to be prepared.

Thank you so much for reading this series and following Jackson, Eli, Lena and Shiloh as they struggle to survive when half the planet goes dark.

Until next time!

ACKNOWLEDGMENTS

First and foremost, a deep heartfelt thanks to the behind-the-scenes readers who give early feedback on the raw manuscript. They are an invaluable aid as I shape the final story that you hold in your hands.

To my fabulous BETA readers: Ana Shaeffer, Fred Oelrich, Melva Metivier, Jim Strawn, Sally Shupe, Jose Jaime Reynoso, Randy Hasting, Annette King, Rick Phipps, Kathy Schmitt, Cheree Castellanos, Cheryl WHM, Mike Neubecker, Bavette Battern, David A. Grossman, and Courtnee McGrew. Your thoughtful critiques and enthusiasm are invaluable.

To Donna Lewis for her excellent line editing skills.

Thank you to Joanna Niederer and Jenny Avery for detailed feedback and proofreading.

A very special thank you goes to David Kepford for his tactical expertise and experience in everything from undercover work to EMT gear and psychological insights into the mind of a killer. And for repeated readings of this manuscript in its various forms. Though the fictional Kepford passed away, luckily the real one is still very much alive. Thank you!

Thank you to Karen Colley Cleaver for sharing what it's like to live with type 1 diabetes. Your experience has helped to shape the character of Lena Easton.

Any errors are my own.

Thank you to our armed forces who put their lives on the line to keep us safe and protect freedom around the world.

To my husband, who takes care of the house, the kids, and the cooking when I'm under the gun with a writing deadline, even when the septic system backs into the finished basement! To my kids, who show me the true meaning of love every day and continually inspire me.

Thanks to God for His many blessings. He is with us even in the darkest times.

Thank you.

ABOUT THE AUTHOR

I spend my days writing apocalyptic and disaster survival novels, exploring all the different ways the world might end.

I love writing stories that explore how ordinary people cope with extraordinary circumstances, especially situations where the normal comforts, conveniences, and rules are stripped away.

My favorite stories to read and write deal with characters struggling with inner demons who learn to face and overcome their fears, launching their transformation into the strong, brave warrior they were meant to become.

Some of my favorite books include *The Road*, *The Passage*, *Hunger Games*, and *Ready Player One*. My favorite movies are *The Lord of the Rings* and *Gladiator*.

Give me a good story in any form, and I'm happy.

Add a cool fall evening in front of a crackling fire, nestled on the couch with a fuzzy blanket, a book in one hand and a hot mocha latte in the other. That's my heaven. I also enjoy traveling to new places, hiking, scuba diving, and the occasional rappel down a waterfall or abandoned mine shaft.

I love to hear from my readers! Find my books and chat with me via any of the channels below:

www.KylaStone.com

www.Facebook.com/KylaStoneAuthor

www.Amazon.com/author/KylaStone

Email me at KylaStone@yahoo.com

Made in United States
North Haven, CT
24 February 2024

49159785R00286